"Why haven't you tried to seduce me?"

"The rules."

"So I'm a challenge for you."

"That, you are." Light blue eyes held hers. "But honestly, if all I wanted was you in my bed, I could have managed it."

"Perhaps," she hedged.

"Very well. Perhaps."

He touched his mouth to hers. It already seemed as though she'd been waiting forever for him to kiss her tonight, but my, it had been worth the wait. Her heart pounded. She'd never felt as desired, or as dispossessed of her senses, as she did now. The surging waves and the lightning and thunder crashing around the ship resonated through her, as though the weather itself echoed the chaos of her feelings.

"You're seducing me now, aren't you?"

"I damned well hope so."

By Suzanne Enoch

Historical Titles

RULES OF AN ENGAGEMENT
A LADY'S GUIDE TO IMPROPER BEHAVIOR
THE CARE AND TAMING OF A ROGUE
ALWAYS A SCOUNDREL
BEFORE THE SCANDAL
AFTER THE KISS
TWICE THE TEMPTATION
SINS OF A DUKE
SOMETHING SINFUL
AN INVITATION TO SIN
SIN AND SENSIBILITY
ENGLAND'S PERFECT HERO
LONDON'S PERFECT SCOUNDREL
THE RAKE
A MATTER OF SCANDAL
MEET ME AT MIDNIGHT
REFORMING A RAKE
TAMING RAFE
BY LOVE UNDONE
STOLEN KISSES
LADY ROGUE

Contemporary Titles

A TOUCH OF MINX
BILLIONAIRES PREFER BLONDES
DON'T LOOK DOWN
FLIRTING WITH DANGER

SUZANNE ENOCH

Rules of an ENGAGEMENT

AVON
An Imprint of HarperCollins*Publishers*

This is a work of fiction. Names, characters, places, and incidents are products of the author's imagination or are used fictitiously and are not to be construed as real. Any resemblance to actual events, locales, organizations, or persons, living or dead, is entirely coincidental.

AVON BOOKS
An Imprint of HarperCollins*Publishers*
10 East 53rd Street
New York, New York 10022-5299

ISBN 978-0-06-166222-5
www.avonromance.com

First Avon Books paperback printing: November 2010

Printed in the U.S.A.

10 9 8 7 6 5 4 3 2 1

For everyone who wanted Bradshaw Carroway
to have his own story.
Enjoy!

Prologue

"Reload! Prepare to fire the deck guns! Take out that damned mainmast before she gets the wind behind her!"

All fourteen of the eighteen-pound cannons on the starboard main deck let fly. A hard heartbeat later the entire ship shook as the larger guns directly below them added their roar into the melee, firing in near unison. In response the French frigate *Revanche* seemed to fly apart, sail and wood and metal exploding out in every direction.

Fifty yards across the water from the privateer, on his own vessel the *Nemesis*, Captain Bradshaw Carroway stood on the upper deck and narrowed his eyes to see through the billowing smoke. For a moment, even with the sound of yelling and musket fire and barked orders spinning around him, everything went still. They wouldn't have time for another volley. He'd have to circle into the wind, and they would lose position. And then the mainmast and foremast of the pirate ship swayed in drunken unison.

"We've got her!" he bellowed. "Bring us in closer, Varley!"

"Aye, aye, Captain!"

"Prepare to board her, Mr. Gerard!"

"Aye, aye!" The first lieutenant snapped a sharp salute and charged down the steps to the main deck.

A musket ball whizzed by his ear, but Bradshaw barely noted it. His *Nemesis* was the smaller of the two ships by a fraction, but she was at least as heavily armed—and his men a damned sight more proficient with the cannons. "Mr. Abrams, I want our big guns aimed below the *Revanche*'s waterline. If I can't take her, I'm bloody well going to sink her."

His third mate nodded and hurried below to deliver the order. At the same time Peter Potter ran up to Bradshaw to hand over his sword. "Here y'are, Captain," the midshipman said, as Shaw buckled on the sword and stuffed two pistols into his belt. "Remind them damned Frenchies that Bonaparte's already had his one escape, and he don't get another."

"That is my intention," Bradshaw replied with a grim smile, having to raise his voice to be heard over the shouts and weapons fire. He looked down at Gerard and signaled before turning his attention to his second mate. "Keep the *Nemesis* as close as you can, Mr. Newsome. Try to avoid blowing a hole through the *Revanche*'s guts unless she's about to do the same to us."

Lieutenant Newsome tugged on the brim of his hat. "I'll see to it, sir."

The grappling hooks were already flying through the air, snagging the French ship's railing and collapsed rigging and dragging the two ships closer together. Working his way through the men and debris, Shaw stepped up onto the *Nemesis*'s railing. At the bellow from Gerard to board the *Revanche*, he jumped.

Most captains would likely remain on their own ship and let others carry out their orders. He, however, wasn't most captains. Pulling his sword, he sliced through a French sailor as the fellow charged at him, musket and bayonet in hand.

Sailing a ship, commanding a ship, was well and good, and he loved the sea. A good fight, however, the roar of chaos and blood and glory, came around far too infrequently these days to be missed. Something burned through his upper left arm, but he ignored it. In fact, he realized that he was grinning as he shot and stabbed his way toward the tall fellow with the oversized hat who crouched behind the wheel on the upper deck. The *Revanche*'s captain didn't seem to enjoy fighting as much as he did.

A sailor came at him low, a saber in one hand. Bradshaw slammed down on the weapon with his own sword, at the same time sending a boot into the man's face. The pirate dropped with a grunt. Scrambling over the fallen mast, Shaw yanked another man off Lieutenant Gerard. "Lead the jollies below decks," he ordered. "I don't want any surprises later."

"Aye, aye, sir. And thank you, Captain."

"I don't want to have to go through the bother of training someone to replace you."

With a grin, Gerard motioned to the commander of the two dozen red-jacketed marines, and they all surged forward.

Heaving another man over his shoulder, Bradshaw charged up the stairs. A saber nearly sliced off his left ear. He ducked the blow and feinted sideways, then with his left hand shoved the muzzle of his pistol beneath the chin of the *Revanche*'s captain.

The man glared at him, and Bradshaw lifted an eyebrow. "*Capitulez*, Captain Molyneux," he ordered.

With an oath the captain threw down his saber. "*Baissez les armes!*" he bellowed.

Below them muskets and swords and pistols clanked to the deck. Bradshaw tipped his hat. "*Merci, Capitaine*."

His own crew began shouting and cheering, then favored the French crew with a rendition of "God Save the King." Bradshaw issued orders to have the prisoners locked up below, and then returned to the deck of his own ship.

"Captain, ye've got a hole in ye," Potter said, his expression concerned.

"Do I?" Shaw finally looked down to see blood trailing from a hole in the left sleeve of his blue jacket. "It'll keep. See that the wounded get down to Dr. Griffeth, and go assist him. And tell him he owes me five quid, because I didn't get killed."

"Cap'n, the good doc got a hole blown through his head."

Damnation. Shaw slowed, the heady exhilaration of battle crumbling into surprisingly sharp-edged sorrow. God knew he'd lost friends before, but they'd been warriors, falling in battle. Simon Griffeth had been a gentle-hearted healer through and through. The two of them had sailed together for the past eight years, and the most pain Simon had ever caused had been with his knife-sharp wit. He drew a hard breath. Those who didn't fight weren't supposed to be killed, damn it all. "Then you're our new surgeon, Potter," he said aloud, keeping his expression cool. Other men had lost their lives today, and he would mourn his friend in private once he returned to his cabin. "Recruit whoever you need to aid you."

With a nod the sailor hurried off. His third mate, Lieutenant Merriwether Abrams, approached, the grin on his face fading as he took in Shaw's red arm. "Captain, you—"

"I know. What's our damage?"

"We'll need a new forward mast and half the starboard railing replaced. No holes below the waterline."

"Good. Men?"

"Nine dead, thirty-seven wounded. Only five seriously, though. Gerard's inspecting the *Revanche*, but she looks seaworthy. I don't know her crew count yet."

Bradshaw rolled his shoulders, wincing as the movement pulled at the wound in his arm. "Tell Gerard to take what crew and supplies he needs. He'll be captaining the *Revanche* back to Southampton. You're to be his second."

The wiry, blond-haired man grinned again. "Thank you, sir."

"Yes, well, don't get too comfortable. I want you back on the *Nemesis* when we get our orders."

"The East Indies this time, do you think?"

"Considering that this is the only pirate we've come across in the last four months, I imagine we've about cleared the Mediterranean of privateers." A week ago, an hour ago, the proposal of seeking more glory in battle anywhere would have had him grinning. At this moment, and for the first time in a long time, he was looking forward to returning to England. *Him*. The man who could barely tolerate dry land. Realizing that Abrams was still eyeing him, Shaw forced a brief smile. "The East Indies would be interesting. So would anywhere, as long as it's not surrounded by land."

Abrams drew himself up to a salute. "Aye, aye, Captain."

Perhaps this was an abrupt and temporary onset of nostalgia. After all, he did miss his horde of brothers after better than a year away. And once he returned to land he imagined that the longing to be at sea would seep into him once more. Battle, though—the East Indies—he wasn't so certain about. Not today. He could only hope that being back in London would remind him that generally he didn't care where the Admiralty might send the *Nemesis* next, as long as they went somewhere.

Five months later

Captain Bradshaw Carroway looked from the missive in one hand to the sealed orders in the other.

"Well?" his youngest brother, Edward, prompted, leaning across the breakfast table on his elbows.

"I'm anticipating, Runt."

"You've been anticipating for five weeks, Shaw. And since you told me if you didn't like your orders you were going to turn pirate, I want to know what they say." The ten-year-old reached over and tapped the back of the orders with one forefinger. "Now. If we're being pirates, I need to go purchase a parrot."

"You're not being a pirate." Their eldest brother Tristan, Lord Dare, strolled into the breakfast room. Wordlessly one of the footmen hurried over to pour a cup of tea and place it at the head of the table. "And you're supposed to acquire a parrot during your adventures, not in advance of them."

"But Shaw's been on several adventures, and he doesn't have a parrot."

"He doesn't have anything from his adventures, thankfully." Tristan sent him a rueful glance before making his way over to the sideboard to select his breakfast. "Do you?"

Bradshaw snorted. "No." He waved the missive, the second surprise of the morning, in the viscount's direction. "Why is the Duke of Sommerset inviting me to his home?"

"How should I know? He doesn't have a wife for you to have . . . danced with," Tristan returned, glancing at their shortest brother.

"I don't care about dancing," Edward broke in again. "Or Sommerset. Open your damned orders, Shaw."

"Edward, do not let my wife catch you using that language." Tristan sent him a mock scowl.

"I already know that foul language is only for men. Please, Shaw?"

He preferred to open his orders in private. Especially when he remained so damned skittish over whether he wanted to sail away again or do something as abysmal as retiring. Hiding his sudden nerves behind a forced grin, he broke the seal and unfolded the thick set of pages.

"Well?" the Runt repeated.

"Apparently I'm to dine on coconuts and native breadfruit."

Edward jumped up from the table. "The Pacific! We're going to be pirates in the Pacific!"

Clearing his throat, Tristan reached out and

grabbed the hopping boy by the jacket. "Go tell Georgiana the news," he ordered. "Quietly. Arabella finally fell asleep an hour ago, and Georgie will string you up from a yardarm or some such thing if you awaken her."

"I'm Arabella's uncle, you know. I look out for her."

Bradshaw waited until Edward was well out of hearing before he let out a sigh. "The Pacific Ocean. I've always wanted to captain a ship around Cape Horn."

"I'm pleased that you're pleased," his oldest brother said quietly. "Are you pleased?"

"What kind of question is that?" Shaw bit back, too strenuously. "I'm a ship's captain. I'm supposed to be at sea."

Tristan continued to eye him. "I'm not an idiot, despite what my wife says. You've been . . . solemn since you returned from the Mediterranean."

If he owed anyone an explanation, it was his oldest brother. "I told you that I lost a friend during that last battle. I've lost friends before, but for some reason it's made me think. And don't laugh."

"I'm not laughing. Think about what?"

"About what I want, I suppose. About whether going about firing cannons at things is enough for a life." He shrugged. "Though I do like firing at things." It was firing at *people* that abruptly had him uneasy. And that was not something a naval captain should be troubled about, for God's sake.

"I know you do." Tristan shifted. "When do you sail?"

Taking a breath, Bradshaw read through the highlights of the first page again. "Four weeks. I'm to take the *Nemesis* to Port Jackson in Australia, where I will be receiving further orders."

"So you're going on a voyage for what, a year and a half, to . . . what?"

Bradshaw frowned. The East Indies certainly seemed likely, but they were sending him on a rather roundabout route if that was the case. "Don't have the faintest idea."

"That would be enough to make *me* question my orders," his brother commented.

"As long as I'm a captain, the wheres and whys aren't supposed to be of any importance to me. Admiral Dolenz is in command out there, so I imagine I'll find out when I arrive."

"Admiral Dolenz, the father of Miss Louisa Dolenz?" Tristan asked skeptically. "The young lady you t—"

"I'm sure she never mentioned that to her father," Bradshaw broke in, scowling. Good God, he could end up stranded permanently in Australia. Perhaps a strategic retirement would be for the best, after all, considering the nonsense they were likely to task him with. "And she said she forgave me. We even danced, last week."

"You'd best hope she has." The viscount paused. "Shaw, you know you don't need to do th—"

"I'm restless, Tristan." That part of him never seemed to fade, whatever his other reservations. It was just that he didn't know any longer what he was restless *for*.

"Then take up estate management. I could use the assistance."

"Scribbling in a ledger isn't my idea of useful. Particularly not when you have clerks to do that for you. Likewise with me serving as the designated minder of the Runt and your menagerie. It's useless."

"One daughter is not a menagerie. And you're not useless."

"I feel useless. I'm one-and-thirty, still living at my brother's home. Even damned Robert's married and moved out, and he spent three years unable to leave the house. And then there's Andrew, who will be finished with Cambridge this year. It's about to be just Edward and me hanging on to your coattails. You don't need me here."

"You're part of this family."

"Which is a lovely thing."

"And if you're unhapp—"

"I didn't say that. I'm contemplating." He folded his orders and pocketed them for a more detailed perusal later. "So who knows? In the next four weeks I may decide you have the better idea, after all." He leaned back to pull his watch from his pocket and flip it open. "And I seem to have an appointment with the Duke of Sommerset in twenty minutes." Standing, he clapped his brother on the shoulder. "Wouldn't you be pleased if I decided I'm becoming too old for adventuring?"

Viscount Dare frowned. "You're not too old for it. But I'd like to think you're becoming too wise for it."

"And how likely is that?"

He and his black Arabian, Zeus, arrived at Ainsley House on Grosvenor Square just before ten o'clock. Whatever it was that the Duke of Sommerset wanted, the man had enough influence that no one in his right mind would ignore an invitation. And despite what his family occasionally claimed, Bradshaw was generally in his right mind.

The square-shouldered butler, smartly liveried in red and black, opened the front door as Bradshaw topped the shallow granite steps. "Captain Carroway," he said. "You're expected. This way, if you please."

Hm. More curious by the minute, Bradshaw followed the man into a comfortable-looking sitting room just off the foyer. The walls and shelves were covered with artifacts and decorations from—well, from everywhere, as far as he could tell.

"His Grace will be with you in a moment," the butler said, and backed out the door, shutting Bradshaw inside.

Shaw strolled over to the window. Many people found a ship to be terribly confining, but he wasn't one of them. On the best of days a ship, his ship, opened the world up before him. Very few people had the ability to sleep in their own bed each night and still see something new out their front door each day. Until the battle with the *Revanche* he hadn't thought he would ever tire of gazing at the horizon. Only since then had he noticed that the view was . . . empty.

The door opened. "Captain, thank you for coming." Nicholas Ainsley, the Duke of Sommerset, stepped into the room and shut the door again. Tall and black-haired, steel gray eyes steady and speculative, he leaned back against the near wall.

"You made me curious," Bradshaw returned.

"You were wounded on your last voyage, as I recall. How is your arm?"

Shaw flexed it. "Good as new. Ball missed the bone."

"I'm glad to hear that. And you're shipping out soon. What, four weeks from now?"

While his specific orders likely hadn't been made public, the fact that he was to sail would be no secret to anyone, much less a man of Sommerset's resources. "Approximately. Are you intending to travel again? I don't shuttle civilians, but in your case I imagine the Admiralty would make an exception."

Sommerset smiled. "If I wished to go somewhere, I would hire my own ship. I find most naval accommodations rather . . . cramped." He gestured at the carvings and pottery on the shelves beside him. "And there aren't many places I haven't been."

"If it's not transportation you want then, Your Grace, what is it?" If Sommerset wanted to reminisce over his travels, the duke might at least offer him a drink. Or a damned chair. "I do have some duties on my ship before we depart," he said aloud, providing himself an excuse if he wanted to leave.

"I have two things to discuss with you, Captain." The duke straightened. "First, you must promise me your discretion."

This was getting odder by the minute. Still, Sommerset, while he'd been a bit wild growing up, had an impeccable reputation. Better than his own, Shaw reflected. "You have my word."

"I am a member of both the Africa Association and the Royal Society. I assume I keep getting asked to chair committees concerning world exploration because of the breadth of my travels—though that doesn't explain why I keep agreeing to serve."

This all seemed rather rhetorical, so Shaw kept his mouth closed and waited. Sommerset wasn't known to prattle on, so hopefully the duke would reach his point soon—or at least offer a tour of his more exotic weaponry. As he'd told Tristan, he did enjoy shooting at things.

"Anyway," the duke continued, "I understand that you're going to the Pacific. That makes sense from the Admiralty's point of view; the Spanish think they own the entire expanse, which is both annoying and troublesome. They would block the rest of the world from exploration and knowledge if they could. And then there's France, which is rumored to be constructing strategic fortifications at the fringes of Spanish occupation."

Or perhaps Sommerset wouldn't reach his point, after all. "If I'm not mistaken, the Royal Society is a bastion of science and learning. What—"

"Yes, I know. I leave the politics for the House of Lords and the battle strategies to the Admiralty. You're here at this moment because I have a debt to settle, and a favor to ask."

Shaw lifted an eyebrow. "What sort of debt and favor?"

"On the main island of Tahiti, a mile or so inland of Matavai Bay, there is a small cluster of huts beside a waterfall. Or at least there was, at one time. If it still exists, and if you find a fellow there with one eye, I'm asking you to give him this." Sommerset dug a hand into one pocket and produced a small mirror, the frame edged with gold filigree and studded with gemstones.

"Does this one-eyed man have a name?"

"The sailors in my party called him King George, because of his resemblance to our monarch. The fellow liked the moniker so much that he adopted it."

"I'll be journeying to Tahiti then, I presume? You seem to know more about my orders than I do."

"I don't know the details. But make your way to Tahiti. King George gave up his most prized possession for my benefit. I promised him that I would replace it. I was also foolish, and said I would do so within ten years." He scowled briefly. "It's been nearly nine. I can't go myself; not now. It seems . . . dishonorable to eschew one duty in order to fulfill another. But I'm not willing to risk being cursed by a man who once saved my life. Not when I can fulfill my oath through you. You have until August twenty-eighth of next year, or we both will have failed."

If there was one thing Bradshaw understood, it was honor and the sacredness of giving one's word. But it stirred him in a different way, as well. Sommerset's little favor gave him a reason to sail one last time. An honorable reason, and one that didn't involve placing men for whom he was responsible in danger for no good reason. The hard, black knot growing inside his chest loosened a little.

"You make a persuasive argument. I think." Shaw took the mirror and examined it. "What sort of curse was that, anyway?"

"He didn't go into specifics, though in my life I've seen some fairly odd things. I'm more concerned about the worth of my word. So don't take this on unless you mean to either see it delivered or die in the attempt. Because I am counting on the worth of *your* word."

"I'll see to it." Shaw pocketed the bauble. "Though I'm at a loss as to why you're trusting me. We aren't precisely friends."

"That leads me to the second discussion. Just under a year ago, I finished renovations to the west wing of Ainsley House here. In the course of my previous travels, I have found that the most difficult part of the journey was returning again to London." He tilted his head. "Do you know what I mean?"

"Yes." Bradshaw took a breath. This was what he'd never been able to explain to Tristan. Their middle brother, Robert, understood, but he'd returned from the Continent so damaged by the war with Bonaparte that communicating with him at all had been nearly impossible until just the last few months when he'd found Lucinda. "London is very . . . small." Especially now, when the most difficult thing to escape from was turning out to be his own thoughts.

"Precisely. And with that in mind, I created a gentlemen's club. I call it the Adventurers' Club, and I decide the membership. At the moment we are fourteen. All men who for one reason or another have found themselves at the ends of the earth and have returned to see London and Society with perhaps a clearer view than most. Would you like to see it?"

"You've built a club here? At your home?"

"Yes. And while you're a bit more . . . civilized than the majority of our members, your career and character and past actions more than qualify you to be here." He hesitated as though he was considering whether to say something more, then pulled back and instead made a sweeping gesture. "I am therefore inviting you to join us."

"I don't quite know what to say."

"Come and see." The duke opened the door again, and led the way back through the foyer and along a hallway running the front of the house. He stopped at a plain, latched door. "This is my entrance. If you wish to join, you will be provided with a key that opens a door directly into the club from outside. The only rules here are firstly, no guests of either sex are allowed and, secondly, no one else is to be told about this place. We are a refuge, and I don't want the general peerage clamoring for entry." He opened the door and stood aside.

That made sense. As Bradshaw stepped through the door, though, he set his contemplation of the rules aside. The room was large and open, the walls paneled with dark wood and liberally decorated with items likely from Sommerset's travels. A trio of tall windows at the far end overlooked a garden, while a pianoforte and a billiards table rested in an open space. Tables and chairs lay grouped across the floor, with a comfortable sofa and pair of chairs clustered in front of a roaring fire and the back wall lined with shelves and shelves of books. "This is very nice."

"There are spare rooms through there," the duke said, gesturing at a door in the back corner, "in case anyone should require a place to sleep. Still interested?"

"Still interested."

"Good." Sommerset glanced across the room, presently occupied by three men plus a fellow dressed like a footman who perched on a stool by a door at the front of the room. "Let me introduce you around."

Two of the four men present were already looking

at him curiously. He recognized one of them, but kept pace beside the duke. "Within a month I'll be leaving for three or so years. You might have waited to invite me until after I delivered your . . . gift and kept both our words."

"I'm asking a large favor of you. In return, I wanted to be certain you knew you could have a drink and a chair or a bed here when you return." Sommerset looked at him for a moment. "Simon Griffeth was my second cousin."

Shaw flinched before he could arrest the motion. He and Simon had chatted about overbearing and aristocratic relations, but— hell, he should have remembered. "My condolences."

"His father showed me the letter you wrote after he was killed. They framed it, as a matter of fact. It was a very . . . exceptional letter."

"Simon was a very good friend."

"He was my good friend, as well. And that is why you're here, and why I'm handing you both a burden and a reward. Simon trusted you. Therefore, so do I."

For once not quite certain what to say, Bradshaw inclined his head. "Thank you."

The duke nodded. Taking a breath, he gestured at the closer of the two men seated in front of the hearth. "This is Mr. Thomas Easton," Sommerset drawled, his voice cool and detached once more. "He spent a year in Persia to encourage the expansion of the silk trade to Britain. Easton, Captain Bradshaw Carroway."

Easton squinted one eye at him. "Carroway. So now the only qualification to join the Adventurers' Club is, what, to survive a rough sea?"

"The only qualification," the duke returned easily, "is my say-so. I see you're awake, Colonel."

The second man sent an annoyed glance at Easton. "Under the circumstances, there's little else I could be."

Sommerset gave a brief grin. "Captain Carroway, this is Colonel Bartholomew James. Tolly served for a time in India."

"Captain."

Bradshaw nodded, straightening. His brother Robert had shown him the article in the *London Times* upon Colonel James's return a few weeks ago. If for no other reason than Bit's reaction, he knew that something horrific had happened to the colonel. "I read about your ordeal. My condolences."

Colonel James gazed at him levelly for a moment, odd amber-brown eyes distant. "Thank you," he said.

"Come, Sommerset," Mr. Easton broke in, "you always have a reason for admitting another uncivilized beast into your club. What's our dear Captain Carroway here for?"

"That's for him to tell, if he wishes to do so—just as I only mention the parts of your tale that you've made public knowledge."

The duke motioned Bradshaw to follow him. "I'm the only navy man here, I presume?" Shaw asked in a low voice.

"Yes. And though you may not be as . . . damaged as some of the other members, I do recognize a fellow outcast—and a man of character—when I see one." He gestured. This is Lord Hennessy."

Smiling, Bradshaw offered his hand. "Malcolm and I attended Oxford together."

The earl shook hands with him. "Not shipwrecked yet, Shaw?"

"Not yet. Last I heard, Malcolm, you were on your way to South America."

Hennessy's expression tightened a little. "One day I'll tell you about that. Good to see you here. We could use someone who still has a sense of humor."

After that, Sommerset introduced him to the footman, Gibbs, who explained that the Adventurers' Club never closed its doors and that any and all of them came and went as they pleased. Then Sommerset held out a key to him.

"Do you wish to join us?"

Given the growing list of things he couldn't discuss with his family members and the fact that he was about to add another three or four years of absence from London to his list of sins and that he didn't even have his own lodgings in Town, a refuge within London seemed a damned fine idea. Especially now when he was occupied with the unfamiliar act of contemplation. "Yes. I believe I would."

With a brief smile, the duke handed him the key. "Join us whenever you like. As I said, however, no one else is to know."

"I understand." Bradshaw dropped the key into his pocket as the duke showed him through the outside door, hidden just off the drive by an archway of vines. "Thank you." He offered his hand. "And I suppose I'll see you in three years or so."

Sommerset shook hands with him. "See that you do. And do as I asked, or I'll be taking that key back." He lowered his voice. "You can keep the curse."

"Yes. Thanks for that."

Chapter One

Then why should we quarrel for riches
Or any such glittering toys?
A light heart, and a thin pair of breeches
Will go through the world, my brave boys.

"WHY SHOULD WE QUARREL FOR RICHES"
TRADITIONAL SEA SHANTY

Eleven months later

A knock came at Shaw's cabin door. "It's Potter, sir."

"Enter," Shaw called, pulling off his worn shirt. According to the calendar it was May, autumn where the *Nemesis* lay in the Southern Hemisphere. By God, it didn't feel like any autumn he'd experienced before. And as someone who didn't particularly like huddling around a spitting hearth while snow blew outside, it was damned pleasant, if on occasion overly warm.

He glanced at the box on his shelf where he'd placed Sommerset's mirror. Taking a possibly cursed item on board a ship was mad, but at the same time he'd felt . . . rudderless since Simon's death. The task the duke had given him at least provided him a sense of purpose, something he could keep in mind when he couldn't stand considering his murky future for another damned minute. A debt of honor—it might be that for Sommerset, but for him it was very nearly the last piece of floating timber on the sea.

"Captain. Shoes so polished I could shave in 'em." The midshipman set the dress shoes on a chair.

"My thanks. Help me with this, will you?" Indicating his formal dress coat, Bradshaw pulled on a clean, freshly pressed shirt.

"Aye. So where d'you think Admiral Dolenz will be sending us?" Potter asked, holding up the dark blue coat with its gold epaulets and white edging.

"From the supplies I would imagine Tahiti, or perhaps Manila."

"No chance he'll send us on to the East Indies?"

"A very slight chance. The Dutch do seem to be misbehaving. From what I've read, however, the ladies in Tahiti wear fewer clothes than the ones in India." His orders hadn't spoken of anything specific other than Australia, so whatever Sommerset had seemed to know was only an assumption. A good one, or he would have detoured to put in at Tahiti during the voyage west. But something was afoot, and he still had enough time to be willing to let it play out. Shaking himself, he grinned. "If they wear anything at all."

"By God, I hope we're off to Tahiti, then."

"I'll mention your preference to the admiral."

The midshipman chuckled. "By the way, Dr. Howard inquired whether he was to join you for dinner this evening."

Bradshaw hid his frown. Of the one hundred eighty-three men presently assigned to his ship, the one he would have preferred to do without was Dr. Christopher Howard. Considering that Howard's older brother was the Earl of Hemswich, however, leaving him behind at Southampton had been out of the question. And since technically Howard ranked higher in Society than he did, leaving him out of any social function was equally difficult. If nothing else, it made the absence of Simon Griffeth even more painful than it already was. "Yes, he's to join me," he said after a moment.

"I believe he's dressing already, actually."

"Not a bit surprised." He finished buttoning his waistcoat, and buckled on his ceremonial sword as Potter brushed any wrinkles from the back of his coat. "Until Gerard returns from his . . . tailor's appointment in town, Newsome has the command. And tell Everett he'd best get that woman out of the bosun's storeroom before Dobbs discovers them and has him strung up from the yardarm by his balls."

Potter cleared his throat. "I'll see to it, Captain. Tailor's appointment. I had one o' those day before yesterday. Cost me three shillings, that bunter did."

Retrieving his hat and the carefully wrapped set of books he'd brought along just for this evening, Bradshaw left his cabin. Giving the brass plaque of Poseidon nailed to the wall a knock with his knuckles, he emerged into the late afternoon sunlight to find Dr. Howard already waiting for him.

As a civilian Christopher could dress as he pleased, and at the moment he wouldn't have looked out of place in London's finest ballroom. Of course Bradshaw, in his dress blues with the fancy braiding on the sleeves and his peaked captain's hat, also looked rather splendid, if he said so himself. He settled the hat on his head.

"Shall we?"

"Are we hiring a hack?"

Bradshaw shook his head. "The admiral's sending a coach."

"Thank God. From the look of things, I thought it might be a hay wagon."

"Mm hm."

He himself rather liked the primitive feel of these new settlements on the very edges of civilization. His first voyage to Barbados in the West Indies, he'd ridden a donkey to accompany his captain to greet the local chieftain. With a grin and a salute to Newsome he descended the steep gangplank and made for the waiting coach.

After a fortnight in port he'd regained his land legs, and mostly he was anxious to discover what the Admiralty meant for him to do. As Howard took the opposite seat and they rolled down the dirt road heading for the hillside on which Admiral Dolenz's home perched, he allowed himself the luxury of speculation.

Under a succession of captains on a succession of ships, he'd fought Bonaparte, skirmished with the Spanish, sunk a pirate or two, and survived rounding the Cape of Good Hope on three different occasions. As captain himself, he'd escorted a trio of supply ships to Belize and back again, and he'd patrolled the Mediterranean against renegade French forces attempting to fund a second escape for their Emperor. He'd written the final chapter of that duty with the interception of the infamous *Revanche*.

That should have set him up nicely for more

killing—Dutch or Spanish pirates roaming through the maze of the East Indies, most likely. He was therefore rather surprised to be out in the middle of the wilderness. And thankful for it. At the worst he would be escorting supply ships from Port Jackson to Tahiti and back, which at the moment he preferred—though he could never admit to that aloud.

"How many of these people are convicts?" Dr. Howard asked, glancing through the coach window at the crowded streets outside, a handkerchief over his nose and mouth.

"Some of them. Don't worry. I'll protect you."

"I only hope I don't get fleas. I've never seen so many damned goats and sheep, even in the Cotswolds."

Bradshaw eyed him. "Just why are you here?"

"Your ship needed a surgeon."

"Yes, and you're sterling at lancing blisters. What I mean to say is, you're the Earl of Hemswich's brother. Why are you a physician, and why are you serving as a surgeon on a naval ship?"

Christopher Howard shifted, but kept his place at the very edge of the seat as though he feared that fleas might even have invaded the admiral's coach. "My father detested the clergy, and only a fool who can't do better joins the military. No offense."

"None taken." *Arrogant git.*

"As for why I'm here, halfway around the world, that's a private matter."

"Ah." It wasn't as private as he'd like to think; Bradshaw happened to know that both daughters of the Marquis of Bregins had gone to take the air in the country at the same time, just before Hemswich had arranged for his brother to earn his passage out of Britain. Apparently Dr. Howard couldn't keep his cock in his breeches, or a French condom on his cock.

Shaw enjoyed female company immensely himself, but he took precautions. At the least, he didn't believe in shirking responsibility. Though after eleven months of enforced celibacy, responsibility and common sense were beginning to plummet on his list. Even the soiled doves who hung about the docks here waiting for sailors were beginning to look appealing. Clearly he needed to shake off his melancholy, reach Tahiti, and then decide what the devil he wanted to do with the remainder of his life.

"I could ask why you're here at Port Jackson instead of fending off the Dutch in the East Indies," Howard commented into the silence.

Shaw shook himself. "I go where I'm sent. As do we both, I suppose."

"I suppose."

"The difference being, I'm not afraid to return to London."

"Bugger off, Carroway."

"*Captain* Carroway. You're on my ship, if you'll recall."

"I recall. Captain."

Thankfully the drive was fairly short, and the coach turned up the long, straight path to the top of the hill before it stopped in front of a broad-fronted sprawl of a white building. The portico stretched the entire width of the house, evenly spaced pillars lending the residence a classical Roman feel. Only the large, open windows on the ground and upper floors spoke of the Tropics and the evening trade winds.

"Now this looks more civilized," Dr. Howard commented, following him to the ground and toward the open double front doors.

"What did you expect?" Bradshaw returned, nodding to the butler and handing over his hat and gloves. "Blue face paint and fur loincloths? The admiral is English, and the Duke of Radcliffe's grandson."

"All I know is that since we've docked I've seen more dirty faces, secondhand clothing, and filth than I ever saw in England."

"And goats and sheep. You mentioned that, as well, I believe." Clearly Dr. Howard hadn't spent much time outside Mayfair. Unpleasant and given to whining or not, however, the doctor was still the most qualified of any on board to bind broken bones and sew cuts closed. Therefore, he needed to be tolerated.

"This way, gentlemen," the butler said, leading them up the stairs.

The servant stopped just outside a set of closed doors. Taking a breath, he pushed them open and stepped through. "Captain Bradshaw Carroway and Dr. Christopher Howard," he announced, and moved aside.

Considering that they were being announced, more than Admiral Dolenz had to be inside the drawing room. Glancing sideways to be certain that Howard wasn't going to trample him to enter first, Bradshaw stepped into the room.

For a heartbeat he thought himself back in Mayfair, in the drawing room of one of the great houses there. A large crystal chandelier hung from the center of the ceiling and made the candlelight sparkle. Scattered about the room beneath it, two dozen ladies and gentleman were gathered, all dressed in the finest silks and linens.

"Good evening, Captain, Dr. Howard."

Admiral Dolenz came forward, and Bradshaw straightened to give his best salute. His orders had already been decided, of course, but good manners couldn't hurt. "Admiral. Thank you for the invitation."

"I would ordinarily say that proper Society is rare here at Port Jackson, but as you can see, at the moment we are overwhelmed with it." The admiral gestured at the room around him.

A tall, well-dressed man stepped up. "We were on our way to Manila, but our boat br—"

"Our ship," a female voice interrupted, and a pretty blond-haired lady wrapped her arm around the gentleman's. "The *Halcyon*. It ran aground on a reef. We've been stranded here for nearly a month, and the captain's said it will be another four weeks before the repairs are completed and we can hope to resume our journey."

"That's a shame," Dr. Howard put in, brushing past Bradshaw. "Manila is poorer for not having you present."

Just barely Bradshaw refrained from rolling his eyes. "Are all of you from the *Halcyon*?" he asked.

"Not all of us, Captain." An older man rose from his seat by the window and walked forward to offer his hand. "Joseph Ponsley," he said. "Late from India."

That name sounded familiar. "*Sir* Joseph Ponsley?"

"Yes, indeed. You've read my book on deciduous plant species, then? Or perhaps my climate and rainfall dissertation."

"My younger brother has. Both of them. I'm . . . not much of a reader, generally."

A faint female snort of derision caught his ear, but with the crowd milling around him, he couldn't tell from where it had come. Perhaps he'd misheard.

"It's a rather narrow field of interest, I admit," Sir Joseph returned with a smile.

Shaking the botanist's hand, Bradshaw forced a grin. "Thank you for saying that." He took the paper-wrapped package from beneath his arm and handed it to the admiral. "You, however, *are* a reader, sir, I believe."

Admiral Dolenz opened the package. "Nicely done, Captain," he said after a moment, turning to the title page of the top book. "A first edition of *Rob Roy*."

"All three volumes," Shaw added, silently thanking his brother Robert for being a voracious reader.

"I suppose now you may sit at my elbow for dinner, then."

"Where would I have been otherwise?"

The admiral sent him a dark look. "In the kitchen, very likely." He winked.

That settled that, at least. The admiral did not know what his daughter had been up to in his absence. Thank God. Feeling a bit easier, Shaw accepted a glass of Madeira from a footman and went to mingle.

Dr. Howard apparently knew at least half the admiral's guests, and considering that a large number of them seemed to be displaced English aristocrats,

Bradshaw wasn't surprised. As for himself, he recognized two of them by name, while three others looked familiar. The remainder of the guests were more than likely recent residents of Port Jackson, because the talk seemed to center around London gossip—though how much of it remained pertinent after better than a year, he had no idea. Apparently old gossip was better than no gossip at all.

The butler rang a gong and announced dinner, and Bradshaw found himself seated at Admiral Dolenz's right elbow. He held the chair on his other side as a petite young woman with brass-streaked chestnut hair came to stand beside him. "Bradshaw Carroway," he said, pushing her chair in as she sat.

"Zephyr Ponsley," she returned, holding up her wine glass for a footman to fill. "I haven't written anything, so you needn't worry about not having read it."

"So you were the one snorting at me before," he commented, reaching for a slice of fresh-baked bread.

"Was I? You must have said something distasteful, then."

This chit didn't seem to be interested in the mountain of gossip still going round the table. "I suppose honesty can be distasteful."

"Perhaps there are some things you shouldn't be honest about. The fact that you don't read, for example, cannot be much to brag about."

He glanced sideways at her. She was pretty enough, he supposed, with a glow to her skin that said she'd spent time out of doors. She had breasts of just the right size to fill a man's hands, and an appetizing curve to her hips. Her mouth, however, seemed to be something else entirely. "Did I shoot your dog or something?" he asked aloud.

"Is that something I should expect?" she returned in the same tone. "You seem to be both ignorant *and* bloodthirsty."

"My point being," Bradshaw commented, finding himself rather amused by the argument, "you're quite unpleasant. I'm attempting to determine whether you speak to everyone you've just met in the same manner, or if I've been singled out for special treatment."

Gray eyes crinkled briefly. "In my experience, people who don't read have small minds, leaving me with very little to say to them."

"And yet you've already spoken volumes to me." He wasn't mistaken; she was enjoying lambasting him. Which as far as he was concerned meant he could respond in kind. "I didn't say that I don't read. I said that I'm not much of a reader. There is a difference. I tend to be occupied with other things." He cleared his throat. "I do read ship's charts, for example. I even keep a log."

She opened her mouth, then closed it again as footmen brought around the baked fish and potatoes. "I read everything. The complete works of Captain Cook, for example."

Bradshaw reflected that the last time he'd attempted an intellectual argument with anyone, he'd lost twenty quid and awakened in Dover with his left foot encased in dried plaster. Damned Simon Griffeth. Still, it had been an entertaining evening, with a kind of joy and exhilaration to it that he'd missed. And arguing with this chit seemed more . . . personal than intellectual. "Those, I've read," he said aloud.

"Captain," the pretty blond woman said from across the table, "do tell us about your ship."

"With pleasure. The *Nemesis* is a one-thousand-seventy-ton frigate. She launched in 1808 and carries forty-six cannons, most of them eighteen pounders. She's outfitted for a crew complement of three hundred twenty, but we're currently carrying only one hundred eighty-three."

"That's a great many numbers," the lady said with a giggle.

The gentleman seated beside her put his hand over hers. "Miss Jones isn't overly fond of numbers, unless they are for counting the waltz."

"Why is your crew so small?" Miss Jones pursued.

"With Bonaparte defeated," Admiral Dolenz took up, "a great many soldiers and sailors have found themselves unemployed. Troops cost money the government would rather spend elsewhere."

"If I might ask, what brings you to this side of the world, Miss Jones?" Bradshaw asked, mostly because the admiral had seen fit to invite her.

"My uncle—my and Stewart's uncle," she amended, gesturing at the shortest of the men, a wispy fellow with thinning blond hair, "is the head of exports for Sheffling in the Philippines. I know how gauche trade is," she said, flipping her hand, "but he's really quite wealthy, and he begged us to come and visit him."

"We decided to make a Grand Tour of it," the fellow beside her, Lord John Fenniwell, if he remembered correctly, took up. "Because I couldn't bear four years without Miss Jones. Could I, Frederica?"

She giggled again. "No, you couldn't."

Fenniwell said something else that made the rest

of his cronies laugh. In the midst of the noise, Miss Ponsley leaned closer to Bradshaw. "I think Lord John couldn't bear to be without Miss Jones's uncle's gauche fortune," she whispered.

Bradshaw grinned, then stifled the expression again. "Are we allied, now? I thought we were deadly enemies."

"I'm still assessing," she replied, a rather compelling sparkle in her gray eyes. "You aren't what I expected a naval captain to be like."

"Well, before the bloodshed begins again, may I say that Zephyr's not precisely a traditional English name? How did you come by it?"

"My mother wanted to name me Patricia, but my father said that a 'warm, following breeze' was always the reason he was able to go the places he'd gone. So they compromised. I was Zephyr Patricia Ponsley to my father, and Patricia Zephyr Ponsley to my mother. Now that my mother is gone, I'm Zephyr."

"So now your father has a warm, following breeze with him wherever he goes."

A smile quirked her lips. "I suppose he does."

"Your father said you were arrived here from India. Are you on your way back to England?" He had several pieces of correspondence, and while there were captains currently docked at Port Jackson who would carry them for him, Zephyr Ponsley and her father were more likely to be able to hand deliver anything to his family. And Robert, at least, would be forever in his debt if he managed to arrange a meeting between his younger brother and Sir Joseph Ponsley. As far as he was concerned, botany had saved Robert's life. Or at least his sanity.

"Oh, no," she replied. "Papa was commissioned by the Royal Society to do a botany study here in the Pacific. This is our starting point."

"That sounds fascinating," he lied, more to keep her smiling and chatting with him than because he meant it. A pretty chit who enjoyed bantering and who had more on her mind than earning a quick shilling—tonight might well prove to be much more interesting than he'd originally expected. He wondered where she and her father were lodging.

"Tell me, Captain," she continued, "what do you do while you're at sea and you're not reading?"

He shifted in his chair. "Generally I tell the ship which way to go, and if I see a storm coming, I make certain some of the sails are taken in. In the evenings, I make notes about where we've gone that day, and I walk the ship to be sure it hasn't sprung any leaks."

Admiral Dolenz burst out laughing. "That, Captain, is likely the most honest description of shipboard life I have ever heard."

Bradshaw had actually forgotten the admiral was sitting there. "Thank you, sir. I did leave out one or two minor items for the sake of brevity."

"You're fairly witty for someone who isn't literary," Miss Ponsley conceded.

"And you're fairly free with your condemnations for someone I only met twenty minutes ago."

To his surprise, she sighed and nodded. "I suppose I am. In all honesty, I've spent more time with scientists and botanists and researchers than with members of the *beau monde*. Pretty words and unmeant flattery is just . . . wasteful."

"Don't let the admiral's other guests hear you say that."

She moved a breath closer to him. "Before you arrived I had to spend thirty minutes listening to them gossip about some unfortunate young lady who thought she could play the pianoforte but actually couldn't. I nearly went out and jumped off the balcony."

Clearly Zephyr Ponsley was not a typical Society chit. And while he was supremely accustomed to moving in those circles himself, he more than understood her cynicism. If he were to choose one of the silk-draped lovelies present to share his bed tonight, it would have been the warm, following breeze on his right. He liked a bit of fire in a chit, and Zephyr Ponsley seemed to have enough to burn his fingers. And she was genuine, a rare quality for either gender in his experience.

Finally, an hour after the ladies had left the table and the men had done their version of gossiping, the admiral climbed to his feet. "Gentlemen, shall we rejoin the ladies? Or rather, perhaps you would all be so kind as to do so. Captain Carroway and I will join you in a moment."

Bradshaw followed Admiral Dolenz into a small study that overlooked the harbor far below. The *Nemesis* was easy to see; she wasn't the largest ship in the harbor, but if he said so himself, she did have the most elegant lines. And far more cannon ports than anything else in sight.

"You've been patient," the admiral noted, sitting behind his desk.

"I've had nearly eleven months to speculate about why the navy wanted me out here on the far side of the world," Bradshaw replied, taking the seat opposite despite the fact that he would rather be pacing. "Pirates, perhaps?"

"There has been some piracy in these waters, as a matter of fact," the admiral conceded. "Spanish and Dutch origin, mostly, though we don't know yet how much—if any of it—is government-sanctioned. And the French have been prowling about lately, as well."

Stifling a smile, Bradshaw sat back in the chair. The Duke of Sommerset had been up-to-date with his list of troublemakers. If all went well, the *Nemesis* would find its way to Tahiti within the month. "So we'll be patrolling? Pirate hunting?"

"No."

Bradshaw opened and closed his mouth again, that unpleasant hesitation touching him again for the first time all evening. "No? The East Indies, then?" he pursued, keeping his expression even.

Admiral Dolenz pulled a paper from a drawer and pushed it across the polished mahogany surface of the desk. "I've been told this is a new era," he went on. "And a new sort of fight for supremacy."

And another damned useless war fought over borderless oceans, no doubt. His gut jolted unpleasantly, but as Bradshaw turned the paper to face him, surprise shoved his uncertainty overboard. "I— Is this a jest?" he asked. "The *Nemesis* is a ship of the line, Admiral. A fighting ship."

"And a damned fine one, with a damned fine captain, from all reports. That's why you're here."

Shaw read through the paper again. It was definitely unexpected. And in a sense, it could be precisely what he'd been looking for. Or it could be the largest disaster since the one Bonaparte had found at Waterloo. "It's better than whaling," he said aloud, knowing something was expected of him.

Dolenz smiled, nodding. "That, it is." He rose again. "Join us in the drawing room. I've even hired a string orchestra. And Captain, you were highly recommended for this venture. I have no doubt that you will perform your duty to the utmost."

Standing, Bradshaw saluted. "Aye, aye, Admiral."

Little in his career had gone as he'd expected; he was too young to have made admiral during the Peninsular War, and now the odds of being promoted had shrunk to almost nothing. His only chance would have been protecting the interests of the East India Company from Dutch interference, and he wasn't certain he had the stomach for that any longer.

He'd been recommended for this duty. Shaw gazed out the window down at the harbor once more. It smacked of Sommerset, in fact, though in that case the only way the orders could have reached Port Jackson in time to meet him was if he'd carried them here himself aboard the *Nemesis*. Hm. If this was all to see a mirror delivered, it seemed a damned lot of trouble to go to. Well, at least with this voyage, he had a chance to see bare-breasted chits, and he wouldn't be hunting down supposed enemies because of poorly managed politics.

Aside from all that, it was likely a fortunate thing that he hadn't already set himself to seduce the warm, following breeze—especially considering that, according to his orders, in two days he would be sailing away with her father to go collect plants.

Chapter Two

I was brought up in London town at a place I know full well,
Brought up by honest parents for the truth to tell.
Brought up by honest parents and reared most tenderly,
Till I became a roving blade which proved my destiny.

"BOTANY BAY"

Zephyr Ponsley stepped down from the overladen wagon and stopped to gaze up at the ship before her. "Are you certain about this, Papa?" she asked.

Her father climbed down from the following wagon and walked up beside her. "The Royal Society wants results, my dear," he said, "and according to the letter I received, they feel we will be better served by a naval vessel than a privately owned one."

While she wouldn't precisely argue with that, especially considering that Captain Napier of the *Destiny* had refused to stop anywhere between Fort William in India and here at Port Jackson, the origin of the vessel was not her greatest concern. "I was actually referring to Captain Carroway. I mean, here he is in the middle of the Pacific Ocean to provide you with transportation, and he can't be bothered to read your book." That wasn't precisely her concern, either, but it sounded like a logical complaint.

Protesting because she'd had the oddest dream about kissing Captain Carroway would earn her a raised eyebrow and a suggestion that she place a higher value on reality than on absurd nightmares. It was only because she'd spent most—all—of her adult life amid scholars, she was certain. A man who answered her jibe for jibe and who wasn't old enough to be her father was a unique experience.

Her father sent her a quick smile. "Perhaps he's been too busy checking for leaks," he replied in a low voice, then straightened, waving, as the captain himself appeared at the railing. "We can't all be intellectuals and scientists. Good morning, Captain Carroway! Permission to come aboard?"

The captain nodded, his black hair lifting at his temple in the morning breeze. Last night, even while she'd been insulting him he'd seemed . . . amused. And a little witty, actually. Today, however, the prospect of placing the success of her father's expedition in the hands of a bloodthirsty warrior in the employ of a country intent on expanding its influence gave her pause. And that didn't even take into account the other flaws of his character. "Are you certain he's a captain?"

"Fairly certain. It's quite a ruse if he isn't one."

"We should look into it. He's too handsome, for one thing. Where are his battle scars and eye patch?"

"Come along, my dear," her father said, chuckling as he nudged her in the shoulder. "I know he cuts a rather striking figure, but you've already decided that he's a barbarian. And there's a great deal of luggage to get on board."

She shook herself. "I wasn't looking at his figure," she retorted, grabbing a satchel and slinging it over her shoulder. "I was wondering how much trouble he'll be."

"That's the benefit of enlisting the navy. He has to follow orders."

"Yes. And nothing more."

A moment later a swarm of sailors descended onto the dock and began emptying the wagons. One by one potted shrubs, trees, and vines vanished onto the ship, together with boxes of notes and sketches and journals, soil samples, and a hopefully ample supply of crates and tubs for the next leg of the expedition.

One sailor toting a small tree caught her attention. "You!" she called, hurrying after him up the gangplank. "Do not hold that by the trunk!"

He kept moving, and the other men seemed to think it amusing not to move out of her way. Blast it. It had taken her father better than a week to talk the fellow who owned the original plant into giving over a seedling. She'd never seen another like it.

Zephyr stepped down onto the deck—and nearly crashed into the dwarf pear. "This trunk?" Captain Carroway asked, holding it out to her by the pot.

She snatched it away from him, holding it to her chest. "Yes. It's irreplaceable."

Light blue eyes assessed her. "Then why are you storing it in my hold?"

"We will be rotating the flora onto the deck, so that each specimen will receive adequate sunlight."

"We?" he repeated.

"Yes, we."

"My orders specify that I am to deliver Sir Joseph

Ponsley to wherever he indicates so that he may fulfill the orders of the Royal Society. They don't say anything about you."

She frowned. "For heaven's sake. You aren't one of those superstitious half-wits who thinks a woman on a ship is bad luck, are you?" Behind him several sailors turned in a circle and spat over their shoulders. Wonderful. They were *all* ignorant heathens.

"You may have noticed that I have a naked woman on the prow of my ship," he commented smoothly. "That is to counter any ill luck that having a clothed woman on deck might cause." The captain took a step closer and leaned down to whisper in her ear. "And the next time you mention bad luck on my ship, I'll throw you overboard." He straightened again. "Lieutenant Abrams will show you where your botanicals are being stored."

A wiry blond man, wearing a blue and white lieutenant's jacket and looking barely old enough to be out of school, stepped forward and saluted smartly. "It will be my pleasure, Miss Ponsley. May I carry that for you?"

Lifting an eyebrow at the captain, she handed the pear over to the lieutenant. "Thank you, Lieutenant Abrams."

"This way, miss."

Not sparing Captain Carroway another look, she followed the young lieutenant into the bowels of the ship. The captain had said he was sailing with half of the full crew complement, but with everyone hurrying here and there carrying her father's things or moving ropes or swishing mops into buckets or stacking boxes or spare sailcloth, the ship looked supremely crowded.

"Will the *Nemesis* be ready to sail tomorrow, do you think?" she asked.

"Aye. We finished taking on supplies last evening. We're just shifting a few things to make room for your plants." The lieutenant glanced over his shoulder at her. "You and Sir Joseph being here explains the extra bits of wood and planks and crates of glass jars. Some of the men were beginning to wonder if they were for rum."

"So you had no idea what your duties here would be?"

"I still have no idea, other than what the captain's told us."

"And what is that?"

Lieutenant Abrams led the way down another narrow stair and around a corner, and abruptly they were in a long, low room. At the rear and stacked to the ceiling were sacks and sacks of flour and grain and barrels of potatoes and pickled cabbages and other supplies, along with six female goats and four large crates of chickens, while to the left were a good portion of her father's things. As she looked on, another half-dozen plants arrived to be set in close-touching rows.

"Captain Carroway said we're to ferry Sir Joseph about while he makes drawings and collects more plants," the lieutenant answered, setting the dwarf pear down. "No doubt there's more to it than that, but I reckon that's all the crew needs to know."

Literally speaking, it was a fair description of her father's work, but as she conjured Captain Carroway's already familiar drawl reciting the *Nemesis*'s orders, she felt distinctly insulted. Clearly he had a heathen's lack of respect for anything that didn't bleed or cause damage. She squared her shoulders. None of this circumstance was Lieutenant Abrams's fault.

"These plants will need to be rearranged," she said aloud. "Some of them will require more sunlight than others. And please keep them away from the goats." She couldn't even imagine how her father would react if one of the animals ate any of his shrubbery.

"Once we get under way I'll have some of the lads assist you with that."

"Thank you, Lieutenant," she said warmly. Captain Carroway might be a savage, but at least someone had manners and common courtesy.

He grinned. "You're a sight prettier than most of the faces I've seen over the past year. I doubt you'll find many objections from the men spending time in your company."

Oh, dear. Assistance was one thing, but she certainly didn't want an entire shipload of men thinking she was only there for ogling—or worse. She'd been distinctly uncomfortable on the *Destiny,* and though that vessel had been owned by a London merchant rather than the British navy, she had a very strong feeling that men were men, whether they wore uniforms or not. And in her admittedly limited experience, most men—the ones who couldn't be bothered to look beyond themselves to learn the secrets of the world—were quite simply useless.

"I should go see if my father needs any more assistance," she said aloud, turning for the stairs again.

Thankfully Lieutenant Abrams joined her, because after only one descent into the bowels of the *Nemesis,* she was fairly certain she would never find her way back on deck without a guide. She blinked as she emerged back into the bright morning sunlight on deck.

A dozen or so sailors climbed about in the rigging around the three masts, no doubt making certain everything was ready for tomorrow. As she turned to look at the ship's wheel on the deck above, she caught sight of Captain Carroway gazing down at her. A slight shiver ran up her spine as he looked away to speak to one of his men.

Her father had noted that Bradshaw Carroway was a rather fine-looking man, tall and lean, with skin tanned by the sun. She saw nothing to argue with in his appearance. And in her dream he'd been rather proficient with his kisses. But it wasn't his looks that gave her pause; it was his willingness to do his duty and enable Sir Joseph Ponsley to do his. She'd seen his sort before, after all. If it wasn't a battle, it didn't merit his attention or his respect.

With the timing of a clock her father climbed the left—port—side stairs to the upper deck. "I was wondering if we might have a word, Captain," he said. "There wasn't a chance last evening."

His expression unchanged, the captain faced her father. "Are you certain you wish Miss Ponsley to accompany us?"

Humph. She'd said she was going, and that was that. And she wasn't about to be left behind in Australia, regardless. Her father nodded. "Zephyr's assistance has proven invaluable."

"She will be the only female on board."

"As a captain in His Majesty's Navy, I presume you will be able to ensure her safety."

"No, I can't ensure her safety. I can ensure that she

will be treated with respect. The rest is up to the sea and whoever might be sailing upon it."

"I hope the sea is more cooperative than you are," Zephyr said aloud, looking up at the two men.

Captain Carroway narrowed his eyes. "As long as *you* follow *my* instructions, we'll all live long enough to find out." He gestured at her father. "I'll show you to your quarters." Blue eyes touched hers again. "This way, Sir Joseph, Miss Ponsley."

As they left the deck, the captain reached out to his left and brushed his fingers across a brass plaque depicting Poseidon. Zephyr opened her mouth to ask whether he was superstitious, then thought better of it. He'd warned her about mentioning bad luck, and while she didn't truly believe he would throw her off the ship, they *were* still in port. And according to him, his orders hadn't mentioned her.

The route the captain took was completely different this time, and she felt as lost as before. "We're not a passenger ship," he said over his shoulder. "If not for the fact that we're sailing at half complement, you might have found yourselves in a storeroom."

"I would hope you would give up your own accommodations before that," she commented.

He muttered something that sounded like "Not bloody likely," but she couldn't be certain. The corridor dead-ended and turned left at a door, but he stopped just short of it to open a pair of doors directly to the right. "They're small," he said, indicating for her to precede him, "but they have actual beds rather than hammocks. Unless you prefer hammocks."

She stepped into the cabin. "Oh, no. Swinging to and fro like that would make me positively ill."

He was correct that the cabin was small; aside from the bed with several drawers beneath it, a trio of shelves, a tiny table, and a chair filled the area completely. Her trunk looked massive in the near corner, and it was just as well that she didn't have a maid, because there would hardly be room for two people in the room while she dressed.

From the captain's expression, he was expecting her to complain. Well, she did have a complaint, but likely not the one he expected. "Is my father's cabin this small?"

"They're identical. Otherwise I would of course have put you in the larger one."

"It's not sufficient. I mean, this one is fine for me, but my father will need room for his books and to do his writing and research."

"Zephyr, as Captain Carroway said, this is not a passenger ship. I shall make do."

"The whole reason we're here is for you to continue your explorations. You can hardly do that in a room with a twelve-inch square table. Or do you think to spend your days in the galley with . . . stews and bread crumbs and black powder getting into everything?"

"We attempt to keep cooking and black powder separate." Captain Carroway sighed. "This way," he said, backing away from the door and turning to the entrance at the end of the corridor. He lowered the handle and pushed it open.

Clearly they were at the rear of the ship, because the four paned windows opposite the door overlooked the dock and part of the harbor. In the center of the room stood a large table strewn with maps and charts, while high-lipped shelves of trinkets and baubles and a few books lined one wall. The other wall was covered with . . . weapons. She took a step closer. Crossbows, spears, rapiers, rifles, pistols, arrows—everything she could imagine, and from at least a dozen different countries. *Oh, dear.* Sometimes she hated being correct.

"During the day," the captain was saying, "you may use this cabin for your research. Just for God's sake don't bring in anything too frilly or sweet-smelling, or I'll be forced to jump overboard."

"This is your cabin," Zephyr commented, facing him again.

"Yes, it is. I would appreciate if you didn't destroy it."

"And these?" she asked, gesturing at the weapons.

"My collection. And be cautious; they're all genuine." He gestured at a crossbow. "I nearly put a hole through my oldest brother's head with that one."

His grin had the odd effect of stealing her breath for a moment until she could recover herself. "You almost sound proud of that fact."

"No, but Dare doesn't surprise very easily. His Lordship nearly piss—" He cleared his throat. "You will have to give me the cabin during the day from time to time so I can consult my charts and discuss matters with my officers."

"Of course. Thank you, Captain."

Captain Carroway squinted one eye. "Call me Bradshaw. Or Shaw. You're not part of my crew."

Her father smiled. "Thank you then, Shaw. With luck, this expedition will advance Britain's understanding of the world. It may not be battle, but that doesn't render it insignificant."

"You might be surprised by what I consider significant."

The captain sent Zephyr a look no doubt meant to convey the idea that he could read her thoughts. Ha. If he could do so, he likely *would* have thrown her overboard already. She lifted an eyebrow at him, and with a twitch of his mouth he faced her father again.

"I run a fairly evenhanded ship, Sir Joseph, but we are part of the navy. And though you aren't a crew member, and however you feel about our methods and discipline, you are now my responsibility." He sent a pointed glance at Zephyr. "In other words, my ship, my rules. Understood?"

"Understood, Captain. Shaw."

Zephyr nodded, as well, mostly because she didn't wish to be tossed into the harbor. His ship, his rules—perhaps, but the expedition was under the auspices of Sir Joseph Banks, and he'd best keep that in mind, the savage.

Up on deck, no one was moving. Or rather, Bradshaw amended silently, they were moving, but not in a productive manner. Instead everyone had crowded up to the dockside railing where they muttered to one another like a swarm of foulmouthed bees.

"Captain," his first lieutenant, William Gerard, said from the wheel deck above, "it's the admiral."

Joining in the cursing, Bradshaw pushed through his men to the gangplank. Down below, Admiral Dolenz stepped down from his coach, put on his hat, and walked toward the ship. "Attention," Shaw hissed.

Immediately the men around him snapped to, and moved back from the gangplank as the order flowed through the sea of sailors. A moment later Bradshaw noted that the admiral wasn't alone; a second and third coach followed. Suspicion ran through him. Twenty minutes ago he'd thought the addition of Zephyr Ponsley to the expedition would be the largest surprise of the day. Now he wasn't so certain that would continue to hold true.

"Permission to come aboard?" the admiral called.

"Permission granted, sir. With pleasure."

He kept half his attention on the two closed coaches. Whoever was inside must be sweltering, but neither door opened. And as far as he was concerned, that meant something ill.

As Admiral Dolenz stepped onto the deck, Bradshaw added his salute to those of his men. "As you were, gentlemen," the admiral said with a crisp return salute. "I believe you have a ship to make ready." He continued directly up to Bradshaw. "A word with you, Captain."

Everyone wanted a damned word with him this morning, and all of it seemed to be either to complain or to add more restrictions and burdens to his command. It could always be worse, as well; Dolenz might have caught a whiff that Shaw had . . . lost his edge, he supposed, and in that carriage could be a replacement ready to take the *Nemesis* away. "I'm listening."

"I'm not a fool, Carroway. I know that every young captain worth his salt wants battle and glory."

Shaw just barely kept from blinking. "I only want to be at sea, Admiral," he said aloud. "The wheres and whys don't much matter." There. That sounded patriotic enough.

"I'm glad to hear that, lad." Dolenz took a short

breath. "Because I am asking you to make a delivery for me."

For a heartbeat Shaw wondered whether it would be a jewel-encrusted comb to go with the mirror. He glanced again at the coaches. "What sort of delivery?"

"Stewart Jones, his sister, and company desire to reach their uncle's home and hopefully his inheritance in Manila. Now they also desire to see the Pacific islands. They want a bit of excitement, and I want the heirs to the Sheffling Export Company to arrive safely at their destination thanks to the Royal Navy. Arrange with Sir Joseph to make the Philippines your second or third port of call."

Which still left him with less than three months to reach Tahiti. "How many of them are there?" he asked, wondering when the Royal Navy had begun a passenger service. A sliver of annoyance pricked at him. Perhaps he didn't wish to engage in a bloody, meaningless brawl, but this did not fit his new definition of anything meaningful. Two civilians, one of them pretty and sharp-tongued, he could tolerate. They had a goal he could fall in behind. Mayfair fops were another category entirely.

"Seven. And five servants."

Damnation. "Is their luggage with them? I truly don't want to delay my departure."

"I made that clear to them this morning. They have a wagon waiting just out of sight, actually." The admiral smiled grimly. "I suggested that it would be better if I made my request before you saw trunks."

"Admiral, if you have no difficulty with a ship of the line becoming a passenger ferry, then I have none, either," Bradshaw replied. Nothing he would say aloud. At least half of his guests would be female, but even that fact seemed insufficient compensation.

"Excellent. These are your people, and I expect you'll be able to manage them better than any other ship in port. I also made it clear to Lord John and the rest of them that once they step onto your ship, you are Lord God Almighty."

"That's something, anyway." A year or so ago he would have shared his reservations with the ship's surgeon, and Simon would have helpfully pointed out that they still had a chance of running across pirates or at least a hostile cannibalistic native or two. It struck him forcibly that he had no one in whom to confide, and nothing to look forward to but settling another man's debt. And to making a few aristocrats grateful to the navy. He shook himself. "As I said before, it's better than whaling."

"Aye." Admiral Dolenz clapped him on the shoulder. "I'll send them up, shall I?"

Bradshaw nodded. "Thank you, sir."

Halfway to the gangplank, the admiral stopped and turned around. "By the way," he said, lowering his voice, "when you return to London I expect you to steer well away from my daughter. Is that clear?"

Christ. "Aye, aye, sir." So he *was* being punished. Dolenz was bloody creative with his tortures. *Damnation*. "Mr. Newsome!"

The square-jawed second lieutenant scurried forward. "Yes, sir!"

"Accompany the admiral down to our new passengers and supervise the loading of their luggage."

Newsome saluted. "Aye, aye, Captain." The lieutenant started off, then hesitated. "Where are we putting them, Captain?"

"Put them in the rest of the port side officers' quarters. No doubt all of the civilians will wish to be grouped together. You and Merriwether will have to shift your kit to the starboard cabins."

Newsome hurried after the admiral. Still swearing under his breath, Bradshaw headed back below deck. Thankfully neither of the Ponsleys was in his cabin, and he stepped inside, closing and latching the door behind him. After a moment spent eyeing a bottle of rum, he sat at his writing desk and scrawled out a last, quick letter to his brother Robert.

The rest of the Carroway clan would have a good laugh at his present circumstance, but Bit . . . understood things about the more frustrating aspects of military service. Bit was the only other brother to have joined the military and left England in its service, and though he'd foolishly chosen the army and ended up in a damned French prison, their experiences had given them a similar outlook. More similar now than previously.

He folded and addressed the letter, then set it with the others that needed to go aboard the merchant ship *Sampson* for its return voyage to England. And then he did pull out a glass and poured himself some rum. Generally he refrained from drinking until dinner or the end of his watch, whichever came last. But damnation, he now had a total of fourteen civilians boarding his ship and settling in for a lengthy voyage. His peers might not count the servants, but they needed to be housed and fed, as well.

Someone knocked at his door. Bradshaw looked up, waiting, but the customary announcement didn't come. His crew knew to tell him who was calling and generally what they wanted before he decided whether to admit them or not. This, then, had to be one of the passengers.

Rolling his shoulders, he set aside his glass and stood, walking to the door. "Yes?" he said as he pulled it open.

Zephyr Ponsley stood there, a large stack of papers in her arms and a grimace on her pretty face. "I have no room for these sketches," she said, patting the papers, "and I can't store them in the hold. Do you have somewhere I could lay them flat?"

He moved back from the door and pulled open the bottom chart drawer set into the large worktable in the center of the cabin. "Will this do?"

"Oh, that would be perfect." She set the sketches into the wide, low drawer, then glanced up sideways at him. "I have to say, despite my misgivings about your . . . commitment to this venture, you've been much more cooperative than the captain of our last ship."

"Ah. Did you insult him at every turn and question his authority and intelligence in front of his men?"

Her scowl deepened. "Actually, I was very polite to him, even though he leered at me several times. He clearly didn't possess an ounce of enthusiasm for anything beyond the front of his own ship."

"The *bow* of his own ship," he corrected, stifling an abrupt grin. "Which ship were you on?"

"The *Destiny*. It was a very smelly ship. I think the cargo was either wet wool or rancid beef. Whatever it was, it was apparently too valuable for him to risk putting in anywhere and allowing my father to collect a few specimens."

"And what about before India? I deduced that you haven't been aboard a navy ship previously. You'll see that I'm quite astute for a near-illiterate."

The quick smile that quirked the corners of her mouth sent him slightly off balance, like an unexpected swell in calm seas. "We traveled over land," she replied. "My father is a botanist, you know. There aren't many collectible plant specimens in the middle of the ocean. The last ship I was on took us across the English Channel to Calais. And that was . . . nearly eight years ago."

He gazed at her for a moment, studying the fresh, sun-touched tone of her skin, the brass highlights in her chestnut hair. Though he'd seen more of the world than she, Zephyr Ponsley had spent nearly as much of her life traveling as he had. He doubted the Mayfair crowd currently being loaded on board could say the same. He'd heard it in their conversation last night; the unshaken belief that they reigned supreme in the world and that nothing could touch, alter, or harm them because they were, after all, English. "How old were you when you left England, if I may ask?"

"Fifteen. We would have left sooner, I think, but Papa waited for a lull in Bonaparte's tantrum."

He himself wouldn't have called the drawn-out Peninsular War a tantrum, though at times it had felt nearly as pointless. The age at which she'd left England explained the directness and . . . artlessness of her conversation. Clearly he'd have to keep an eye on her, or her fellow passengers would eat her alive. "You're fairly tolerable when you attempt to be civil," he noted.

Amusement touched her face. "As are you. *Fairly* tolerable." She shrugged. "I suppose I'm used to people telling me I'm mad to roam the world rather than marry or that I have no business assisting my father as though I'm some sort of expert. And then there's the you-collect-plants? statement and the accompanying incredulity. I . . . tend to strike first now."

He grinned. "Well, don't stop striking on my account. I happen to think both of you are mad, to spend your time looking at shrubbery."

"Which makes you an unsophisticated barbarian."

Shaw inclined his head, rather liking the moniker. "You heard we're to carry more passengers," he said, realizing he was still looking at her rather intently.

"Yes. We didn't actually wish to journey to Manila, because the island there has been so well explored, but perhaps we'll find something interesting on one of the neighboring islands."

So she didn't care about other civilians, as long as they didn't hamper her father's expedition. Clearly Miss Ponsley was a very single-minded chit. "I need to speak with your father," he said aloud. "Charting a course isn't like crossing a street. And as captain, I'd like to know where we're going." And to make certain that one of their early destinations would be Tahiti.

She nodded. "He actually told me that he didn't wish to step on your toes, and he would wait until you asked rather than simply telling you where we are to go. Personally I think that's a waste of time, but I've noticed that men seem to require a certain amount of blowing and stomping before they reach a mutual decision."

"Mm. While I begin stomping, then, would you be so kind as to ask Sir Joseph to join me at his convenience?"

"Yes, I will." She hesitated. "Thank you for helping me find a place for the sketches."

"You're welcome."

As she left the cabin, Bradshaw sank into his chair again. If it had been only the Mayfair crowd on board, he would have made a point of simply avoiding them. Now, though, that had become more problematic. Zephyr Ponsley annoyed, intrigued, and amused him all at the same time, and the idea of abandoning her to the sharp tongues of Society's darlings actually troubled him. To himself he could admit it; she and her father might be the explorers, but he found himself rather curious to figure her out. And curiosity was a welcome change to the general doldrums that continued to circle him like a school of hungry sharks.

Chapter Three

She's a deep water ship with a deep water crew,
She's a deep water ship with a deep water crew.
She could hug the shore but damned if we do, .
Aboard the *Roseabella*.

"THE ROSEABELLA"

I have to say, the *Halcyon* was a much more luxurious vessel," Lord John Fenniwell said, squinting as he gazed over the ocean.

"I don't particularly require luxury," the other man, Stewart Jones, returned, "though the ladies seem to be sorely lacking in amenities."

A few feet away from them, Zephyr looked up from her perch on an overturned bucket. Sliding her pencil behind one ear, she flexed her fingers over the half-finished sketch of the *Nemesis*'s busy main deck. "I'm not lacking anything," she said. "In fact, I find ocean travel rather . . . invigorating."

Both men turned to look at her. "Miss Ponsley. I didn't see you there," Lord John returned, inclining his head. "You may change your opinion if we hit rough seas. We were very fortunate on our journey here, but I've heard tales that would turn your hair white."

She'd heard her share of tales, as well, though they didn't have much to do with ocean travel. Rather, her father had been very fond of telling her how empty-minded most members of the peerage prided themselves on being. "Hopefully your good luck will continue," she said, deciding she didn't care to ask for an embellishment.

"I was wondering, Miss Ponsley, if you would care to join us for luncheon later. We've asked for and been granted our own table," Mr. Jones took up.

She sent a glance toward the raised deck at the bow of the ship, where Captain Carroway stood looking over a chart with her father. Many of the men had shed their shirts once they left port, and while the officers had refrained from doing so, they had replaced their crisp blue uniforms with plain cotton shirts and trousers. The captain's was open at the neck, the wind buffeting his collar a little.

"My father and I will be moving some of our plant specimens up on deck, but thank you," she said, offering a smile.

"So what have you and your father discovered?" As Mr. Jones spoke, the third man in their party, Lord Benjamin Harding, joined the other two. "Some new, prettier roses?"

"Some roses, yes," she returned, disliking the way they loomed over her. She stood up, cradling the sketch pad against her chest. "And a great many semi-arid plants that have never been seen in England before."

"Explain something to me," Harding put in. "Captain Cook journeyed to most of these islands. Why would anyone wish to plod along the same trails that he already blazed?"

Ah, that argument again. "Have you seen every plant native to England?" she asked.

"I have no idea."

"And yet nowhere has been better explored. I would hazard a guess that whatever Captain Cook saw, recorded, and collected was only a fraction of what exists out here. And who knows whether one of the plants he never set eyes on will prove to be the most significant find of the decade?"

Lord John grinned. "I'm only here for the scenery. And I have to say, the sights on this ship are an improvement over the last one." Light green eyes took her in from head to toe.

She gripped the sketch pad just a bit tighter. "I'm sorry your trip to Manila is further delayed. The currents and the time of year made it imperative that we travel to Fiji and its environs before heading northwest."

"Time spent in your company will make the journey easier," Stewart Jones commented, his expression nearly identical to that of his two friends. "How is it we never caught sight of you in London?"

"I haven't seen London since I was fifteen. And I daresay I have bett—"

"Gentlemen," the low, already familiar drawl of Captain Carroway came from directly behind her, "we're about to attempt a bit of fishing for dinner, if you'd care to try your hand aft."

"Oh, that's sporting of you, Captain."

The trio strode off, making wagers over who would catch the most fish and the largest specimen. Zephyr turned around, shading her eyes as she looked up at the captain's face. "You interrupted me."

"I'm prepared to wager that you were about to say something insulting to them. Perhaps that you have better things to do than bat your eyes and giggle at the quips of men who wrongly think themselves amusing."

She furrowed her brow. He was a very good guesser. "Not necessarily," she lied. "It would only be the truth if I did say that, however."

"Mm hm. You'll be sailing with these gentlemen for at least several weeks, Miss Ponsley. I suggest not insulting them until closer to the end of the voyage."

"I insulted you almost immediately," she countered, amusement pushing aside her previous annoyance.

"Yes, but I have a sense of humor. Be a little cautious around them, for your own sake."

He *did* have a sense of humor, clearly, and while she didn't generally appreciate advice, perhaps she could stand to measure her words a bit more closely. Her father owed his present assignment to the aristocracy, after all. She cleared her throat. "Thank you, Captain."

"Shaw," he returned in the same easy tone. "What are you sketching?"

"Some of the shipboard activity. There will be a thorough report and likely another book, and sketches and drawings of our surroundings will be a part of them."

"'Painting is silent poetry,' I believe," he drawled, holding out one hand. "May I?"

"For someone who isn't much of a reader, you're fairly handy with ancient Greek poetry," she commented, turning the sketch pad to face him.

"I never said I was completely illiterate." He eyed her drawing. "That's rather good. And you've drawn Hendley eating, which is highly accurate."

She was beginning to wonder whether he was being intentionally amusing, or if it was his natural character. "Do you sketch?"

"If I say no, will you accuse me of being unskilled at everything?"

"I might."

"Ah. Then I sketch on occasion. I actually prefer carving. That's fairly barbaric and uncivilized, isn't it?"

Zephyr tried to stifle her smile, but couldn't quite manage it. "It does involve knives." She didn't recall seeing any carvings in his cabin, but then the weaponry along the wall had taken up most of her attention. "Highly barbaric, I think."

"Excellent." He glanced away for a moment, then looked at her again. "You requested some assistance in moving plants onto the deck."

"Yes. They won't survive down in the hold."

Bradshaw nodded. "How many men do you require?"

"A half dozen, for an hour or so."

"Hendley!" he called, and the fellow eating the turnip straightened into a salute. "Find five more volunteers to assist Miss Ponsley. There's an extra draught of rum in it for the lot of you."

"Aye, aye, Captain. With pleasure."

The captain turned on his heel and started up the stairs to the wheel deck. Zephyr cleared her throat again, abruptly and oddly reluctant for him to leave. "How long until we reach Fiji?" she asked.

Pausing, he faced her again. "Another five days, I would guess. We're making nearly twelve knots at the moment." He stood silent for a breath. "I would ask you what it is your father isn't telling me about this expedition, but I imagine you're more inclined to keep his confidences than to enlighten the ship's captain."

"Naturally," she returned, hiding her sudden concern. There hadn't been any secrets that she knew about. If her father was truly keeping something from Bradshaw Carroway, then he was also keeping it from her. And that was unacceptable.

"Just so you know then, I'm not fooled and I know something's afoot."

"Very well. If you'll excuse me?"

"I've been doing that for three days," he drawled, and went to stand by the wheel.

As soon as she and the volunteers finished placing a portion of the plants in the sun and out of the worst of the wind, she went to find her father. He was in his tiny cabin, bent over a map showing all known detail of the islands of Fiji. "You should be in the captain's cabin," she said, squeezing in to join him. "The light in here is abominable."

"I'm just making a quick check to be certain Shaw and I concur. You know Cook only saw the southern islands. I've a mind to head a bit farther north. The only concern seems to be the reefs. And luckily enough, that is not *my* concern."

Zephyr nodded, looking over his shoulder as he ran his finger across several of the larger islands. "Reefs and cannibals," she added. "Isn't that what

Captain Bligh said? That his crew was pursued by war canoes and nearly eaten?"

"Hopefully that was an exaggeration. If not, I've yet to meet a man who absolutely could not be reasoned with."

"Still. To risk being eaten for botanicals seems . . . well, a touch mad," she pressed.

With a brief smile he looked around at her. "So you've guessed we're after a bit more, then."

"Are we? The captain thinks so."

"He's a cleverer fellow than I gave him credit for, Bradshaw is. Just before we sailed from India I received my own orders from the Royal Society." He dug through a satchel beside the bed and handed a paper over to her. "In short, we're to cultivate as many alliances among the native peoples of the South Pacific as possible. In addition, we will be expanding our collection to include not only interesting flora, but fauna, as well."

"Animals? That is not going to make Captain Carroway any more fond of us."

"It'll be birds and insects mostly, I would imagine, going by the information Captain Cook and his ilk have recorded. But anything new and undiscovered that we can collect, my dear, will be what puts the Ponsley name into the annals of exploration."

"That's why you brought along all that extra timber and wire. For cages. You're going to have to tell the captain eventually."

"He's been fairly agreeable thus far."

She shook her head. "That's because he likes being at sea, and we're giving him a reason to sail. Cages of animals littered about the ship—no, I don't think he'll like that."

"Well, I intend to delay telling him for as long as possible. But we will have to begin constructing cages in the next day or two in order to be prepared for our arrival in Fiji." He sent her a brief grin. "I don't suppose you wish to tell him," he suggested.

"He might throw me overboard," she returned with an amused snort. "I think he finds you more tolerable."

"Coward."

"Papa, as you've said several times, I am merely wise beyond my years." All twenty-three of them. "How is it that the Royal Society is concerned with diplomatic advances? You're a naturalist, not an ambassador." He preferred botany, but she understood why the Society would seek out his expertise in zoological matters, as well. But as for the other—he communicated well with other scholars, but he'd never attempted a diplomatic mission before.

"I'm only to attempt to establish a general friendly relationship and to assess the usefulness of future endeavors. I'll leave treaties and land agreements to those more qualified."

"So they leave the danger to you, and keep the glory for themselves."

He smiled. "I will find my share of glory out here, I believe." He blew out his breath. "And so I will go and find the ship's carpenter, and see how long our captain will remain ignorant."

Privately she thought that was a very poor idea. Captain Carroway had been more cooperative thus far than she'd expected, but she had to imagine that if there was anything that could make him dislike the current venture, it would be animals on board his precious ship. And she was *not* going to be the one to tell him.

Bradshaw sat in his writing chair and one by one pulled off his boots. Admiral Nelson had once recommended that all officers wear shoes rather than boots in case of leg injury, but he hated the pinching things and only wore them with his full dress uniform. In this heat, though, he was tempted to change his mind.

At the end of a day he welcomed the exhaustion and the relief that came with finally being able to relax and sleep. For the past four days since he'd sailed away from Port Jackson, however, two things had stood between him and his relief at being in oceans he'd never traveled before simply to explore them.

The first of those things was the fact that after having complained to his brother about how useless he felt being assigned to watch over his youngest brother, he now found himself serving as governess to better than a half-dozen daft aristocrats. He was almost certain he'd danced a quadrille with Juliette Quanstone during his last leave in London, and now the most frivolous part of London was sailing with him. Scowling, he removed his open waistcoat and then yanked his shirt over his head, casting them both aside.

The second thing troubling him was the chit. Zephyr Ponsley. If he hadn't received his orders that night at Admiral Dolenz's residence, he would have done his damnedest to bed her. He still wanted to do so. But now, on his ship, she was rampaging among the aristocrats like a chicken in a fox den.

Technically only her safety was his responsibility, but maddening as she was, she was also the . . . freshest breath of air he could recall. He didn't want to see her cowed or ridiculed by the Mayfair mob.

There were several ladies on board, of course, if all he wanted was a chit in his bed. He was fairly certain at least two of those females had left their virginity back in England. They, however, weren't creeping under his skin like an itch he couldn't scratch.

His door rattled. "Captain? It's Ogilvy. Do you have a moment?"

"Come."

The ship's carpenter opened the door and stepped inside, closing it behind him again. Even in a room as large as the captain's cabin Ogilvy seemed to fill the space. How he fit in his tiny hammock in the crowded crew's quarters, Bradshaw had no idea.

"What is it?" he prompted after a moment.

"Sir Joseph asked me to put together a few things for him with that timber and wire he brought on board," the big man said. "I wanted to know if I had your permission to hammer together his cages."

"As long as it doesn't interfere with your duties, give him whatever he . . ." Bradshaw trailed off. "Cages?"

"Aye. A dozen birdcages, and about half that many for—what did he call it?—possible animal encounters."

Bradshaw felt his muscles clenching, and made himself relax again. "In your estimation, how many cages could you construct from all the material Sir Joseph has on board?"

"Two hundred or more, depending on the size."

"Thank you for informing me, Ogilvy. Carry on."

The carpenter saluted, then left the room again. Bradshaw, though, stayed where he was, standing in the middle of his cabin and glaring at nothing. He could follow his first inclination, which was to stride two doors down the corridor and confront Sir Joseph Ponsley over precisely what his expedition's goal was and then decide if he wanted this nonsense to continue aboard his warship. Or he could wait and see how the botanist meant to go about collecting animals in secret, especially once they needed to be fed and the cages cleaned.

He scowled. Either way it didn't seem flattering for the *Nemesis*, especially with her already serving as the *ton*'s luxury yacht. In addition to the insult of making the ship a haven for pigeons and snails, hunting animals would take immeasurably more time than digging up a few shrubs. Sir Joseph had put Tahiti fifth on his list of islands to be visited. That was already a problem, and it had just become worse.

He had eight weeks remaining to complete a task that might have seemed petty, but had become the main reason he'd been able to make this journey without going mad. He would deliver that mirror to one-eyed King George, or— No. There was no "or." He would do it. "Damnation," he muttered, pacing back and forth.

Another knock sounded at his door. Bradshaw paused, but no one called out his identity or reason for pounding on the captain's door at twenty-three hundred hours. One of the civilians, then. Taking a breath, he walked up to the door and pulled it open.

Zephyr Ponsley stood there, a dark green dressing robe tied about her waist with a matching ribbon.

Her feet were bare, her chestnut hair with its streaks of brass loose down her back. The sight forcibly reminded him that he'd been imagining her naked for nearly five days, but he kept his abrupt lust tamped down. "Miss Ponsley. It's a bit late to be storing away sketches, isn't it?"

She swallowed, her eyes focused on his bare chest. "May I come in for a moment?" she whispered.

He jerked his chin toward the interior of the room. Zephyr walked past him, and he caught himself leaning in to smell her hair. She was even more of a damned annoyance because he couldn't quite figure her out, blast it all. Bradshaw folded his arms across his chest. "If this is a social call, shouldn't you have closed the door?"

"It's not a social call." She faced him again, scowling. "Not precisely. I mean to say, I was awake, and I heard Mr. Ogilvy come to see you."

"And?"

"And you're angry now."

"I was angry before."

"No, you were amused before."

Despite her presumption at deciding she knew his emotions, having someone there with whom to argue was infinitely more satisfying than stewing on his own. "If I'm angry, then what am I thinking?" he asked, leaning one hip against the worktable.

"You're thinking that my father should have told you earlier that he would also be collecting wildlife specimens."

"That would have been nice to know, yes," he agreed.

"I only found out today, myself," she returned, "after you commented that something was afoot."

At least his instincts were still reliable, small comfort though that was. "And?" he prompted.

Zephyr reached into the pocket of her dressing robe and pulled out a folded piece of paper. "The Spanish and the Prussians and the Dutch are all attempting similar voyages of discovery," she said, holding the letter out to him. "The Royal Society didn't want anyone at Port Jackson to know that we were doing more than a botanical survey."

Bradshaw took the paper, his fingers brushing hers as he did so. Warmth swept beneath his skin, but he willed away the sensation. Instead he opened the paper and tilted it toward the lantern so he could skim his eyes across the Royal Society's orders to Sir Joseph Ponsley.

He suspected that the Duke of Sommerset had dictated them; the tone sounded very familiar, at least. If His Grace wanted his damned mirror delivered so badly, he might have considered throwing fewer obstacles in the way of his messenger. "We haven't been at Port Jackson for four days," he commented, handing it back. "The next time your father feels the need to keep something from me, make certain he reconsiders."

"No."

He lifted an eyebrow. "Beg pardon?"

"I told him that he needed to discuss matters with you, as this is his expedition. Likewise, I am telling you that you need to discuss matters with him, because this is your ship." She tucked the letter back into her pocket. "And now, good night."

"So you came in here to tell me that you're not going to tell your father anything?" he asked skeptically.

"I wanted to make certain you understand that you're not the only one following orders. And I agree that he should have told you—and me—earlier. The object is to make this expedition successful; too much stomping and blowing is simply counterproductive."

"And there's nothing else you wish to say or do?" he prompted.

"No. Nothing else. Good night."

For several minutes after she closed his door again he stood staring at it. Evidently there was a reason apart from ill luck that encouraged captains to keep women off their ships. They were damned distracting. Despite his—and apparently her—best efforts, this one kept reminding him that he'd been celibate for better than a year, across two oceans and thousands of miles.

Finally he shrugged out of his trousers, finding them a bit snug, and dropped onto his bed. One thing was becoming painfully clear. In more ways than he'd anticipated, this was going to be a very long voyage.

Bradshaw Carroway, shirtless. In those gothic tales she tended to read whenever they paused their travels for a day or two, he would have perfectly fit the part of the pirate who captured the princess, took her to bed, and then fell madly in love with her after her rescue. At the same time, she couldn't quite imagine him driving his ship onto the rocks in despair of ever seeing his princess again.

But goodness, he was attractive. She sighed as she bit into the sausage soaked in very thick gravy. It tasted a bit . . . indescribable, but she'd eaten enough odd foods during her travels that she could have her breakfast without blinking. Something about the salt-tinged air made her dreadfully hungry anyway.

"Good heavens," Miss Juliette Quanstone murmured, looking at her from across the table, "how can you eat that?"

"It's not so bad." They'd asked her to sit with them. She would have preferred to be on deck, but she hadn't chatted with young ladies her own age in what seemed like forever. "And I like a good breakfast."

"I certainly wouldn't call it good," Miss Juliette countered, nudging her sister Emily in the shoulder and giggling. "You do eat with a great deal of gusto."

Zephyr nodded. "I'm hungry."

Frederica Jones shook a fork at the untouched lump on her plate. "I told Lord John that we should have brought along our own cook again, but that stupid fellow deserted us once we reached Port Jackson. Can you imagine? He simply fled into the wilderness."

"I know," the fourth of the Mayfair friends, Lady Barbara Prentiss, took up. "It's awful enough to be so long with only three maids between us. But now to have to eat food cooked by a . . . a man with only one leg—it's too much to be borne."

"That, however," Miss Jones whispered, indicating something past Zephyr's shoulder, "is not too much to be borne."

"You know his oldest brother is a viscount," Miss Juliette commented, giggling again. "And nearly as handsome."

Hiding her frown, Zephyr glanced behind her. Captain Carroway stood in his open shirt and white trousers, his blue and white waistcoat hanging open, as he took a generous slice of meat pie from the cook. "Did you know Captain Carroway in London?" she asked the four ladies in general.

"I've danced with him," Miss Juliette returned, "though he seems to be pretending that he doesn't remember. He actually told me that I was pretty as a rose."

Miss Jones waved. "Captain! Do join us, won't you?"

"Frederica, what are you doing?" Miss Emily whispered. "You know I've a sour stomach this morning."

"Then don't eat anything."

The captain strolled over to stand at the front of the table. "Good morning, ladies," he drawled with a slight smile that didn't touch his light blue eyes.

"Captain, dine with us," Miss Jones said, indicating the bench beside her.

"I'm on duty, I'm afraid. Feel free to take a turn up on deck this morning; the weather is very pleasant."

"It's so hot," Miss Juliette complained, fanning her face. "And the sun will turn us as brown as Miss Ponsley."

Zephyr's cheeks heated. Of course she'd been in the sun too much; it was a hazard of her father's duties. She'd never thought of her coloring as something to be ashamed of, however.

Bradshaw's gaze touched hers, then slid away again. "The natives on these islands will think you sickly and avoid us altogether if you don't add a bit of color to your palette," he said to no one in particular, "and some of their curatives are said to be ghastly." He inclined his head. "If you'll excuse me, ladies."

"Well." Miss Jones made a dismissive gesture. "I think Captain Carroway has forgotten that we are English, and as such, need to set an example. Of course we will look as proper as possible, whatever the savages might think." The other ladies chuckled, but she reached over to cover Zephyr's hand. "And I have a parasol to spare for you. We'll have you looking like a proper English lady again in no time at all, won't we, ladies?"

"Oh, yes." Juliette smiled. "It is a shame about your name, though. What was your father thinking?"

"He was thinking that he was an explorer, and he named me after the most fortunate thing a traveler ever encounters."

"It seems rather unfortunate to me," Emily put in.

"Well, I can take neither credit nor blame for it," Zephyr said, rising before she could forget Shaw's advice and say something less than polite, "so instead I will go and see to my father's botanicals."

Juliette began fluttering again. "Oh, on your way out, send dear Dr. Howard over here, will you? His brother is an earl."

Making her way through the dozen men heading into the large, low room among the lower deck cannons for breakfast, Zephyr deliberately avoided the rather handsome Christopher Howard as she stepped out to the corridor. Even after six days she had to think for a moment which way led deeper into the bowels of the ship and which way led up to sunlight and fresh air.

A hand grabbed her arm and yanked her sideways.

Before she could shriek, a second hand swept across her mouth. In a blink she was inside a small rope closet, the door closing her inside with her attacker. Furious and frightened, she kicked backward, aiming high.

"Damnation." Bradshaw's low voice came from behind her in a smothered grunt. "Stop it."

Pulling free, she squeezed around to face him. In the tiny closet there was barely room for the two of them to breathe. "What are you doing?" she demanded.

"Hush. I wanted to inquire whether you want me to move you and your father to the other side of the ship, away from those harpies," he whispered.

"You heard that, did you?" she asked in return, somewhat mollified.

"They weren't precisely being subtle about it. They don't know what to make of a chit who has a purpose in life other than to marry well."

She felt distinctly complimented. "And you? You're not very nice to me, either."

"Yes, but I'm the captain. I'm supposed to be crusty."

There was that humor again. It was quite disarming, really. She grinned. "You're very good at it, then."

"Hm." With a glance past her at the closed door he leaned down and touched his lips to hers. "I like a warm, following breeze," he murmured, straightening again. "I find you refreshing." Then he set her bodily aside so he could leave the closet.

Zephyr stood there in the near dark for a moment, her heart beating as loud as thunder. She wasn't even certain whether she liked him or not, and yet she suddenly felt shivery all over. *Good heavens*. Taking a deep breath, she pulled open the door and slipped back into the corridor.

Whatever that kiss had meant, if it was anything more than a tease from a man who'd spent far too much time at sea, she abruptly cared very little what those other silly ladies thought of her name. And all because aggravating Bradshaw Carroway liked it.

Chapter Four

Attired in sailor's clothing
She boldly did appear,
And engaged with the captain for
To serve him for a year.

"THE HANDSOME CABIN BOY"

"Call out the depth, Mr. Abrams!" Bradshaw shouted, shading his eyes with one hand as he guided the *Nemesis* around a rather alarming and haphazard grouping of reefs. He sent a quick glance at the masthead high above the deck, where he'd sent his first lieutenant, William Gerard, to keep a close eye on the water beyond the bow.

"Four fathoms, Captain!" young Mr. Abrams called from his position just to the port side of the bow. He dropped the knotted rope back into the clear blue water, counting knots as it lowered again. "Holding steady at four!"

"Is that good?" Sir Joseph asked from beside the wheel, his expression a mix of worry and anticipation.

"So far it's good. The current's fast as the devil

here, but if I can maneuver us in past the northern tip of the island there, we can set anchor without worry over being dragged."

"Three and a half, Captain!"

"Quarter sail, Mr. Newsome!"

"Aye, aye, Captain!"

The second lieutenant gave the order to furl all the topsails. Immediately the pull on the wheel lessened as they slowed. "Set the anchor," Shaw ordered, turning the ship to starboard as Gerard signaled in that direction. "And furl the rest of the sails."

A minute later the ship rocked to a halt, gently as a baby in a crib. At least he hadn't run them aground at their first destination. Sir Joseph looked as though he wanted to applaud, but thankfully he didn't do so. Miss Ponsley had been standing at the bow for the past thirty minutes, no doubt ready to dive in and swim for shore if he should be unable to make anchor.

"May we go ashore now?" Sir Joseph asked.

If it had been just him, or even him and his well-trained men, Shaw would have been sorely tempted. A new land, new horizons—his heart sped at just the thought of charging on shore, devil take the consequences. It was a welcome sensation, and one he needed to be cautious of.

"No," he said aloud. Shaw signaled Newsome again, and the second mate blew a quick series of two-toned blasts on the whistle. Almost immediately the three dozen jollies traveling with them trotted up on deck, rifles at the ready, and lined the railings.

"Marines, Captain?" the botanist stated, frowning. "We are not here to begin a war or to take anyone's territory."

"Neither are we here to be eaten," Bradshaw returned. "If the natives haven't seen us already, they will do so any minute. I prefer to know their temperament before I allow a nationally treasured, world-renowned botanist for whom I am responsible off this ship. And so you're aware, a dozen of the eighteen-pound cannons are also primed and ready to fire."

"This is not what I want, Shaw. We—"

"In the morning, Sir Joseph. And wherever you go, you will be accompanied by armed marines." He sent a glance at Zephyr, now stalking back toward them, a deepening frown on her face. "And by me, for the first day, anyway."

"Oh, if they're friendly, I think we should go, as well."

Without turning around, Bradshaw knew that the other party of civilians had gathered behind him, on *his* damned wheel deck. *Christ*. "We'll assess the situation in the morning," he repeated, and turned on his heel. "If you'll excuse me."

Miss Ponsley looked as though she was ready to chase him down, so instead of heading below to check on the cannons, he strode up to the mainmast and began to climb. Given the lack of undergarments most English ladies wore during the summer, he doubted she would join him up on the masthead.

"Captain?" Lieutenant Gerard exclaimed, moving aside on his perch to allow Bradshaw to step onto the platform.

Shaw bent over, trying to catch his breath. "I used to climb this all the time," he panted. "I think the mast has gotten taller."

Gerard grinned. "It's the new ships, sir."

With a snort, Bradshaw straightened again. "How does it look?" he asked, doing a slow turn.

Before them and less than a hundred yards to the south, green land and rugged cliffs marked the closest point of land. Just to the west of that lay a curved white-sand beach bordered with palm trees, an undulating stretch of dense hills just beyond. The ocean all around them was dotted with reefs and small islands. It was something of a miracle that they'd made it to anchor without the benefit of detailed charts. He supposed that task would fall to him, as well; Sir Joseph might know fern species, but reef charts were clearly not his forte.

"It's pretty," Gerard said. "Dangerous, but pretty."

"Any sign of natives?"

"I was looking at the reefs, sir. Nothing that I noticed."

"I want a watch up here. Two sets of eyes at all times. Bligh reported fast war canoes, and Cook says there was a great deal of evidence of cannibalism on the southernmost islands. I reckon we were seen from both of the larger islands on our way in, so keep a lookout behind us, as well." He blew out his breath.

"And we're here for plants?"

"And birds and grubs, apparently." He glanced back down at the deck to see that the Ponsleys had vanished, more than likely to one of their cabins to say disparaging things about him. As long as they stayed alive for the duration of the voyage, he supposed he didn't much care. "I'll send your relief up here, and then schedule the watch, William. Four-hour shifts."

"Aye, aye, Captain."

Once he returned to the deck he sent one of the

sailors up to relieve Gerard, then headed below to personally tell the men manning the cannons that they were not to fire without his direct order. Whatever Sir Joseph might think, he didn't have any interest in beginning a war here, either.

By the time he had the ship secured both for a possibly lengthy stay and for a quick departure if necessary, the sun was directly overhead. In the lee of the island the breeze was slow and light, and heat seemed to radiate up from the deck. It would be even warmer down below, but the Ponsleys remained out of sight, presumably sulking.

Or, he supposed, they could be planning a swim to shore. One of them could be, anyway. Tapping his fingers against Poseidon's beard, he descended into the ship. As he made his way down the long corridor he immediately realized that his cabin door was open. And he never left his door open.

Of course his cabin wasn't entirely his any longer, either. As he stepped inside, Sir Joseph and Zephyr were both bent over his worktable, his chart of the Fiji Islands spread out before them. "May I be of assistance?" he asked.

"You seem to be concerned that we will be attacked," Sir Joseph stated, straightening. "Where was it, precisely, that Bligh was pursued by war canoes?"

Bradshaw stepped up to the table and pointed at the passage between the two largest islands. "Here."

"And we're . . ."

Glancing at the botanist, who'd chosen precisely which island he wanted to explore, Bradshaw moved his finger east, just to the north side of the third largest island. "Here."

"That's a good hundred miles from where those war canoes were reported."

"A hundred and twenty miles, approximately." Shaw straightened. "My theory of war canoes is that they exist because one faction dislikes another. The canoes Bligh reported represent one side. I'd like to know if the other lies just up the coast or not before I unleash anyone for whom I am responsible into the wilderness."

"Then bring guns and men and accompany us," Zephyr put in, gazing out the cabin's windows as though she longed to be ashore.

"I intend to. After I give anyone who may have spied our approach time to make themselves known. At the moment the *Nemesis* is our mobile fortress." He folded his arms across his chest. "Are we going to have this argument every time we set anchor?"

"That would depend, I imagine," Zephyr returned, facing him, "on whether you continue to stand as our overcautious nanny."

Shaw liked to argue. He did not, however, like being called a nanny simply for doing his damned duty. Clearly the chit had no idea how . . . tenuous life aboard a warship could be. "I have one task, Miss Ponsley. And that is to see your father returned safely to England at the end of this voyage. Therefore, if nothing hostile rears its head, we will disembark at eight hundred hours tomorrow morning." He inclined his head and turned for the door.

"Captain? A moment, if you please."

Out in the corridor he stopped to wait for Zephyr to catch up to him. "I'm not going to debate you," he said.

"That's wise. You would lose."

"Not today. I did read Cook's journals. We're between war canoes and cannibals, and more than likely surrounded by them."

She raised both hands. "I concede that point."

"You're not required to," he returned, wondering briefly whether his brothers would ever believe him—*him*—spouting rules and regulations. Sweet Lucifer, the last year had changed him. "You only need to follow my orders."

For a heartbeat or two she scowled at him. "Before you began acting so stuffy," she whispered, glancing past him down the corridor, "I was about to ask if you might consider not allowing the Jones party to accompany us tomorrow morning."

"Stuffy? I'm being cautious. For your own good, I might add. And I have no intention of allowing them to accompany us tomorrow."

"Oh." She blinked, looking up at him. "Why not?"

"Because I doubt they know the difference between a cricket and a scorpion." He took a step closer, setting a hand against the wall past her shoulder. "I assume you do."

"Of course I do. In most cases. The thrill of exploration is encountering that which has never been seen before. I would, however, look for a stinger before I picked it up."

A smile tugged at his mouth. "*That* is the difference between you and them." He realized that he'd focused his gaze on her soft lips, and so he straightened again and turned away. "Now if you'll excuse me."

"Is that why you kissed me?" she murmured at his back. "Because I'm not like them?"

Bradshaw stopped his retreat. Thank God most of

his men had already realized it was cooler on deck, and they'd made their way out of the ship's depths. "I didn't intend to kiss you," he returned in the same tone. "The closet was smaller than I recalled."

"So it was a matter of square footage, rather than you thinking I don't know the rules of propriety."

"Precisely. And if you're staying down here, open my cabin's windows to catch the breeze." With a nod, he headed for the galley.

A soft footstep sounded behind him, and then he was shoved into a side corridor. Since he was fairly certain who it was, he didn't make a sound as he whipped around. "Square footage?" Zephyr hissed, shoving his shoulder again. "Do you expect me to believe that?"

"Do you want me to apologize?" he asked, lifting an eyebrow. "Because I don't have any intention of doing s—"

She threw an arm around his shoulder, rose up on her toes, and kissed him. His mouth found hers in return, heat cascading through his body. He wanted to devour her. With a stifled groan he grabbed her shoulders, clutching her closer while the deck seemed to spin drunkenly beneath his feet. *Christ.* Then he set her away from him, taking a second to catch his breath. "You're still not leaving the ship until tomorrow," he drawled.

Zephyr stuck her tongue out at him, then with a swish of her skirts headed back toward his cabin. Bradshaw, though, stayed where he was. Good God. Whatever insanity had been pulling at his insides had clearly found its way into the open. He was aware that he'd become obsessed with the safety of his passengers and crew. Chasing after this mouthy, headstrong chit who seemed determined to charge into trouble—he had the distinct feeling that he couldn't possibly have made a worse decision. Except that it wasn't his mind that seemed to be leading the way.

Zephyr leaned over the side of the ship and dropped her satchel into a sailor's lifted hands. The launch below looked rather small from the height of the deck, but neither it nor the rope ladder hanging down to it was what concerned her. Rather, it was the fact that three sailors were already on the bobbing craft, and she was wearing a gown.

Drat it all, she was the daughter of a famed botanist, and she was on the adventure of a lifetime. And yet she hesitated because she didn't want men looking up her dress.

"Here," Captain Carroway said, taking her arm.

She faced him, then blinked as he knelt down in front of her. "What the devil are you doing?" she demanded. If this was a marriage proposal, he needed to invest much more than two kisses. And he needed to be considerably nicer.

"I'm holding out breeches," he returned, flapping out the white knee-length trousers. "Step into them."

Oh. "I am not dressing on deck, you ninny. And those are men's clothes."

With an audible sigh he stood again. "Then go put them on in your cabin. You have five minutes. Once we get to shore, you may remove them again. Or leave them on. I imagine they'll be handy protection against insects."

"He makes a good point, Zephyr," her father said, climbing over the railing and descending, clearly eager enough to be off that he would be willing to leave her behind, as well.

"Will they fit?" she asked, grabbing them out of Bradshaw's hand.

He shrugged. "Don't have any idea. They belong to a twelve-year-old cabin boy."

Swearing under her breath, she fled the deck. He might have suggested that she wear breeches beneath her skirt before the moment she was to step over the side of the ship. Once inside her cabin, she slammed the door, pinned her skirt up under her chin, and shrugged into the breeches.

They felt odd and confining and scratchy, but at the same time rather . . . bold and wicked. It took her a moment to button the flap, and then she experimentally wriggled her hips.

Zephyr stepped back into her shoes and hurried onto the deck again. Both the marines' launch and her father's small boat were already halfway to shore, and everyone had boarded the third one except for her—and the captain. "I won't even ask if you're wearing them," Shaw said, holding out a hand to help her over the railing.

His lean face was perfectly serious, but his blue eyes danced. As she scowled and clambered down the swaying rope ladder, she had no idea why she'd been seized by the desire to kiss him yesterday afternoon. The man was impossible—arrogant, overbearing, and happy in his ignorance of science. But if he was such a bloodthirsty barbarian, why did he seem so determined to keep her father and her bundled up away from any trouble? It made no sense.

"Oh, she is," came from below.

She pretended not to hear, but couldn't help the

heat creeping up her cheeks. Letting go of the ladder, she seized one of the marine's shoulders for balance and took her seat.

Bradshaw, though, stopped halfway down the ladder above her. "Who said that?" he demanded, all humor gone from his expression. "Hendley?"

"Aye, sir. Just an observation," the sailor returned. "I meant no harm."

The captain set both feet onto the boat. "Get back onto the ship. Now." He glanced up. "Eddings! You're taking Hendley's place."

"Aye, aye, Captain!"

"That isn't necessary," Zephyr whispered, as Bradshaw sat beside her.

"As I've said before, I'm not interested in your opinion, Miss Ponsley," he returned, not making any attempt at all to be subtle. "I won't have anyone disrespecting the passengers on my ship."

As Eddings descended the ladder, Hendley leaned over the railing to look down at her. "Apologies, Miss Ponsley," he said, tugging on his forelock.

"Accepted, Hendley," she replied, and turned her gaze to the shore as the boat shoved away from the *Nemesis*. Captain Carroway had stated his annoyance with her on purpose, she abruptly realized, so that the crew wouldn't be angry with her. And at the same time he'd fairly well assured that no one else would look askance at her. None of *his* men, anyway.

"Thank you," she said quietly enough that only he would be able to hear her.

He gave a short nod. "How *do* they fit?" he returned in the same low tone.

Zephyr grinned; she couldn't help herself. "I'll never tell."

She looked toward the nearing shoreline, excitement running through her. All across Europe and even into India, she and her father had traveled well-marked trails. Englishmen had walked there before. And the only reason her father's collecting of botany specimens was important was that almost no one had bothered to gather them or make such detailed notes about comparisons and contrasts within species before.

Here, however, they could be the first. Captain Cook had landed to the south, and even if some French or Spanish sailors had perhaps touched this very shore, no one knew it. No one had heard of or benefited from anything they might have discovered. And whoever had set foot here before, she was very likely the first Englishwoman ever to do so.

"I have to ask, Captain," she said aloud, as the boats turned shoreward just beyond where a deeply cut river flowed into the sea, "what do you think of the local warrior cannibals? They don't seem to be anywhere about."

His gaze remained on the beach-lined shore. "No, they don't," he returned absently. "Not that we've seen, anyway." He faced her again, his light blue eyes as serious as she'd yet seen them. "Promise me that you will not go anywhere alone. I or one of my men will keep one eye on you at all times."

She cleared her throat. "There are moments when a lady requires privacy," she returned as delicately as she could.

"Inform me in enough time to find you a safe place," he said, no reflection of her own embarrassment on his lean face.

"You're a ship's captain, Bradshaw. Watching after me hardly seems a fitting occupation for you."

"It is today. Promise me, Miss Ponsley. Nowhere alone."

She tried to be affronted, because very likely he hadn't had this conversation with her father. But setting foot on an unexplored island was a new experience, and she wasn't a fool. "I promise. Just please try to keep up with me."

His mouth quirked. "I shall do my best."

Their boat reached the waves as they crested and foamed onto the white sand beach. Four sailors jumped overboard on some unspoken signal, sinking up to their thighs in the roiling water. Zephyr grabbed on to the side as the boat rocked violently.

With the sailors charging for shore, a heavy rope running between them and the bow of the boat, she couldn't do anything but hold on. A second later the hull bumped and scraped onto the sand and rocked to a halt.

Bradshaw stood, stepping out of the boat and onto the sand. "Miss Ponsley," he said, offering his hand.

"That was quite exhilarating." Grinning, Zephyr rose, slung her satchel over her shoulder, and gripped the captain's fingers to step over the side of the boat and onto the beach. She'd arrived. And yet, exciting as that was, she wasn't entirely certain that the tingle down her spine was because of the Fiji Islands and not the warm hand holding hers.

"Is it what you imagined?" he asked.

"It's better." Fifty yards up from the water, the beach ended. From there onward, everything was green with splashes of bright color. Palm trees, ferns, shrubs, vines—green and lush and tangled and covered in exotic flowers as far as she could see. She glanced at her father, already at the tree line and crouched down to examine the littering of coconut shells there. For him, this moment and this place would be absolute paradise.

"Miss Ponsley?"

She looked up at Captain Carroway. "Hm?"

"I need to issue some orders, and gesturing with both hands is more manly."

Oh, dear, she still held his hand. "Goodness," she squeaked, releasing him. "I quite forgot everything but my eyes."

"Understandable." With a brief grin he moved a few feet away to order the marines to form an armed perimeter surrounding them, while several men were to remain with the three boats. The remainder of the sailors began lifting cloth sacks and cages and nets, together with a box of instruments for determining altitude and small jars for insects and soil samples.

"Captain," her father called, straightening, "I would like to make my way up there," and he indicated the tallest of the hills behind them, "so I can assess where I might find the greatest variety of flora and fauna."

Bradshaw nodded. "Major Hunter, you heard the botanist. Lead away."

The senior officer among the marines nodded. "Stay at least twenty yards behind us, Sir Joseph," he said, motioning to his fellows. A group of the red-jacketed soldiers trotted into the trees, assuming a half-circle pattern as they moved inland.

The captain reached back into the boat for his

sword, which he buckled around his hips. Then he gestured for Zephyr to precede him. She caught up with her father as they entered the trees.

"With this army about us," he muttered, "we won't find anything that isn't rooted to the ground."

"Hopefully if the marines don't spy anything alarming, they'll quiet down a bit and allow us to explore more freely tomorrow."

"Hopefully. This is the only thing, you know, that made me hesitate to embark on a navy vessel. Too damned many rules and regulations."

Zephyr glanced over her shoulder. In his open-necked shirt, blue waistcoat, and white trousers, the sword hanging on his left hip, Bradshaw looked more like a pirate than a captain in His Majesty's Navy. The marines were the only ones wearing their full uniforms, though even if she'd just happened upon them she would have a very good idea of who led the group.

"Oh, look at that." Her father pulled his arm free and hurried over to examine some sort of moss or fungus on one side of a tree.

"So you don't run hither and thither collecting sticks?" Shaw's voice came from just beyond her shoulder. "I'm somewhat disappointed."

"I sketch," she returned. "I or someone else does need to keep an eye on my father, or he'll wander off."

"You're finally taking my warnings seriously, then, are you?"

"I'm more concerned that he'll get lost. He went out looking for seedlings just outside of Istanbul, and it took me and a party of local soldiers nine hours to locate him." By now she'd gotten past the abrupt, panicked feeling of being utterly alone in a faraway place, but at the time she'd almost wished she'd been the sort of woman who fainted and let others see to things.

"That does not make me feel any better." He motioned behind him. "Eddings."

The sailor hurried up. "Captain?"

"Stay not more than ten feet from that man at all times," he ordered, pointing a finger at the botanist.

"Aye, aye, sir."

"And take a pistol in case you need to signal the rest of us."

"Aye, aye."

He might have looked after her father himself, she supposed, since as the captain had said, his orders didn't even mention her. Apparently, however, Bradshaw Carroway had assigned himself to *her* protection.

They had topped the lowest and closest of the hills when one of the marines appeared. "This way, Captain. It's safe," he said, heading off toward the east.

"Well, then," Bradshaw muttered. "Wait here," he said to the rest of the party, then offered his arm to her. "It's safe, I believe."

It wasn't the direction her father had said he wanted to go, but since he fell in with them, she decided not to object. Aside from that, she was curious.

They emerged into a small, level clearing, and she stopped. Before them a badly dilapidated hut overlooked the beach and the shallow lagoon below. The roof was gone except for a pair of roughly cut beams holding up a feathering of palm leaves, while a circle of low stones approximately ten yards across lay in front of the most regularly shaped of the openings in the walls.

Clearly the place hadn't been occupied in some time. If anyone had been there, they would have had a grand view of the *Nemesis* sailing in to anchor. Zephyr started to point out that since the place had been abandoned, the captain's caution was no longer necessary.

As she turned to look at him, though, he stepped into the center of the ring of rocks and squatted down, ruffling his fingers through the dirt and grass. A moment later, he lifted a long, white stick. No, not a stick, she amended, a chill running down her spine. A bone. A human femur, if she remembered anything of anatomy.

He straightened, facing her father. "Anything you wish to collect from here?" he asked, dropping the leg bone to the ground again.

"Actually, yes," her father returned, going to a small, overgrown patch of weeds at one side of the square hut. "This looks to be some sort of garden. I need to collect one of each."

Several of the sailors looked dismayed, but the marines had declared the clearing safe. Zephyr moved around behind the hut where she could see both the structure and the ship below, then leaned back against the nearest tree trunk and pulled her sketchbook and pencils from her satchel.

"I told you to stay in my sight," Bradshaw said a moment later, striding up to her.

"I was in sight of at least a dozen men," she returned, keeping her gaze on the setting before her.

"They aren't me." He gestured, and one of the men trotted over to set a folding chair down beside her. "There."

She hadn't realized he'd seen fit to provide her

with a seat. "Thank you. It's easier to sketch on my lap." She sat on the stretched canvas chair.

"Does your father even care that there are human bones lying about?"

"I think he was considering that if these people are cannibals, this may be the closest he will be able to get to a deliberately planted garden. He isn't obtuse; merely . . . focused."

"It is pretty up here," he conceded, turning his attention toward the hills still above them.

"It's beautiful." Tomorrow she would have to bring her watercolors with her; the black lead hardly did justice to the lushness around them.

"Yes, beautiful."

When she glanced up at Bradshaw, he was looking directly at her.

Chapter Five

When I was a little boy so my mother told me, to me
Way haul away, we'll haul away Joe
That if I did not kiss the girls,
My lips would all grow mouldy, to me
Way haul away, we'll haul away Joe.

"HAUL AWAY JOE"

Someone was watching them. Every instinct Bradshaw possessed told him that they were not alone on this island, and with the *Nemesis* visible from nearly every hilltop on the north side, someone had seen them. The only logical conclusion was that the natives were either waiting for or gathering reinforcements.

"This is a rather handy game trail," Sir Joseph noted, puffing as he ascended the hill just in front of Shaw.

"It's not a game trail," Bradshaw returned, half his attention on the young lady tramping beside him. Yes, he'd been an idiot and called her beautiful, but at least she hadn't made fun of him for it. Then again, she was just as likely to agree—not because she was vain, but because a fact was a fact. And she was, in fact, pretty.

"It's not?" she put in.

"I've only seen one sort of footprint, and it's human. And I haven't seen anything but spiders and a lizard or two on the ground. They don't make game trails."

"Spiders? And lizards?" the botanist broke in, slowing. "You must point them out to me. I am collecting fauna specimens as well, if you'll recall."

"Ye can have every mosquito that's bit me," Eddings commented, swatting the back of his neck.

"I'll give ye the flies," another one added.

"Yes, I must have insect specimens, as well," the botanist agreed. "And please alert me to anything else you see. All of you."

"How fresh are the footprints?" Zephyr asked after a moment, her voice pitched low.

"Since the last time it rained." He glanced up at the cloud-speckled sky. "Two days, three perhaps."

"You know my father is supposed to attempt to gauge the friendliness of any natives he encounters," she continued. "But I have to admit that you have me, at least, a bit nervous."

And it had taken only human bones, documented attacks, and a dozen dire warnings to convince her. "That's what the marines are for." He slapped yet another bug off the back of his hand. The things seemed to be able to find every inch of uncovered flesh. Zephyr was looking at him, and so he sent her a quick grin. "We won't tell him about that one," he muttered.

"I've done away with a few of th—"

"Look," he interrupted, stopping as color up in

the branches of a tree ahead of them along the trail caught his attention. Bright red lifted from one branch to another. A second red splash joined the first.

"Oh, birds," Miss Ponsley murmured, stopping beside him. "Father," she called softly.

Sir Joseph turned around. "What is it?"

"Shh. Up there."

The botanist turned and looked where she indicated. "Beautiful," he said. "Some variety of parrot, I would guess. One of you fetch me a net, will you?"

"Father, you can't climb up there. You'll break your neck."

One of the marines hefted his rifle. "I'll fetch it for you."

"No, no. I want it alive."

Bradshaw stifled a sigh. "I'll fetch it," he said, unbuckling his sword and handing it to Miss Ponsley. "Where's a net?"

"They may be breeding pairs, Captain. If at all possible, I want a quantity of them."

Slinging the net over his shoulder, Shaw walked slowly to the base of the tree. " 'I want a quantity of them,' " he repeated under his breath, scowling. "And *I* don't want to fall on my arse and set that damned chit laughing at me."

He'd been a proficient tree climber as a youth, and in more recent years a strategic branch near a window had spared a lady or two's reputation. Generally, however, it wasn't something he did with an audience. Since he'd volunteered, though, he supposed he had no one to blame but himself.

As he started up the winding trunk he could make out at least a half-dozen crimson-chested birds. They seemed interested in his presence, but not particularly worried by it. Then again, they quite possibly realized just how ineffective a net would be in a tree full of leaves and twisted branches.

Halfway up he moved out along a likely branch. Small green fruits hung in groups everywhere, with the birds above dropping seeds on and around him. With that much food about, bribing them into the net wouldn't work. At a crook in the branch, however, he nearly put his boot on a handful of fuzzy black caterpillars.

Sighing, he scooped them into his hand and laid them out again on the branch where the birds could see them. Then he sank back and attempted to look as small and innocent as possible.

With a squawk, several of the birds descended onto his branch and began plucking up the caterpillars. Waiting until about half of them had their vibrant green- and blue-colored backs to him, he flipped the net out from his chest and along the branch.

Five minutes later, he lowered the tangled net and the five parrots thrashing around in it carefully to the ground. "Well done, Shaw!" Sir Joseph congratulated him as he hopped down from the last branch. "You, bring up one of the cages. Oh, they're lovely."

Bradshaw wiped his dirty and scraped hands off on his trousers. When he straightened, Zephyr was eyeing him. "What?" he demanded.

"I had no idea bird-trapping expertise fell under the purview of the Royal Navy."

That was the problem; it didn't. Shaking off the thought that he was having a grander time straying outside the navy's blasted purview than he'd managed lately following it, Shaw grinned. "My youngest brother badly wants a parrot and an eye patch. The Runt keeps encouraging me to turn pirate."

"The Runt?"

"Edward. He's eleven now and very proud of his nickname, so don't frown."

"I'm not frowning. And you'd likely make a grand pirate."

She was grinning as well, so he decided not to be offended. "My thanks." Bradshaw checked the angle of the sun. Though the day was turning out to be much more interesting than he'd anticipated, he didn't want to see what became of them during the night. "Sir Joseph, we need to return to the ship."

"But we've just begun," the botanist protested.

"We'll head out again in the morning with more men and supplies, and some tents." He sent a glance around the lush, covered hills again. "This place may look deserted, but I'm not willing to test that theory without a defensible place to spend the night."

Of course the botanist didn't like the decision, but neither was he foolish enough to insist on staying inland on his own. As for his daughter, Zephyr was talking soothingly to the parrots in their cage.

"They were eating the fruit," he said, and took his sword back to hack off a sizable bunch from the tree.

"You should have made provision for us to stay the night," Zephyr noted, shouldering her satchel. "Clearly you know nothing about exploration."

"And clearly you know nothing about leadership or strategy. Jollies toting tents wouldn't be very effective at protecting you and your father, now would they? And I don't believe in sacrificing men for no good reason. So we'll set out again tomorrow."

She opened her mouth to say something he expected to be insulting. Instead her face paled and her gaze focused just beyond his shoulder. "Shaw," she whispered.

Every muscle in his body tensed. "How many?" he asked, not moving. Damnation. For once he wouldn't have minded his instincts being wrong.

"I see one. A man. Behind the tree just beyond you."

"Look away from him." He waited, but she didn't even blink. "Zephyr. Look at me."

With a slight gasp her gray eyes met his again. "What do we do?"

"Start down the hill." Resisting the urge to look behind him, to attack first, he laughed aloud. "Major Hunter," he said in a tone of casual conversation, "stay at ease, but we have at least one man watching us from about thirty feet behind me." He caught up to Miss Ponsley, putting himself between her and the one threat he knew of. "Let's retreat in an orderly fashion, but be ready."

"Aye, aye, Captain," the marine returned. "Slow and easy, boys. Let's not begin something if we don't have to."

"My specimens," Sir Joseph broke in, clearly attempting to keep his voice calm, and not succeeding nearly as well as the major. "We can't leave them behind."

Damned plants and birds. "My men, take what you can carry, and easy does it," Shaw instructed, putting a hand on Zephyr's shoulder. She was shaking. "Do you sketch people?" he asked conversationally.

"What?" She looked up at him.

"I'm curious. Do you sketch people, or only plants and scenery?"

"I sketch people, when they're interesting."

"When we get back to the ship, could you sketch the man you saw in the trees?"

She hesitated. "You may be rather more clever than I originally thought," she finally said.

"Don't bandy that about. I have a reputation to maintain."

All the way back down to the beach Zephyr expected to be pierced through the back with a spear or an arrow or something. It would be a difficult shot, of course, since Captain Carroway stayed close enough behind her to touch the entire time. She could feel him back there, warm and solid and steady. For heaven's sake, he joked with her as they descended the hill.

"Captain, my men and I will take the third boat," Major Hunter said, his profile to the tree line as they loaded her father's specimens and tools into the launches. "After you're safely away."

Bradshaw nodded. "Get them into the water, lads," he ordered, in the same easy tone he'd been using since she'd told him about the figure hiding in the trees.

Keeping her back to the jungle and the very real danger behind them gave her the shakes, but thus far the captain's strategy of being cautious and pretending to ignore the fellow had been working. As the first two boats left the beach and floated free into the water without them, though, she abruptly felt very vulnerable.

"Shall we, Miss Ponsley?"

Without waiting for an answer, the captain swept her up into his arms and waded into the water.

Zephyr grabbed him around the shoulders, hanging on to his neck. The waves slapped against his thighs, and he shifted her higher so that their cheeks nearly brushed. With a heave he set her on her bottom onto one of the benches, then leapt over the gunwale to sit beside her.

She hadn't even gotten wet. "Thank you."

"Don't look back yet," he said. "Hunter and his men aren't out of spear or dart range."

"How did you know we wouldn't be attacked?" she pursued.

"Captain Carroway had no idea that we *would* be attacked," her father broke in with a frown. "With all that talk of cannibals and war canoes, you turned even me skittish. I daresay the fellow was curious about us."

Bradshaw frowned, then wiped the expression away before she could be certain she saw it. "I hope you are correct, Sir Joseph. But I intend to keep you and Miss Ponsley alive, whatever your thoughts on the subject. We'll give it another go tomorrow."

"You cannot know—"

"That is final, Sir Joseph."

Jaw locked, his gaze on his ship, Shaw looked every inch the formidable captain of a formidable naval vessel. That was what she'd first imagined he would be like, she realized, and he'd surprised her by being otherwise. Except that he wasn't. Unless he was.

That was the question; deciding which man was the true Bradshaw Carroway. At the moment, she was grateful to whichever of them had gotten her and her father off the island without a shot being fired, or a spear thrown. For a barbarian, he'd shown a great deal of restraint.

As soon as they were back on board the *Nemesis*, Shaw issued orders for the watch to be doubled, and then he went below decks to his cabin, where he locked the door behind him. She knew that, because she'd followed him.

For a moment she stood looking at his door. Blasted maddening man. Instead of simply making declarations he might at least explain himself from time to time. Or once. She made a fist. They would just see how he felt crossing someone who didn't let him retreat.

"Some say a ship's captain is inscrutable by nature," a low voice drawled behind her.

Stopping with her knuckles halfway to the door, she turned around. "Dr. Howard," she exclaimed, putting her hand over her heart. "You startled me."

"I do apologize, Miss Ponsley." He smiled rather charmingly. "I heard that you encountered a native."

"Not so much encountered as caught sight of," she corrected, grinning back at him. "The captain thought it best to be cautious."

"I'm certain that's for the best, then." He started to turn around, then hesitated. "I wonder, Miss Ponsley. Would you care to join me for tea? I have a box of fine English leaves I've been saving to make everyone jealous."

She couldn't remember the last time she'd had a cup of genuine English tea. Or chatted with a genuine English gentleman—a man of science, no less. Because while she'd had conversations with Captain Carroway, she certainly didn't consider him a gentleman. "That would be lovely, Dr. Howard."

"Splendid. I shall meet you on deck by your plants in fifteen minutes."

"I'll be there."

As he left the corridor, a trio of sailors hurried by, tugging their forelocks as they passed her. Well, she couldn't simply stand there and scowl at the blasted captain's door. Blowing out her breath, she returned to her own cabin where she could remove her boy's breeches. Hopefully whoever they'd been borrowed from could do without them, because they had solved a number of difficulties in traveling on boats and over rough terrain.

When she returned to the deck, she was surprised to find that every passenger on board seemed to be taking tea with Dr. Howard. Her father was the only one absent, and he was undoubtedly occupied with his finds of the day. "Hello," she said, accepting a cup from the doctor.

"This is the most civilized I've felt in a week," Lady Barbara Prentiss commented, eyeing Lord Benjamin over the rim of her cup. "Weeks."

"Tell us about the savage you saw, Miss Ponsley."

She glanced at Stewart Jones. Word spread on a ship with rather alarming speed. "I only saw his silhouette."

"At least you set foot on land," Mr. Jones returned. "We've been forbidden to do so."

"I think the captain will change his mind about that," Lord John put in. "After all, we requested passage on this ship to see some of the sights. And Admiral Dolenz would not be pleased to hear that we were kept captive in our cabins for months."

Zephyr hadn't been terribly impressed with these people; they didn't know how to dress properly for the Tropics, and if anything they seemed less well-read than Shaw. But they were being pleasant, which was more than she could say for the captain. "There were a great many mosquitoes and stinging flies," she said, rubbing her arm for emphasis. "And very large spiders."

"Oh, that sounds unpleasant." Juliette Quanstone shivered delicately.

"And human bones in front of an old hut." There. She could be friendly, too, and at the same time hopefully convince them to stay on the ship and out of the way.

It wasn't so much that she wanted them kept captive as it was knowing that with them present the attention of the crew would be divided, with everyone forced to look after and cater to the half-dozen lords and ladies skipping about the island. That left less help for her father, less exploration they'd be likely to manage, and a greater likelihood that something would go wrong.

The fact that Captain Carroway's attention would also be divided was only a minor concern, because he did seem rather capable of seeing to several things at once. And he had proved to be handy at avian capture, so keeping him close by her and her father would likely be the wisest idea.

As the sun set, the scattered clouds darkened to reds and purples more vivid than any oil paints. Zephyr sat on a barrel to watch the colors deepen, and ignored the conversations going on around her. She'd never been this close to the center of London Society before; her father had been knighted by King George, but other than a great uncle who was a baron, she had little connection to these people. Perhaps if they'd remained in London long enough for her to have her debut Season it would have been different, but that hadn't happened. And now she was more comfortable with seeds and soil than waltzes and gossip.

"—Dare married money, and that is how Captain Carroway managed to get his own command," Miss Quanstone was saying as the sunset faded enough to lose Zephyr's attention.

"You know his younger brother was accused of treason," Lady Barbara added, sipping her tea.

Dr. Howard nodded. "I remember that," he said. "Though he was found to be innocent."

"Of course he was. Otherwise our good captain would be a cabin boy on an American whaling ship somewhere." Lord John chuckled.

"All hands on deck!"

Zephyr jumped at Lieutenant Abrams's yell, and then again as the bell behind the wheel began clanging. Everything went into motion—sailors running to their stations, the marines charging up on deck, weapons at the ready—and in the middle of it all, Bradshaw Carroway sprinting onto the deck. Someone tossed him a spyglass, and she finally looked in the direction Mr. Abrams pointed.

A fire burned on the shore, approximately where they'd landed earlier. As she watched, a second fire flared thirty feet farther up the beach, and then a third approximately the same distance in the other direction. "Any sign of canoes?" Shaw barked.

"No, sir."

"Lieutenant Newsome, I want you at the bow, and Keller on the gun deck. Make certain no one takes a shot without my orders."

With a quick salute the thin, blond-haired man and another officer with flaming red hair disappeared below. Zephyr continued to watch, her fascinated attention divided between the beach and the *Nemesis*'s captain. The jaunty, easygoing fellow had vanished, replaced by a commanding, levelheaded officer who radiated competence and calm.

Behind her, the London group chattered nervously, their jests pointed and clearly meant to show how unafraid they were. Well, she *wasn't* afraid. Cautious and concerned, yes. But not afraid.

After several minutes, a total of seven fires burned along the beach, the silhouettes of bodies moving in front of them the only proof that people manned them. Bradshaw closed his spyglass and walked down the deck toward his passengers.

"I would recommend that you leave the deck," he said coolly.

"Is that an order, Captain?" Lord John asked, lifting an eyebrow.

"No. We haven't been threatened, and we're out of dart and spear range, so do as you will. But they may have keener eyes than we do, and you lot are dressed differently than everyone else on deck. You may attract attention. Not to mention that we have very few women on board, and you're all in one spot."

"Oh, heavens, John." Frederica Jones clutched Fenniwell's arm and squeezed her eyes closed.

"Very well. Ladies, let's get you below. Don't worry; we'll protect you."

Lord Benjamin gestured at Zephyr, but she shook her head. "They've already seen me," she said. "And I'd like a look at them in return."

Whatever Lord John said about worry over the females, the men seemed in as much of a hurry to escape the supposed view of the natives as the ladies were. Shaking her head, Zephyr watched them retreat. She doubted they had an ounce of spleen among them.

"Here."

She turned around as Bradshaw held out his spyglass to her. "Thank you," she said, pulling it open and lifting it to her right eye.

"Don't look directly at the fires; you'll be too blinded to make out anything around them. Focus just to one side or the other."

She looked. "I can't make out any features," she said after a moment, moving her gaze slowly up the beach. "But I do believe there are both men and women there. And children. They seem to be eating."

"That's what I gathered, as well," Shaw's low voice commented. "It doesn't look hostile, but I don't know anything about their customs. And Cook wasn't much help, I'm afraid. I looked through his journal entries again, but he barely paused at the Fiji Islands long enough to restock the water barrels."

"And all Bligh saw was the men pursuing him on the water." She sent him a glance before she resumed her gaze through the spyglass. "I thought all navy captains wanted to fire their cannons and shoot at things."

"Sorry to disappoint." He cleared his throat. "Though in all honesty, I do generally like shooting at things."

Zephyr clamped her lips shut to keep from laughing. The view through the spyglass shook and danced in her hands. "I believe you; I saw your wall."

"Will you sketch the figure you saw for me?"

he asked after a moment. "And your father would likely appreciate it, as well."

"Certainly." She closed the spyglass against her palm and handed it back to him.

To her surprise, he accompanied her down to her cabin and then stood in the narrow doorway as she gathered her sketch pad, pencils, and watercolors. "The light's better in my cabin than in the galley," he said.

"But it's evening. You said we were to flee your cabin at night and leave it to you."

"I didn't say 'flee,' and this is a special circumstance." He gestured her toward his door. "If you please."

She pushed open his door and went to sit at the worktable while Bradshaw lit the room's four lamps. He'd left the door open, and while the rules of propriety didn't much seem to matter this far from the drawing rooms of London and even less to her, she did appreciate the gesture. After all, if she'd learned anything about her fellow passengers today, it was that they loved to gossip. She didn't care to be made the subject of their tongue wagging. Not now, and not when they returned to London.

"He was mostly in shadow," she said, glancing up at the captain as he sat opposite her.

"Draw what you remember. It's the best look I'll get until tomorrow morning."

Zephyr bent her head, first sketching a rough outline of the tree so she could situate the man standing beneath it. As she drew she felt herself sinking back into the day, hearing the wind through the tops of the trees, smelling the humid air and the rich scent of plants and earth.

"You're not going to simply sail us away toward the horizon tomorrow, are you?" she asked, keeping her attention on the sketch.

"No. But I prefer to avoid slaughtering anyone if I have the choice. I'm also aware that sitting here in the water looking at the shore isn't going to do your father much good. If the entire population of the Fiji Islands is on the beach in the morning, however, I may change my opinion about the fleeing bit."

"Why d—"

"Captain?"

Bradshaw turned to look at the doorway as her father stepped into the room. In his hands were two large birdcages, red-breasted parrots hopping to and fro inside. "They are not staying in here," Shaw stated, rising.

"They can't stay in the hold," her father protested. "And I'll have to sleep standing up if we have one more day's success at collecting."

Blowing out his breath, Bradshaw glared at the cages. "Tonight they may stay here," he said. "Tomorrow, if we haven't been attacked and eaten by the natives on the beach, I'll see about putting some shading up on the deck."

"That would be magnificent. Thank you, Captain. And I apologize for questioning your judgment today. After seeing those fires burning tonight, I daresay you may have saved our lives." He set the cages down against the front wall. "Zephyr, when you finish sketching, I need some assistance labeling specimens."

"I'll be there shortly." She looked from Shaw to the cages as her father returned to his own cabin. "At least they aren't rodents," she offered. Just as she finished speaking all the birds began squawking, the sound like a rusted saw on metal. She clapped her hands over her ears. "Oh, good heavens!"

"I knew this was going to happen," Shaw muttered, striding to his bed. He reached into one of the drawers beneath it, yanked out a blanket, and returned to the birds. Swearing, he dropped the blanket over the cages. The parrots fluttered, then began to quiet down.

"Well done, Captain," she said, grinning.

"Damned birds."

Twenty minutes later she blew the excess lead and erasures off the sketch and turned it to face Bradshaw. "That's what I saw."

He pulled it toward himself. "Bligh mentioned feathers and face paint," he said almost absently, "which I assume would be in honor of doing battle. This fellow isn't wearing either."

"Not that I recall."

"Then he was either surprised to see us, which I doubt, or he wasn't leading an attack party." He studied the drawing for another moment. "Or he's from a completely different tribe that dislikes feathers and face paint, no matter the occasion."

Zephyr gazed at him. He'd thought the entire encounter through, and he'd made his suppositions based on what she'd seen. She hadn't known what he wanted to see the sketch for, but of course it made sense now. "I hope the first part is correct," she said aloud.

"As do I." He stood again. "May I escort you to your father's cabin?"

For a moment she was disappointed that he wasn't going to attempt to kiss her again. "It's twenty feet away."

"And?"

"Very well. I suppose if you wish to look silly, it's your own affair."

She crossed in front of him. Abruptly he took hold of her arm and backed her into the wall beside the birdcages. Tilting her chin up with his free hand, he lowered his mouth to hers. Slow, hot, and lingering, the kiss sank all the way down into her bones.

Finally Shaw lifted his head again. Zephyr looked up into his eyes, swallowing. "You are very aggravating," she managed, her voice shaking a little.

"As are you." Moving away a step, he gestured her toward the open door again.

"I don't even like you," she continued, walking into the corridor and thankful she didn't have to grab on to the wall for her abruptly uncertain balance.

"I don't like you, either."

Chapter Six

She is a frigate tight and brave
As ever stemmed the dashing wave.
Her men are staunch to their favorite launch,
And when the foe shall meet our fire,
Sooner than strike we'll all expire
On board the *Arethusa*.

"THE SAUCY ARETHUSA"

By morning the canoes arrived.

The crew had heard enough stories about spears and cannibals that most of them were armed, and Bradshaw made a show of smiling and clapping sailors on the back as he stepped onto the main deck shortly after sunrise. "Easy, boys. They don't know what we're about any more than we've deciphered them."

Walking to the railing, he looked down. Two dozen broad, thick-hulled canoes, half of them equipped with rudimentary masts and sails, sat between the *Nemesis* and the shore. Some of the men wore face paint, and from his vantage point he could see axes and spears in the bottoms of the boats.

Only men sat in the canoes, but a mix of men and women and children lined the shore. A great many of them were talking, and some were shouting, but he couldn't make out a word of what they said. Clearly it wasn't Spanish or French or German, or even any mix of the three.

"Fascinating," Sir Joseph said, stopping at his elbow. "Are they hostile?"

"Not so far," Bradshaw returned, turning his head as a chorus of "miss" sounded behind him. If it had been any of the London chits he likely would have warned them that the sight they were about to gaze upon might be offensive to their sensibilities. But it was Zephyr, and so he shifted sideways to give her room at the rail.

"They don't seem to be attempting to kill us," she noted, lifting her gaze to look at the beach. "Oh, my."

Most of his crew had been looking in the same direction since sunrise. The men there wore a minimal loincloth of undefined material, some sort of woven . . . tube running from the waist and curving down like the handle of a teapot to sheath the cock. Balls were left apparently to enjoy the tropical breeze. The women had on grass skirts of various lengths, and nothing else. "I do like warmer climes," he said with a faint grin, glancing sideways at her.

"That is uncalled for," she retorted.

"Yes, it is. My apologies."

"How do you mean to proceed, Papa?" Zephyr asked, turning her back, deliberately or not, on Shaw.

Just because she was pretending to ignore him, however, didn't mean that he would ignore her—or what she said. "Sir Joseph isn't going to do anything until we determine whether they want to invite us to *eat* dinner, or to *be* dinner."

"I have an idea about that, Shaw, if I may."

His brief acquaintance with Sir Joseph Ponsley left Bradshaw less than convinced that giving the botanist free rein would be a good idea. The fellow had a brilliant mind, but his caution and common sense were much more questionable. "Does it involve anyone being eaten?" he asked aloud.

"Ideally, no. There are some things down in the hold that might suffice."

Shaw nodded. "Dobbs, go assist Sir Joseph."

"Aye, aye, sir."

The bosun's mate and the botanist trotted off. Whatever Ponsley had in mind, he'd best hurry. The longer everyone had to wait about beneath the hot sun, the shorter nerves and tempers would become. Little chance as he had to be remembered for anything he might accomplish here, Shaw did not want to be known as Bloodbath Bradshaw or Cannibal Killer Carroway.

"What do you think they want, sir?" Newsome asked, his voice tight.

"Considering that they haven't attacked, I would say they want the answer to that same question themselves. Calm yourself. If the officers panic, the men will follow."

Newsome squared his shoulders. "Aye, aye, Captain."

"Would it be odd if I wanted to sketch this?" Zephyr asked.

He glanced at her. Of course she wasn't afraid; she'd been shaken yesterday, but had been nowhere close to panicking. Today she was merely curious.

But curiosity killed felines, and he would do anything to be certain no harm came to her. Or her father, of course. "Odd? Not for you," he returned. "Do it from my cabin, though; I want you below decks."

"And I want the view from right here."

Bloody hell. He did not want an argument over his authority now. Bradshaw jabbed a finger up toward the wheel deck. "Up there. And stay back from the railing."

Scowling, she folded her arms across her chest. "Very well."

One argument successfully dodged, then. As she turned to fetch paper and pencils, though, her father reappeared, Dobbs on his heels and toting a crate.

"May I?" the botanist asked, gesturing at one of the long gaffing poles.

"That looks rather weaponlike, don't you think?" Bradshaw countered.

"I'll be cautious. And I don't believe I appear nearly as dangerous as you do, Captain. Neither of us wants bloodshed."

"Which is why I'm concerned." Bradshaw eyed Sir Joseph. He'd met a share of explorers before, men who were more than willing to sacrifice everyone around them for their own glory. The botanist might be a bit single-minded, but he wasn't one of those men. And Shaw was about to wager all their lives on the theory that his assumption was correct.

He picked up one of the poles himself and handed it over. "Have at it."

Opening the crate, the botanist pulled out a handful of blue and red and green necklaces made of cheap glass beads. Hooking them with the end of the pole, he slowly and carefully lowered them over the side of the ship. After a moment's discussion among the canoes, a single craft approached. One of the loincloth-wearing men stood up precariously and snagged the treasures with one hand.

Excitedly they passed them around the canoe, and then the standing fellow removed the shell necklace from around his own neck and placed it over the gaff's hook. Sir Joseph lifted the pole again and removed the necklace.

"Lovely," he said, examining it. "We shall have to collect some shell specimens, as well. This yellow one is mag—"

"Put it on," Shaw interrupted, just refraining from rolling his eyes. *Scientists.*

"Beg pardon?"

"Put the gift around your bloody neck before you offend them."

"Oh. Yes, of course." Removing his floppy straw hat, Sir Joseph placed the shells around his neck, touched them with his fingers, and bowed.

"So far, so good," Bradshaw murmured. Moving a step forward, he patted his chest, then the botanist's, and then he pointed at the island.

Immediately the natives began motioning them to come forward, jabbing fingers from the *Nemesis* to the shore. With still no indication of whether they were the guests or the main course, Bradshaw glanced at his first officer.

"Lower one of the boats. I want four volunteers. Levelheaded ones."

"But Captain," Gerard returned in a low voice, "these people are *known* cannibals."

"And I like a good leg of lamb. That doesn't mean

I take a bite out of every sheep I come across." He took a breath. "If something should happen, you are to take every able-bodied seaman and come and get us. I do not wish to be roasted and eaten. Now get to it, William."

With a quick smile, the lieutenant saluted. "Aye, aye, Captain."

Bradshaw turned around to order his sword brought up to him. Other than that and his boot knife, he meant to go unarmed. No pistols or rifles that the natives might not understand. His family would be amazed at his diplomacy—or they would have been, before his duty in the Mediterranean.

Both Tristan and especially Robert seemed to have realized that his perspective had rather significantly altered. He wasn't certain why he'd thought of them just then, unless it was because his family felt like the only rock-solid thing in his life on the rolling sea.

He caught sight of Zephyr handing over a satchel to her father. Did she have an anchor to hold her steady? She certainly didn't have much of a home, if she'd been away from it for eight years. Once the two Ponsleys parted, he approached her himself. "You aren't going to ask to come along?"

"I may enjoy exploration, but I'm not a fool, Captain. If you aren't eaten, I'll join you tomorrow."

"That's encouraging." He accepted his sword from one of the cabin boys and buckled it on. "What did you give your father?"

"Some plant and seed samples from here and elsewhere. I thought it would help him explain what we're about."

"Good thinking. Now stay away from the railing."

"I will. For heaven's sake. I just finished saying I wasn't a fool."

Shaw tipped his hat to her. "Are you going to wish me luck?"

She lifted her chin. "I'll wish that you return my father safely to the ship."

For a moment he wanted to kiss her upturned mouth again. He found women distracting at the best of times, but he could generally separate business, as it were, from pleasure. Perhaps the confusion here was that Zephyr Ponsley *was* his business. She irritated and interested him by equal turns. "Stay out of trouble while I'm off visiting."

"You are im—"

"Ready, Captain," Gerard called, with impeccable timing.

Bradshaw sketched a bow. "Good day, Miss Ponsley."

Zephyr did climb the steep steps to the wheel deck, but she did not stay back from the railing. Considering that her father had just launched into an ocean full of very real danger, she didn't think Shaw actually expected her to go and hide.

The small launch with the six Englishmen aboard was immediately surrounded by war canoes. Her father looked worried as he clutched the satchel she'd given him, the small crate of various-colored glass beads at his feet. Captain Carroway—Bradshaw—however, wore a slight smile and looked no more concerned than if he was poling along the Thames at Kew Gardens.

He was so full of contradictions that she was beginning to have the devil of a time deciphering him. First he ordered her about like she was one of his sailors, then he did something thoughtful, while the next moment he seemed as likely to dismiss her as to kiss her. And oh, my, that man knew how to kiss. She perhaps didn't have much experience with such things herself, but he far surpassed that silly count in Spain and Mr. Michael Fordham, her rather determined suitor at Fort William. Far, far surpassed them.

But being courted meant marriage and children and a home, and she had yet to meet anyone for whom she would be willing to give up traveling and exploring with her father. However little she knew about Society, she was very aware that daughters of knights rarely had the opportunities for science and travel that had been given to her. And it would certainly take more than a few excellent kisses to convince her to give up her freedom.

She shook herself. There she was, witnessing a possibly historical moment and not even documenting it because she was contemplating a very aggravating man and a life she hadn't even been asked to relinquish. Swiftly she took a seat on the chair someone had left up there. Since it was the same chair Shaw had provided for her on the island yesterday, she assumed it was meant for her. With a glance at the tense faces around her, she began sketching the English boat at the center of the scene, with the war canoes around it and the crowd on the shore, waiting.

"He's actually gone with them?" Dr. Howard exclaimed, stopping next to her.

"The captain and my father, yes," she returned, slowing her sketching to concentrate on rendering Bradshaw's confident profile.

"That's damned foolish. The captain is responsible for the safety of his ship and his crew. All we need do is fire a few cannons and the primitives will scatter to the winds."

"They would also be angry. I have no wish to be ambushed while collecting insects. And the captain *is* being responsible for his crew. He's risking himself, not his men." And he did that a great deal, she'd realized. Were all navy captains so willing to risk their own lives to spare their crew? She doubted it.

"Allowing them the opportunity to kill and devour an Englishman isn't doing a favor to any of us."

Finally she glanced up at the physician. "I'm certain you're perfectly safe here on the *Nemesis*, Dr. Howard."

"Please, call me Christopher."

"Christopher, then."

"And you've misunderstood my concern, I think." He smiled charmingly. "It's not myself I worry over, Miss Ponsley, but rather you and the other ladies on board. These are the wilds of the world."

She rather liked the way he said that. The wilds of the world. Perhaps her father could use that as a book title once they were finished with this expedition. "I've spent time in India and the Ottoman Empire and Persia, Christopher. I am accustomed to this sort of life."

"Even so, I believe one only meets unfriendly cannibals once."

"We don't know th—"

"If I may, I have spent time in London with the other passengers, and with Captain Carroway. He has something of a reputation for wild and . . . ungentlemanly behavior." He moved closer, squatting down beside her chair. "I tell you this in confidence, so you'll know that if you should require my assistance or my friendship, it is available to you."

She refrained—just—from calling him a nickninny. Bradshaw had warned her to show some restraint, and the doctor did own some very nice tea. "Thank you, Christopher," she said aloud. "I appreciate the information, and your friendship."

"It is my pleasure," the surgeon said, straightening. "And now if you'll excuse me, I have some duties to see to."

As he left, she returned to her sketch. She had to draw from memory now, since the boat had reached the shore. Bradshaw Carroway might have been wild and ungentlemanly in London, but at the moment he was responsible for her father's life. And she would not have let her father leave the safety of the ship if she hadn't trusted that Shaw would be able to protect him.

Pushing a pencil behind her ear, Zephyr stood. "Mr. Abrams?"

The young man fourth in line for the command of the *Nemesis* turned away from the view. "Miss Ponsley? What may I do for you?"

She gestured at the spyglass he held. "Might I borrow that for a moment?"

Instead of handing it over, he reached into his belt for the glass that, as far as she could tell, belonged to Captain Carroway. "Cap'n said you might be curious," he commented, as he gave it to her.

"Thank you." So he'd taken a moment to think of her curiosity while preparing to embark on what could possibly be his last trip to shore, ever. Opening the glass, she lifted it to look over at the beach.

Whatever else was transpiring, the natives seemed quite pleased with the glass beads. Hopefully her father would remember to save back the prettiest of them for the chief or king or whoever their ruler was. The men held spears, but none of them seemed to be pointed at the Englishmen—which made her feel only a little easier.

"Does your captain do this often?" she asked.

"Do what, Miss Ponsley?"

"Offer himself up to cannibals without an armed escort?"

"He once had us paint and re-rig the ship to look like a merchant vessel so the French would try to board us," the lieutenant noted. "If it'd been me, I would have opened fire as soon as the Frenchies came in range, but the captain said we were to take the ship and not sink her." He chuckled. "You should've seen the look on that Frog captain's face when Captain Carroway ordered the planks covering the cannon ports dropped and he saw all those thirty-two pounders pointing straight at him."

It wasn't quite what she'd meant, but Zephyr understood what the lieutenant was saying. Captain Carroway didn't frighten easily. She could add that to the reluctantly growing list of things she found admirable about him. Upon boarding the *Nemesis* she'd expected to find him to be full of regulations and completely lacking in imagination or even curiosity. And he still continued to surprise her.

After ten minutes or so, the large crowd on the beach disappeared inland. Lieutenant Gerard cursed, then called up to the two men perched on the tiny platform at the top of the tallest mast. "Any sign of where they headed?"

"South and easterly, Lieutenant!" one of them called back. "Can't make out anything now."

"Keep a sharp eye, Everett!"

"Aye, aye, sir."

Zephyr looked into the dense green tangle of the island's interior for another twenty minutes, but no one appeared, no one came running onto the beach yelling for assistance, and no smoke appeared from a likely cooking fire. Finally she set aside the spyglass and went back to her sketching, this time adding splashes of color so she would remember the sight when she finished it later. Down on the main deck below several of the sailors were constructing some sort of awning out of an old, patched sheet and some of her father's wood supplies, multiple enclosures taking shape beneath it.

So Bradshaw hadn't forgotten about his promise to put some shelter on deck for the animals they would be collecting. Of course if the parrots in his cabin were as noisy as they had been last night, forgetting might have been impossible for him.

As she sketched, the conversation going on several yards away from her slowly seeped into her mind, lifting her from the fresh memory of watching her father and Shaw greeting the Fijian natives. She looked up.

"—long do we sit here before you either go in and retrieve our people, or decide they've been devoured and sail us the devil away from this place?" Dr. Howard was saying in a hard, sharp voice.

From his expression, Lieutenant Gerard would rather be bailing out a leaky boat than conversing with the surgeon, but he kept his voice low. "I am under orders from my captain," he stated evenly. "I am following them. I will continue to follow them."

"This is ridiculous," the physician returned, his fists clenched and his body canted forward. "A few muskets would send those savages fleeing, and Sir Joseph could collect whatever damned plants he wanted in peace. And the other passengers could go ashore instead of being locked in their cabins like animals."

"I am not going to stand here and debate with you, sir," the lieutenant said. "The captain's orders are law. At the moment, *I* am the captain of the *Nemesis*. Control yourself, or I will have you removed from the deck."

"You? What are you, a farmer's son? A fishmonger's boy? You should know by now who your betters are."

Taking a breath, Zephyr stood. "One of my father's goals on this expedition," she said, tucking her pencil behind one ear again, "is to attempt to instigate friendly relations with the natives of the islands we visit. So while I am sorry that Miss Jones and her friends aren't able to go ashore today, I place the orders of the Royal Society above sightseeing."

Dr. Howard sketched a bow. "Miss Ponsley. Very diplomatic of you. I think you'll recall, however, that your opinion wasn't asked for."

How typical—a man who didn't agree with a female but didn't have an argument to support his stance simply resorting to bullying. She lifted her chin. "Nor was yours."

Narrowing his eyes, the physician turned on his heel and descended the steps. For heaven's sake, she hadn't even been stating an opinion. She'd been reciting the facts. Clearly Dr. Howard was not as science- or logic-minded as she'd thought.

"Do you require something, Miss Ponsley?" Mr. Gerard asked, his own expression still tight.

So he didn't want her assistance, either. *Men.* She shook her head. "No. I'm just stretching my legs."

"Very good, then." Nodding, he excused himself and headed off toward the fore of the ship.

Well, clearly someone wasn't communicating well with others, and under the circumstances that someone seemed to be her. And that troubled her—not because she longed to speak with spoiled and frivolous-minded people, but because once she and her father finally returned to England, she would have to be able to do so.

Sighing, she resumed her seat and continued with the watercolors. Unfortunately, the person who seemed the most likely to agree to assist her with learning social niceties was Bradshaw. *Oh, dear.* Perhaps she could approach one of the other ladies on board. They certainly knew how to comport themselves in polite Society.

By sunset she was becoming less concerned about diplomacy, and she was beginning to reconsider Dr. Howard's suggestion. Muskets and marines would be against everything her father wanted, but she'd been watching the shore for better than eight hours, looking for him and for Shaw to reappear. It was odd, but when she imagined what might be happening to them, it wasn't her father's face she saw, but Shaw's. Was he being hurt? Tortured? Killed?

Of course she worried about her father, as well, but from what she'd learned of Bradshaw Carroway, he would put himself between those for whom he was responsible and any danger they might face. During the course of the day she'd also realized something else about the *Nemesis*'s captain—he listened to her.

The other men on board seemed to view her as a chit who was more attractive with her mouth shut. Shaw, though he constantly disagreed with her, had never dismissed what she said. And that only added to her confusion about him.

"Goodness, you've been out here all day?"

She looked up as Juliette Quanstone topped the steep steps. "My father is out there somewhere," she returned, gesturing at the island. "Where else should I be?"

"But you're not even wearing a bonnet." Julia lifted her own delicate white parasol. "Use this," she said, glancing past Zephyr at Lieutenant Newsome. "Otherwise the natives will think we've kidnaped one of their own."

Zephyr wanted to point out that she couldn't paint and hold a parasol at the same time, but before she could do so, Miss Quanstone jammed the handle into the knot of ropes tied to the railing.

"There. A young lady should always keep her complexion as flawless as possible." She clapped her hands together. "You know, I always carry a copy of *A Lady's Guide to Proper Behavior* with me. I will be happy to lend it to you."

Juliette smiled prettily, clearly thinking she was performing a good deed. Zephyr smiled back at her. It had been a great while since she'd had a female friend, and never as an adult. Though she couldn't help but think that she would have preferred someone with whom she had more in common, perhaps it would be better that they didn't. "Thank you," she said aloud. "What brings you up here?"

"Oh, the others are playing whist. I needed a breath of fresh air." She started to lean back against the railing, then brushed her finger against the wood and made a face, straightening again. "Do you play?"

"Sometimes, with my father. I don't have a great deal of patience, so I'm not very good at it."

"I'll be happy to teach you. I'm quite good at it myself."

Zephyr gritted her teeth. "Thank you. And I would very much appreciate if you would lend me that guide. I'm afraid my . . . polite conversation is rather rust-covered."

"I noticed that, though I didn't want to say anything. I would be happy to serve as your tutor. All of us could. Oh, Barbara and Frederica would so enjoy having a project."

Good God. "I—"

One of the lookouts whistled. Zephyr stood up so fast that her sketchbook fell to the deck, but when she looked toward the shoreline she couldn't make out anything but trees. The sailor up on the mast would have a better view, of course, but until someone came into sight now she didn't think she'd be able to sit still.

"Does that mean that Captain Carroway is returning?" Juliette asked.

"I'm not certain."

"I do hope so. It was quite brave of him to voluntarily step among savages. And I know for a fact that he dances exceptionally well."

Zephyr's grip on her pencil tightened, and she forced her fingers to relax. So stepping among cannibals and navigating a quadrille were of equal importance. She would have to keep that in mind. "I thought you and your friends considered the captain wild."

"Oh, he was. He still is, I suppose." Juliette wrapped her arms around her shoulders in an apparent imitation of an embrace. "Wild is rather delicious, don't you think?"

She'd begun to think so—which both baffled and annoyed her. But her more immediate concern was over the still empty beach. "I prefer disciplined and dedicated," she said aloud. Zephyr took a breath. "Now if you'll excuse me, I'd like to keep a lookout for my father."

"Oh, of course." Placing a kiss just an inch or two shy of Zephyr's right cheek, Miss Quanstone left the deck again.

Zephyr supposed the conversation had been pleasant enough, if a bit backhandedly insulting, but perhaps she was giving it too much thought. One thing she did know for certain, however, was that she didn't like the way Juliette made it sound as though Shaw skulked about the corridors of the *Nemesis,* kissing all his female passengers willy-nilly. If that was so, she had a little something to say to that impossible man.

Everyone not on duty seemed to be crowding up to the port side railing, but that didn't stop her from squeezing in to find her own spot. The sailor at the top of the mast whistled again, and she lifted onto her toes.

There, just inside the line of palm trees and other greenery, she glimpsed movement. Her heart hammering, she leaned over the railing, trying to make out the tan jacket of her father and Shaw's dark blue uniform.

Finally, as they emerged onto the white sand beach, she saw them. Bradshaw's jacket was open and his hat was missing—as was her father's—but other than that they looked intact. Thank heavens.

Canoes appeared from up the river and around the peninsula, and the *Nemesis*'s launch pushed into the water to be escorted by two dozen of the fierce-looking vessels. Beside her, Lieutenant Gerard ordered the marines to be ready, but to keep their rifles at their sides.

Most of the natives, she noticed belatedly, wore glass bead necklaces that sparkled in the lowering sunlight. Even with the cheap ladies' jewelry, they still looked like warriors—as did the man seated in the middle of the English launch, a necklace of what looked like shark's teeth around his own neck.

Finally the boat reached the side of the *Nemesis*, and Dobbs flung the rope ladder over the side. Swiftly Zephyr made her way down the stairs and through the excited sailors to the railing on the main deck. It seemed like forever, but must have been less than a minute before her father's head appeared, and the sailors surged forward to help him onto the deck.

"Zephyr! It was glorious," he said, handing her back the satchel. "I must have half a hundred new plant specimens. They showed me one meant to quiet coughs and fevers."

"That's wonderful, Papa."

"And we weren't eaten," Bradshaw added, regaining the deck in a rather athletic fashion.

"Well done, Captain," Lieutenant Gerard said with a grin.

"Will they allow us on shore again?" Zephyr asked, half her attention on the loud calls coming from the canoes paddling around them.

"Yes," Shaw answered, since her father was clearly occupied with overseeing dozens of plant specimens being lifted up from the small boat and several of the canoes below. "From what we could decipher, they think we're very amusing, and they mean to provide us with guides. Or escorts. Or guards. I'm not entirely certain of which."

"That's excellent." A shiver of excitement went through her. Nervousness was there, as well, but she refused to be left behind this time. "I want to hear all about your visit."

Bradshaw nodded, then blinked as he seemed finally to notice the excited sailors around them. "Guests and officers in my cabin for dinner in one hour."

While sailors hurried off to alert Winstead the cook and remove the front wall paneling of the captain's cabin in order to fit the expanded table, Zephyr stood back. Yes, she wanted to know about their adventure, but she didn't much like the idea of being relegated to just another member of the audience.

She didn't want to share Bradshaw with another four admiring ladies who'd danced with him in London and could say flattering and proper things to him so he would wish to kiss them instead of her, either.

Chapter Seven

You can search the world for pretty girls
Till your eyes are weak and dim,
But don't go searching for a mermaid, son,
If you don't know how to swim.

"THE MERMAID"

Bradshaw wondered for the fiftieth time or so what Captain Bligh had done to be set upon by war canoes.

Had someone taken a shot at a canoe when the craft approached for a closer inspection? Had the *Bounty*'s launch strayed into waters sacred to the Fiji natives? Had the moon been full, or waxing, or waning, and signaled some dire portent or other?

"A penny for your thoughts," Zephyr said, looking up from her sketch of the busy village just down the rise from where they sat in the shade of a large tree. Sir Joseph had told him the thing's species and genus, but "tree" rolled off the tongue—and through the brain—much more efficiently.

"Just wishing Bligh had gone into more detail. I'd prefer not to inadvertently repeat his mistakes."

"We've been traipsing about for better than a week now, and no ill has come to us," she returned in her usual matter-of-fact tone.

"Yes, but the Mayfair mob is ashore again today." If he stood, he would have been able to see them at the far end of the village, where they were apparently bartering hairbrushes and torn, useless bits of fabric for necklaces and paintings done on flat-pounded bark.

"You should likely be keeping close by them."

"I'm keeping close by you, because you're more likely to wander off into the jungle." She was also a much more interesting companion, but he wasn't about to tell her that.

"If wandering is your measuring post, you should be with my father."

"I have twelve men chasing Sir Joseph about the countryside, toting satchels and boxes of soil and birdcages." He leaned sideways to look at her sketch. Zephyr had a wonderful eye for detail, but more than that, she seemed able to convey mood and movement. Just by looking at her rough outline of the village he could almost hear the swish of grass skirts and the chatter of the natives. "Are you attempting to be rid of me?" he asked belatedly.

"Yes, I imagine I am."

"And why is that?"

She glanced up at him, squinting one gray eye against the sunlight. "I know I must seem like some kind of a curiosity, some chit badly in need of—what's the term?—a little Town bronze? Simply because I've never had a London Season, however, doesn't make me a fool."

Bradshaw met her gaze. "I never said any such thing."

"Have you been kissing any of your other passengers, then?" Zephyr returned to her sketch.

The question stopped him. Until that moment, kissing Miss Jones or Lady Barbara or the Quanstone sisters had never even occurred to him. Which was exceedingly odd, given his off-duty reputation. And the line of her shoulders was stiffening. "Are you jealous?" he asked, genuinely curious.

The point of her pencil snapped off against the sketchbook. "Actually, I've been attempting to decide whether you're genuinely interesting or merely extremely lucky. So thank you. I believe you've just answered my question, half-wit."

"I will confess that conversing with the ladies of the Mayfair set is much easier than chatting with you." Finding that he was only mildly annoyed even with the direct accusations, Shaw reached into the leather satchel she'd set between them and handed her another pencil. "I always know just what they're going to say. You're more complicated. And unpleasant."

"Juliette loaned me a booklet on proper behavior. For your information, it says that you and I should not be sitting here together without a chaperone."

Zephyr shifted her borrowed parasol, putting it between them to block him from her view. He'd never seen her use it for anything practical, except perhaps for the trips to and from the *Nemesis* on the launch. She had managed to brain him with it at least twice. And then there was the present blockade.

"And yet here we are, with no one even looking at us askance." Pushing the parasol back behind her, he grinned. "Though I'll admit that the bare-breasted and cock-handle-wearing natives likely know very little about the rules of polite Society."

"But you know the rules, and there you sit."

"I think it's because I've known you for well over a fortnight and I still haven't figured you out. It's very annoying."

"If I'm so annoying, why do you keep kissing me?"

In some ways it would be a shame if she did learn all the nuances of propriety, because that would signal the end to conversations like this one. "I don't know why I keep kissing you," he said aloud, shifting closer to run a finger down her soft cheek. "I can't seem to help myself."

"I hope you have a better idea of what you're about when you're captaining the ship."

"As do I." God, her skin was soft.

She hunched a shoulder as if brushing him off. "Stop that." When he lowered his hand, she drew another few lines. "I meant to ask you. What happened to your hat? Did it fall off and you forgot about it?"

"The chief liked it. Apparently he only means to wear it during ceremonial occasions."

"So you simply gave it to him?"

Bradshaw shrugged. "I have another hat. Your father has half a garden stowed in the hold. And no one has any holes in them or has been boiled or roasted."

For a moment she gazed toward the village again. "Apparently it's bad form for a lady to ask a gentleman his reasons for doing something, but I believe this concerns the expedition."

"Stop sidestepping and ask your question then, Zephyr." He found her directness charming, and if she actually began following the advice of that damned guide she'd borrowed, he was going to throw it overboard.

She folded her hands into her lap. "If you insist, then. I've read Cook's journals, and Admiral Nelson's, and the biography of Wellington."

"That's rather bloodthirsty reading for a chit who calls *me* a barbarian," Shaw noted.

"Well, with traveling so much, I suppose I have a great deal of time to read." Her brow furrowed, then smoothed again. "My point is that with very few exceptions most military commanders would not have risked themselves the way you have been since we arrived here. And if they *had* made their way on shore, they would have shot any natives threatening their safety."

Had she figured him out already? He'd known her for a mere fortnight, and he'd spent most of that time simply seeing to his shipboard duties. "Your father's instructions are to be friendly."

"There's a difference between diplomacy and risking yourself unnecessarily." She edged a breath closer to him. "So explain yourself."

Now would have been a good time for chaos to erupt, but despite his sudden wish the village and surroundings remained calm and bathed in sunlight. "You complained about me being a savage, and now you're annoyed that I'm not one?" he ventured, deciding to parry rather than surrender.

"You're the one with the wall of war in your cabin. And you said you like to shoot things. But I don't think you do."

Shaw studied her face for a long moment. This was the sort of conversation he might be cornered into having with his brother Robert, but no one else. Except, surprisingly, for the painfully intelligent young woman sitting beside him. He blew out his breath.

"Before this duty the *Nemesis* was in the Mediterranean chasing down pirates. The most notorious of them, Captain Molyneux of the *Revanche*, kept eluding us. It was very . . . aggravating. We finally ran her down, took out her mainmast, and boarded her. Within twenty minutes we'd taken her."

He shifted a little, keeping his gaze turned away. After better than eighteen months it should have faded, but he could still smell the black powder and blood. "A very good friend of mine was serving as my ship's surgeon. Simon was belowdecks patching up some powder burns and he caught a stray ball through his skull. It killed him so instantly he didn't even drop the gauze he held in one hand."

"I'm so sorry, Shaw."

He cleared his throat. "Thank you. Simon was a very kindhearted soul. We'd served together for eight years. I always told him he would have made a fine pastor, and since he wasn't strictly a member of the crew, he was the one I could always confide in and chat with. His death just seemed so . . . senseless. Useless. And I suppose I lost my taste for bloodshed."

For several hard beats of his heart they sat in silence. He was acutely aware of the sound of birds and the distant chatter from the village. He'd just handed this woman the power to end his career with the navy, which tended to frown on captains who hesitated to fight. But if he'd learned anything in his years of service, it was how to read people. And however mad it seemed, he trusted Zephyr Ponsley.

"That explains several things," she finally said.

"Good things or bad things?"

"When we were assigned a navy ship I was convinced you would be firing cannons at everything that moved. So as much as I hesitate to hand you a compliment, I continue to find myself pleasantly surprised. I believe you've already saved lives. I find that admirable, Shaw."

"Just keep it to yourself, if you please. Not the bit about you admiring me, but the rest of it. I am the captain of a warship, and if I decide to retire I would like it to be honorably and by my own choice."

"But what will you do if you have to fight?"

"I'll fight." Actually he wasn't entirely certain what he would do, but that was something he had no intention of sharing with anyone.

"You are more complicated than I imagined." She reached over to pat his knee as she would pet a dog. "And I shall be the soul of discretion."

He was *not* a puppy. "I have been in battle, you know. More times than I can count—which is a very high number, I assure you. I've shot, and been shot at. I've been hit a time or two, as well. It's only that I've come to the conclusion that a great deal of this . . . stomping and blowing, as you call it, is for no damned good reason." Shaw sent her a smile. "And if you do speak a word of this, I'll toss you overboard."

She grinned back at him. "You're still a barbarian, aren't you?"

"Yes." And that was much better than being a lapdog. "And now that I've told you something intimate, I think you should reciprocate."

"Ah." Shifting to face him more squarely, she

tucked her pencil behind her ear. "First, might I ask you another question? It's actually luck related, but I don't wish to be left behind to be eaten."

To anyone else, Shaw would more than likely have made a flip answer and turned the conversation back to her again. Zephyr Ponsley, however, liked knowledge. In some ways, she reminded him of his closest brother. Robert, before love had saved him, had practically lived off information—and nothing else. In other ways she reminded him of Simon, who always seemed to know precisely when he didn't want to discuss something and then plowed in anyway. "I actually believe the natives here only eat their enemies, and only as a form of revenge," he said aloud. "So don't make them angry, and you won't be dinner."

Amusement, and relief, touched her face. "Then I'll ask my question and risk stranding, shall I? At the worst I'll have to wear a grass skirt."

And nothing else. The abrupt image stopped his brain for nearly half a minute. He could see her creamy, sun-touched skin, a shell necklace hanging between her nicely-sized bare breasts. His trousers began to feel snug again, and he mentally shook himself. "What is your question, then?"

"The brass plaque just outside the main hatchway," she said. "Poseidon, I presume. Everyone touches it as they go to and from the deck. It makes a kind of sense, asking for luck from the god of the sea, but do you believe it actually makes a difference?"

"I know that the *Nemesis* has been through several actions where other ships haven't survived, and I know that her first captain, Jonathan Strake, nailed Poseidon up there before her keel ever touched the salt water. So to answer your question, it doesn't hurt to give the sea god his due, and it might just help."

Zephyr regarded him for a long moment. "I simply cannot decipher you," she finally admitted. "It is very aggravating."

"Yes, it is that. And now it's your turn. Something intimate."

"I don't have anything intimate to share."

He doubted that. "Very well," he said anyway, "answer a question. Did you always wish to be an assistant botanist?"

"I'm not an assistant botanist. I'm my father's assistant. His work is important, and he needs me. I daresay he would forget to eat if I didn't remind him."

"But is this what you wish for yourself?" he insisted, aware that she'd dodged the question.

"How many women have the opportunity to explore the world as I have? And what else would I wish for? To be stranded in London doing embroidery?"

"I was thinking more of whether you missed having a home."

She looked down for a moment, something wistful crossing her delicate features. "I daresay I miss it no more than you do."

"Th—"

"No. I'm finished. Discuss something else."

Shaw pulled out his pocket watch and opened it, knowing it would tell him he'd already put off leaving this spot for too long. "We'll have to postpone that. I need to get back to the ship to take my shift at watch," he said, hiding a frown as he stood.

No one would say anything if he shirked his duty

and stayed in Zephyr's company for the remainder of the afternoon, and that was precisely what he wanted to do. But he was the captain, and he couldn't very well expect anyone to perform his duties if the senior officer couldn't be bothered to do so.

"I suppose I have to leave then, as well."

"Yes, you do." Shaw took her sketchbook and then offered his free hand to help her up. "Though I will give you the choice of staying in camp or returning to the ship for the night."

Her lead-dusted fingers were warm in his, the callus on one side of her middle finger clear evidence that she used a pencil frequently. He rubbed the pad of his thumb against it. In an odd way the knowledge that she was an educated, very bright woman aroused him.

Generally, in London, anyway, he preferred the brainless but worldly-wise chits who knew how to chat about the weather at soirees and please a man in bed—and little else. Here in the middle of the Pacific, however, even with several of those very ladies sleeping only a foot away from his cabin, the opposite seemed to be true. It was the contrary one he'd been working so hard to know better.

Bradshaw blinked, nearly stumbling over an exposed root. Getting to know anything more about a female than what would entice her into bed went against every fiber of his confirmed bachelor beliefs. Women were for leave, a respite from the celibacy of the sea. Bothering to learn details of someone who would be an acquaintance for a night or two, and then be left behind for years, made no sense.

Yes, he'd been considering retirement. But that

didn't mean he'd become softheaded. Nor did it mean that he had to begin considering marriage. He shot her a sideways glance. If he'd ever met a woman with marriage less on her mind, he couldn't recall her. Desire, lust, was one thing. But— He shook himself again. For God's sake. *Stop thinking about bloody marriage.* Especially not with a woman who aggravated the devil out of him with every other sentence she spoke.

"Do you think Miss Jones and her friends will be staying on shore tonight?" she asked, breaking into his thoughts.

"My men shuttled an entire boatload of clothes and servants to the tents, so I would imagine so," he returned, grateful to have something less problematic to contemplate.

"I think I'll sleep on the ship, then."

Zephyr thought she saw quick interest flicker in the captain's eyes, but it might have been the sunlight through the waving palm trees. When he offered his arm, she took it. After all, the ground was very uneven.

A warship captain who had determined to look for opportunities to avoid a fight. In a sense she'd known there was something . . . additional to him, but she'd put her bafflement to his alternating humor and autocracy. For a moment as he'd spoken of his friend Simon, she'd very much wanted to kiss him. And then to ask about her own wishes . . .

Thank goodness she'd managed to put a stop to that before she could begin to weep and confess that she had never taken the time to examine her own hopes or dreams or convictions and that she had no idea what she was other than her father's assistant.

Until very recently, the question had never even occurred to her.

It was odd to find herself both admiring Shaw and feeling thankful that she and her father had been assigned the *Nemesis,* because generally she very much enjoyed sparring with him. Most men either realized they were being picked at and ridiculed and left with all due haste, or they simply found softer-witted prey. Captain Carroway, however, seemed to find her amusing, and to appreciate her efforts. And he hadn't hesitated in returning her jibes with his own. He might prefer diplomacy, but he certainly knew how to answer her shot for shot.

"Has your father mentioned how long he wants to remain here?" he asked into the silence.

"I think he would be happy to stay here for the rest of the year," she returned, "but the Royal Society specified that he explore the entire region. I'll ask him this evening, but I would imagine that another three or four days will give him enough samples and specimens to make him think this visit has been worthwhile." She glanced up at his lean profile. "Why, are you ready to sail away again?"

"Yes. I have a great curiosity to see Tahiti."

"Are the women more naked there than they are here?"

"That's hardly possible. I'm actually more concerned that the longer our people are ashore here, the greater the odds are that something will go wrong."

"That's very pessimistic of you."

A quick grin curved his mouth. "I prefer to think of myself as an experienced realist."

"Does everything I say amuse you?"

"Nearly everything," he returned. "Why shouldn't it? You're rather witty."

"I hope you do take this expedition seriously," she stated, abruptly beginning to remember why he annoyed her. "Do you know that one of the plants my father discovered just outside Constantinople has the properties to ease hysteria in women? And I know for certain that at the end of the expedition we will be bringing species and information to London that have never been seen or heard of before. It's important."

He inclined his head. "For you, perhaps. I sail the ship and attempt to stay out of trouble. With everyone but you, of course."

"And you check for leaks," she retorted, with what she hoped was dripping sarcasm. "Don't forget that part."

"Are we enemies again, then?"

"You're the one who confided in me and then decided to become cynical."

"I didn't just become cynical," he retorted. "Didn't you listen to what I said? Or did it pass by you because I didn't use the word 'shrubbery,' or 'rhododendron'?"

"Oh, do shut up, you . . . simpleton."

That seemed to put a halt to his amusement, and they spent the next twenty minutes in near silence. She didn't care a whit, as her attention was on their lush, wild surroundings and not on the handsome, possibly troubled man stalking beside her. He, of course, was more than likely deciding which trees would be adequate for shooting arrows or cannonballs at, as that wouldn't cause any injury to his crew.

"Thank God," he muttered, as the tents just inside

the tree line came into view. He pulled his arm free of hers. "I'm leaving for the ship in ten minutes, if you still care to go."

"I'll have to see if perhaps my father's caught a toad or a snake. Either would be more interesting than you."

"And more fitting company for you." With that he made his way over to one of his officers, leaving her to stand near the fire pit.

"Impossible man," she growled, and went to collect the paints she'd brought ashore with her, not that she would have enough light to paint by this evening. Gathering them made her look busy, which was all she required at the moment.

The sailor, Hendley, approached her. Like most of the crew he was shirtless and barefoot, a strand of shells around his neck. "Lemme carry that for you, Miss Zephyr," he said, indicating her heavy satchel.

"Oh, that's not necessary," she returned. "I'm only going to the boat."

"Aye, but the boat's taking the captain back to the ship, and me and the lads could stand a bit of a holiday." He glanced to one side of the small cluster of tents, where two of the female villagers were handing woven baskets of fruit to one of the cook's mates.

An odd, uncomfortable flush went through her. She knew the sailors looked on her kindly since Shaw had made it look as though she disapproved of his heavy-handedness, but this could be a bit more serious than a fellow stealing a look at her legs while she climbed down a ladder. *Drat.*

With a forced smile she handed over her satchel and followed Hendley to where the fruit was being loaded into the small boat. "Thank you, Hendley," she said, as he stowed her things beneath one of the seats.

He tugged on his forelock. "My pleasure, Miss Zephyr."

Zephyr tapped her palms against her thighs, waiting for Hendley to leave and Bradshaw to appear. If she told the captain what the sailors seemed to have planned, though, everyone would know she'd been the one with the wagging tongue. And there was still a great deal of ocean between her and the end of the voyage. As she debated whether it was better to remain friendly with the crew or to prevent a possible "incident," as Shaw referred to it, she saw him emerge from one of the tents, his coat in one hand.

"Blast it," she said for Hendley's benefit. "I forgot to check my father's supply of jars."

With that she trudged back over the sand to the tents. As she crossed by Shaw, she swished her skirt. "I need to speak with you," she murmured, trying not to move her lips. "Now. Without anyone knowing."

He continued on, apparently not hearing her. Zephyr pushed into the tent that had been set up for her father. Now what the devil was she supposed to do? Write the captain a note? What if someone saw it? She paced. Twelve jars were easy enough to count; she couldn't very well claim to be delayed by arithmetic.

Something scratched against the canvas at the rear wall of the tent. "Zephyr?"

She hurried toward the low voice just outside. "What's your excuse for being back there?" she whispered.

"It's private and very manly," Shaw returned in the same tone. "What do you want?"

"I believe that some of your men are planning to visit the village tonight. The women there, to be more specific."

What sounded like profanity rumbled into the tent. "Hendley?"

"I prefer not to say."

"Get to the boat. I'll see to it."

How he meant to accomplish that without giving her away, she had no idea, but she could have examined and counted every jar five times by now. Stifling her questions but not her curiosity, she left the tent and strolled back to where Hendley still stood by the boat.

"Jars all counted, miss?"

"Yes, and why he wants another dozen for tomorrow, I have no idea. How many different beetles could there possibly be on one island?"

The sailor laughed. "No idea. But if he wants all the biting flies and mosquitoes, he's going to need barrels."

She smiled back. "I do hope we won't be collecting those beasties."

"Which beasties are we not collecting?" Shaw's voice came from behind her as he approached.

"The biting ones."

"Ah." He paused, lowering his brow. "Speaking of which, Mr. Abrams!"

The young lieutenant approached. "Yes, Captain?"

"Our guests have decided to remain on shore tonight. I'm sending you another half-dozen jollies, and I want a careful watch kept around the camp. And only one draught of rum per man. We need sharp eyes. If Sir Joseph or any of the well-dressed horde is injured, they'll send the lot of us off to Botany Bay."

Lieutenant Abrams saluted. "Aye, aye, Captain. I'll see to it. No one in or out of camp tonight."

"Thank you." With that, Shaw signaled, and four sailors pushed the boat into the surf. Again before she could do more than gasp, he swung her into his arms. "Crafty enough for you?" he murmured.

"Yes. Thank you."

Wading through the water, he set her onto her seat and then clambered in after her. "Do I still compare unfavorably to a toad or a snake?" he asked in a more normal tone, dumping water out of his boots.

"Papa hadn't returned, so I couldn't see one to find out. I'll decide in your favor for the moment." After all, he'd allowed her to do the right thing and not pay for it. She was obligated to view him a bit more kindly, at least for the time being.

Once they boarded the *Nemesis*, Bradshaw ordered the additional marines to shore and relieved Lieutenant Gerard of the watch. "Potter, tell Winstead that Miss Ponsley and I will be dining in my cabin," he added, then went below, presumably to check for leaks.

He hadn't even asked if she cared to dine with him. On the other hand, she was once more the only female on board—and even her father had decided to sleep on "Garden Island," as he'd dubbed it. So unless she wanted to dine alone in her tiny cabin, it would have to be dinner with Bradshaw.

She procured a pitcher of water and closed her cabin door to remove her boy's breeches and wash her face and hands. Considering that this was autumn sliding into the winter season here, she could only wonder how warm the summers must be. In another few weeks they would all undoubtedly find out.

The Mayfair ladies would all dress for the occasion of dining with the captain. Her borrowed guide said a lady should always look her best, no matter the company. Perhaps if she more closely followed the rules of Society, Captain Carroway would stop taking so many liberties with her . . . with her mouth. She frowned into her small hand mirror. Those kisses heated her insides, and she wasn't entirely certain she wanted to give them up.

"Silly girl," she muttered at her reflection. When they arrived back in London her father would be famous and celebrated, and she refused to go from being a valued assistant to a sharp-tongued embarrassment. With an irritated sigh, telling herself that she was practicing for the benefit of Sir Joseph Ponsley's future social engagements, she stripped out of her simple orange sprigged muslin and dressed in the blue silk gown she'd worn to Admiral Dolenz's dinner.

She'd always dressed herself and put up her own hair, and by the time Potter knocked on her door to summon her for dinner she'd managed what she decided was a pleasing knot at the top of her head, wavy strands of her red-streaked brown hair falling down her back and brushing her temples. There. At least she didn't *look* like some madwoman who traipsed off on expeditions because she was unfit for polite Society.

Shaw's door was open, and she walked in to see him buttoning his magnificent blue dress jacket. *My goodness.* "Hello," she said aloud.

He faced her. For a long moment he didn't say anything, just took her in. Heat stole through her veins. "We seem to have had the same idea," he commented finally. "That's an alarming thought, isn't it?"

"Exceedingly." She gestured at the small table set for two, a trio of lit candles in a small brass candelabra standing at its center. "Thank you for deciding I should dine with you."

"I believe in self-sacrifice." With his attractive, amused smile, Shaw pulled out one of the chairs for her. "Miss Ponsley."

She sat. "Captain Carroway."

"We—"

"Here ye go, Captain," the ship's cook, Winstead, chortled, limping into the room on his wooden leg. He carried a platter in his arms, with another crewman behind him bearing still another plate. "The best lobscouse I think I've ever made."

Bradshaw grinned as he took his own seat opposite her. "Then it must be very fine indeed."

With great care, pride obvious in his face, the cook set two covered plates on the table, one in front of each of them, and then with a flourish removed the lids. The other fellow placed the fresh bread with a tub of butter between them.

Winstead closed the door as he left. It was more than likely merely habit, and heaven knew she'd spent most of the day alone with Bradshaw, but this felt . . . different. More intimate. She cleared her throat. "What is lobscouse, anyway?"

"Corned beef and pork, potatoes, nutmeg, juniper berries, and God knows what else." He picked up his fork and knife and gestured at her with them. "Enjoy."

The muted sound of a fiddle began a tune from somewhere above them, and a moment later male voices began singing. She could only make out a few of the words, but they sounded very naughty. Across the small table from her, Bradshaw scowled.

"Well, that's rather inappropriate," he grumbled, lifting his napkin from his lap and pushing back his chair. "Excuse me for a moment."

Zephyr put out a hand. "They've all been on constant watch for over a week now. I can certainly tolerate a raucous sea shanty or two."

Shaw lifted an eyebrow, but resumed his seat. "Just don't listen too closely." He shoveled in a mouthful of lobscouse.

"You know, after spending such long stretches at sea without any . . . social contact, I'm not surprised that their song lyrics discuss what they miss."

"Very circumspect of you. If they did some of the things in port that they're singing about now, they would be arrested." With a grin he downed a swallow of rum. "Speaking of which, thank you for setting me on Hendley. There's no surer way to begin a fight than by one man stealing another's woman."

"Ah, yes. The Trojan War, for example." Despite its peculiar name, the lobscouse wasn't bad at all. In fact, it was actually quite good.

"Or any skirmish where the natives might make a meal of their opponents." Shaw gazed at her for a moment. "I forget whether we are allied or at sword points this evening. Do you recall?"

"I recall that you said something annoying," she returned, taking another bite to cover her grin, "though I couldn't say precisely what it was."

"Undoubtedly I was being autocratic, and you were being direct."

"Undoubtedly."

She took another bite, her attention half on the maddening, compelling man seated across from her, and half on the occasionally discernable lyrics wafting down from the deck above. At the tail end of one loud verse, she choked. "Drag your *what*?" she coughed, reaching for her glass.

He eyed her. "You actually want to know?"

She nodded, still trying to drown her cough with the weak Madeira.

"You *are* the adventurous sort," he commented, then cleared his own throat. "*Drag yer nuts across me guts*," he recited. "The shanty's sung by three dockside whores, comparing the size of their . . . comparing their qualities." He pushed away from the table again. "Nelson forbade singing on naval ships, but it's crept back in. I'll put a stop to it."

"I don't mind it, really," she protested. "I was only a little startled."

"Mm hm. I'll be back in a moment."

Shaw left her sitting there. As soon as he left the cabin she stood up and hurried to throw open one of the rear-facing windows. She heard the screech of the violin as it abruptly stopped, the captain's deep, annoyed voice, and then the beginning of a very correct shanty about a sailor faithful to his young lady on shore.

Zephyr shut the window again. Laughing, she hurried back to her chair. At times she found Bradshaw Carroway's unflagging tolerance of nearly everything just . . . maddening, but on other occasions it left her feeling very bubbly inside, like fine champagne or sea foam.

The cabin door opened again. "That should do it," Shaw commented, closing them in once more and returning to his seat. "I instructed them that no lyric was to mention anything below the heart and above the knees. That may leave mermaids, but I'm not certain."

"Ah. Mermaids. Have you ever seen one?"

He regarded her for a moment. "I've seen a great many things at sea," he offered, lifting his fork and then setting it aside again, "some of which I can't quite explain."

Zephyr nodded. "That is because you don't read."

Shaw took several swallows of his rum, then put the mug down and leaned both elbows on the table. "I would wager I have more knowledge of some topics than you do." His blue gaze lowered to the swooped neckline of her gown. "And I've been told I'm an exceptional teacher."

She swallowed hard, nearly choking again. "Are you propositioning me, Captain?"

"Yes, I suppose I am." He glanced down, then straight at her again, his gaze full of amusement and challenge. "You're the science-minded chit. Don't you find it maddening to be so ignorant of such an . . . integral part of life?"

"Even if I did, what makes you think I would choose you to educate me?"

His grin softened. "I suppose that's for you to answer, Miss Warm, Following Breeze. Yes, or no?"

Chapter Eight

Well, Sally is the girl that I love dearly,
Sally is the girl that I spliced nearly.
For seven long years I courted Sally,
All she did was dilly-dally.

"BULLY IN THE ALLEY"

Zephyr Ponsley gazed at Bradshaw, an alluring mix of surprise and appreciation in her eyes.

"What, precisely," she said, "makes you think for one minute that I would hand you my virginity and any hope for respectability I might have back in England?"

Shaw straightened a little. Perhaps that was anger rather than appreciation he saw in her pretty gray eyes. His snug trousers loosened a shade. "You're a forthright chit. I thought a forthright query would be welcome."

"Perhaps, if I were purchasing a horse. Or you were." She glared at him for another moment, then took another bite of dinner. "Is that what you think of me? That I'm a softheaded idiot who has no thought of anything but pleasing you? Even if I hadn't read

Miss Juliette's booklet on proper behavior I would not succumb to so . . . flat-footed a proposition." She sipped delicately from her glass of Madeira.

This was exceedingly odd. "Isn't this where you storm off in a fit of righteous indignation?"

"*I* didn't say anything inappropriate," she returned. "And this dinner is quite delicious. You storm off if you must."

Good God, he'd been lusting after a lunatic. "This is my cabin and my ship. I'm not going anywhere." He picked up his own fork again and took a large bite.

"Fine."

"Fine."

They ate in silence, accompanied only by the church hymn now being sung on deck. So what if he had been imagining the two of them naked and sprawled together in his bed, moonlight through the windows bathing her soft skin in silver? She was more than likely akin to a praying mantis, ready to bite his head off after mating—if she bothered to wait that long. He'd only made a suggestion, and it had been a very good and logical one if he said so himself. Which he did.

Shaw set down his knife. "So is it the proposition to which you object, or the way it was delivered?"

From her abruptly thoughtful expression, she was actually considering. "A bit of both, I think."

Perhaps he was the mad one. At any rate, he couldn't help but be intrigued despite the insults she'd just handed him. "How so?"

"Well, I may have lived a great part of my life outside England, but I do know a few things. My uncle is a baron, and so I'm considered a lady. And a lady does not throw away her virginity. Not without an expectation of . . . well, of compensation." She frowned. "And don't you dare presume that I'm referring to money."

"I wouldn't dream of it. Go on."

"You're fairly good at kissing, and I would imagine you've bedded females of good birth."

Briefly Shaw reflected that he'd never had a conversation like this in his life. Clearly she expected honesty, and he had nothing to gain by lying even if he'd had the inclination to do so. "Yes, I have. And therefore, your argu—"

"Were you discreet?"

He closed his mouth again. "Yes."

"And to achieve your goal were you at least charming and complimentary?"

"I suppose I was. Would you care to tell me the point of this, or should we continue fishing?"

She leaned forward on her elbows. "Certainly I'll tell you my point. If you want me, which I presume you do, you must follow the rules."

" 'The rules,' " he repeated dubiously.

"My father's work is simply too important for me to risk a scandal for no good reason. There must be an expectation of something. Marriage, for example. Or at least the belief that an engagement will follow."

"I have never lied to a chit about my intentions, and I refuse to begin doing so now. Especially not when we will be living on the same ship for at least the next eighteen months."

Zephyr lifted both eyebrows. "You've never lied?"

"Not about my intentions."

She considered that for a moment. "That's admirable, I suppose. But there are several gentlemen on board who, outwardly at least, are nicer to me than you are. If one of them was . . . interested in me, I would expect to be wooed. Those are the rules. And they apply to you, as well. So if all you want is to satisfy your baser urges, I'm afraid I must turn you away."

Brandy. This conversation called for brandy rather than watered-down rum. Ignoring the way his gut had tightened when she'd mentioned other men pursuing her, Shaw stood and stalked over to empty his mug out the window. That done, he retrieved the bottle of brandy he kept inside the knight's helmet on one shelf.

"I want to be certain I've heard you correctly," he said, pouring himself a drink and offering to replace her Madeira with something more substantial. When she shook her head, he clanked the bottle onto the table. "You aren't interested in a single evening of pleasure. I'm supposed to convince you that I wish a marriage, whether I'm being truthful or not."

"Well, clearly you could never convince me, regardless, because I'm aware of your ulterior motive."

He didn't much like that. "But I refuse to surrender without a fight."

A swift, excited smile touched her mouth. "Then follow the rules, and we shall see how persuasive you are."

Her smile stopped him for a moment. She *wanted* to be seduced. Apparently even the most logical of chits required flattery. Even logical chits who were learning about propriety from booklets.

"Do I receive any credit for inviting you to a private dinner in my cabin? And there have been several kisses you said you enjoyed."

"You actually didn't ask as much as you simply expected. And the memory of kisses fades so quickly in the face of all of the wonders of Fiji."

"Is that so?" he murmured, standing. He walked around to her side of the table, took her by the nape of her neck, and kissed her. It was a damned fine kiss, teasing, nibbling, hard and soft all at the same time, and her fingers dug into his forearms as she held on to him. Shaw lifted his head a little. "Say that again," he taunted, his gaze focused on her mouth.

Her breath was uneven against his cheek. "Goodness," she gulped, swallowing. "I do find you annoying."

"Yes, I know. The feeling is mutual."

"Please return your mouth to your side of the table."

He still counted that kiss as a point to his side. Narrowing his eyes, Shaw released her. Even so, he couldn't keep himself from brushing her cheek with the backs of his fingers. After all, she wanted a seduction. "Now what?"

"I believe, Captain Carroway, that I shall leave the next step up to you. I have an expedition in which to participate." With a rather alluring smile she picked up her fork again. "I wish to be wooed according to the rules. I think that's a fair expectation. If it isn't of interest to you, then perhaps another gentleman will step in. But how far this seduction goes will of course be up to me."

"You damned chit. It's of interest to me. *You're* of interest to me, though at the moment I have no idea why."

"Excellent."

* * *

Bradshaw walked the deck as Potter cleared the dishes and candelabra from his cabin. *Follow the rules.* He'd never followed the damned rules in his life. And not for a chit he found compelling but wasn't even certain he liked.

Shaw blew out his breath. At least the evenings here were glorious. The warm breeze took the chill from the night air and washed away the day's humidity. On the island the insects would be feasting, but here on the water he saw only the occasional moth attracted by the ship's lanterns.

The multiple bird and animal cages and their shelter going up on deck were nearly finished, thank Lucifer, because he was ready to hand the damned squawking parrots still lodging with him over to Winstead for a dinner of roast tropical bird. Sir Joseph seemed to have realized that his other creatures would not be welcomed in the captain's cabin, because they currently remained ashore with the botanist.

Back in his own quarters he stripped out of his shirt and waistcoat, having left his coat behind with the remains of dinner, then sat at the worktable to write out the day's log. Generally that consisted of noting the ship's heading, speed, and the weather conditions, together with any unusual observations and notes on supplies.

Since Zephyr kept throwing the importance of the expedition at him, he made an attempt to expand on his thoughts—or at least the ones he wanted the Admiralty to know about. He'd found himself more contemplative lately, but he couldn't allow much of that to creep into the expedition's official record. His superiors would read it, and as he'd told Zephyr, he wanted his future to be his own decision.

He paused, gazing through the window at the rising moon. If he did retire, did he wish to marry? And if he did marry, would he consider Zephyr Ponsley? He wanted her. And this wasn't even the first time he'd thought of marriage and that maddening, annoying woman together. "Damned chit," he muttered.

"Damned chit."

He looked up from the logbook. His door remained closed. Two of the windows were open, but he more than likely would have spied any sailor hanging over the aft of the ship. With a slight scowl he lowered his head again and resumed writing.

"Damned chit."

Bradshaw set down his dipped pen. "Who's there?" he demanded, standing. He would not tolerate eavesdropping from his crew. Striding to the door, he yanked it open. Except for a pair of sailors making their way toward the galley, the corridor was empty. Taking a breath, he shut the door again. "Bloody hell," he muttered. Perhaps the tropical heat was melting his brains.

"Bloody, bloody. Damned chit."

This time he could make out the source of the voice. Squatting down, Shaw lifted the blanket off the parrot cages. "Damned chit," he said deliberately.

One of the three red-breasted parrots in the larger cage cocked its head and peered at him with one beady orange and black eye. "Damned chit," it squawked, in a fair impression of his own voice.

"Hm. Isn't that interesting?" he mused, pulling

one of the fruits out of a bucket and wedging it through the stick enclosure. "Pretty bird."

"Bloody hell." The parrot eviscerated the fruit, leaving the scraps for his cell mates.

Straightening again, Shaw walked over to close the windows. Then he returned to the cage, lured the talkative male parrot to the front with another slice of fruit, and then pulled open the little door. The pigeon-sized fellow darted out, fluttering about the large room as Shaw closed his friends back inside.

Returning to the table, he sliced up another fruit with his boot knife, holding it in the fingers of his left hand as he wrote with his right. He'd never tamed a bird before, though he had trained horses and several hunting dogs in his youth. He imagined the process was much the same—patience and a large quantity of food.

As the parrot swooped down to perch on his wrist and nibble, Shaw sent another glance at the door. If only women were as simple to decipher. Though in all honesty, he'd seduced enough women to know that if sex was all he wanted from Zephyr Ponsley he could have managed it by now, whatever rules she wished him to follow. Apparently, however, he wanted to still be able to banter with her and share a meal with her. That was exceedingly odd, because maintaining a friendship with a female had never even occurred to him before. Perhaps he should borrow that blasted booklet to refresh his memory regarding the rules.

"Damned chit," the parrot said.

"Precisely," Shaw agreed.

* * *

Zephyr made certain she was on the first launch back to the island in the morning. However boldly she'd spoken last night, she was well aware of her own shortcomings where conversing with gentlemen and proper behavior were concerned. Hopefully she would be able to snatch a moment to chat with Juliette Quanstone before her father dragged her away for the day's explorations.

"Good morning," her father greeted her, as he glanced up from the stack of specimen jars in front of him. "Come take a look at this."

"How did you sleep last night?" she asked, kissing him on the cheek. She took the proffered jar and lifted it. "Good heavens! Is that a millipede?"

The long, black, plated creature that coiled around the bottom of the jar and halfway up the sides was clearly deceased, but she couldn't help a slight shudder, anyway. As big around as a broom handle, it had to be more than a foot long.

"It may well be the largest millipede ever recorded," her father said with a grin, taking back the jar and carefully setting it down with the others. "And I hadn't thought entomology would compare with botany. Life out here seems to be full of surprises."

"Yes, it does," she agreed. And some of them she couldn't discuss with her father.

That idea stopped her for a moment. He thought of her the same way she did—as his assistant. She'd dared a rather formidable man to seduce her, and as her father held a magnifying glass up to the millipede, she realized that Sir Joseph more than likely wouldn't be concerned with that, if he could even be bothered to notice, as long as it didn't interfere with the expedition. It was a marriage that he wouldn't like, because that *would* interfere. What she hadn't deciphered was how *she* felt about a lover, or a husband, or Shaw.

"—part of my collection on board. It's beginning to stack up in camp, and I worry that the natives will begin shopping here for dinner."

She blinked, forcing a grin as she caught up to her father's conversation. "As long as they're after the birds and lizards rather than the crew, I suppose it would only be an annoyance."

He furrowed his brow. "A tragedy, you mean."

Whether he was speaking of the importance of his collection or the unpleasantness of his fellow camp mates, she had no idea. Knowing him as she did, it could be either one. "I believe my launch is still here, if you want to begin this morning."

"Excellent. Ask them to remain here, will y—"

"Good morning, Miss Ponsley." Lord John Fenniwell appeared from the direction of the river, Mr. Jones and a trio of marines with him. "You'll be happy to know I only received three insect bites last night."

"That's an improvement, then," she returned, smiling. "I'd hoped the additional fires might keep them at bay."

"I wasn't bitten at all," Stewart Jones put in. "I stayed directly downwind of the fire."

"That explains while you smell like baked cod." His sister and the two Misses Quanstone made their appearance, all of them looking as if they'd just stepped out of a salon rather than a tropical jungle. Miss Jones nodded at Zephyr. "We're going to walk a mile or so up the river and have a picnic, if you'd care to join us."

"Thank you, but I'll be joining my father today. I did wonder if I could have a word with you, Juliette."

"Oh, certainly. I'll be along in a moment, Frederica."

Zephyr led the way to the edge of the camp. The other ladies and gentlemen looked on curiously, but hopefully they were out of earshot. "Might I ask your advice about something?"

"Of course." Juliette Quanstone twirled her parasol. "I saw you using your parasol on the launch," she commented. "In a few weeks you may have a proper lady's complexion again."

"I only wish someone would invent a parasol that kept biting insects away."

"How clever that would be!" Juliette exclaimed. "What is your question, dear?"

Zephyr cleared her throat. "Yes. I . . . find myself attracted—slightly attracted—to a man. I—"

"Oh, goodness! And you've had no mother, no governess, and no friends to advise you! You unfortunate darling!" Juliette wrapped her arm around Zephyr's. "You must tell me everything."

Abruptly this didn't seem such a very good idea, after all. "There isn't much to tell. I only wondered if you had any suggestions over how I should proceed."

"I assume you're speaking of either Dr. Howard or Captain Carroway. You needn't tell me, because of course I understand discretion. I commend you in either choice, because both are brothers to titled gentlemen. The Howard family is wealthier, but considering your own lack of close connections and the distance from England, you should definitely encourage a suit."

She hadn't been asking anything of the kind, but it was interesting. *"The Lady's Guide to Proper Behavior* says a lady should do nothing but comport herself admirably."

"That guide was no doubt written by an unmarried lady. It's useful from time to time, but if you truly wish to net a wealthy husband you must be certain he knows of your interest. In the best of circumstances you should remind him of what he wants on every possible occasion, driving him to the edge of madness, so that taking you before an altar is the best and only solution that occurs to him."

"Juliette, do hurry," her sister Emily called. "The day will be too warm for walking, soon."

Miss Quanstone released Zephyr's arm again. "You may consult me about anything," she said cheerily, "because of course I know a great deal more about such things than you do."

Zephyr watched her prance away. Well. She wasn't certain how she felt about throwing herself at Shaw, but she did like the idea of driving him mad. She only needed a little time to develop a strategy. Because while she'd ordered him to follow the rules of a seduction or a betrothal or whatever it turned out to be, she'd made no such promise herself. And a quiet, deeply buried part of her wanted to know whether he considered her worth the effort of a difficult pursuit or not. Because perhaps she admired him a bit more than she was willing to admit.

Two hours later, on her hands and knees looking over the top of a boulder, she was still considering her plan of attack—or possibly counterattack. "Shh, Papa," she whispered over her shoulder. "And send Hendley around with the large net."

More muttering continued below and behind her, but she ignored it as she gazed at the creature perched on a tree branch just a few feet beyond the tip of her nose. It had the low body and long tail of a lizard, but also a soft green coloring with white stripes and a crest worthy of a dragon running down its spine. And if it was a lizard, it was by far the largest one she'd ever seen.

Her father crept up beside her. "What is . . . Oh. Oh, my."

"It looks like an iguana from the Southern American continent, does it not?" she whispered. "But I didn't think they climbed trees."

"Nor do they grow three feet long. What a find, Zephyr! Well done."

The eyes with their ring of yellow swiveled in his direction, and the thing opened its mouth and hissed. Below, in the hollow in front of their rock perch, Hendley and another sailor reached the base of the tree and began climbing.

"Very good, Hendley," her father said in a low voice, waving his hands to keep the creature's attention. "There seems to be a sturdy branch directly below the animal."

Abruptly the lizard seemed to realize it was being stalked. It sprang off the branch, leaping forward—onto the boulder where Zephyr and her father perched. Yelping in surprise, Zephyr straightened onto her knees. The last thing she wanted was to be bitten in the face.

"Look out!" her father yelled belatedly, scrambling backward.

With a hiss the iguana scampered between them. Before she could do more than think they were about to lose their largest find, Zephyr twisted and threw herself forward.

She landed with her hands around the base of the thing's neck, her body pinning down the length of it. "Oh, goodness," she gasped, feeling the cool, scaled skin and the strength of the thing as it wriggled, trying to escape her grip.

"Stay right there, Miss Zephyr!" Hendley jumped to the ground and charged around to her side of the boulder.

The animal's tail whipped against her thigh, hard enough to bruise. She wanted to yell for someone to hurry, but that would likely frighten the beast still further—and it would make her look cowardly.

While her father yelled nonsensical, contradictory orders, Hendley dropped the net and grabbed up a cloth sack. Clambering up to her, he opened the mouth of the sack. "Lift his head, and I'll shove this over 'im. Ready?"

"Yes," she panted, shifting. At his nod she heaved the heavy lizard up, and Hendley got the creature's front half into the sack. Moving fast, she let it go, grabbed its tail, and pushed. A second later the sailor knotted the sack closed and whooped.

"Better than Saint George and the dragon, Miss Zephyr."

She laughed. "Thank you."

"You've got a scratch there." His grin diving into a scowl, the sailor gestured at the inside of her left arm.

Now that he mentioned it, her arm did sting a bit. Dusting herself off, she glanced down. A thin line of blood oozed from just below her armpit to the inside of her elbow. "Oh, one of his claws must have caught me." She brushed at the scratch. "It's fine."

"Hendley, let's get that beauty into a cage," her father instructed, hovering about the sack as though he wanted to open it and look inside. "We don't want to frighten it to death." He glanced over at her. "Make certain to get a good sampling of those red flowers. That's what it appeared to be eating."

Zephyr shook out her arm. "Yes, Papa."

Taking a sharp blade and one of the other sailors, she hacked off several branches covered with the pretty red blooms. She collected seed pods, as well, so her father could identify and perhaps cultivate the tree later.

"You should have Dr. Howard take a look at that cut, Miss Zephyr," the stocky sailor with light blond hair commented as he helped her gather their scattered supplies back together.

"Thank you . . ."

He tugged on his forelock. "They call me Peaches, Miss Zephyr."

"Thank you, then, Peaches, but it's only a scratch. And if we turn back now, my father will forever lament the things we might have seen today and didn't."

"Aye, Miss Zephyr. All the same, I would appreciate if you would tell the captain that me 'n' Hendley said you should get it seen to."

"Certainly, but I don't see why it's any of Captain Carroway's affair."

Hendley walked past them, the cage and lizard balanced on one shoulder. "Because the captain said any of us what let anything happen to you would have hell to pay."

Peaches was nodding. "Aye. We're all to look after you."

Fleetingly she considered asking Peaches and Hendley whether Shaw had given the same order regarding his other guests, but she wasn't certain she wanted to know the answer. Because as uncivilized as Bradshaw Carroway was, she couldn't help but feel the tiniest bit flattered at the idea that he might have singled her out for special care and attention even before their conversation of last night.

The sun, haloed with long strands of purple and red clouds, hung low in the sky by the time they returned to camp. Before they reached the clearing, Zephyr heard shouting. At the same time the marines with them hurried forward, weapons at the ready.

"What the devil is this?" her father asked.

What looked like half the village was gathered there along with the ship's crew still ashore, everyone speaking at the top of his lungs. Zephyr looked with some trepidation at all the spears and guns present. "What's happened?" she asked, taking Juliette Quanstone's arm.

"One of the natives stole Lord John's pocket watch and won't return it."

Zephyr sent a glance at Lord John, standing toe to toe with the village's chief. So they were all going to be killed and eaten because of a stupid silver pocket watch taken from a nobleman who could afford hundreds of them. Uneasiness ran up her spine.

Almost without realizing it, she looked about for Bradshaw. A moment later she spied him several yards away from the main commotion. He sat on a mat made of woven palm fronds opposite a half dozen of the older boys, taking turns shaking and tossing a handful of what looked like painted bones and shells and then exchanging trinkets based on the results.

Gathering her skirt in one hand, she circled the argument and stalked up to the captain. "Wagering? We're all about to be eaten and you're wagering?"

"I'm learning how to play," he returned calmly, keeping his gaze on the game. "It's fairly straightforward, luckily. Fetch Lord John, will you?"

She wasn't part of his crew, but neither was she mad enough to begin another argument at the moment. Especially since Bradshaw seemed to be the only one who knew what he was doing—whatever that might be. Cautiously she made her way forward.

"Lord John, Captain Carroway asks that you join him."

John Fenniwell's rather fair complexion had gone red and mottled. "I am not shifting an inch until my property is returned to me."

Her father stepped into the mix. "It's a pocket watch, John. I'll purchase you another, for God's sake."

"It has an inscription from my father. And if you allow these savages to steal from us, we'll all be naked by sunrise. Worse, for the ladies."

"If you keep up this nonsense," Shaw said, materializing beside Zephyr, "we'll all be dead by morning."

"You—"

Nudging Lord John aside, Shaw pointed from the bones and shells in his hand to the man clicking the pocket watch open and closed and then to the parasol Zephyr had shoved into her satchel. Realizing what he was up to, she pulled out the delicate white thing and opened it, twirling it enticingly.

The chief said something to the man holding

the watch. After a short conversation the islanders formed a circle and produced another mat. Shaw took a seat, folding his long legs and looking as relaxed as if he was playing charades in some Mayfair town house. The warrior sat opposite him.

"If I lose, Fenniwell," he said conversationally, shaking the items in his fist, "you will nod and smile and walk away, or I will shoot you in the head. Is that clear?"

"Yes, Captain," the marquis's second son returned, looking as though he would rather eat a millipede.

Shaw and the native took turns tossing bones and shells for several minutes, apparently wagering on whether they would land marked side up or down. She found it rather baffling, but Bradshaw could obviously add inveterate gambler to his list of sins. And thank goodness for that.

Finally with some laughter and conversation she couldn't begin to decipher, the islander handed over the watch and the bone necklace from around his neck, while Shaw pulled a button off his uniform jacket and gave it to the man. With an exaggerated bow the native turned and walked away. Zephyr let out the breath she'd been holding and stepped up as Shaw stood again. For a heartbeat she nearly threw her arms around him—until she remembered just how many people were still standing about, and that he was supposed to be wooing her, not the other way around.

"Well done, Captain," she said instead, occupying herself with closing the parasol.

He tossed the pocket watch to Lord John. "Thank you. I . . ." His voice drifted off, his gaze in the direction of the village. A half-dozen men left the chieftain's hut, glanced in their direction, and then disappeared into the jungle. A moment later another dozen men followed them.

"Shaw?" she whispered.

"I want all passengers into the first launch and on their way back to the ship. Now." He glanced at her father. "I'll see your things brought safely aboard, Sir Joseph."

Evidently her father realized that arguing at the moment wouldn't be wise. "I know you will, Captain."

"It seems to me the danger is over with, Carroway," Lord Benjamin Harding commented, looking on as Lord John examined his pocket watch, perhaps for scratches. "You're shutting the stable door after the horses have fled."

Shaw faced him. "Get in the boat," he snapped. "We'll discuss the new rules for disembarking once we get under way."

Zephyr retrieved her satchel, then started as Shaw grabbed her wrist. "I'm going, for heav—"

"You're injured." He took her left arm and turned it gently.

"I wrestled a lizard. A large one."

Blue eyes lifted to meet hers. "Who won?"

Her cheeks warmed. "I did."

With a brief smile he released her again, fingers brushing hers as he did so. "I am not surprised. Have Dr. Howard take a look at it."

"I will."

"Good. I want you in fighting form for our next conversation."

Apparently he *had* decided to follow the rules as she'd laid them out. She liked that idea, even though it very likely meant she was either going mad or she was falling for absolutely the wrong man. Either way, it looked as though she was in for a very long voyage.

They weighed anchor just before sunset, and then spent an anxious forty minutes maneuvering in the fading light around reefs and sandbars. As soon as they reached open water Zephyr went below, anxious to finish up her watercolor of the village before she forgot the nuances of color.

Someone knocked at her door, and she jumped. "Come in," she called, blinking in the dim lamplight.

The door opened. "You shouldn't be painting in here," Shaw said, scowling. "The light will have you going blind."

"I can't paint in the galley while everyone's dining. And you—"

"Don't remind me." He sighed. "Use my cabin whenever you wish. I only ask that you knock first."

Wiping her fingers on a cloth, she smiled. "Thank you."

"I'm being nice to you. Please make a note of it."

Her heart sped just a little. "Very well."

"Oh, and one more thing." He reached behind him, then held out a handful of flowers. Beautiful, tropical flowers unlike anything that would ever be found in a London florist's shop. Yellows and reds and oranges brighter than sunset even in the tiny, dim room. "These are for you," he said.

She stood up, her paintbrush falling somewhere onto the floor. "That . . . they . . . What lovely specimens. My father will be very happy to see them," she finally stumbled.

Bradshaw shook his head. "Don't you dare. I didn't pick these for your father, and you damned well know it. Now take them and put them in a jar, and don't press them or write a treatise about them. Just enjoy them for what they are—flowers from a man who admires you." With a grin he put them into her hand, then ducked out of the cabin and closed the door behind him.

"Oh, goodness," she whispered. A very long voyage, indeed.

Chapter Nine

Sing ho for a brave and a gallant ship
And a fast and favoring breeze.
With a bully crew and a captain too,
To carry me over the seas.

"Ten Thousand Miles Away"

"You have heard the story of the *Port-au-Prince,* I assume," Bradshaw said, leafing through his charts for a better look at the portion of the ocean they were entering.

"Yes, but that was twelve years ago."

"The Tongans captured a British vessel, set it on fire, and killed all but one of the crew. I don't care if it was a hundred years ago; there's been no news since to convince me that it won't happen again. I recommend we bypass Tonga in favor of Tahiti."

After Fiji and two minuscule islands inhabited only by crabs and some scrub brush, only a fortnight remained until the next full moon and his failing to fulfill the Duke of Sommerset's mission. It would be much easier if the botanist went along willingly, but by God, they would be in Tahiti before that happened.

"But they say Tonga is part of the Friendly Islands, do they not?" Zephyr put in, experimentally feeding the parrot a piece of melon.

The bird hadn't spoken in front of anyone else, so he hadn't mentioned it yet—especially considering the red-feathered fiend's choice of vocabulary. "They only call them that because when Cook landed there he didn't realize the feast they laid out was to keep him occupied while they murdered him."

"Which they didn't." Sir Joseph sat at the writing desk to dissect a stem of something or other. He turned with the magnifying glass in hand, making his left eye look huge.

"You can't be that naive, Sir Joseph. William Mariner told the story of the missed Cook massacre and the *Port-au-Prince* disaster when he finally escaped the island. I'm not taking you there."

"No one's explored the flora or fauna there beyond looking at the coastline through a spyglass. We have to go."

"Then we have a disagreement." Finding the chart for which he'd been looking, Shaw slammed it down on the worktable, making the parrot squawk and the two Ponsleys jump. "And the ship goes where I say. We are not going to Tonga. I can have us to Tahiti in a week. Less, if the fair weather continues."

Zephyr straightened. "How many islands comprise Tonga?"

"No one knows. At least a hundred." He could guess what she was going to say next, but short of throwing her out the window he didn't know how to stop her from speaking.

She approached the chart. "And on which one was William Mariner held?"

Squaring his shoulders, Shaw indicated one of the three largest islands, close to the center of the grouping. "This one. Lifuka."

"Then we go somewhere else. According to you, there are at least ninety-nine other islands from which to choose." She sent a sideways glance at him. "Unless you can only find the large islands."

Damnation. "We know even less about them than we do Lifuka."

"No, no," Sir Joseph said, rising to join them at the worktable. "Zephyr makes a very good point. In fact, I would like samples of the vegetation from a northern island and a southern one." He gestured at the tiny dots decorating the Pacific Ocean. "We'll choose small ones, preferably with hills high enough to trap rainfall and protect any vegetation from the trade winds."

Shaw glared from one of them to the other. "I will choose the islands, and I will decide when and if and for how long we go ashore." Which would be three days at the most, just to be certain.

Evidently realizing that he wasn't going to receive a better offer, Sir Joseph nodded. "You may have saved our lives on Fiji, Shaw. I don't mean to second-guess or argue, but you know I have my own orders. If this is what you're willing to grant us, then we will take it."

We. So he meant to drag his daughter on shore again, as well, despite knowing that Tongans had killed Englishmen before. And since she was going, then Shaw would go, as well. Someone needed to keep a damned eye on her. "Then excuse me for a moment. I need to order a change of course." And order full sail. The swifter they traveled, the better.

Halfway down the corridor, Zephyr caught up to him. He contemplated not stopping, because he didn't feel particularly charming at the moment, and he didn't want to lose the ground the flowers and the sugar biscuits he'd ordered Winstead to bake had gained him. "What?" he asked, turning around to face her.

She skidded to a halt. "I . . . I just wanted a word with you, Captain," she said, glancing at the sailors passing around them. "In private," she added, much more quietly.

Well, that sounded better than he'd expected. "Let's go see how the plants in the hold are faring, shall we?" He offered his arm, and with a slight grin she wrapped her hand around his sleeve.

He stepped into the hold, seeing only Browning, the cook's assistant, gathering eggs for dinner. "Captain," the boy said, straightening to salute so quickly he almost dropped the pot he carried.

"Browning. Give me the room."

"Aye, aye." Clutching the eggs to his chest, the lad hurried out of the hold.

"Very adept of you," Zephyr commented.

"It's good to be the captain." He brushed a strand of her hair back from her face. "Now, what did you want to talk to me about?"

"I wanted to thank you."

Shaw opened his mouth and then closed it again. It was about damned time. "You're welcome."

She lifted an eyebrow. "What am I thanking you for, then?"

He slowly drew her into his arms. "For the flowers, I presume. And perhaps the sweets. Or I suppose it could be in advance. For this." Lowering his head, he touched his mouth to hers. Slowly, gently, he tilted her face up, deepening the kiss as her arms slid around his shoulders. Shaw closed his eyes, sinking into the sensation of her. Whatever he'd done previously and with whom, no moment that he could recall had ever left him feeling both so . . . aware and so satisfied all at the same time.

"I meant," she said, still leaning into him, "thank you for saving us. I saw the same thing you did on Fiji, whether anyone else noticed or not. Those men did not have anything pleasant in mind."

"No, they didn't. Which reminds me." He took her arm, turning it so he could see the inside of her elbow. The cut had scabbed over, and looked healthy, thank God. "You had Dr. Howard clean it for you?"

"Yes. And having rum poured over an open cut is not a sensation I care to repeat."

He grinned. "Try having whiskey poured over a stab wound in your side." Shaw shifted to kiss her again. "You might have thanked me in front of your father," he said in a quieter voice, his pulse stirring. "I think we're here for precisely this."

"Perhaps. You've made a fairly good beginning, for a barbarian. Not that I have anything with which to compare you, of course."

"Well. That's something, I suppose." Shaw wound a finger into the material of her green skirt and tugged. "I have to admit, you're beginning to annoy me a bit less."

"Is that so?"

"I've never courted anyone before," he admitted, his heart skittering again, tense and excited as he was when the *Nemesis* left a still harbor for a swift current. He was about to plunge straight in, and he couldn't quite fool himself; it wasn't just because he wanted her body. There was more to it than that.

"I'm not fooled. You're only courting me toward a seduction."

Loosening his grip, Shaw took a half step backward. "I'm not so certain about that," he drawled, and walked away before she could open a wound and pour whiskey on it.

They circled the island before the captain ordered the anchor to be set. From a distance it looked like a green, roundish dot on the ocean. The fact that Shaw had found it—well, that was only one of several things she couldn't deny she was beginning to like and admire about him.

Boot steps approached behind her and stopped. "Are we going to sit here until someone discovers us?" she asked without looking.

"I see this as more of a run-in-quickly-and-then-flee expedition," Shaw's easy drawl returned.

"My father won't like that."

"I don't precisely give a damn." He moved up another step, putting his hands on the railing beside her. "A hundred or so miles from here Captain Bligh lost his ship to damned mutineers. And at nearly the same spot another captain and his entire crew save one were slaughtered."

"So it's bad luck for captains?" she queried, keeping her voice low so he wouldn't threaten to drop her over the side.

"I'm generally not overly superstitious, but I'm not blind to the odds, either." He lifted his spyglass. "You're joining us, I suppose?"

"Of course. I'll bring my watercolors, as they dry more quickly."

From his brief scowl he understood her sarcasm, but he didn't say anything in return. Instead he collapsed his spyglass and turned to face her. "Let's go then, shall we?"

"You're not going to argue with me?"

"I'm certain we'll have a plentitude of other things to disagree over, my warm, following breeze." With a slight grin he walked away to speak with his first mate, take his saber from a cabin boy, and clap Major Hunter on the shoulder.

My breeze. The presumption should have had her responding in kind, but instead she had to occupy herself with wiping the ridiculous smile from her face. It was frustrating, really, when she found him so blasted aggravating and contrary. Most of the time, anyway. Since she'd already donned the breeches beneath her gown and gathered all the materials she was likely to need for the day, Zephyr headed for the starboard side of the ship where sailors were lowering three launches. Her father was there already, handing over his things to be passed down to the first boat in the water.

"What do you think of the captain's choice of island?" she asked.

"I was worried we would be stopping by a sandbar or an exposed bit of coral reef. I must say, while this island is small, it has quite varied terrain. On the east side I even thought I saw some evidence of volcanic activity. This could be a splendid day."

She smiled at his clear enthusiasm. "I do hope so."

As had become usual, Shaw ended up seated beside her on the launch. With her father seated directly behind them she tried to make a point of ignoring the captain, but as he didn't seem to be looking at her, it obviously wasn't working. With a sniff she opened her parasol and held it between them like a shield.

Halfway to shore, she felt his thigh stiffen where it brushed hers. Immediately alarmed, she looked toward shore, but no painted natives waving spears were anywhere to be seen. Then a fist knocked at the white parasol. Scowling, she lowered it again. "Yes?"

"Look over there," he said, pointing to the north of where the *Nemesis* lay. Then he whistled, drawing the attention of the other boats to the same spot.

"What am I look—" A spout of mist shot into the air, followed by the loud sound of an exhalation. Then a much smaller puff right beside the first. "Oh!" she exclaimed. "Whales!"

"Do you know the species, Shaw?" her father asked, sitting forward.

Shaw shook his head. "I can't tell from here. I'm used to seeing them from the deck."

More puffs and exhalations began all around them. "I smell fish," Zephyr commented, wrinkling her nose.

"It's what they eat, my dear. But keep your voice down."

"Why?"

"Because those are very young calves. I've heard of cows overturning launches if they think their young are in danger." Raising up a little, he gave a hand signal to the other boats, and they slowly began rowing toward the shore.

A whale surfaced just yards away, its large black eye looking directly at her. Zephyr held her breath, not afraid, but . . . awestruck. She'd never seen anything so huge, with so much intelligence behind it. After a long moment of contemplating each other, the whale sank below the surface again.

"The sea's got a good look at you now," Bradshaw whispered, his breath warm against her ear. "And you didn't flinch. Well done, Zephyr."

A shiver of surprising excitement ran down her spine. She liked the way Shaw had said that, that she'd been eye to eye with the largest creature ever known, and she hadn't blinked. She unclenched her fingers, and realized she'd been grasping Shaw's hand. "Oh, my apologies," she exclaimed, her cheeks heating. "I was merely . . . absorbed."

He grinned. "Understandable. We seem to have stumbled onto a calving ground. This is not something seen every day."

The boat lifted a little and slid sideways, and the sailors began muttering nervously. Hendley surreptitiously crossed himself. Another whale surfaced not an oar's length from them, the spout of its breath warm and damp and very fishy smelling.

"Captain?" Hendley said tightly, pulling his pistol from his belt.

"Put it away," Shaw returned. "Keep rowing. Don't splash." He leaned closer to Zephyr. "Can you swim?" he breathed.

She nodded, her heart beating faster. This was not the danger she'd expected to face here. Shore was less than fifty yards away; she *could* swim it if she had to, but the idea of doing so among dozens of whales made her distinctly uneasy.

Finally the boat scraped bottom. The sailors began talking again, and she blew out her breath. "That was quite exciting," she offered, taking Shaw's hand as he helped her over the gunwale.

To her surprise he kept her hand in his, leading her up the shallow beach and the line of greenery. "If we should flip over on the way back to the *Nemesis*," he said in a low voice, "keep clear of the men. Most of them can't swim, and they'd pull you under."

He said it so matter-of-factly that it took a moment for her to realize that he had just stated she was to let men drown. "That's awful."

"I prefer as few deaths as possible. Needless ones make me angry." Shaw took a breath. "I believe your father could use your assistance."

Zephyr turned around. Her father was already on his hands and knees, peering under some shrubbery while one of the sailors approached from the opposite side. Shaw seemed perfectly content to observe with faint amusement, so Zephyr hurried over for a sack and a jar.

"What is it, Papa?"

"A lizard. Dash it, I've lost sight of it. Everett?"

"I don't think it got past me, Sir Joseph, but I don't see it."

Her father straightened again. "Well, let's move on. Eyes open, everyone."

With the help of some ropes and the very nimble sailors they made it up the top of the low cliff that ringed the west side of the island just inland from the beach. At the top she turned and looked back toward the *Nemesis*. All around the ship whales spouted, as if they'd simply followed the frigate in and then stayed to see the sights.

"It's moments like this when I realize how far into

the wilds we are," Shaw commented, following her gaze. "I doubt those animals have ever seen a whaler."

"And I hope they never do. It's too . . . enchanting here for shooting or harpooning anything."

"I agree," he commented with a grin, then bent down and picked something up. "Nearly as lovely as you are," he said, straightening.

"You'd best not be describing a snail or a worm."

He handed her a three-inch-long feather of a nearly iridescent green. "Not a snail," he murmured, running a finger along the feather and across her palm. Blue eyes held hers. "I have the oddest desire to learn what you want from life," he continued.

Warmth slid down her spine. "I don't know what I want," she answered truthfully. And she'd avoided thinking about it for a very long time.

"You should consider it. I'd like to know whether you see me there or not. In your life, I mean."

It was very unlike Shaw to leave himself so exposed to a possible broadside, but she could see nothing but sincere curiosity and affection in his gaze. "I w—"

"What have you got there, Zephyr?" her father broke in, making his way over and taking the feather from her fingers. "Extraordinary. Well found, my dear. Gentlemen, we must find the bird that goes with this feather."

Shaw stepped forward. From his expression he was about to remove the feather from her father's possession. Taking a quick breath, Zephyr stepped between them. "Let me put that in my satchel," she said, "so it won't get frayed."

With an absent nod he returned it to her and then caught sight of something else and hurried away. She knew Bradshaw continued to gaze at her, because she felt . . . warm inside, and nearly ready to begin giggling at nothing. Rather than look back at him, she carefully slipped the feather between two pages of a sketchbook and continued along the trail. After all, they were on an expedition—not strolling through Hyde Park. And she could add the feather to the small collection she'd begun to acquire, along with a dried flower taken from the bouquet Shaw had given her a few days earlier. They weren't mementoes, though. No. They were . . . a record of her travels.

The island was sheltered from the worst of the winds here, and the trees grew taller and more densely. Fluttering brilliant green caught her attention, and a moment later they'd tracked a group of fifteen or so small birds to a stand of hibiscus bushes.

"Oh, they're lovely," she said softly, noting their ruby red chests and the tufts of brilliant blue on their heads. Clearly they were the owners of her feather.

"A subspecies of parrot, I would assume." Her father freed one of the bird nets and handed it to Hendley, who'd become rather adept at catching animals of varying sorts. "Nectar eating. We'll have to dig up a supply of the plants to take with us."

As Zephyr sat down to sketch, Bradshaw actually picked up a shovel and helped to dig out a pair of hibiscus bushes. They might have shied away from attempting to establish a conversation with the natives of these islands, but at least they were able to collect flora and fauna. In her experience traveling with her father, that was by far the most interesting part of the expedition, anyway.

Something tickled across her foot, and she looked down. And froze. A large spider with long black legs and yellow joints walked across her toes, then paused as if to look up at her. She hissed in a breath. "Shaw," she squeaked.

"What? Do y— Oh. Don't move."

"I'm not going to move. Do something."

Good heavens, the thing looked nearly eight inches across. Her ankle jumped despite her determination to remain extremely still, and the spider began moving again—up her calf and beneath the edge of her gown. "*Shaw.*"

He squatted down beside her, a jar in one hand and his sword in the other. While Zephyr tried not to scream and fling the thing away from her, he carefully lifted the hem of her gown with the sword point.

"Just pick it up," she ordered, her voice still squeaking.

"I don't want to get bitten," he returned in the same calm voice he'd used when she'd first spied that man on Fiji. The voice he used when they were all in danger and he didn't want anyone to panic.

"Don't kill it, Shaw." Her father appeared, the net in his hands large enough to capture both the spider and her. "It's magnificent."

"It's on my leg," Zephyr ground out.

For a moment she thought Shaw meant to attempt to coax the monster into the jar. Before she could protest that course of action, however, he slipped the saber forward beneath the spider's abdomen and flicked the beastie into the air. It landed several feet from her and started to scamper back in her direction. Shaw stepped in between them and plunked the jar down over the spider.

"Oh, well done," her father complimented, moving in to finish securing the animal.

Zephyr screeched and jumped to her feet, brushing at her legs and shuddering. Thank heavens she'd been wearing breeches, or everyone there would have gotten a splendid view of her unmentionables.

"You look a whale in the eye, but a spider gives you the shakes?"

Whipping around, she shoved Shaw in the chest. "You didn't want to get bitten? What about me? I didn't have any damned boots on, you know, and I don't like spiders! Particularly ones large enough to eat small dogs!"

Bradshaw chuckled, grabbing her hands before she could hit him again. "I apologize, Miss Ponsley. Truly. You held so still. It was quite brave of you. I'm all admiration. Honestly."

"Ha. Very amusing."

"I am utterly serious. I'm not a great fan of spiders, myself. Th—"

A tremendous, deep boom reverberated through the jungle. For a heartbeat, every other sound ceased, as if the entire island was listening. Then Bradshaw turned and ran back the way they'd come.

"What—"

Major Hunter grabbed up her satchel and half tossed it at her. "That was cannonfire, Miss. We need to follow the captain. Now."

Her father looked at the gear spread around them. "But my—"

"Grab something and move!" the marine commander bellowed, lifting one of the cages in his free hand.

Everett caught her under the elbow. "They was to signal in case of trouble," he said, moving them into a run. "We'll be able to see from the ridge."

Had one of the whales rammed the ship? She had no idea how much damage that might do, but she couldn't imagine that firing a cannon would be very effective. Slinging the satchel over her shoulder and across her head, she picked up one of the remaining boxes as they passed by it.

They reached a break in the trees, and she caught sight of Bradshaw standing at the top of the ridge. He had his spyglass raised, and every inch of him looked poised for battle. Nervous and worried as she was, she would have had to be dead not to notice how utterly magnificent he appeared. He might detest the idea of battle, but he certainly looked prepared for it.

He turned as the rest of the group reached him. "Ready the ropes," he barked. "Lower Sir Joseph and Zephyr. Make directly for the boats. No delays."

"What's happened?" Zephyr asked as marines and sailors both began playing out the ropes and rigging some sort of seat.

Shaw handed her the glass. "There," he said, pointing slightly to the south and west of where the *Nemesis* still lay at anchor. "Damnation. They must have seen us this morning."

She looked through the spyglass. Eight canoes—no, nine—fast and low to the water, approached from the direction of the island she could just make out in the distance. Even with no weapons or face paint visible, they looked . . . threatening. Dangerous.

"What are we going to do?" she asked, as she handed the glass over to Major Hunter.

"Get back to the ship before they can cut us off," Shaw answered. "Lift your arms." When she set down her things he slipped the makeshift seat over her, settling it around her hips.

"Hand me one of the cages," she said, when he'd finished. "I can take it down with me."

"If you start to lose your balance, drop the cage," the captain instructed, handing it over to her as she sat down at the edge of the ridge, her legs dangling into space.

"Thank you for your concern," she returned, nodding at the sailors to begin lowering her, "but I'll manage."

"I dread the reports I'll have to write if you break your head." A half smile on his face, most of his attention clearly on the fast-approaching canoes, he looked down at her from above.

A few moments later her feet touched solid ground again, and she swiftly climbed free of the ropes and sent them up again. As they lowered her father and the rest of their finds and supplies, Shaw and most of the others clambered down the cliff on their own. Before the last of them had descended, they began their run for the beach.

By the time they made it to the edge of the water the canoes had nearly reached the *Nemesis*. Deep dread hit Zephyr as she realized that the launches would not make it to the ship before the Tongans could reach them. Shaw scooped her into the launch as they pushed off. He helped the sailors and marines shove the boats into the water, then jumped into the one where she and her father sat.

"Once they come into view, keep your heads down and sit still," he instructed, grabbing up a spare oar and helping to paddle.

"I have more glass necklaces," her father said, clutching the satchel that held his journal and most recent notes. "We made friends with cannibals. I am willing to attempt to do so here."

"We were tolerated by cannibals because we were something out of the ordinary," Shaw returned. "Once they realized we were just as petty and small-minded as anyone else, we lost our appeal."

"If we were able to—"

"You may get your chance, Sir Joseph. Here they come." He turned to glance at the two boats directly behind them. "Make ready, but do not fire unless I give the word."

All of the *Nemesis*'s cannon ports were open, and the ship looked absolutely bristling with power. The frigate, though, held her fire as well, apparently waiting for Shaw's command. How reluctant was he to fight? Enough to risk their safety? One canoe, then a second and a third, came into view around the bow. Each carried nearly a dozen men, and now she could see the face paint. A spear flew out, landing in the water only a few yards short of them.

"Do you still want to exchange gifts?" Bradshaw asked her father. He whistled toward the ship, then made a circular gesture. Immediately the anchor began lifting. A second later the cannon closest to the bow on the port side fired. Water erupted just in front of the nearest canoe.

Clapping her hands over her ears at the thunderous sound, abruptly Zephyr remembered the whales. As she looked about, though, she couldn't see any blows. Perhaps the noise of the first cannon had frightened them away.

The canoe swung wide, but continued closing the distance between them. One of the natives lifted a tube to his mouth, and a feathered dart struck the gunwale. Shaw cursed. "Garnett, your weapon," he ordered.

One of the marines handed over his rifle. Bringing it up to his shoulder, Shaw sighted and fired. Wood splinters shot into the air as he chipped a good chunk out of the side of the canoe. He'd hit almost exactly the same spot on the canoe that the natives had hit on his boat. New admiration touched Zephyr. She certainly recognized that as a warning to keep back. Would the Tongans?

"Excellent shot, Captain," Garnett commented, taking the rifle back and reloading it.

"Thank you. Let's hope it suffices."

The canoes slowed as a great deal of loud arguing commenced. The launches kept up their pace, and hers hit the side of the *Nemesis* quite hard. For a moment Zephyr thought they might overturn. Then arms were grabbing her and practically lifting her up the rope ladder. As she reached the deck she abruptly noticed that another three canoes were circling the ship from the aft. They were nearly surrounded.

"Warning shots!" Major Hunter bellowed, and in a unified crack a dozen rifles fired from the deck.

"Hoist the boats!"

On the tail end of that order, Shaw erupted onto the deck and tossed a cage at her. She caught it by reflex. A second later a dart whistled past her ear.

"Get away from the railing," he snapped at her. "Make sail!"

A lit torch hit the rigging and then bounced down and back into the water. "Buckets!" Lieutenant Newsome ordered.

Abruptly Zephyr realized what it meant to be

on a warship. And she was very glad to be there. What at first glance seemed like absolute chaos was anything but. These men knew precisely what they were doing, what their ship could do, and what their captain was likely to do.

Another torch flew in, this time hitting the deck and rolling. A spotty line of fire followed it. Hendley and another sailor tossed the thing back overboard and dumped a bucket of sand over the burning line of some sort of tar substance.

Zephyr wanted to help. Clearly, though, the best thing she could do was stay put and not trip anyone. She clutched the birdcage to her chest, the anxious chirping of the birds echoing her own heartbeat.

As another torch sailed over the railing, she heard Shaw swearing again. "Sink one of those damned canoes," he ordered.

Her father dropped his satchel. "Captain!"

"Encourage them to leave it first," Shaw amended. "Strongly."

Another volley of shots rang out, followed a few seconds later by the boom of one of the smaller deck cannons.

"That discouraged 'em, Captain!" Mr. Gerard yelled from his vantage point to port.

"I damned well hope so. Keep an eye out. Leavey, head us southeast. I believe we have another island to find." From up on the wheel deck he sent a grin at her. She smiled back at him. After all, he'd managed to extract them from another difficult situation without killing anyone. She admired him for it. More than that, she liked him. Rather a great deal.

Chapter Ten

A captain bold from Halifax
Once left his captain quarters
Seduced a maid who hanged herself
One morning in her garters.

"THE UNFORTUNATE MISS BAILEY"

Bradshaw peered at the half mirrors of the sextant and made another adjustment to the delicate instrument. Once he had his sighting, he checked his pocket watch against the measurements and handed the sextant back to one of the cabin boys. "Make us two degrees to port, Mr. Leavey," he said.

The pilot spun the wheel. "Aye, aye, Captain. Two degrees to port."

As he turned his gaze to starboard and the growing wall of clouds filling the horizon, he could almost smell the coming storm. They'd been lucky to this point; fairly mild weather had followed them all the way from England and out to the middle of the Pacific. Silently he sent up a prayer that the worst of it would pass to the south of them, but not only were they due, but he'd cut his deadline to reach Tahiti to almost nothing.

He could blame it on Sir Joseph, who wanted to stop and linger at every island they sighted, but it wasn't the botanist's gray eyes lit with the joy of wonder and discovery that had him setting anchor when they should have been moving. Whatever he'd embarked on with her rules, at the least it seemed to be affecting him. He enjoyed women, but he'd never had one as a friend before. A friend he wanted, but a friend nonetheless.

It was for that reason he could wish that Zephyr hadn't become so friendly with Juliette Quanstone; the London chit knew far too much about his past reputation for his comfort. And he was fairly certain that somewhere during this voyage he'd ceased to be that man. On the other hand, once they returned to England it would help if Zephyr knew some of the nuances of Society, because she simply couldn't go about speaking to dukes and earls the way she spoke to him.

He supposed he could blame these new and odd feelings on those nebulous rules of hers, but he wasn't certain that "blame" was the correct word. If he'd simply seduced her straightaway he would of course have remained polite and amiable toward her, but in becoming acquainted with her first he'd discovered some things about her and about himself that he would never have had cause or opportunity to otherwise experience.

Material swished behind him, and he turned around. At the sight of the blond hair and parasol, the anticipation stirring through his muscles faded again, and he nodded. "Miss Jones. What may I do for you?"

"Lieutenant Gerard said we won't see another island until we reach Tahiti. Is that true?"

"Yes. There's nothing between us and Tahiti but four days of large, empty ocean." And a rather alarming-looking storm front.

"That sounds terribly dull."

Shaw just refrained from rolling his eyes. "After our reception in Tonga, a bit of boredom sounds rather refreshing to me."

"But I haven't done anything the least bit amusing since we were in Fiji, and even that ended far too abruptly. We've only been ashore once since, and a crab pinched my toe and completely ruined my shoe."

Thank Lucifer he'd never pursued Frederica Jones. Whether it was the absence of the Mayfair setting or his own altering perceptions, his so-called peers annoyed him more every day. And not in the amusing way that Zephyr did. "We have orders, and a schedule to keep. That, unfortunately, must remain my priority."

She sighed, then lowered her head to bat her lashes at him. "Do your orders say anything about dancing?"

"I beg your pardon?"

"I know that several of your men play instruments. I think we should have a dance. With waltzing. It would be a touch of Society in the middle of the wilderness. But Miss Ponsley says I need to receive your permission before I plan anything. So do I have your permission?"

As far as he was concerned, there was far too much Society in the middle of the wilderness already. Of more interest was the information that Zephyr knew about the suggestion of a dance and hadn't ridiculed it. "When did you wish to hold this soiree?" he asked.

"Tomorrow night. Then we would have time to pull our gowns from the hold and have them pressed, and to ask your . . . cook to prepare something festive."

With another glance toward the southeastern horizon, Shaw shook his head. "I suggest tonight. We're going to be in for some foul weather, more than likely before morning."

"Havc our soiree tonight?" Miss Jones lifted both eyebrows, the portrait of affronted female. "We'll never have time to prepare. I refuse to wear a wrinkled gown."

"Then you may wait until the weather clears again. Perhaps after we arrive at Tahiti. I imagine the natives would be fascinated to see an English soiree."

As he'd expected, she frowned and stomped one foot. "I do not wish to be stared at by . . . primitive persons." When he didn't give in, she sighed. "Very well, then. I will require more assistance if we're to have a soiree tonight. I can only hope it won't be an unmitigated disaster. If it is, it certainly won't be my fault."

He inclined his head. "You may blame me for the rush." And thank Zephyr that he'd agreed to it at all.

Finally she smiled again. "Well then, Captain. I suppose, then, that you may attend. As may your officers."

"Make the arrangements, Miss Jones. I'll appoint Lieutenant Newsome as your liaison."

She curtsied. "Thank you, Captain."

As she walked off, Shaw sent another glance at the gray on the horizon. "I'm going below," he said, motioning young Mr. Keller to step forward. "You have the command, Jamie. Send Newsome down to my quarters, will you?"

The lad saluted. "Aye, aye, sir."

"And don't tell him why; I don't want him jumping overboard."

As he'd expected, his cabin was already occupied, today by a botanist, his daughter, a foot-long deceased millipede, and a parrot. "Good morning," he said, pulling off his coat and sitting at the small writing desk to note the course change in his logbook.

"Good morning." Sir Joseph looked up from the millipede. "Are we still on course for Tahiti?"

"For the moment."

"You haven't gotten us lost, have you?" Zephyr asked, continuing to work on her painting of a living version of the millipede in its natural surroundings.

He grinned. "Not yet. A storm is coming."

Finally she faced him, slipping a pencil behind her ear in that absent, attractive way she had. "Did you smell it on the wind?"

"I saw it in the sky. To the southeast. A rather foreboding bank of clouds. The wind will send it in our direction." He shrugged. "Another reason I wish we'd reached Tahiti already."

"It has seemed cooler today," the botanist noted. "What about the animals on deck?"

"We'll fasten down the coverings. They should do as well as the rest of us."

"Bloody hell."

Clearing his throat, Shaw rose and went over to

pull open the door of the one parrot cage that remained in the cabin. Red fluttered into the air and then circled to land on his bookshelf. "Pretty bird," he said encouragingly, walking to the worktable.

"Damned chit."

"You taught it to say that, didn't you?" Zephyr asked accusingly.

"I didn't. Not intentionally. I think you inspired him."

Sir Joseph gazed at the parrot. "It's remarkable that he's begun to mimic you after such a short acquaintance. You must tell me your technique, Shaw. It could be invaluable in the future."

"My technique is food and patience. The same method I use to . . . captain this ship."

He'd almost said it was the same method he used to woo a woman, but with the woman he wanted in the room, that would have been a poor idea. He looked at the creature in the jar. The damned millipede looked dangerous even soaked in alcohol. "Have you painted the small parrots yet?"

"Everything will have its turn," she replied. "Just because the birds are pretty and that spider rather frightening doesn't make one species more important than the other." She lowered her head still further, but not before he saw the curve of her mouth. The damned chit enjoyed an argument, that was for certain.

"I prefer the birds." Realizing he was still gazing at her, he offered an arm to the red parrot. "We have a very small chance of reaching the islands before the storm, but if the reefs are anything like those at Fiji, it'll be safer to remain in deeper water until the weather clears."

"I shall leave the specifics up to you, Shaw. I daresay you've saved our lives on two separate occasions now."

"And you got to shoot a rifle," Zephyr added with a grin.

The bird fluttered back into the air, then gripped its small clawed feet into his forearm. It was lighter than he expected, and even the claws felt more like pinpricks than anything else. He offered the bird a piece of hard tack bread. "And no one's been killed. Don't forget that." The determination to leave that statistic unaltered was his main reason for not racing the storm to Tahiti. Whatever his personal reasons for hurrying, the sharp-eyed female with the brass-streaked hair needed to remain safe.

Zephyr set down her pencil again. "You should name your friend there," she commented.

"I was thinking of calling him Fiji. Or Niu. As far as I could determine, that's the Fijian word for 'coconut' or something similar."

She eyed him. "Goodness. You learned a word in Fijian? I'm very impressed."

"Then you should see me do arithmetic. I don't even use my fingers to count." He used his forefinger to scratch the parrot at the base of its scarlet head. "Niu. Say 'Niu.' "

"Bloody hell."

The botanist's daughter laughed. It was a merry, light sound he immediately memorized and wanted to hear again. As he watched, she set down her sketch paper and stood up. "Papa, if we're heading for poor weather, I'd best go see that your plant specimens are secure in the hold."

"Yes, oh, yes. I'll join you in a few minutes, after I finish my notes."

When she sent a glance in Shaw's direction, he nearly felt as though she'd poked him in the ribs. He certainly understood the message in her eyes, anyway. Clearing his own throat, he set Niu onto Sir Joseph's shoulder. "I'll escort Miss Ponsley," he said aloud. "No need to trouble yourself, Sir Joseph."

"Oh, very good then, lad. I shall continue on here. Perhaps I might attempt to improve Niu's vocabulary."

Before Shaw could wish him good luck with that, Zephyr sent him another glance and left the room. Whatever was afoot, at least it seemed interesting. Following her down the corridor, he wasn't certain whether he was in for an argument or more kissing or both.

"Are we going to be in for a squall, a tempest, or a typhoon?" she asked over her shoulder.

"You're quite the storm thesaurus this morning."

"Does that mean you don't know?" Turning the corner, they descended the steep stairs into the hold. At the bottom, she faced him. "How do you think we're faring, Captain?"

He decided that she had remarkably pretty eyes. He'd always been partial to gray. They reminded him of the sea. "We'll be fine. I'll keep a close watch. If the waves begin well before the storm then we're likely in for a more direct h—"

"Not the weather, nickninny. You and I."

"Ah. I think we're faring quite well." He shifted a little, balancing his weight over both feet on the chance he was wrong about that and she meant to kick him in a sensitive area. "What's your opinion?"

Zephyr liked the sound of his voice, the low, cultured drawl that seemed to resonate with her own heartbeat. Being close to Bradshaw Carroway was like . . . It was like nothing she'd ever experienced before, and she'd begun to realize that she felt less lonely here in the middle of the ocean than she had since her mother died.

"I think *you're* faring better than I expected," she said aloud, straightening his shirt across his broad shoulders because she wanted to touch him. "I occasionally believe that you're actually wooing me."

"I think I may be," he returned. "After all, if this is indeed my last voyage I need to begin considering more domestic things, don't you think?"

Zephyr stared up into his light blue eyes. "You're bamming me."

Shaw snorted. "You could stand to improve your skills at flattery," he noted.

"I'll admit that you may be more worthy of flattery than I first believed." She wanted to kiss him. And if he'd just been discussing marriage—*marriage?*—that required thought. Kissing was better than thinking.

"I've merely been following the rules, as you ordered me to." He tilted his head. "That doesn't mean I wouldn't rather peel you out of that gown and put my hands on you." His gaze took her in from head to toe. "Every inch of you."

Oh, my. She felt her cheeks warm. "And what about after that?"

"I'll have you again, I imagine." He took a slow step closer. "I imagine it very much."

Then he advanced another step, and she abruptly

found the flat of her palm against his chest, over his heart. The slow, deep beat thrummed against her fingers. Goodness, he was fit. And tall, and tanned, and imposing. And capable. And very, very handsome.

She tried to shake off the sensation that she was swaying on her feet, drowning in blue eyes. "My concerns are more long-term. Juliette says a lady should tease a man with what he wants until he's willing to give anything to achieve it."

"That strategy presumes dishonesty on both sides. You asked me to woo you. I took that as a request to be more attentive and to better our acquaintance before you risk your reputation at my hands. That's a logical request, Zephyr. And I'm rather glad I've embarked on it. It's been a unique experience for me. You don't have an ulterior motive, do you?"

Zephyr swallowed. If he'd been some dull, close-minded, jaundiced, and warty captain, she wouldn't have bothered showing him anything but contempt. Bradshaw Carroway, however, was maddening and stubborn and at the same time far more clever and insightful than she'd ever anticipated. "No, I don't. And I like that we've become friends."

"Not just friends. Keep that in mind as well, my breeze."

With a grin full of humor and . . . and naughtiness, he turned on his heel and left the hold. Left her standing there with her father's plants. Well. Now she felt like someone had just dumped a bucket of cold sea water over her, and she didn't like the sensation.

Shaking herself, she glanced about at the plants. If a storm was coming, she wanted assistance in securing them. Preferably, persons who knew about strong knots. With an irritated sigh, she went to find Hendley.

By evening the wall of clouds to the southeast had become mountainous. The sea, though, remained nearly as calm as a pond. According to Shaw that meant they likely wouldn't receive a direct hit, which Zephyr had to see as good news.

"Stap my anchor."

She chuckled, looking at the parrot perched atop an old musket mounted on the captain's wall of weaponry. Niu was clearly a clever creature despite his immediate liking for Shaw, but he was also a very contrary one. He seemed to want to say nothing pleasant at all. Even her absurdly patient father had given up the attempt to teach the parrot some more polite phrases.

"Aren't you worried the little beastie will fly away?"

Jumping, Zephyr looked quickly toward the half open door. "Dr. Howard."

The earl's light-haired brother inclined his head. "I apologize if I startled you, Miss Ponsley."

"No need. If you're looking for Captain Carroway, I believe he's on deck." And it took all of her concentration and willpower to remain below and work.

"I was looking for you, actually." He stepped farther into the room, stopping beside where she sat at the worktable. "You've been invited to the soiree tonight, I presume?"

"I have." According to the bell that chimed every hour she still had just under three hours before the festivities were to begin. She'd attended dances in other countries, but this would be her first proper English to-do. Or as proper as it could be, under the circumstances. "I'm quite excited to dance."

"That's handy, as I wanted to ask if you would save a waltz for me. Frederica means for several to be played, I believe."

"I haven't waltzed since I was fifteen, Dr. Howard, and that was only with my father when I was learning the steps."

He smiled charmingly. "It will be my honor to reeducate you, then. Do say yes."

Goodness. An actual waltz at an actual Society soiree. With an actual gentleman. An odd gathering catered by a one-legged man and with music provided by a group of sailors who preferred naughty sea shanties, but a party nonetheless. "Yes."

"Excellent. And I ask you again to call me Christopher. We have been and will continue to be close neighbors for quite a long time, after all." When she nodded, he reached over and took her fingers, brushing his lips against her knuckles. "You have pretty hands," he noted, releasing her again. "A gentleman likes pretty hands on a lady. You should take better care of them."

Mortified, Zephyr clenched her hands into her lap. "I've been drawing with charcoal," she said, though that had to be obvious.

"Of course." He sketched a shallow bow. "I'll see you this evening, then."

Once he'd gone, she sat back, sighing. She'd become used to backhanded compliments from Juliette and her less-friendly companions, but she failed to see why those sugarcoated insults were so popular with the *haute ton*. At least when Shaw insulted her, he simply said it, and in the most cynical way possible. And his compliments were . . . sincere.

"Pretty hands."

"Niu, be quiet. I have enough men teasing at me. Don't you join the mix."

"Damned chit."

Zephyr drew a breath. So she had a partner for one waltz tonight. The men—both passengers and officers—outnumbered the ladies, so it was entirely likely that she would be able to dance every dance tonight if she chose to do so. If she felt charitable, she might even save a waltz for the captain. Though she would have felt more charitable if he'd kissed her earlier in the hold instead of just grinning at her like a half-wit.

She glanced about the cabin again, empty but for her, the parrot, and an alcoholically preserved millipede. Then she rose and walked to the door to close it.

Generally, while she was a curious person, she wasn't a nosy one. But Shaw had begun speaking about the two of them beyond the moment when he expected her to give in to his charms and . . . be with him. He did tease, however, and for heaven's sake, she wanted to know if he was serious. Zephyr hurried to his writing desk, keeping in mind the fact that either Shaw or her father could make an appearance at any moment.

The logbook was filled with entries discussing the weather, heading, depth of the ocean, and any disciplinary action or exemplary behavior on the part of the crew. She flipped back to the days they'd been anchored at Fiji, but while he'd noted the attire and behavior of the natives along with their estimated military strength and the island's value as a supply station, he hadn't gone into much more detail. In fact, he'd actually written that Sir Joseph would provide a more rounded study of the Fiji Islands and islanders. The entries for Tonga were a bit more exciting, but then there had been shooting involved.

With a scowl she closed the book again. Considering that the log was an official document and would be turned over to the Admiralty at the end of the voyage, she didn't actually expect to find any mention of herself—or of his opinion of or feelings toward her. Or of his reticence about battle. A note about her competence or something would have been nice, though. And helpful.

As she set the log back in its place she spied the piece of paper tucked inside the back cover. Brushing aside the brief feeling of guilt, she pulled it free and unfolded it. Shaw had several times mentioned his rather large family, and in particular his closest brother, Robert. This was clearly part of a letter addressed to Bit, as Shaw referred to him.

Dear Robert, she read to herself, *On the good chance you receive all of my correspondence at once, this is my third letter to you since Australia.* From there he went on about the fair weather they'd been experiencing, and about his happiness at being in a poorly explored part of the world without being assigned the task of hunting anyone down.

Someone clumped past outside. Zephyr caught her breath, ready to stuff the paper back where she'd found it and flee to the worktable. The boot steps, though, didn't slow, and she angled the letter to the lamplight again.

You'll be glad to know we've survived Fiji intact, no

thanks to Lord John Fenniwell and his idiot companions. The man could barely navigate the tables at White's; I don't know what made him think voyaging would be a good idea. If I ever behave in such a dim-witted manner, please shoot me.

Well, that sounded reasonable. *I trapped a large spider in Tonga. The creature had the good sense to climb up Miss Ponsley's leg, but thus far no one has suggested it be pickled for such temerity.*

Zephyr snorted, then quickly covered her mouth. The first mention of her didn't sound all that flattering, but it was rather amusing.

Sir Joseph has been living up to the reputation of which you repeatedly informed me, she continued to read. *I will attempt to convince him to name a newly discovered weed or shrubbery after you.* Zephyr chuckled again at that; clearly Shaw was fond of his brother.

I seem to have acquired a parrot, red and green in color. I've named him Niu, the Fijian word for "coconut." Please tell the Runt that thus far he only repeats foul language. That should please Edward greatly. His most-often repeated phrase is "damned chit," which I attribute to my own frequent summation of Zephyr Ponsley.

"The feeling is mutual," she muttered, leaning her hip on the desk. Shaw wrote fairly lengthy letters. And rather humorous ones—to this point, anyway.

Good God, she aggravates me, Bit, she read on, scowling. For a moment she debated putting the letter back right then, but she also had the very illogical desire to know precisely what he *did* think of her, and if he'd somehow been fooling her after all.

She lifted the letter again. *She questions everything I do and say, and delights in ridiculing me. The odd thing is, though, that while I wouldn't tolerate such anarchy from anyone else, from her I find it amusing. Even endearing. Yes, I'll say it—I enjoy arguing with her. More than that, I genuinely like her. Laugh if you will, and I know you are, but I intend to discov—*

The letter stopped there. She had a fairly good idea how he would finish the sentence, however, because she felt much the same way about him. Annoyed and aggravated, excited and aroused and . . . hopeful all at the same time.

Once she'd put the letter back where she'd found it, Zephyr returned to her chair. Before she could do more than pick up her pencil again, the cabin door opened. "Captain," she squeaked, jumping.

Lifting an eyebrow, Bradshaw paused in the doorway. "Were you expecting someone else?"

"No. Of course not. I was concentrating."

"Mm hm. Why was the door closed?"

Yes, why was that? "To keep your parrot from flying off," she returned, deciding Christopher Howard's query made as good an excuse as anything. She gestured at the crossbow on which Niu now perched.

"Are you going on deck for the party tonight?" he asked, shutting the door behind himself.

"Are you?"

His mouth twitched. "I asked first."

She set down her pencil again, glad that it looked like he'd interrupted her work rather than that he'd nearly caught her snooping through his private correspondence. "Fine," she said aloud. "Yes, I am attending. Dr. Howard has already requested a waltz."

He stopped halfway to the parrot. "Are you going to waltz with him?"

A small thrill ran down her spine. She wanted to ask whether he was jealous, but she was fairly certain ladies didn't say such things. "Yes." Zephyr took a breath. "He said there were to be several waltzes. Apparently Miss Jones is very fond of them."

"Thank you for alerting me." Shaw grabbed a chair and changed course, setting it in front of one of the built-in bookcases. For a moment she thought he might be looking for a book, improbable as that seemed, but instead he stepped onto the chair and reached behind the top row of tomes. As she watched, he retrieved a full bottle containing an amber-colored liquid.

"Brandy?"

"Very fine brandy," he returned, stepping down and returning the chair to the worktable. He pulled two glasses from a drawer and sat beside her. Uncorking the bottle, he poured an inch or so of liquid into each glass. He nudged one of them toward her.

"Is this an attempt to render me inebriated?" she asked, eyeing the glass and then him.

"I would use the cheaper stuff if that was my goal." He took a swallow from his own glass, half closing his eyes in obvious appreciation as he drank. "I think we need to have a conversation."

"A conversation," she repeated skeptically. "Are you certain you wish to attempt that? I'm rather formidable."

"Yes, you are." He poured himself another inch of brandy even though he hadn't finished off the first of it. "You and Juliette Quanstone chat quite a bit, do you not?"

"Yes. She's been quite helpful in teaching me about men and Society."

"That's good," he returned, "as long as you realize that what she offers is only an opinion, and not necessarily the correct one."

Zephyr hooked the tip of one finger over the rim of the glass and pulled it closer. "What shall we converse about, then?"

Shaw motioned for her to take a drink. "A little thing I like to call *my* version of Society," he said.

Chapter Eleven

One day there came a sailor, just an ordinary bloke
A-bulging at the trousers with a heart of solid oak.
At sea without a woman for seven years or more,
There wasn't any need to ask what he was
looking for.

"BELL BOTTOM TROUSERS"

"What I'm attempting to say," Shaw commented a quarter of a bottle later, "is that in the middle of the Pacific Ocean or not, nothing you do or say in the presence of these people will remain private. All of London will hear about any misstep you make the moment we return. That includes your supposed friends and any and all gentlemen who want to dance with you."

"But they're on their way to Manila."

"Howard isn't. And you heard the gossiping at Admiral Dolenz's house. Word spreads. Nothing can stop it. Not even oceans."

Zephyr stood. "You're a fine storyteller yourself, Shaw." Picking up her sketch pad and the jar with the millipede inside, then tucking a pencil behind her ear, she faced him. "And if that is good brandy, I would hate to taste an inferior bottle."

"It's an acquired taste." As was she, actually. And he'd acquired it.

"I shall be cautious with Dr. Howard. Though how you can stand to live in London when you have such a low opinion of your fellows astounds me."

"Why do you think I'm out here?" Bradshaw pushed his chair back, blocking her escape. "And for God's sake, I'm trying to be helpful," he grumbled, straightening to glare down at her.

"No, you're not," she returned, lifting her chin. "You're trying to be certain I don't find any other man on this ship as interesting as I find you."

"Aha." Keeping his expression even, he took the paper and insect out of her hands and put them back on the table.

"What now?" she demanded, her cheeks darkening.

"You find me interesting." Moving slowly, he freed the pencil from her hair and set that down, as well.

"Perhaps, when you're not telling me what to d—"

Shaw kissed her. The soft "oh" of surprise melted and molded against his mouth, arousing and more intoxicating than any glass of brandy. Not kissing her when she'd invited him to do so in the hold had sent him on a long, brisk walk through every recess of the *Nemesis*. Not kissing her now likely would have stopped his heart altogether.

She moaned, sweeping her hands up his chest and around his shoulders. He wanted to kiss her senseless, then pull her out of her gown and explore every inch of her warm, naked body. God, he hoped she was wearing those boys' breeches. He'd dreamed of her wearing them and nothing else for the past two nights.

He lifted her onto the worktable. "Zephyr," he murmured against her mouth, moving in between her legs to hold her around the waist. Those other men on the *Nemesis*—he might have been like them once, and for quite a long time, but he'd changed. Some of it had been because of Simon's death, but Zephyr Ponsley had altered his course so greatly that he'd never return to where he'd begun. He didn't want to.

Someone knocked at his door. "Captain, them ladies want us to move the water barrels so they have room to dance."

If he didn't answer, Eddings would simply walk in. And fool that he was, he hadn't latched the door. Very reluctantly Bradshaw took a step backward. "Move them, Eddings."

"Aye, aye, but they want to hang lamps in the rigging, too."

Zephyr hopped down from the table, straightened her skirt, and gathered her things back into her arms. Then with a flip of her head that would have looked magnificent had her long, brass-touched hair been down, she walked away and pulled open the door.

"You've become quite convincing," she said over her shoulder. "But not completely."

He grinned. "Miss Ponsley?"

She faced him. "Yes?"

"I'm happy to follow your rules. Not everyone else would feel so bound. All I ask is that you keep that in mind."

With a nod, she brushed past Eddings and disappeared into her own cabin. Shaw was fairly certain he heard her lock her door as soon as it closed.

Whatever she thought of his argument, verbal and otherwise, he hoped she had at least listened. Eddings cleared his throat, and Shaw shook himself. "Women do not belong on ships," he stated aloud.

"They're ill luck, aye," the sailor agreed, surreptitiously crossing his fingers.

"Not ill luck. They're annoying." He blew out his breath. Time for another long walk. "At least we're not likely to sink with chits on board; Davy Jones couldn't stand the tongue wagging. Now. No lamps in the rigging, but set a half dozen along the port railing."

Eddings saluted. "Aye, aye, Captain."

Once he was alone, Shaw sank back into his chair. It had used to be that captaining a ship absorbed him completely. Somehow since she'd come aboard, Zephyr had dug her way into him so deeply that he couldn't imagine how dull and ordinary a voyage without her would be.

And with her and his ship and the weather, the expedition, and his mission for Sommerset all rattling about together in his mind, he was beginning to consider that he was going mad. At least that would explain why thinking of her and his future linked together didn't cause him to drop dead. It didn't even frighten him—though there were so many things between his now and his future that anything could happen.

"Damned chit," he muttered.

"Damned chit," Niu echoed, flying down to land on the table, lift his tail, and shit on the map of Tahiti.

"Exactly," Shaw agreed.

By the time he'd finished the day's log entries and his rather convoluted letter to Robert, then summoned Peter Potter to help him into his dress uniform, the sun had set and the wind had begun to rise. The night sky directly above them still glittered with starlight, but to the south and east a heavy blackness stretched from well below the horizon to well above it.

"What do you think, Captain?" Lieutenant Newsome asked as Shaw stopped beside him.

"What I think, Albert, is that we're going to be in for it by tomorrow. I want everyone not on duty or catering to the Mayfair mob in their hammocks by ten bells. I want them to sleep while they can."

"Aye, aye, sir." Newsome glanced toward the well-dressed group gathering on the main deck. "And the off-duty officers, sir? Are we to retire, as well?"

"I believe all officers have been invited to attend the soiree. It would be rude not to at least make an appearance."

The young lieutenant grinned. "We can't very well be rude."

"I suppose not. But I'm ending this at midnight, regardless of manners or who hasn't danced with whom."

"Understood, sir. I'll inform the men."

"While you do that, assign someone to watch the barometer. I want a report every thirty minutes."

Nodding, the lieutenant hurried away. Shaw kept his gaze on the blackness curving around to head them off. If he had his preference they would be heading for the lee side of the nearest well-charted island to take shelter. The closest set of islands at the moment, however, was Tonga, two days behind them and anything but reliably mapped. And considering their reception there, he would remain on the open ocean.

"What are you looking at?" Miss Juliette Quanstone asked as she topped the steps. "I don't see anything but black."

"And that is the problem," he returned. "We should see stars and the moon rising." The moon that would be full in less than a week, signaling that he'd missed Sommerset's deadline.

"Oh." She glanced east again. "Are we in danger?"

"We're on a piece of wood in a very empty ocean, Miss Juliette. We're always in danger."

Any chit with sense would have looked at least momentarily thoughtful. The older Miss Quanstone, though, played with the pearl necklace about her throat, no doubt to draw attention to her low neckline. "Then I shall have to keep a close eye on you, Captain," she returned with a flirtatious flutter of her eyelashes. "In fact, for my own safety I shall secure a dance with you. The third waltz of the evening will do well, I think."

There was only one female with whom he was interested in dancing, but as Zephyr seemed to like Juliette, he would be polite. "Three waltzes?" he commented, more surprised at the quantity than the request. "How many are there to be? I can't have the *Nemesis*'s name bandied about as a stage for scandalous behavior."

Juliette giggled. "There are to be four waltzes. With no Society mamas about to frown at us, we are indulging ourselves."

Four waltzes. Four chances to secure one with Zephyr. Or three, rather, since she'd already given one away. "In light of that," he said aloud, "please do me the honor of partnering me for the evening's third waltz."

She sank into a curtsy. "With pleasure, Captain."

"And please inform our hostess that this soiree will end at midnight."

Miss Quanstone scowled. "Midnight? That's hardly—"

"Midnight," he repeated.

As she hurried down to the main deck and the hastily cleared dance floor, Shaw sent another glance at the horizon. He'd just made himself less popular, but it didn't signify. In the next day or two everyone on board was bound to curse his name at least once.

Seeing the ragtag orchestra gathering at the bow, he crossed the main deck and climbed the stairs to them. Three fiddlers, two hornpipers, and a drummer—hardly anything Mayfair would tolerate back in London, but they were half the world away from Almack's and Vauxhall Gardens.

"You have your orders, lads?" he asked, noting that they all looked more apprehensive than they had when they'd repelled the Tongans.

"Aye, Captain," Dobbs returned. "We told the lady we only know one waltz, but she said we could play it four times. Don't know none of them quadrilles, but we've been practicing three country dances."

Bradshaw stifled his grin. Even without considering the setting, this was going to be an unusual evening. "Just play loudly, and no mermaid shanties."

The group laughed, visibly relaxing. "Aye, aye, Captain."

A swish of skirts approached him quickly from

below. He turned around, unsurprised to see Miss Jones glaring up at him, hands planted on her hips. "Miss Jones. You look quite enchanting this evening."

She blinked, belatedly curtsying. "Thank you, Captain."

"You wanted to tell me something, I believe?" he prompted, descending to join her on the main deck.

With her initial roaring approach interrupted, the best she could do now was sputter. "We cannot end the soiree at midnight. In London we would have barely begun by then. We wouldn't have time for even a dozen dances."

"Then I suggest you begin. We end at midnight. I want my crew well rested for tomorrow."

"For your silly storm?"

"Have you been on shipboard during a storm?"

"We had rain rounding the cape."

"That is not a storm. If you prefer, I can end your soiree now. My ship, my rules, Miss Jones."

She frowned mightily. "Oh, very well. But my uncle and the Admiralty will hear of your . . . autocratic behavior." Miss Jones jabbed a finger up at the so-called orchestra. "You lot. Play a country dance. Now."

The group tugged their forelocks in near unison. After a ragged note or two, they began a passable if very unusual-sounding dance piece. With a sniff Miss Jones flounced away, no doubt to complain about him to her friends.

Shaw stayed where he was, watching as the group paired off and took to the temporary dance floor. If he had to pick a moment when the *Nemesis* had gone from being a British warship to an odd, chaotic combination of pleasure yacht and floating zoo, he would choose this one. But the oddity had actually settled into the ship's bones by degrees since their last voyage on the Mediterranean.

And maddening as it was, in all honesty he couldn't say he would be willing to trade it away. In a sense, it might even have saved his life. At the least, that odd melancholy that had followed him from London hadn't touched him in weeks. Of course the main reason for his acceptance of the proprietorship of this floating Bedlam was. . .

He paused in mid-thought as his reason stepped onto the deck. For a chit who'd spent all her adult life traipsing across Europe and the Near East, Zephyr knew how to wear a proper evening gown. The violet and gray dress was just bright enough to show its colors in the lantern light, while the delicate violet-dyed lace at the sleeves and neck gave her entire appearance an . . . ethereal softness that seemed both fitting and at odds with her character.

His mouth went dry as he took her in, and it was the first time he could remember that happening, ever. Heat skittered beneath his skin. The sensation was distinctly unsettling. And welcome, whatever he might be in for.

Zephyr stopped at the edge of the deck. Minstrels, dancing aristocrats, cannons, the muffled sound of squawking parrots under their night tarp, and a warship of the Royal Navy. At both first and second look it all seemed so very odd. And so unexpectedly delightful.

As she lifted her gaze, she caught sight of Bradshaw. *Oh, my.* He'd donned his dress uniform once more, and looked tall and lean and even deadly in deep blue and white. Not for the first time she considered that being naked in the arms of such a man might not be such a bad thing.

"Miss Ponsley."

She jumped as the *Nemesis*'s first mate appeared at her elbow. "Mr. Gerard. Good evening."

The lieutenant also wore his formal attire; in fact, now that she looked, she noticed that all the officers wore their dress uniforms. He bowed to her. "This country dance is half finished, but would you do me the honor of dancing the remainder of it with me?"

At the edge of her vision Bradshaw started toward her. She'd had more than enough of his advice, however, about how she should conduct herself in front of the Mayfair group. Zephyr smiled and held out her hand to the lieutenant. "Yes, please."

With a grin Mr. Gerard took her hand and pulled her into the middle of the dance. She hardly had time to worry if she knew the steps before she was dancing them. The other four ladies glittered with beads and jewels; evidently even a tiny soiree called for diamonds. Or perhaps they hadn't had the opportunity to wear them for a time. She had on her mother's pearl necklace and ear bobs, but they were the only fancy jewelry she owned. Nor did she have much of an inclination to collect more.

While she was dressed a bit more simply than the other ladies, she didn't feel the lack. Whether that had something to do with the way Shaw was gazing at her from the edge of the cleared deck, she didn't know—but she felt pretty.

No, not pretty. More powerful than that. Even if she couldn't put words to it, the feeling was definitely heady. And in the swirling breeze around them, the effect was even more exhilarating.

The dance ended too soon, and she and Lieutenant Gerard joined in the applause. Before she could even look about for him, Shaw gripped her elbow. "Give me a waltz," he said in a low voice, his light blue eyes shimmering gray in the flickering lamplight.

The . . . possessiveness in his expression was mesmerizing and thrilling all at once. "You may have the last waltz of the evening," she said, knowing she was smiling and excited and unable to stifle either.

"The infamous fourth waltz," he returned with a brief grin of his own. "I accept." He looked past her at the hatchway. "I hope someone invited your father."

"Oh, yes. He declined. I believe he has one of the miniature parrots in his cabin, to see whether Niu's conversation is unique. And he prefers not to dance, these days."

A very unusual hornpipe-led waltz began, and Lord Benjamin walked up to them. "Are you spoken for, Miss Ponsley?" he asked, his back half turned to Bradshaw.

The captain looked like he was about to take exception to the slight, so Zephyr wrapped her hand around Lord Benjamin's arm and led him away. "I am now," she said aloud.

"Good." The Duke of Autledge's fourth son put a hand on her waist, took her other hand in his, and they began dancing.

"You seemed rather put out with the captain," she noted.

"Yes. He's ending the dance at midnight, which

has Frederica nearly in hysterics. I'm determined to disapprove of such autocratic behavior."

"I believe he only wants everyone to be safe," she commented, but Lord Benjamin clearly didn't want to hear it.

For a few moments she concentrated on remembering the steps and on trying to keep from frowning in concentration. She didn't think she was very successful, because her partner's pained expression became more pronounced. "I haven't waltzed in a long while," she offered, trying to count the steps in her head rather than aloud.

"You dance divinely," he returned. "And you look lovely, which compensates regardless."

Thank goodness she'd combed her hair, then. And even managed to pin it up. "You are very kind," she said aloud. Lord Benjamin more than likely wouldn't appreciate her barbed comments, so she would save them up for Bradshaw.

By the halfway point of the dance she felt comfortable enough not to glance at her feet every few steps. And it was then she noticed that the captain had also taken to the improvised dance floor. Miss Emily Quanstone danced in his arms, so graceful her feet didn't even seem to touch the wood planking. And her tall partner clearly knew what he was about, as well. The easy, athletic way he moved translated quite well to the waltz, and for once he was actually smiling at one of his civilian passengers.

Taking a breath, Zephyr looked away. The other dancers were quite fine, too, though Mr. Jones seemed a little plodding in his steps. It rather fit her assessment of his entire character, actually. Lieutenant Abrams had claimed Miss Juliette, and while his steps lacked a little finesse, he was supremely exuberant. She would have to remember that if the two of them should dance, or they might end up falling overboard.

As soon as the waltz ended, Miss Jones called for another country dance. Frederica seemed determined to force as many dances as she could into the smallest amount of time possible. Clearly no one was happy to have the dance end at midnight, and she wondered whether Shaw was simply being contrary until she caught sight of him standing at the bow and gazing out over the ocean. One of his officers approached. The two men spoke for a moment, and then the younger man hurried back to the wheel to chatter at the pilot.

"The captain says a storm is coming," Mr. Jones observed, circling her. "Don't be alarmed."

"I'm not alarmed," she returned, winding around Juliette Quanstone before returning to her partner's side. "I'm only wondering if we could be doing something more useful than prancing across the deck."

"Considering that he's sent most of his men below decks to sleep, *I* think Captain Carroway is only attempting to bully us." Frederica Jones frowned in Shaw's direction. "Who ever heard of a soiree ending at midnight? It's not as if anyone has Parliament in the morning."

"I think you simply have to accept that we are all subject to the captain's whims, Frederica," Lord John Fenniwell commented easily. "When he feels the need to flee, we flee. When he says we must cower in our cabins, then we must at least return to them."

Zephyr didn't like the way he said that, or the way

the others chuckled at his supposedly droll comments. She started to point out that Lord John was the reason they'd left Fiji so abruptly and that Shaw had deliberately chosen to depart Tonga rather than begin a war. His actions had made sense. Yes, she knew of his private reservations, but they certainly hadn't prevented him from doing his duty, and performing it well.

"I prefer to keep in mind the fact that no one's been killed," she said aloud.

"Of course you have nothing to complain about," Lady Barbara noted. "You get to go ashore and do as you please."

Well, that was rather sharp. "I assist my father. And as you know, he is the reason the *Nemesis* is out here to begin with."

"And how fortunate you are that the *Nemesis*'s captain is such a fine specimen of a man," Barbara returned, sending a quick grin at Juliette.

"A specimen who indulges you and ignores us," Mr. Jones put in.

Zephyr was more concerned with the idea that Juliette might have been relaying their conversations to the rest of her friends than with the sharp comments of her dance partner. She hadn't said anything terribly private or embarrassing that she could recall, but she'd thought that Juliette had understood how long it had been since she'd had a female friend in whom to confide. Had it all been fodder for laughs?

"Have you been carrying tales?" she asked, frowning at Juliette.

Miss Quanstone swept forward, taking her arm. "Nonsense. We have eyes, you know. And clearly there is some . . . connection between you and Captain Carroway."

That did make sense. "Very well," she said aloud.

"Which is no reason, Stewart," Juliette continued, "for you to be blaming Zephyr for the captain's unfortunate decisions."

"Yes," Frederica seconded, taking Lord Benjamin's arm. "And we mustn't waste our evening with complaints." She waved at the orchestra. "Play another waltz!"

The second waltz sounded exactly the same as the first one. According to Stewart Jones this was the height of barbarism, but she rather liked the way the odd orchestra played the tune. And personally she thought the decision to rush through the soiree as though their lives depended on completing ten dances before midnight was exceedingly silly.

"I hope you know I was only bamming you," Mr. Jones said. "You're a pretty thing, and you ain't to blame for Carroway treading all over us like we ain't just as good as he is."

Zephyr could debate that, but it seemed wiser to only smile. "As your sister said," she returned, wishing he would stop gripping her waist so tightly, "perhaps we should dance rather than complain."

"Well, I'm nearly ready to be in Manila," he countered. "If Tahiti is as disappointing as Fiji, I will be happy to put an end to this holiday. I daresay we paused at Tonga so briefly I'm not even certain I saw it."

They'd stayed at the southern island for two days, but given the dangers, she'd heartily agreed with Shaw's decision to keep the Mayfair group on board the *Nemesis*. "It was fairly barren," she offered aloud.

"And a waste of time. After all, if we don't reach my uncle's house, he may will his company and holdings to Frederica's and my other cousins—and they are nothing but grasping social climbers."

"How dreadful." Clearly Stewart had his nose so high in the air that he couldn't see his own absurdities.

"You have no idea." Mr. Jones gazed at her; they were nearly eye to eye, which was easier on her neck, but in this instance she would have preferred being able to spend the waltz examining his cravat. His brown eyes were . . . pleasant enough, she supposed, but she simply didn't like the familiar way he looked at her.

Out of the corner of her eye the sky flashed. No one else seemed to notice, and she supposed the lightning might have been her imagination, but she didn't think so. By the time Dr. Howard walked up to her and the waltz music began for the third time, the ship had begun an irregular roll quite different from the slow, soothing rise and sink to which she'd become accustomed since they'd left Australia.

"I imagine you've been complimented quite a bit this evening," the physician commented as they began their swirling circle around the deck, "but I feel the need to add my own. You are breathtaking, Miss Ponsley. Please do me the honor of allowing me to call you Zephyr."

"Certainly." Evidently her ink-stained fingers were passable when sheathed in violet-colored gloves. Across the deck Shaw danced with Juliette, and the elder Miss Quanstone seemed to have no complaint about him—not to his face, anyway.

"Thank you, Zephyr." The physician gazed at her, light green eyes glittering in the lamplight.

He was a bit more difficult to decipher than Mr. Jones, or even Lord John and Lord Benjamin. For one thing, as a physician he was obviously a man of science—the sort of fellow she'd encountered most frequently while accompanying her father. He'd actually done something with his life instead of making a career of wagering and idleness. They should have been great friends by now, and she had to wonder why they weren't. "May I ask you a question?"

Christopher nodded. "Please do."

"Did you always want to be a physician?"

"Ah."

"You've been asked that before."

"Let's say I'm aware that my career is not a typical choice for an earl's son and younger brother." He smiled easily. "As a boy I was certain I would be a famous hunter. As I grew up I realized it was the physiology of things that interested me. My specialty is actually ladies' maladies, but I serve where and how I'm needed. Even as a lowly surgeon on a navy ship."

A gust of wind put out two of the lanterns lining the railing. Zephyr stifled a shiver; if not for all the frantic dancing, she would have been cold. "The captain may have been correct about the storm and its arrival," she said, noting that the silver brushstrokes of the stars had vanished now.

"I wouldn't worry," Christopher returned. "The waves and tides around Cape Horn were quite formidable, and the *Nemesis* managed it without difficulty."

"Have you been at sea during many storms?"

Brief impatience crossed his face. "No, I haven't. Nor have I attended a soiree on shipboard. Talking about the one won't change its course or duration. Thanks to the second event, however, I believe I have found a friend and perhaps a kindred spirit." He pulled her a little closer. "I would like to know you better, Zephyr."

She blushed. Thankfully she could blame her red cheeks on the chill now touching the air. "We *are* becoming better acquainted."

"No. This isn't sufficient. For one thing, there are far too many other people about. I don't wish to share you."

Abruptly she realized what he was talking about. Christopher Howard wanted the same thing of her that Shaw did. And he didn't seem to know the rules, either. "That's very kind, I'm sure," she stumbled, reflecting that all she'd wanted of him was friendship. The other didn't interest her in the least. "My only aim on this expedition is to assist my father."

"And there's no reason you shouldn't do so. I only ask to share your company from time to time in the evening." He lowered his mouth close to her ear. "And as a physician I can inform you that it is unhealthy for a gentleman to go without female . . . companionship for any length of time. You would therefore be assisting me in performing my duties."

Beginning to feel distinctly uncomfortable, Zephyr tried to edge a little away from the man who held her in his arms. "Have you made the other ladies on board aware of this?"

"They already know. I daresay they're doing their

duty. But there are too few ladies, and frankly I prefer a female who is less . . . practiced."

Before she could conjure a response to that, the waltz ended. Zephyr backed away from her dance partner as swiftly as she could without drawing undue attention or unwanted questions from any of the other guests.

"What's wrong?" Bradshaw asked from just behind her.

That figured. Shaw wasn't even one of the guests. "Nothing."

"Mm hm. What did he say to you?"

She faced him. "Nothing. Truly. If anything, his reasoning about a man requiring female companionship for his health only helps your own cause."

"I don't need his help." Bradshaw narrowed his eyes. "He suggested that you fulfill his so-called requirement, didn't he?"

"Shaw, it doesn't signify."

Slowly he turned his gaze from her to look across the deck at the physician. "I disagree."

With that he stalked away, directly up to where Dr. Howard stood speaking with Lord John and Miss Jones. Shaw tapped Christopher on the shoulder, waited until the physician turned around, and then hit him in the jaw.

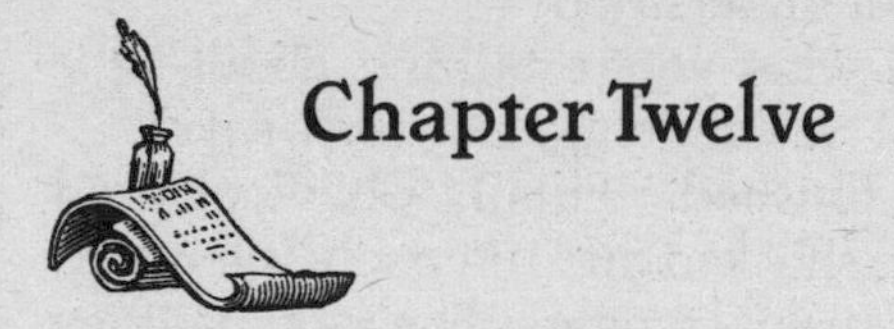

Chapter Twelve

> The wind is piping loud, my boys!
> The lightning flashes free,
> While the hollow oak our palace is,
> Our heritage the sea.
>
> "A WET SHEET AND A FLOWING SEA"

Rain began pelting the deck around them. Bradshaw scarcely noticed, however. Every ounce of his attention remained on Christopher Howard sprawled on his arse.

"What the devil is wrong with you?" the physician sputtered, putting a hand to his jaw and wincing. He scrambled to his feet. "I'll see you thrashed for that, Carroway."

Shaw's hands were still clenched, and he worked on loosening his fingers one by one. Concentrating on that was the only thing keeping him from leveling Howard a second time. He knew why he was angry; the puzzling, disturbing question was why seeing Zephyr upset left him *so* angry he could barely see straight. "You may not be a part of the navy, but you are on my ship and you will behave as a gentleman. Is that understood?"

"I have no idea what you're talking about," the doctor snapped. "I was dancing, for God's sake!"

"This dance is finished." Finally Shaw glanced away, taking in the shocked and intensely interested faces of the rest of his passengers. The fact that they remained out in the rain was indication enough that he'd begun something that wouldn't be forgotten. "I would put you in the brig, Dr. Howard, but your services will likely be required in the next few hours. Return to your quarters. All of you."

"Not so fast," Howard snarled, wiping water from his face. "I demand an explanation!"

Shaw lunged forward, slamming down the arm Howard lifted in protest and wrapping his elbow around the physician's neck. "An explanation?" he hissed in the man's ear. "I know why you're here. I know that you seduced both of Bregins's daughters and then fled like a rat when they became pregnant. And you will not play your game with someone on my ship. If I catch you sniffing around Miss Ponsley again, I will keelhaul you." Shaw shoved him away again. "Is that clear?"

Howard stumbled back a step. "Yes, it's clear. Hypocritical of you, but clear." Before Shaw could go after him again, he retreated below decks.

Shaking the water out of his hair, Bradshaw looked around again. His crew was going about finishing making the ship ready for foul weather. All his passengers had fled below, likely more because of the rain than because of his orders.

He amended that thought as he turned around. Zephyr Ponsley still stood on deck, her wet hair falling down from the pretty knot she'd fashioned and hanging past her shoulders. Lightning flashed, thunder booming close behind. Every other woman he could think of would be fleeing in tears over the ruin of her dress and her hair. Zephyr, though, just looked at him.

"You should get below," he said, something tumbling about in his chest as he approached her.

"You punched him."

"Yes, I did."

"Why?"

"Because he insulted you."

"You want the same thing from me that he did, do you not?"

"No. I don't want one night, one damned romp. Aside from that, I know more about Christopher Howard and his character than you do. And that's enough for the moment. Get below."

Thunder rumbled again, closer. She nodded. "Be careful. You—"

The ship abruptly nosed skyward and then pitched down again.

Zephyr stumbled, and he grabbed her arm, pulling her back against him as a wave broke over the bow, spraying them with cold, salty water. Sheltering her with his body, he guided her to the rope his men had just finished stringing across the length of the main deck.

"Hold on, and keep your feet under you," he instructed.

"You shouldn't have hit him," she said over her shoulder as she led the way toward the hatch. "I wasn't the least bit interested."

Feeling somewhat mollified, he ordered the fore

topsails to be furled. "Be cautious of him, anyway. And it's not jealousy, if you're going to accuse me." Not entirely, anyway.

"Then what is it?" Another wave sprayed across the deck, and he tucked her closer against his chest. In nothing but that wet silk gown, she must be chilled to the bone.

"I should have known I needed to be more straightforward with you. He seduced two sisters, got them both with child, and then fled to sea and left both of them to face the consequences on their own."

She blinked her pretty, insatiably curious gray eyes. "He did that?"

"Yes, he did."

Potter approached with his oilskin coat, and Shaw took it to wrap the heavy thing around Zephyr's shoulders. She hugged it to her, for once apparently speechless.

"See her to her cabin, Potter," he ordered. "Then bring me back my coat."

"Aye, aye, Captain. This way, Miss Zephyr. Watch your footing."

With a nod she started off, then paused again. "Keep an eye on the birds, Shaw."

The animals were the least of his concerns at the moment, but he would do what he could. "I will."

After she disappeared below, Shaw made his way to the sheltered aviary they'd constructed on deck. With the oiled tarp tied tightly over the cages, the animals were likely better off there than anywhere else on the ship, but if the weather worsened he would consider moving them.

Bracing himself against the rising wind and the

pitching deck, he climbed up to the wheel deck. "How is she handling, Leavey?"

"As long as we're heading into the wind she's happy as a lark," the pilot returned, blinking rain out of his eyes. "I think she likes this dance."

Potter returned, and Shaw peeled off his sopping wet dress coat to don the slicker. "Is Miss Ponsley safe and snug?"

"Aye, Captain. The rest of 'em is already howling for extra blankets and wishing they hadn't ate so much baked marlin for dinner."

"Locate Mr. Newsome and inform him that he's to keep our passengers as safe and quiet as possible. Make certain all lanterns are secured and that no one's using bare candles." He'd warned the civilians about that already, but they'd clearly been expecting nothing more than a cool English rain.

By two o'clock in the morning they were riding mountainous forty-foot waves, and the sleet was traveling horizontally. Even with his slicker on he was wet through, and when William Gerard came on deck early to take his watch, Shaw didn't protest.

"Keep her into the wind," he instructed his first mate, having to yell to be heard over the storm. "Both the mizzen topsails look ready to tear, but don't furl them or we'll lose steering."

"Aye, aye, Captain."

"And if you can, keep an eye on the birds. If you can manage it safely and you think it necessary, get them below."

Bradshaw patted Poseidon and closed the hatch behind him, cold and tiredness nearly leached into his bones. Shaking out his hair again, he put one hand on the wall for balance and headed aft to his cabin. Sailors hurried to and fro seeing to their duties, several of them carrying foul-smelling buckets.

Some of his men regularly became seasick in rough weather, but from the moans behind the guest cabin doors and Newsome's harried expression, the passengers were faring far worse. Hopefully that meant they would leave him be for the next day or so.

With a tired sigh he reached his cabin and shut the door behind him. Niu squawked at him, then went back to demolishing the bowl of peanuts someone—more than likely Zephyr—had left lodged on the worktable. Shaw brushed some of the shells off a chair and sat down to pull off his boots. An inch of water poured out of them when he turned them upside down.

After he stripped out of his sopping wet clothes and dried off, he threw on an old shirt and pair of knee breeches. Hopefully Gerard would be able to deal with the storm, but if conditions worsened he needed to be ready.

Once he put out the lamps and sank onto his bunk, he expected to fall asleep swiftly. He actually liked rough weather, and he'd already become accustomed to Niu's late-night barking. Tonight, though, tired as he was and with warmth seeping back into him from the toes up, he found himself wide awake.

He'd had his own command for three years. In that time he'd had to order men to be lashed for flagrant and dangerous disobedience. It was part of being the captain of a ship at sea—the only law for thousands of miles. In some cases a captain and the rules of discipline were the only difference between fighting for King and country and pure piracy.

In his entire career he'd never punched anyone under his command. Yes, he'd flattened a fellow officer on occasion, but he'd never abused his position. Until tonight, apparently.

Did it matter that Christopher Howard was a poor excuse for a gentleman? Shaw frowned. He had his own reputation in London, and it wasn't for celibacy. On the other hand, he'd never lied to an innocent or set one sister against another. And he'd never left a chit pregnant and fled to escape the consequences. Christ, the man was a physician. But it wasn't about past misdeeds. This had been very much about the present.

The ship rolled hard to starboard, then righted itself again. He sat up for a moment, listening, but no one sounded the alarm bell. A few books escaped over the high lip of the shelf and hit the floor, but he was likely to lose more of them before daylight. Of more importance was the box with Sommerset's mirror, but it hadn't budged. He sank back again and left the fallen tomes where they lay.

After another few minutes he sat up once more, reached over and grabbed one of the fallen books, and relit the lamp close by his head. "Damned chit," he muttered, glancing toward the door as he cracked open the book. She made him insane. That was the only explanation—both for his punching Howard and for the knot of . . . fury in his gut when he'd heard that the physician had set his sights on her.

"Damned chit," the parrot squawked, scattering still more peanut shells about.

"I concur." Shaw nodded at the parrot, then settled in to read about Odysseus's seven-year attempt to return home after the siege of Troy. He seemed to have his own Siren aboard the *Nemesis*, which made him want to dash not his ship but his head against the rocks. Repeatedly.

Where previously he and Christopher Howard had disliked but tolerated each other, tonight he'd made an enemy. And he was still mad for a chit whom he'd become determined to woo properly. As the ship rolled hard over again, he began to consider that sinking might be the best outcome he could hope for.

Zephyr sat squarely in the middle of her narrow bunk. She braced one hand against the wood bed frame and the other against the wall. It was likely her imagination, but she thought she could feel the pounding of the ocean beneath her fingertips as it roared just inches away from her.

She'd looked in on her father to find him already asleep, the noncommunicative miniature parrot back in its covered cage. The weather had worsened since then, and falling asleep now seemed virtually impossible. And that didn't take into account the way she couldn't stop thinking about Bradshaw's violent behavior.

Whatever terrible thing he'd said Christopher Howard had done back in England, it didn't make sense that he would react so strongly to a poorly executed request for her . . . favors—unless he *was* jealous, whether he claimed to be unaffected or not. *Goodness.*

The ship lurched hard over. Her sketch pad and pencils slid off the table and crashed to the floor. Crawling off the bunk, she picked them up again. As she straightened, the *Nemesis* pitched forward. Losing her balance, she banged her head on the trunk jammed into the corner.

"Blast it," she cursed, rubbing her temple.

At the same moment she dimly heard Niu squawking. *Oh, dear.* Was the poor parrot alone in Shaw's cabin? There was certainly a plentitude of things in there to fall and frighten or even injure him.

Pulling her dressing robe off the foot of the bunk, she shrugged into it. Bracing herself, her head still thudding, she stood up and opened her door. The corridor was dimmer than usual; apparently the crew had doused every lantern possible. Belatedly she blew hers out, as well, then staggered the few feet to the door of the captain's cabin.

Walking normally was simply impossible. With one step the deck rose two inches higher than she expected, with the next it was three inches lower. Pushing away from the wall, she grabbed the door handle and shoved.

A second later she lay sprawled on the floor in the middle of the captain's cabin, the door banging against her foot. "Damnation," she muttered.

As she lifted onto her hands and knees the door finally clicked shut, so at least it wouldn't be knocking her over from behind. She shoved a book out of her way and looked up—to see Bradshaw leaning back in his bunk, an open book braced against his thighs, and one eyebrow lifted as he looked back at her.

"Hello," he said, amusement dripping from his voice.

"I hit my head." It certainly wasn't that serious, but at the moment she would take any excuse to explain why she happened to be crawling on the floor.

Immediately he was beside her, his large, lean form kneeling at her shoulder. "Just now?" he asked, brushing hair back from her temple with surprisingly gentle fingers.

She twisted to sit upright, her knees folded beneath her. "No. In my cabin. I was picking up my sketches, and then my head slammed into my trunk."

"Don't bother to pick anything up until the weather calms."

"Well, I know that now, don't I?"

"Where does it hurt?"

Zephyr pushed two fingers against her sore left temple. "Here. But it doesn't signify. I actually came to see whether Niu was well. I didn't know you were in here."

"Stop moving about and let me look."

Shaw tilted her chin with his fingers, brushing her hair back from her forehead and leaning in close. His expression was genuinely concerned, and his touch gentle and careful. "You'll have a bruise, I think," he murmured after a moment, drawing her hair down over her shoulder. It was still a bit damp, so she'd left it loose to do as it would.

His touch made her feel shivery. Zephyr rather liked new experiences, but this was the most . . . personal connection she could recall. She cleared her throat. "The weather didn't cooperate with Frederica's four waltzes, did it?"

"No. I thought it might hold off for another few hours, but evidently Poseidon thought four waltzes was too scandalous."

She chuckled. "Perhaps we should invite him next time."

"He'd sink us for certain." Shaw continued toying

with her hair. "That reminds me. You owe me a waltz."

Oh, she felt deliciously warm, despite the chill in the air. "Don't expect it tonight. We'd both break our legs."

"Let's try this." Still on his knees, he moved directly in front of her. "Put your hand on my shoulder," he instructed, taking her free hand in his and slipping his other beneath her dressing robe and around her waist.

"This is silly."

"Humor me."

With an exaggerated sigh Zephyr placed her hand on his shoulder. Through the thin cotton shirt his skin felt warm beneath her fingers. Slowly he drew her closer, until they touched hip to hip. It seemed the most natural thing in the world then to rest her cheek against the side of his neck.

"Your hair smells like the sea," he said quietly, his voice husky and deep.

"Yes, I got it all over me." She took a rather unsteady breath. "Is this your idea of dancing?" The *Nemesis* rolled again, and she pressed closer into him to keep her balance. "Unless your plan is to have the ship turn circles beneath us."

"It may yet." He flexed his fingers where they touched her waist. "Tell me you'll steer well away from Christopher Howard from now on."

She nodded. "All those Mayfair people baffle me. Even Juliette. I thought we'd become friends, but I think even she merely finds me amusing. Someone with whom to pass the time until she can recite our conversations back to her friends."

"I can't help but notice that you didn't include

me in that condemnation." His lips brushed her temple.

The ship's motion and the way they had to lean and flex to stay upright *was* a kind of dance. A very intimate, very intoxicating one. "I thought that was implied," she said, her voice oddly breathless even to her own ears. She rubbed her cheek against him.

"Whatever you are to me, Zephyr, it is not simply a way to pass the time."

Zephyr lifted her head to look him in the eye. "That still leaves a great deal of gray space, Shaw. Why haven't you tried again to seduce me?"

"The rules."

"So I'm a challenge for you."

"That, you are." Light blue eyes held hers. "But honestly, if all I wanted was you in my bed, I've spent my life with amiable women who don't ask much of me. I could have managed it."

Given the way he kissed, he more than likely could have. And yet he'd honored her request. "Perhaps," she hedged.

"Very well. Perhaps."

She liked the way he didn't deny that; in fact, as far as she could tell, he'd never attempted to lie or even to flatter her with those biting, backhanded compliments the other passengers handed out so readily. "If it's not because you're bored and felt like playing a game and it's not because you prefer contrary women, then what is it, Bradshaw?"

He touched his mouth to hers. It already seemed as though she'd been waiting forever for him to kiss her tonight, but my, it had been worth the wait. Her heart pounded. Even when they'd kissed before she'd never felt as desired, or as dispossessed of her senses, as she did now. The surging waves and the lightning and thunder crashing around the ship resonated through her, as though the weather itself echoed the chaos of her feelings.

"I don't know what it is, Zephyr," he returned huskily, putting an arm around her shoulders as he lowered her onto her back among the sliding books. "But I feel . . . compelled to be close to you."

Oh, it sounded very good. And as his mouth moved to the base of her jaw, it felt even better. Was she making a mistake? When they finally returned to London she expected to be pushed by her father's accomplishments into the middle of proper Society—hundreds of Christopher Howards and Lord Benjamins. If nothing else, experiencing with Shaw what he claimed they all wanted from her would aid her in dealing with them. And that could be invaluable.

Zephyr tangled her fingers into his damp black hair. She'd never been one to delude herself, and as soon as the thought occurred to her she had to admit that this wasn't about fortifying herself against the future. This was about discovery—discovering what it was, precisely, that compelled her toward this man who charmed and aggravated her by turns.

"Dr. Howard said it isn't healthy for a man to be celibate for an extended period, and that I would be doing something noble by allowing him to . . . visit me. I almost laughed in his face."

"I never would have attempted that bilge with you. You're far too brilliant for anything but the truth."

"Did you just call me brilliant?" she breathed, trying to sound skeptical. The words came out more giddy and aroused, though, than cynical.

He chuckled against her breastbone, the low sound echoing into her chest. "I did. You've knocked me off my feet. Literally."

"You're seducing me now, aren't you?"

"I damned well hope so. Though we could blame it on the weather, if you like." Shaw kissed her mouth again, lowering his lean length along her body.

Oh, goodness. "How do we go about this, then?"

"I'm not a book of instruction." With another kiss he sat up beside her.

She sat up as well, abruptly annoyed that he might have changed his mind. "I'm only asking because I don't know."

"Mm hm." Shaw stood, then bent down and swept his arms beneath her shoulders and her knees. "First times shouldn't happen on the floor."

For a moment she wondered whether the *Nemesis* would pitch them both onto their heads, but Shaw was far steadier on his feet than she would have been. Sliding her arms around his neck, Zephyr tried kissing him along his jaw as he'd done with her. She was rewarded by a low groan that sent a responding heat all the way through her insides.

Shaw set her down on his bunk, then climbed up beside her. For a moment he leaned his head on his bent arm, simply looking at her. "Damned chit," he murmured, then swooped over her with another assault of achingly intimate kisses.

With his free hand he pulled her arms free of her dressing robe, leaving her in only her thin night rail, already tangled up around her knees. Common sense told her to run—after all, while she didn't know the particulars of his reputation, Dr. Howard had mentioned some things. And Bradshaw himself had admitted to being something of a rake and a rogue. But she couldn't help one thing, damn it all. She liked him. A great deal more than she felt ready to admit.

Shaw ran his hand from her thigh up along her waist to her shoulder, brushing his fingers across one breast as he did so. Sensation and excitement crashed through her. Zephyr gasped.

"If you like that," he said, drawing the shoulder of her night rail down her arm, "you'll enjoy this." He bared her other shoulder, lowering the shift to her waist. Shaw trailed his fingers down her breastbone, then swirled around and around, closer and closer, until he brushed across her nipple. He did the same with her other breast, touching and caressing her until she couldn't breathe.

"Shaw," she whispered, digging her fingers into his shoulders, "if you're doing nothing but teasing me, I am going to be extremely annoyed with you."

"I'm not teasing," he returned in the same intimate tone, leaning down and taking her right breast in his mouth.

Jumping at the warm, sucking sensation, Zephyr arched her back, pulling him closer against her. *Good heavens*. When she could breathe again, she caught hold of the bottom hem of his loose shirt and lifted. Fair was fair, and she wanted to put her hands on his warm skin.

Grinning, Shaw straightened onto his knees, straddling her hips. Shirtless, his suntanned skin glowing in the light of a single lantern, and his hair tousled by her and the weather, he looked utterly magnificent. Above the thrill and power she felt at being desired was the keen excitement at being wanted by *him*. Captain Bradshaw Carroway, wild and decorated and surprisingly compassionate captain of the *Nemesis*.

"Lift your hips," he said, tugging her night rail down further.

She did as he asked. "Do I get to finish undressing you?" It seemed only fair, after all.

"Please do. I'm feeling a bit constricted, as it is."

Lowering her gaze from his light-colored eyes, she could see what he meant. The tent at the crotch of his old-fashioned breeches was unmistakable. Licking her lips, Zephyr reached up to unfasten the dark material. Outside the ocean raged and the skies thundered, but she could feel it inside her, as well. An excited grin curved her mouth as she tugged Shaw's breeches down to his thighs.

"See? Not teasing." He bent forward onto his hands and knees, kissing her deep and openmouthed.

Zephyr wanted to touch every inch of him, warm, smooth skin and hard muscles beneath. She especially wanted a good look at— How did men seem to refer to it most frequently? His cock, she decided. It sounded manly and naughty all at the same time. And in traveling from England and then overland to India, she'd heard men call their . . . nether regions quite a few interesting things and in several different languages.

Shaw lifted his head a little. "What are you thinking?"

She tangled her fingers into his hair again, drawing his face down to hers once more. "I was thinking that I saw the statue of David and some very provocative drawings in India," she answered, nibbling at his lower lip, "and that an actual naked man is much more interesting."

"Thank you for that. And I doubt any statue could do this." With a wicked grin he bent his head to run his mouth over her breasts again, then slid lower to kiss her stomach, then lower still. His fingers joined in as he moved to her inner thighs and then up . . . there.

Zephyr squealed. Immediately she clapped both hands over her mouth. Luckily Niu barked in response, flapping about the room before he settled in again at the worktable. Shaw lifted his head, eyes dancing, to look at her before he returned to his task.

Not even worry over being discovered could keep her from moaning and wriggling her hips. This was much, much better than anything she'd imagined. She clutched her fingers into the blankets, all coherent, logical thought blasted into oblivion by the heat searing through her. Except for one niggling little point.

"Shaw," she squeaked, "this is not sex."

"I beg to differ," he said, his voice muffled. "And how do you know, anyway?"

Oh, God. He expected her to be able to carry on a conversation? "I've seen drawings. And I've seen animals. It's not your . . . oh . . . It's not your mouth that goes down there."

"No?" Removing his mouth, he slipped a finger inside her. "This, then?" He wiggled his finger.

"Oh!" Spasming, she tried to close her mouth around the keening, panting noises that she couldn't seem to help making. "Now . . . you're . . . teasing."

"Does it feel good?"

"It feels . . . very nau . . . naughty."

Shaw lifted up, moving over her until he could take her mouth with his again. His finger, though, kept up its motion. "Yes, but does it feel good?" he insisted.

"You know it does."

"Then stop complaining."

A second finger joined the first. When he closed his mouth over her breast, sucking and nibbling in time with the motion of his fingers, she broke loose. Shivering and shuddering inside and out, all she could do was dig her fingers into his hair and gasp for breath. "Shaw, Shaw," she rasped.

"There you go," he murmured, kissing her deeply.

He moved again, settling over her with his knees between hers. Still kissing her ferociously, he sank down, his cock brushing her thighs and then slowly sliding inside her. Pressure, a sharp pain that made her gasp again, and then him filling her inch by inch. Now *this* was sex.

"Does that feel good?" she asked him shakily, running her hands down his back, feeling the play of muscles beneath her fingers.

"Yes." He pulled away, then pushed forward again. "Very good. Very, very."

As he moved he continued kissing her, his expression intense—as though he couldn't stop looking at her, couldn't stop caressing her and moving inside her. Tension tightened his muscles beneath her touch, and began creeping through him into her again.

Shaw felt so good, his warmth and weight on her so indescribably . . . necessary to her that she didn't think she could have pushed him away if she'd wanted to. And heaven help her, she didn't want him going anywhere. Nowhere but deep inside her.

His pace increased, deep and pounding to the same hard rhythm of her heart and the crashing waves just beyond the windows. All at once she broke loose again, pulsing and shuddering, stifling her cry of ecstasy against his shoulder. Then Shaw shuddered, too, his muscles tensing mightily and then relaxing again. He sank down, resting his forehead against her neck.

The waves continued to heave and rumble outside, but there in Shaw's cabin with her arms around his strong shoulders, her breath and heartbeat returning to something close to normal, she felt much more relaxed and peaceful. And content. Very content. Her, naked with Bradshaw Carroway. And enjoying it. Perhaps the sea had driven her mad. If it had, however, at the moment she wanted to remain that way.

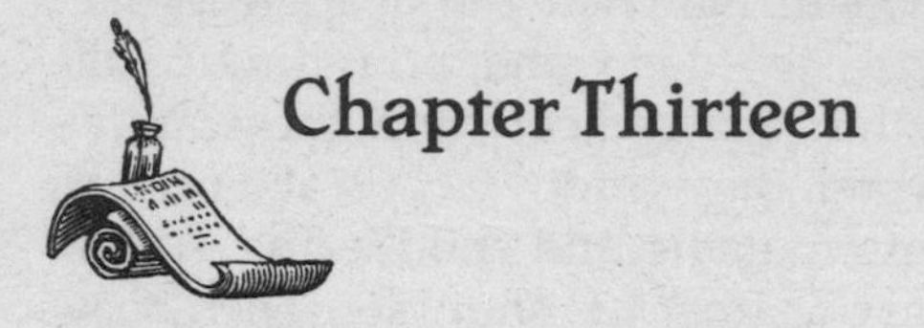

Chapter Thirteen

Her face it was a work of art,
I loved that girl with all my heart.
But I only liked the upper part,
I did not like the tail.

"THE MERMAID"

Bradshaw rolled onto his side, reaching down to grab the blanket and drag it up over both of them. He wasn't surprised when Zephyr didn't cling to him or cry, but rather ran an exploratory hand down his chest to his abdomen. Generally this was the time when he made a bit of pleasant small talk and vacated the lady's bedchamber. After all, he'd never made a secret of the fact that he wasn't interested in anything more than a pleasant romp.

Tonight he felt oddly enthralled, every nerve attuned to the woman lying in his arms. It seemed the height of importance that he remain there, however much the wind howled and pushed at the ship. He gazed, unmoving, at her face until her direct gray eyes lifted to meet his.

"Hello," she said softly, smiling.

He twined his fingers with hers. "Hello. How is your head?"

"Oh." She lifted her free hand to touch her temple. "I forgot all about it."

Shaw grinned. "That was my goal, you know."

"Ah." She chuckled. "Well done, then."

Shaw leaned forward and kissed her again. Where before she'd been tempting and troublesome, now he couldn't seem to kiss her enough or touch her enough to satisfy him.

"What do we do now?" she asked.

"Attempt to get some sleep."

"I can't stay here."

He nearly protested that, but of course she was correct. "I suppose not."

"Are you still going to be nicer to me, or is that finished with now?"

"As long as we may argue from time to time, I'll continue following your rules."

"But you got what you wanted."

"What I want continues to be somewhere just in front of me. Like having you again. And after that, well—I'm not finished with you, Zephyr." Aside from that, he . . . he knew, deep down in his bones, that he was gazing at his future wife.

He'd begun following her rules as a way of seducing her. Now he meant to do whatever was necessary to bring her all the way to an engagement. And beyond. How he'd manage it when his career was at sea and her intention was to follow her father across the land, he had no idea. At this moment, none of that signified. It would happen, because he couldn't imagine otherwise.

She turned onto her stomach. "What were you reading when I fell through the door?"

Bradshaw traced her spine with his fingertips. Her skin was soft and smooth and warm, and rather mesmerizing. Even more so because he'd been in this situation—or close to it—before, and he'd never felt like this. He wanted to protect her and chat with her and see her smile and simply gaze at her.

"Shaw?"

He shook himself. *"The Odyssey."*

"Ah. Is it an illustrated copy?"

And she still aggravated the devil out of him. "Slightly."

Zephyr laughed, burying her head in her arms to muffle the sound. "At least you're honest," she chortled.

"As I keep tell—"

The *Nemesis* went over hard to starboard, laying them down nearly ninety degrees. Cursing, Shaw grabbed Zephyr around the waist and braced his shoulders against the side of the shelf that bordered the head of his bunk.

Everything went flying, and only his free hand clenched into the windowsill behind him kept them both from crashing headfirst to the floor. She gasped, flailing to try to catch her own weight as they slid to the head of the bunk. He could hear both the screams of his passengers and crew and the awful creaking of the *Nemesis* as her ribs strained to hold her together at the unnatural angle.

The window directly behind his head broke in. Freezing water cascaded over both of them. Then with a mighty groan the frigate righted herself. "Good girl," he muttered, even as he and Zephyr tumbled to the floor. Shaw rolled beneath her to break her fall, and a bare elbow dug into his ribs.

"Shaw," she rasped, shaking as water washed against them.

He sat up, pulling her out of the sloshing inch of water with him. "Are you injured?"

"I— That—"

"Are you injured?" he repeated more forcefully, gripping her bare shoulder.

Zephyr blinked. "No. No, I don't think so. Are y—"

"Good." His breath returning in a rush, Shaw scrambled to his feet. His tossed-about clothes were lodged beneath the table, and he dug them out. They were sopping wet, but it hardly mattered. "Get dressed, and get to your cabin. The crew will be everywhere in moments."

Crawling across the floor, she grabbed her night rail. "I'll go see to my father."

With a nod he stomped into his still-wet boots, then reached down to pull her to her feet. "Be careful," he said, squeezing her fingers. "There'll be debris and likely panicked passengers and crew."

He was halfway to the door when she grabbed his shoulder and turned him back to face her. She was as wet as he was, her night rail nearly transparent as it clung to her form. Her long hair hung over her shoulders and across her face, obscuring one gray eye. He took it all in at once, in a single heartbeat, but he knew he would remember it forever.

"You be careful," she said, and rose up on her toes to kiss him.

Shaw summoned a brief smile. "You look like a mermaid," he murmured, then wrenched open his cabin door and slipped into the corridor.

"We're sinking!" Lord John wailed, staggering into him, spittle and vomit on his chin. "Do something!"

"Calm yourself, Fenniwell," Shaw snapped, pushing the marquis's son away from him. "Return to your cabin. Now."

"I will not! We should be the first to the launches!"

"In this weather a launch would overturn before it could cast off from the ship. If you're too frightened to be alone, go to the galley."

Still wild-eyed, Fenniwell nodded. "If we die tonight, Captain, you'd best hope you don't survive, either."

Shaw took a hard breath. He damned well had better things to do than argue with this fool and coward. "I'll remember you said that." Beyond Lord John, Zephyr emerged from his cabin and snuck over to open and then close her door.

"My goodness, that was unsettling," she exclaimed, continuing on to Sir Joseph's closed door.

"Miss Ponsley, I see you've survived," Shaw commented, his temper easing at the sight of her.

She nodded. "I have to admit, Captain, the *Nemesis* is a very fine ship." With a veiled glance at him, she rapped on her father's door. "Papa? Papa, are you well?"

"Yes," his muffled voice came. "The bird is loose, and I can't get the door open."

However much Shaw wanted to stay and assist her, every life on the ship was his responsibility. And men had been on deck when they went over. "I'll send you some help," he said, then pushed past Fenniwell.

The wind nearly blasted him off his feet as soon as

he stepped onto the deck. Almost dreading what he would see, he looked up. The jib sails were tangled and flapping around the rigging, but to his surprise all three masts still stood.

"Captain!"

Sheltering his face from the stinging rain and spray, he climbed up to the wheel deck. "Gerard," he said, relieved to see his first mate still on his feet. "Did we lose anyone?"

"No, sir. Not up here," the lieutenant returned, having to shout to be heard. "We all tied on not twenty minutes ago. Pettigrew went over the side, but we hauled him back in again."

As they spoke, Dobbs approached him from behind and knotted a stout rope from around his waist to the railing at the fore of the wheel deck. "Some of the boys has broken bones, Captain," the bosun's mate said, "and we've some water in the fore hold."

"We can manage that. Send some lads to see to Sir Joseph's plants in the aft hold."

"Aye, aye."

"Gather the wounded into the galley. Rouse Dr. Howard if he's managed to sleep through this, and have Potter give him as much help as he can."

Dobbs saluted. "Aye, aye, sir."

"And one of my windows shattered. Get it boarded up and see if you can mop up the water. And see to my parrot."

The bosun's mate nodded again and hurried off, bracing himself against the wind. Shaw listened as Gerard and then Newsome and Keller arrived to give him the latest status of his ship and crew. They had several serious injuries, but the fact that no one had been washed overboard or killed below decks was miraculous.

"Gerard, go below and get yourself warmed up. You as well, Leavey. Send Davies up to take the wheel." As the two men stumbled past him, he caught his first mate by the arm. "You saved lives tonight," he said. "I'm beginning to think you're ready for your own ship. Well done, William."

The lieutenant chattered a smile. "Thank you, Shaw. And you're wet as I am. I'll change into something dry and finish my watch."

There was stubbornness and there was stupidity, and Shaw was already shivering, himself. "Very well. If the kegs haven't broken, see that everyone gets a draught of rum. That should calm some nerves."

The moment Shaw took the wheel the sea nearly ripped it from his hands again. Bracing his legs, he kept them facing into the towering waves. If they were caught broadside again, they likely wouldn't be as lucky the second time.

Once the struggling crew got the jibs cut loose and rehung the steering improved, and the sickening lurch of the ship at least evened out a bit. Even after Davies made his way up on deck Shaw kept the wheel. In the past he'd done so because he loved the challenge of it, the struggle against the wild sea. This time it was more—his skill at the wheel kept everyone down below safe. Beyond that, it kept that damned annoying and delicious chit safe.

"Cap'n," Davies finally spoke up, "give yerself a rest there. I'll take 'er, and I'll keep 'er upright."

Shaw couldn't feel his arms any longer. With a reluctant nod he stepped sideways to allow the pilot to take the wheel. Slowly the black sky lifted to deep gray, and the waves became visible as they rolled in to lift the *Nemesis* into the air. Stretching his back and abruptly aware that he'd been awake now for just over twenty-four hours, Shaw handed the deck back to Gerard, untied the line securing him to the ship, and went below.

Just being out of the wind left him warmer, and he handed his slicker to one of the cabin boys. He wanted to lie down for a minute or two, but that would wait. Instead he followed the sounds of complaining and groans of pain to the galley. Two dozen men lay or sat on the floor and tables wedged among the cannons, while another fifteen or so helped out with bandages and hot tea and rum.

"Excuse me," Zephyr's voice came from behind him, and he automatically stepped aside. Sending him a look full of secrets, she brushed past him, toting an armful of gauze and bandages. He followed her to the table where she set them down.

Seeing him, the sailors and jollies present started to rise to attention, but he waved them back down. "As you were. I believe we've seen the worst of it, lads," he announced, "and the *Nemesis* has weathered the storm better than you lot."

Amid the general laughter, Potter approached him. "Not as bad as we thought," he said, wiping his hands on a cloth. "Thank God most everyone was in their hammocks."

Shaw started to reply, then realized that someone was missing from the scene. "Where's Dr. Howard?"

Potter cleared his throat. "He's feeling poorly," the midshipman said, then took a half step closer and lowered his voice. "The doc says as he ain't a part of the crew he ain't coming out of his cabin until you apologize for flattening him."

Shaw took a breath. "I see." He motioned to the closest of the jollies. "I need a word with Major Hunter at his earliest convenience."

The marine nodded and made his way out of the galley.

As Shaw waited, he visited with the men, making his own assessment of both morale and injuries. He didn't like this, didn't like that his crew had been hurt, but he couldn't blame the weather. Waves weren't expected to make sense or to choose arbitrary sides. They simply were, and he could accept that.

His attention kept shifting to Sir Joseph sewing up a sailor's gashed arm while Zephyr cleaned and bandaged other wounds. Then there was the Mayfair group, huddled together at a table and not doing anything worth a damn. The worthy and the unworthy—as if he needed additional proof to know that.

Evidently seeing that they were being observed, Lord Benjamin stood up from the miserable bunch. "Captain Carroway," he called, motioning.

With another glance at Zephyr, Shaw made his way over to the corner table. "Yes?" he asked, noting that Mr. Jones had a bandage across his forehead and that he seemed to be the only injured member of the party.

"We've taken a vote," Harding continued. "We are not willing to risk our lives to find a new species of shrubbery. Admiral Dolenz ordered you to deliver us safely to Manila. That is where we wish to go. Without further delay."

He'd actually been expecting this. "You are an addendum to my orders, Harding. Tahiti first. Then Manila." Even if he hadn't had business in Tahiti, he wouldn't have given in to their simpering.

"That is not acceptable." Lord John stood up, his fists clenched.

"If we cross paths with another ship willing to take you, you're free to leave. Until then, sit down and drink your tea, go back to your cabin, or help patch up these men."

Before any of them could reply to that, Shaw turned his back and walked over to Sir Joseph. "I had Merriwether check on your botanicals," he said, bracing his legs as the ship rolled hard again. The aristocrats behind him began their panicked chattering again, but he ignored it. "You've had some branch breakage and will need to do some repotting. I wouldn't allow him to explore further into the hold than that. I recommend you wait until the weather calms. I don't want anyone trapped down there if we roll again."

The botanist sat back from wrapping Mr. Beesley's left ankle. "I would like to take a quick look, regardless. The botanicals are of primary importance."

Briefly calculating whether arguing that one concession would be worthwhile or not, Shaw nodded. "A quick look. Abrams will escort you, and you will remain for no more than five minutes."

"Agreed. What of the birds on deck?"

"They were moved below thirty minutes before we went over. I suggest you thank Mr. Gerard for looking after them." He sent a glance at Zephyr, catching her quick smile before she looked away.

"I will do so."

Shaw accepted the cup of hot tea Potter brought him. "I have one or two more things to see to, and then I am going to attempt to find a dry place to sleep for an hour or so."

As he turned for the door, Major Hunter staggered through the doorway. Straightening, he saluted. "You wanted to see me, Captain?"

"Dr. Howard has declined his assistance. Please put a sentry outside his door and make certain he remains in his cabin. If he has nothing to offer the *Nemesis*, then we have nothing to offer him."

"Understood, Captain. I'll see to it."

"You can't mean to starve him," Zephyr exclaimed, as the major left the galley again.

"No, but I can make the remainder of his voyage as unpleasant as possible. That is, Sir Joseph, if I may impose on you to stand in as our surgeon."

The botanist inclined his head. "I believe between Zephyr and your Mr. Potter and myself, we can manage it."

"Then excuse me." He turned to face the table holding his peers again. "You may remain here or return to your cabins, but I don't want anyone other than my crew in the hold or on deck until further notice."

Miss Emily Quanstone lifted her head from the table. "I am not going anywhere," she said in a miserable voice, and sank down again.

Even the chits who weren't ill sat moaning and complaining, sending the three maids they shared to fetch blankets and tea and to tidy up the disheveled cabins until he ordered the servants to remain in the galley, as well. Only Zephyr moved among his injured men, the knot she'd tied into her hair coming loose and the simple gown she'd donned streaked with blood and plaster from the bandages. And by God, she was the most compelling woman in the room. In the entire hemisphere.

She lifted her gaze from wrapping Everett's arm, her bright gray eyes meeting his for a moment that seemed to last a heartbeat and a lifetime all in the same space of seconds. Her lips curved up at the corners, and then she returned to her work.

After he left the galley he spent the next hour checking that the cannons remained secure, inspecting the damage aft where one of them had broken loose and cracked a beam, picking his way through the mess of the forward and aft holds, and setting the carpenters to make the birds a secure place below decks to be used during foul weather.

By the time he returned to his cabin, his broken window had been boarded up and the water and glass mopped away. Niu chattered quietly to himself in a cage hung from a pole someone, more than likely Ogilvy, had built across the corner of the room behind the door. It was fairly ingenious; if the ship rolled on its side again, Niu and the sailors in their hammocks would be the only ones whose roosts would swing around and allow them to remain upright.

The bed had been changed, as well, and Shaw pulled on a dry pair of trousers and sank wearily onto the mattress. He fell asleep thinking not about the storm or the damage to the *Nemesis*, but about a troublesome young lady who'd crept beneath his skin without him even being aware of it. It was beginning to seem that it was time to decipher the question of if and when he might retire.

* * *

Zephyr awoke as her cabin door opened. Sitting straight up, she swiped a hand across her eyes. "What's happened?"

"More than enough already," Shaw returned, remaining in the open doorway.

She grinned, her heart skittering excitedly. "Are you going to stand th—"

"I knocked, Miss Ponsley," he interrupted, "but someone told me you'd taken a blow to the head yesterday. I worried when you didn't answer."

Belatedly she noted Potter standing behind him. "Oh." Anticipation flashed into embarrassment. "Thank you for your concern, Captain. I feel quite well, especially after getting some sleep."

"I'm pleased to hear it." He straightened from his slouch against the door frame. "The weather's begun to clear, and I thought you might want a first look at our next destination."

"Tahiti?" She sprang to her feet and would have run straight up on deck if not for Shaw's rather intense gaze at her low neckline. "I—I'll get dressed and be up in a moment."

He nodded. "No hurry. We've an hour or so of daylight remaining."

Goodness. Had she slept that long? Of course she'd sat in the galley with the men all day yesterday and well into the night, and it had been nearly morning before her father had declared her to be asleep on her feet and sent her back to her cabin. When Shaw continued to grin at her, she closed the door on him before she could blush and give herself away to Potter. Then she dug into her trunk for a clean muslin to wear.

Tahiti had actually been fairly low on her father's list—after all, its abundant supply of breadfruit trees was already well known. Shaw had been the one pressing for a visit. His argument that several indigenous species waited to be discovered made sense, but she thought it likely that he was more interested in experiencing the famed naked hospitality of the islanders. That idea had previously made her scoff and shake her head, but now it rather annoyed her. It annoyed her a great deal, actually.

The sea remained unsettled, and she braced her hands against the walls as she climbed the steps and emerged onto the main deck. Shaw and her father both stood at the bow, discussing something and gesturing. As she joined them it was Shaw who took a step back to give her access to the view. She could feel him standing there just behind her, and the hair on her arms lifted. Zephyr took a breath. She'd never felt anything so heady in her entire life. It took every ounce of willpower she possessed not to lean back against him and pull his arms around her.

"There," he said, pointing ahead and just to starboard. "The storm put us off course, so we're approaching from more westerly than I'd planned."

A low bank of pillowy white and gray clouds rimmed the horizon. One of them, however, was much darker and lower on the horizon than the others. So that was it. Tahiti.

As she took in the sight, she noticed her father glancing at her. Zephyr shook herself. Shaw and she were antagonists. Even if she felt momentarily agreeable, no one else could know that or they would begin to wonder why. "I'm rather amazed you managed to find it at all," she said aloud to the captain. "Are you certain we haven't simply circled back around to Tonga?"

"I'll send Dr. Howard out at first light just to be certain, shall I?" Shaw returned easily.

"You must be thrilled to finally be here," she pressed. "You've certainly been more anxious to see Tahiti than anywhere else we've been."

"No one's likely to attempt to murder us here. And I can get the damned civilians off the ship for a time. Present company excluded from my general annoyance, of course."

"Peace on board is the only reason you're happy to be here?"

She could feel his scowl. "Are we arguing again?" he asked.

"No, you're not. After the past two days I am declaring a truce between you two," her father broke in. "At least until we reach solid ground again."

"How long will that be?" she asked.

"Tomorrow morning," Shaw replied, then turned his attention to her father. "You seem to have weathered the storm quite well, Sir Joseph. And thank you again for seeing to my men."

"I did what I could. In truth, though, I shook in my boots all that first night. I'm afraid I'm rather pleased that botany is a land-based science."

Something crossed Shaw's face. She could almost hear what he must be thinking; his life was on the sea. As helpful as he'd been, and as troubled as his thoughts were about his choice of career, he likely couldn't imagine spending the remainder of his life on land.

A chill ran down her spine. If she continued as her father's assistant, her life would be on land. Oh, she didn't like the abrupt thought of half the world dividing her from Shaw.

"I'm going to put in at Matavai Bay," the captain was saying. "There's some talk of a better harbor to the south, but the Matavai charts are better."

"I have no preference," her father returned. "I bow to your expertise."

Shaw's expression eased a little, as though he'd anticipated an argument. "I intend to have my men camp at the village. We can travel overland from there. The lads could likely use a bit of a holiday after the past fortnight."

Her father frowned. "I don't approve of what you're intimating, Shaw. This is a scientific expedition."

The captain shrugged. "My men aren't scientists. And whether I approve or not, I'm not fool enough to try to prevent them from behaving like men." He backed up, brushing his hand against Zephyr's as he did so. She didn't know whether it was intentional or not, but she liked it. "If you'll excuse me," he continued, "I need to finish a rather lengthy log entry. Miss Ponsley, when you've a moment, your sketches ended up scattered across my cabin. I'd rather you organized them than have my men attempt it."

She wanted to join him immediately, but that wouldn't have been very seemly. "I'll join you shortly."

"Very good." As he walked away, she couldn't help but watch. So much had happened, she could hardly believe she'd had her hands all over him two nights ago. And she wanted more.

When her father cleared his throat, she jumped. *Blast it all.* "Did you inspect your specimens, Papa?"

"Yes. Shaw's assessment was accurate. Broken branches and stems and flowers with petals fallen off, but only three completely destroyed."

"Oh, I'm so sorry."

The botanist drew a breath. "I would be more concerned, but after setting a dozen broken bones, my perspective has widened somewhat. At least for the moment."

Her world had become a bit larger during the last two days, as well, though not because of the storm. "I know what you mean," she said aloud.

"Would you send a dozen or so men to join me in the hold, my dear?" he said after a moment. "I think I'd best organize all the supplies we'll need now. Once we arrive at Matavai Bay I have a feeling that you and I will be more or less abandoned."

"I'm certain Shaw will arrange for us to have assistance, Papa. He may be barbaric, but he does know his orders."

"Unless he joins his men in . . . frolicking with the native women. He does have a reputation, you know."

Zephyr's muscles tightened across her shoulders, and she fought to keep from scowling. It had been bad enough that she had her own doubts. Hearing her botany-obsessed father voice them made it even worse. An unpleasant knot thudded into her stomach, cold and angry all at the same time. "Yes, I suppose he does," she forced herself to say.

After her father left the deck and she'd sent assistance for him, she stood there alone at the bow to glare at Tahiti. Now she almost wished they'd risked more time at Tonga and had to miss this so-called friendly island altogether. And of course it wasn't jealousy. Her only concern was that here no one would pay any attention to the expedition. Yes, that was it.

"Blasted Tahiti," she muttered, and went below to find Shaw.

"Close the door," he said, rising from his seat at the writing desk.

"Everyone knows I'm here. And I should go assist my father."

With an annoyed glance he moved past her and shut the cabin door himself. "I want to show you something."

Perturbed with him or not, her body remembered the first night of the storm. "What might that be?" she asked, trying to keep her voice even and not entirely succeeding.

Rather than take her into his arms, Shaw crossed to his bookshelf and pulled down a box tightly wedged behind several books. "This is why I've wanted to reach Tahiti," he said, and handed it to her.

She opened it, reaching inside to pull out a hand-sized mirror rimmed in gold and encrusted with gemstones. "A mirror? Do you plan to trade it for a woman or something? You could likely purchase a chieftain's daughter with this."

He started to say something, then shut his mouth again. "You're beginning to make me a bit angry, Zephyr," he finally commented. "I thought I'd made it clear that you have all my attention. If you're going to argue with me at least choose a topic that makes sense."

Well, that was a very nice thing to say. She hefted the mirror. "What's this for, then? It must be worth a hundred pounds or more."

"I'm to deliver it to a local fellow who goes by the name King George. It's to settle a debt on behalf of the Duke of Sommerset, who apparently knew my orders before I did. He claimed there would be a curse if he didn't repay this King George within ten years. It's some sort of traditional, mystical mark of the passage of time, I believe."

She looked at the mirror again. "From your hurry, might I assume that this mystical ten-year period has nearly passed?"

"I have two more days. The next full moon marks the end of it." He took the mirror back and replaced it in its box. "Do you want to keep traveling with your father?" he asked, meeting her gaze again.

She swallowed. "He's my family."

"That's not what I asked."

Zephyr put her hands on her hips to cover her sudden discomfiture. "Yes, it is. If you want a better answer, ask a better question." She turned around and opened the door again. "I'd like to join you when you go see this King George," she said over her shoulder, and went to assist her father.

At least traveling with the botanist gave her something purposeful to do. And it kept her from wondering what her life would be like if she'd had a more conventional upbringing—or at least a family, a home, and friends. That was not something she needed to be dwelling on at the moment.

By morning the waters were calm enough for the *Nemesis* to sail into Matavai Bay. And they weren't the only ship present, either. A small merchant ship flying the British flag had already put in, and at the far end of the wide harbor a French frigate rode low in the water.

"Will that be trouble?" her father asked, climbing the steep steps ahead of her to the wheel deck.

Shaw already stood at the starboard railing, his gaze on the French ship. "She's a good match for the *Nemesis*," he said calmly. "We'll take the middle of the harbor, which gives us better position. Their captain would be foolish to begin something."

"And what about *our* captain?" Zephyr prompted, looking for a trace of reluctance in his gaze and not seeing it. Then again, the stronger he appeared, the less likely anyone was to attempt to move against the *Nemesis*—or so she hoped. She was fairly certain he did, as well.

"I'm here for lizards and birds." He faced forward, then angled his chin in the same direction. "Our welcoming party is on the way."

The difference between the Tongan greeting and the one they received now from the Tahitians couldn't have been greater. At least as many women as men filled the large, double-hulled canoes, all of them calling greetings in broken English and waving and blowing kisses and throwing flowers at the *Nemesis*.

Zephyr took a spot at the bow both for a better view and because she had no wish to be trampled by eager sailors. As the boats reached them, women actually began climbing aboard, and the chaos on deck increased tenfold. "Good heavens," she murmured, not certain this sight was something she wanted to sketch.

Fingers brushed her elbow, sending a warm shiver through her. Without looking she knew Shaw stood there beside her. "They're a good lot, you know," he said after a moment. "But they've been at sea for quite a while, telling tales about Tahiti that've been spun about so many times there's likely no truth left in them at all."

"I'm beginning to feel overdressed," she commented, noting the woman with a pair of golden breasts who placed a flower necklace around her father's neck and then hugged him.

"You'd look very fine in a grass skirt and shell necklace and nothing else," Shaw murmured, amusement touching his deep voice. "Because whether you believe me or not, I prefer your delights to anything else I see, my delicate flower." He straightened again. "And now if you'll excuse me, I believe that is the chief currently inventorying your father's birds."

Zephyr watched the chaos unfolding below with abruptly renewed interest. *Oh, my.*

Chapter Fourteen

The Muses, still with freedom found,
Shall to thy happy coast repair;
Blest Isle! With matchless beauty crown'd,
And manly hearts to guard the fair.

"RULE, BRITANNIA"

King George, the mighty English father?"

Shaw shook his head, keeping his voice low as the chief continued giving his tour of the foliage outlying the village, explaining the uses of the various plants in broken English while Sir Joseph took notes furiously. "No. He lives here, in a village near a waterfall. He has one eye, and some Englishmen call him King George." He put a hand over one eye to demonstrate.

The voluptuous young lady with whom he was speaking clapped her hands and gestured inland. "Yes! Yes. Rafiti. Very old man. He live close by." She ran her palm along his cheek. "I show you."

Thank God the fellow was still alive. He had the distinct feeling, though, that if this maiden led him into the jungle it wouldn't be to find a one-eyed man. "I will find a guide," he said. "Thank you."

"Any luck?" Zephyr asked, falling in beside him.

"I believe so. I'll ask for a guide to the waterfall after the greetings are all finished."

Whether because she'd decided that the other English ladies on the ship were correct or she was merely attempting to be amusing, she'd brought the white parasol along with her. In her white and yellow muslin gown with the matching parasol on her shoulder, she looked as if she was just out for a stroll along Park Avenue in Mayfair. At the same time, he would never mistake her for such. Her gray eyes were too bright, too inquisitive, and far too comfortable with her surroundings for her to be anyone but . . . herself.

"For fever, you said?" Sir Joseph was commenting, bending down to clip off a leaf and press it between the pages of his notebook.

"Yes. Fever. Make a tea, much sugar because of . . . of . . . sour."

"It's bitter?"

"Yes. Bitter."

This was all fascinating, Shaw was sure, but they didn't need him there, and today he definitely had better things to do. The large-breasted chit took his hand and tried to lead him off into the village, but with a smile he declined. He'd allowed three dozen sailors a bit of leave for the day, and he could hear a number of them singing down by the main fire pit.

A half-dozen marines and four of his sailors accompanied them on the botany tour this afternoon, but he was ready to wager that an elephant could stumble through the middle of the group without any of them noticing. He could hardly blame them, but at the same time he'd yet to see a Frenchman. Before he left for his personal mission, he needed to know what was afoot, if anything.

"The French ship," he finally said aloud, breaking into some sort of discussion about black stool. "Where is the crew?"

"Le Courageux?" the chief asked. "They across harbor. Other ship down to Papeete, they wait."

Shaw frowned. "Papeete?"

"Yes. English there. Build big church, say no . . . how you say, *sein nu*."

"Bare breasts," Shaw translated, hiding a grin as Zephyr blushed. "Missionaries."

The chief nodded. "Yes. Missionaries." He frowned. *"Papaa."*

Whatever that meant, it didn't sound very flattering. More troubling was the fact that there were two French ships in these waters. True, England and France were no longer at war, but that didn't mean they had to like each other. And now the *Nemesis* was outnumbered.

"Ah. This Captain Wright." The chief gestured at the stocky man approaching them up the trail. "From English ship *Swift*."

The captain doffed his hat. "Welcome to Tahiti, Captain Carroway."

"Do I know you?" Shaw asked.

"I recognized the name of your ship. You're the one that finally stopped the *Revanche*. God bless you, Carroway. Damned pirates."

He didn't particularly care to be reminded of that, even with warships and possible danger close by. "Just doing my duty, Wright."

"Doing it dashed well." Captain Wright fell in

with them as they continued on their botanical tour. "Glad to see you here now. Those Frenchies have been bloody high-handed since they sailed in. I'm already nearly a fortnight late leaving for the West Indies, but I can't get my breadfruit trees aboard. They've got most able-bodied men cutting timber."

"For what purpose?"

Wright shrugged his square shoulders. "Some say it's for building a fortress on one of the other islands hereabout. Some say it's for building one here. But it's something large and solid and permanent."

"Shaw, I do not want us entangled in political squabbles," Sir Joseph said, lowering his pages of notes. "We will be here for a fortnight or more, and then we must move on."

He didn't particularly want to stay any longer than that, either. Both Sommerset and Admiral Dolenz had mentioned uncomfortable French activity out here, however. This was the first evidence of it he'd seen, but in truth he was somewhat relieved to be responsible for a group of pampered aristocrats and a world-famous botanist. And the botanist's daughter, of course.

"We'll move on," he said aloud, "but I'd still like to know the good local gossip. Captain Wright, walk with me."

He walked toward the nearest beach, Wright keeping pace with him. "You're ferrying civilians?" the merchant captain asked.

"More a matter of convenience than choice," Shaw replied, forcing a grimace. Captain Wright was likely an honest merchant, but Shaw didn't intend to be the one to inform him that the *Nemesis* was carrying nearly a dozen civilians worth a sizable ransom. He'd leave the fools to make that mistake themselves—after he warned them against it, of course.

"Ah. Used to sail with the navy myself, I did."

"When did the second French ship depart?"

"The *Audacieux*? Two days ago. They arrived here the day after I did. And I should tell you, the *Courageux* there in the harbor is captained by a fellow named Phillipe Mariot de Gardanne. Heard of him?"

Bloody hell. "I have."

Wright squinted one eye. "I thought so. I know he's heard of you. And he does not seem to be a man who's here to see the sights, regardless."

Whether Admiral Dolenz's concern over the growing French presence in the South Pacific was warranted or not, Shaw had sailed into more trouble than he needed—or expected. And he'd thought to be able to concentrate on Zephyr once he delivered the mirror.

Shaw took a breath. Whatever the French were up to, he had a duty to at least do what he could to throw some stones in their path. "I promised my lads a few days here," he said aloud. "I wouldn't object if you used our presence to discourage the French from coming about, if you think that would help you fill your hold."

Wright inclined his head. "I hoped you would say that." He gave a mock salute. "In fact, I shall see to it immediately."

The stout captain hurried back toward the village, but Shaw remained on the shore. Just north of the harbor, he couldn't see any of the ships anchored on the far side of the point. No, at the moment the world consisted of jungle, beach, and ocean. And him.

He stood there, welcoming the solitude that sank

into his bones. Back in London the Season would just be ending, with his large extended family leaving to see the derby races and then traveling home to Dare Park. In fact he was gazing nearly straight at them, across India and Arabia and most of Europe. Half the world away.

Material rustled behind him. Shaw turned around. "You shouldn't be wandering about here on your own," he said, holding out his hand.

Zephyr twined her fingers with his. "I wasn't wandering. I was purposefully walking in your direction."

"Don't do it again without an escort. Promise me."

Her brow furrowed. "I promise. What's amiss?"

"The captain of the *Courageux* is Phillipe Mariot de Gardanne."

"That's quite a mouthful. He's not a nice man, I presume?"

"He's something of a lunatic. It was his cousin I captured on the *Revanche*. Molyneux was hanged shortly before I left England."

"So you've managed to find a mortal enemy halfway around the world." She moved closer, wrapping her free hand around his arm. "What will you do?"

"I will remain alert and wait to see what he does. Whether I'm a barbarian or not, my first duty here is to your father."

"But?" she prompted.

"You're very inquisitive."

"It's one of my most charming qualities." She leaned her cheek against his shoulder. "I know you'd prefer not to fight."

Shaw nodded. "I'll behave if he does. The Admiralty's worried about the French presence here, however, so I need to keep my eyes open."

"And what about King George?"

"I'm going on a hike this afternoon, before the second French ship can return and before Gardanne can realize that the *Nemesis* is only at half strength."

"I'm still going with you."

Taking her on a trek through the jungle would have made him uneasy, except for the fact that with Frenchmen wandering about he wanted her close by and safe. "Then let's collect a jolly or two and go."

They seemed to have finished their conversation, but he continued to hold her hand in his. Considering all the activity in and about the village, the privacy they'd found on this quiet beach was rather astounding. Zephyr brushed her cheek against his shoulder. Whatever troubles he had on his mind, she liked that he still took time to tell her his thoughts. Her father almost never did that. She was never Sir Joseph's partner or his equal; and honestly it had never occurred to her to be other than his follower. He'd even named her that. A following breeze, he called her.

She had no connection to Shaw other than an almost alarming degree of affection, but with him she felt more . . . equal. More listened to, more included. More cared for, even.

"It's very pretty here, isn't it?" she commented, mostly to break the silence and to escape her own flying thoughts.

"I'm going to say a word, just for your general opinion and consideration," he said, his light blue gaze touching hers.

"I'm listening."

"Marriage."

Zephyr blinked. Had he actually just suggested a proposal? A marriage? With her? A thousand thoughts all flitted through her mind, none of them making any sense, but several of them centering on whether she was reading too much or too little into one blasted word. "I think"—she stumbled, backing away from him and toward the village—"that if you mean to ask a question, you should ask it. And you shouldn't make it so stupidly ambiguous just on the chance that a negative response might embarrass you or wound your feelings."

"Is that so?" He stalked after her.

"It *is* so. And another thing. Before you ask such a question, consider giving me—or whoever you intend on asking—a reason to say yes."

She turned away, but Shaw put his hand on her arm and twisted her back to face him before she'd even reached the trees. Zephyr started to protest, but his mouth lowered over hers before she could utter a sound. Good heavens, the man knew how to kiss.

It was blatantly unfair. Simply because she couldn't seem to resist him didn't mean that she found him acceptable. And the fact that she generally enjoyed his company more than that of anyone else on the ship—or in the entire South Pacific—didn't signify. She sighed against his mouth, sliding her arms around his shoulders.

"You are wearing too many clothes," he whispered, backing her up against a palm trunk and kissing her again.

Heat coiled down her spine. "Someone will see," she protested, digging her fingers into his jacket and feeling the hard play of muscles beneath.

She wanted to be with him, wanted him again so much that she ached inside. The strength of her desire was even a little dismaying considering that just a moment ago she'd been arguing with him. Clearly the sea voyage had rendered her mentally unbalanced—even though she'd never enjoyed anything as much as she had since she'd boarded the *Nemesis*.

Shaw lifted his head a little, his blue eyes glinting. "No one will see," he murmured, and abruptly slung her over his shoulder, then strode into the jungle.

"Shaw!" she squeaked, trying for a handhold and settling for swatting him on the arse. "Put me down!"

"Hush, Zephyr." He sounded distinctly amused as he clambered through the trees along the coastline and over a set of boulders. When he stopped, she took an upside-down look at what seemed to be a small glade.

He set her onto her feet again. Zephyr smoothed out her skirt and tried to summon a scowl. "That was very uncivilized of you."

"Yes, it was." He grinned. "Come here."

"I think I'm still angry with you."

A bright-colored bird flitted overhead to perch at one end of the small clearing. She turned to watch it, and Shaw moved up behind her. "You like me again," he returned, nibbling on her ear. At the same time he untied the ribbon at the back of her gown, then went to work on the half-dozen ivory buttons running down her spine.

"You're very uncivilized."

His mouth trailed along her shoulders as he pulled her dress and her shift down her arms. "A young lady doesn't leave England and travel half the world to look for something civilized," he commented, drawing her back against his chest and putting his hands over her bared breasts.

"I'm looking for plants," she managed, putting her hands over his.

"And birds. Don't forget the birds." Shaw stripped out of his jacket and laid it down over the short grass. Taking her hand, he lowered her down, the blue jacket beneath her still carrying his warmth.

"And lizards, too. And insects."

When Shaw sank down on all fours over her, she lifted up to kiss him again. Touching his skin seemed very important, even vital, and she untucked his shirt to stroke her hands over his chest and stomach. She supposed she could attempt to decipher why it was that she continued to find him so interesting when he teased her with the one word every young woman was supposed to want to hear and she'd never expected to have spoken to her, but at this moment she had no trouble answering that question at all. He felt very, very good.

His mouth closed over her left breast, his fingers still playing with her right one. Mouths were quite wondrous, really. She'd had no idea, prior to a few days ago. Zephyr arched her back, trying to stifle the moaning sounds she very much wanted to make. After all, he might say no one would see them, but he hadn't mentioned hearing.

"Unfasten my trousers," he murmured, turning his attention to her other breast.

She didn't like being told what to do, but she had enjoyed the results last time. Her fingers shaking, she unbuttoned his white trousers and tugged them down past his hips. Feeling bolder this time, Zephyr experimentally stroked her finger down the length of his large, stiff cock.

He hissed out a breath. "Do that again, Zephyr."

This time she ringed her fingers around his girth, rubbing against him with her palm. His muscles shuddered, and she did it again.

"Where did you figure that out?" he asked, sitting back on his knees to grasp the hem of her gown. Then he moved up along her again, pulling her skirt up with him as he went.

"I told you I've seen drawings." She lifted her hips, leaving her gown and shift bunched around her waist.

"You're very astute, then." Shaw settled himself between her thighs.

She grinned breathlessly. "Thank you. I do try."

Shaw bent his arms and kissed her, slow and deep. At the same time he angled his hips forward, sliding tightly inside her. This time she felt no pain, only that same hot, delicious filling sensation as their thighs met. No, not the same. It was more . . . just more. This time she couldn't help the moan that escaped her lips, the sound echoed by a lower-pitched sound from Shaw.

As he slowly withdrew and then stroked forward again, tension and then abrupt release speared through her, leaving her shaking and clinging to him helplessly. "Oh, God," she groaned, arching again.

When her muscles began to relax and somewhat rational thought returned to her mind again, the first thing she noticed was the look in Shaw's eyes. The possessiveness and . . . affection in his gaze shook her all over again. At the same time, she felt abruptly powerful and lighter and so many things she couldn't describe them even to herself.

Bradshaw found that moment again, when he

wanted the earth to stop and time to still and everything just to remain precisely where it was—for him to remain where he was. And yet he wanted her too much to remain motionless. Keeping his gaze on her face, Shaw drove into her again and again, everything narrowing to where their bodies connected.

Finally he couldn't hold off any longer, and he held himself deep inside her as he came. Breathing hard, the back of his shirt damp with sweat, he lowered his head against hers, keeping his weight on his knees and elbows.

Twice. He could explain feeling that oddness once—after all, he'd been celibate for well over a year. But twice now, and with her, and in the exact same way . . . It shook him.

"You're very quiet," Zephyr observed, eyeing him.

He shifted off her and sat up. "Apologies." Unable to stop himself, he leaned over and kissed her. She brushed her fingers into his hair, kissing him back.

Shaw sighed. Considering that his bout of madness showed no sign of abating, and considering that he'd punched a man with a reputation for seducing and abandoning chits, he couldn't simply stand up and walk away without proving to her and to himself that he wasn't like Christopher Howard.

"Come here," he said, motioning for her to turn around so he could button up the back of her gown. "At the risk of another verbal thrashing, I need to say something serious to you."

The muscles across her shoulders tensed. "You're not going to sling that word about again with no context or verbs to clarify its usage, I hope."

"No. The next time I use that word, I won't be ambiguous."

After a moment she nodded. "I am listening seriously, then."

Now came the difficult bit. "We've been together twice now, and I hope to repeat the experience several more times, at least. The—"

"This is a serious conversation?"

"Hush. The problem is that I didn't take any . . . precautions, and neither did you."

"I could be with child, you mean." Her head lowered briefly and then she turned around to face him. "I'm not an idiot. Why didn't this occur to me before now?"

"I'm the more experienced party. I should have mentioned it."

"Yes, you should h—"

"My point being," he cut in, "that if—that I would marry you." Ha. No ambiguity that time. "There would be no scandal."

For a long moment she gazed at him, though he couldn't decipher what she might be thinking. It seemed likely that she would hit him, and he braced himself for that. He deserved it, after all—on this count, at least. Christ, he'd never forgotten something so vital to his continued . . . bachelorhood before. By all rights he should be terrified. But he wasn't. Not at all.

"Are there precautions you can take?"

"The bird has already flown the cage, love."

She scowled. "Are there any precautions you can take?"

Shaw nodded. "Yes."

Zephyr climbed to her feet and brushed out her rather wrinkled skirts. "Then in the future you will take them."

That was extremely unexpected. And extremely welcome. He stood as well, buttoning his trousers and tucking in his shirt once more. "In the future."

"Now finish buttoning me."

He did as she asked, bending to kiss her smooth, bare shoulders only once before he pulled her gown together in the back and fastened the remaining buttons. "I thought you would be . . . hysterical," he noted, even though he knew damned well that he should keep his mouth shut.

"I do know something of biology," she returned, facing him. "And addition and cycles. I believe we are in the clear, as you sailors say. But as that is only by good fortune, I will be more cautious. As will you."

"As will I." He retrieved his jacket and pulled it on.

"Don't we need to go find your one-eyed man?" she prompted, and he realized he'd been gazing at her for a rather lengthy time.

God, he'd forgotten for a moment. "Yes, we do." Shaw offered his arm. "Come along, my dear."

Just before dusk Shaw, with Zephyr, three jollies, and a village guide, descended a hill strewn with worn outcroppings of lava rock and reached the small group of huts tucked up against a stream and wide, low waterfall. He glanced up at the rising moon to the east. It was full; he'd reached his destination just in time. If King George was elsewhere, he hoped it was very close by.

A pair of naked boys scampered up to them, and their guide said something Shaw couldn't decipher, followed by the old fellow's name. "Rafiti," Shaw echoed for emphasis. "King George."

The lads hurried away, yelling and laughing. A

moment later an elderly man ducked out of a hut, peered at them through his one brown eye, and then disappeared inside once more.

"Perhaps he doesn't want a mirror," Zephyr commented.

"He'll take this one, regardless." She didn't understand, of course, that the damned mirror and the peaceful mission surrounding it had been the only thing that kept him sane on the voyage from England to Australia. Since then she'd taken the pretty thing's place in every imaginable way, but he hadn't forgotten. He owed the Duke of Sommerset a debt he would likely never be able to repay, and he would bloody well hand King George his mirror.

The old man emerged again, and Shaw blinked. Now he wore a cape made of feathers and palm fronds, while a crown of more feathers and fronds adorned his head in a rather obvious imitation of the English royal crown. With his high forehead and jowly cheeks he did bear a marked resemblance to the last portraits of King George before Prinny had locked him away somewhere.

Zephyr made a sound. "Goodness," she whispered. "Should I curtsy?"

"Yes, you should. Salute," he ordered his men, and the jollies snapped to. Technically Shaw should salute as well, but given the faux monarch's bearing, he would likely better appreciate a bow. Wishing he'd brought a hat, Shaw swept down in the most elaborate flourish he could manage. Beside him Zephyr sank almost to the ground with her low, reverential bow.

Rafiti said something, and their guide stepped forward. "He say up to your feet, Captain."

Shaw straightened again. "We're very happy to finally meet you," he said to the old man.

He nodded. "Nicholas dead?"

Nicholas. The Duke of Sommerset. "No. He could not make this voyage, so he sent me to find you."

The fellow pulled a strand of twine from around his neck and held it out. A dark blue button hung from the loop. "I have this for long time. He promise me to return. This his promise." He shook the necklace.

Shaw produced the box from the satchel he carried. "He made *me* promise to give this to you."

His gaze shifting between the box and Shaw, Rafiti held out his hand. With as much ceremony as he could manage, Shaw opened the lid and then handed it over, box and all. A small crowd had gathered around them, the torches they carried providing the only light now that the sun had set.

King George pulled the mirror free and held it up. Then, to Shaw's surprise he tucked the small thing against his cheek, a tear sliding down from his one eye. "He remember old King George. He keep promise."

Zephyr took a step closer, brushing Shaw's fingers with hers as she did so. "We do not know the story of the mirror, King George. Would you tell us, or is it private?"

He was glad she'd asked; he wasn't certain how he would have gone about it. King George motioned them to the open fire pit at the center of the huts. "Come. I tell you."

While women handed out banana leaves holding a fine roasted pork, Bradshaw sat on the ground so close to Zephyr that their knees bumped. "We'll still have to walk back to the shore after this," he said in a low voice. "It's going to be a late evening."

"He was so happy to see that mirror," she returned, smiling as one of the youngsters sat on her other side. "I want to know why. Don't you?"

"Yes."

"Then don't complain."

"I wasn't complaining. I was commenting." He glanced sideways at her happily eating a dinner roasted by half-naked women while insects and frogs chirped around them in the growing darkness. "Thank you for joining me here."

Zephyr met his gaze, a slow smile on her face. "You're welcome."

Once they'd finished eating, King George stepped up beside the fire. Still in his full royal regalia, he lifted the mirror over his head. "Many, many years ago, an English explore our island. He a good English, called Nicholas. Him and friends give gifts to us, give to me a shining mirror."

"I was wondering where he'd gotten a mirror in the first place," Shaw murmured, pretending not to notice as Zephyr's fingers crept around his.

"One day he come to eat, and then boom! Gun shoots at him. More gun. More gun. Three gun shoot at him. Nicholas say, 'Pirates!' and his other friend fall dead. Nicholas in big trouble. Say, 'King George, I need mirror for save me.' I love mirror, but I give it. Nicholas look into mirror and see pirates behind. Boom! He shoot one. Put more powder and ball in gun. Boom! He shoot one more. Put powder and ball in gun again. Then, two boom! He shoot pirate, and pirate shoot mirror. All broken. Nicholas, he promise me fine mirror again, but all he have is blue button." Rafiti held up the twine necklace holding the button. "I know he live very far away, but he say no more than ten year and I have best mirror. Mirror of King George, English father."

With that he lifted the mirror again, and everyone cheered. A tear in his eye, King George swept forward and threw his arms around Shaw. "Nicholas brother, and now Captain Bradshaw brother. Is good, good day."

Just beside Shaw, Zephyr was laughing, clearly caught up in the general . . . joy of the people around them. "You see," she said, gripping his arm as Rafiti left to show off his new treasure to the rest of the villagers, "you did a good thing. And you had the right of it, Shaw. This is better than any battle."

He was glad she'd said that quietly, because with three jollies close by he didn't want to hear of a rumor that he'd lost his nerve. But as he looked about him, and especially at the woman seated beside him, for the first time he realized that he hadn't actually lost anything. Or if he had, he'd gained much, much more.

Surrounded by torch-carrying natives, they navigated their way back to the harbor. Zephyr wrapped her hand around his arm, for once content to walk silently beside him. It was past midnight, but he didn't feel tired. And he liked having her there with him, the unexpected satisfaction of sharing an unparalleled experience in an only half-discovered paradise. The entire experience left him feeling oddly domestic—and even more oddly content.

"I suppose I do find you occasionally acceptable," she finally mused, leaning her cheek against his shoulder. "Especially on evenings like this. But declaring that I like you seems a bit of an exaggeration."

"Mm hm."

"Why are you being so agreeable? It's rather off-putting."

He grinned. "I'm lulling you into thinking you've bested me, so my next verbal strike will be even more devastating."

"Well, it won't work now, because you've warned me."

"Perhaps that was a part of my pl . . ." He trailed off as the sound of booted footsteps approached them along the path. Shaw stepped in front of Zephyr, pulling free of her grip and putting his hand on the hilt of his sword as the jollies fanned out to either side of the trail.

A flash of blue trouser and red sash in torchlight caught his eye through the lush vegetation. It was enough. A French naval officer's uniform.

The figure came around the bend and into clear view. Shaw swiftly took in the uniform; he'd seen countless incarnations over the years, both through a spyglass and eye to eye over the point of his pistol. And this was a captain. He had a good idea which one. "That's close enough," he said, curling his fingers around the hilt.

The tall, thin man in his French naval attire stopped, his own gaze glancing over the jollies and then settling on Shaw. "*Bon soir,* Capitaine . . . Carroway, *oui?*"

"Yes." Shaw nodded. "And you are?"

"Ah. *Pardon.* Capitaine Phillipe Mariot de Gardanne, of *Le Courageux.*" The cool brown gaze flitted beyond Bradshaw. "Your lady, Capitaine?"

"Yes. Do you often go strolling alone in the middle of the night, Gardanne?"

"You are also away from your friends quite late."

"Not all of my friends. Are we going to dance, Captain, or are you going to tell me why you were looking for me?"

Gardanne smiled, though the expression didn't touch his eyes. "I am here only to welcome you to Tahiti, Capitaine, and to say that I am acquainted with your reputation and your past deeds. Very well acquainted."

"I know who you are, as well. And I hope for your sake that you are a better student of the law than your cousin was."

"I am an exceptional student," Gardanne returned. "Do you plan to stay here long?"

"As long as necessary. And I suggest you keep to your ship until I go. For your own sake."

"I shall consider that. I'm glad we understand each other, Carroway."

"I understand you quite well, Gardanne. Good evening."

"Good night, Capitaine." With a precise pivot on his heel, the French captain turned around and strolled back the way he'd come.

Shaw drew a hard breath. Damnation. For a few hours this evening he'd found the peace that had eluded him for so long. Peace, and something more. With Zephyr's hand in his again, they resumed their walk back to their campsite. Now he had the distinct feeling that Gardanne meant to hand him precisely what he didn't want—a fight.

Chapter Fifteen

Steel sparkle, pikes rattle, and swords loudly clash,
And the blood on her decks like salt water did dash.
Her scuppers with huge streams of crimson did pour,
And the blue seas all round us rolled purple with gore.

"BOLD DIGHTON"

Something very odd was afoot.

Zephyr looked up from her sketchbook to gaze across the village. It wasn't the tension of having a French warship anchored just across the harbor, and it wasn't the doubts Shaw relayed concerning Captain Wright and the *Swift*—though the portly captain didn't look like any pirate she'd ever imagined.

No, the oddness was batting about in her chest, fluttering and shivering whenever she looked at Shaw—which seemed to be almost constantly. Even when they chased about the shoreline trying to catch insects, even when the colors and sounds and beauty of Tahiti surrounded her, begging to be sketched, she stayed close by and gazed at him.

She'd been with him before yesterday afternoon, and while that had been an extraordinary and eye-opening experience, it hadn't made her lose her mind. Of course the first time she had dwelled more on the physical sensations and then the ship had nearly capsized. Since yesterday, however, her mind stayed filled with the look in his eyes, his touch, his scent, his weight, the way he seemed prepared to go to any lengths to protect her. Even the way he was the only man she'd ever met who both could and dared to hold up his side of a conversation with her.

He was certainly the only man to ask what she wanted for her life and her future. She only wished she could decide. But she did know that since she'd met him, she'd begun considering the same questions, herself.

"I don't like the way our captain keeps looking at that French ship," her father commented, as he placed a handful of seeds into a jar. "I hope he remembers that the war is finished, and that his duty at the moment is to aid our exploration."

"I told you Captain Gardanne confronted us last night," she replied, glancing again at Shaw where he stood on the slight rise and gazed toward the harbor. "He only wants to make certain we're safe."

"That's very diplomatic of you, my dear. I'm glad to see you two dealing together better these days. We still have several months of exploration ahead of us."

She blinked. Dash it all, unless she wanted to give her father an apoplexy she couldn't let him guess that she and Shaw were dealing so well together they'd become lovers. Zephyr glanced sideways at her father. "I have to admit, Shaw has surprised me."

"Indeed. The Admiralty may have known what it was about when they assigned the *Nemesis* to us. I only hope he doesn't lose sight of his true responsibilities."

Zephyr nodded. "What do you think of Captain Carroway as . . . as a man?"

"His men certainly respect and love him. I'd like him better if he had more of a scholarly bent, but I suppose that's not a requirement with the navy, eh?" He chuckled, then abruptly sobered again. "If not for his treatment of Dr. Howard, I daresay I would have no qualms about him, at all."

But he'd flattened Christopher Howard because of her, whatever claims he made about his general dislike of the physician's behavior. Even now, after nearly five days, the man remained confined to his cabin.

Shaw finally turned away from the harbor to approach her and her father. "I need to return to the ship for my watch," he said. "Do you intend to remain here, or do you wish to accompany me?"

"I'm going for a stroll with the chieftain's brother," her father replied. "And I'd like Zephyr to sketch some of the specimens in their natural habitat."

A brief frown crossed Shaw's face and then vanished just as quickly. "I'll have Major Hunter join you. And until I know for certain what Captain Gardanne has up his frilled sleeves, I'd like you back at the village by sunset."

"We'd best leave now, then. Bring your sketchbook, Zephyr." Her father hurried over to indicate which cages and tubs he wanted brought along, and Hendley with his half-dozen mates began gathering the equipment.

"I'd join you if I could," Shaw said in a more intimate voice, brushing his fingers against her skirt, "but Gardanne meeting up with us last night wasn't a coincidence. He has people watching us. I need to do the same to him. Stay close to Charles Hunter, will you?"

"I thought all the Frenchmen were on the opposite side of the harbor."

"That's what Captain Wright said. I don't believe him," he returned. "Gardanne managed to avoid being captured by the English fleet on and off for a decade, and he sank half a dozen English ships."

"And you captured his cousin."

"There is that." He put a hand on her shoulder. "Be back here by sunset."

Zephyr nodded, trying not to smile at him. "I'll see to it."

A dozen native men and women fell in with them, and her father quickly recruited their assistance in finding the best places for wildlife and unusual plants on the northwest part of the large island. Hendley and his companions were clearly more interested in the bare-breasted women than in finding any lizards or spiders, but in some ways she could hardly blame them. This was the first landing they'd made since Australia where the natives hadn't attempted to kill and likely eat them.

She sat on a rock to draw her father examining a flowering vine while two of the Tahitian men attempted in broken English to explain its medicinal uses. None of Shaw's troubles concerned Sir Joseph as long as they didn't affect his search for plants and fauna.

As for her, well, the past few weeks had seen her embarking on her own journey—and for the first time in her memory her path was moving in a different direction from her father's. It had begun so gradually that at first she hadn't even noticed. Yes, she enjoyed traveling and exploring, but knowing the Latin name of every fern didn't have the same significance now. The minutiae of things had made even her large world small, until Bradshaw had given her genuine friendship and affection, and her gaze had lifted.

When they returned to England at the end of this voyage the botanist would have years of research and papers and planting and dissecting ahead of him. He'd looked forward to it for years, and in all his descriptions she'd been at his side taking notes and painting tropical blossoms—and now birds and insects—to illustrate his books and papers. He'd never actually asked, and she was no longer certain what her answer to such a request would be, anyway.

It was such a blasted conundrum. She had no idea how she would even manage settling into London life. The only people she knew were Juliette Quanstone and her companions—and Shaw, of course. Shaw, who'd begun bandying about words like "marriage" and asking her what she wanted for herself.

Well, perhaps what she wanted was to not always be on the way to somewhere else, her nose buried in books and sketches in all the between times. Perhaps she wanted acquaintances she had actual time to develop into friendships. Perhaps she wanted . . . Perhaps she wanted Bradshaw Carroway, not just for an arousing night or two, but to stay in her life forever.

"Zephyr. Zephyr!"

She started. "Yes, Papa?"

"Make certain you sketch both the open flower and the bud. The coloration is quite different, and I want it documented."

"Certainly. Of course."

Trying to shake the future from her mind, she pulled out her watercolors. The one thing she couldn't dislodge, didn't want to dislodge, was that her future now seemed to have widened to show her paths she'd never expected to see, much less want to follow. And at least one path had a wild, blue-eyed ship's captain sailing along it with her.

Within three days the crew and passengers of the *Nemesis* had settled into Tahiti. Shaw warned Lord John and his circle to stay well clear of any Frenchmen and to watch their tongues around Captain Wright, just on the chance that the *Swift* wasn't quite what she appeared to be. The last thing he wanted was for his idiot passengers to end up on a pirate ship and held for ransom.

Whether they would take his advice or not, he had no idea. Avoiding the crew of the *Courageux* was turning out to be easier than he'd expected, as Captain Gardanne seemed to have stopped gathering his rocks and timber and retreated with all his men back to their ship. He could speculate over the reason for their secrecy, but unless or until they made an aggressive move he had no cause to take action. And that suited him quite well.

Only an hour or so of daylight remained this afternoon as he finished his daily duties and left the ship for another night ashore. To his surprise, the chieftain and his retinue stood grouped on the beach looking in his direction as the launch reached the shore.

"Captain," the chief greeted him, nodding solemnly. "You honor us. You keep Frenchmen off island."

"I'm pleased my presence could help you. Hopefully they'll decide to sail away in the next few days."

"We give you honor back. Come."

"That isn't necessary, sir. The—"

"No. You come. For protect you and your blessed crew."

Apparently the influence of the missionaries down in Papeete was spreading, after all. He didn't intend to offend the chief by refusing to drink fermented coconut milk or some such thing. "Very well. Lead on."

The next two hours were quite possibly the most excruciating of his life, even taking into account several bullet holes and sword slices he'd experienced over the years. By the time he realized that protection entailed having native symbols tattooed around his neck in a permanent black necklace, it was far too late to refuse without offending everyone present. A sea urchin spine dipped in some sort of plant-based ink and hammered into his skin over and over and over—in a sense he *did* feel invincible, because if he survived this, nothing else could kill him.

Finally they returned his shirt to him, sprinkled him with water and flowers, and declared him a blessed protector. He understood that it was a great honor; only the chieftain himself had tattoos in a similar pattern of diamonds and swirls. But sweet

Lucifer, it stung. Pulling his shirt on over his head and trying not to wince, Shaw thanked his torturers and made his way to the clearing where his crew had set their tents. He left his shirt untucked, because pulling it any closer against his skin would have left him whimpering like an infant.

"There you are, Shaw," Sir Joseph said, coming forward to clap him on the shoulder. "We've had quite a remarkable day."

Wincing at the contact, Bradshaw sent a glare at Hendley, who sat on an overturned crate directly beside Zephyr. The sailor shot to his feet, saluting at the same time. "Sit here, Captain, why don't ye? Might I fetch you some dinner?"

"Rum," Shaw grunted, sitting. "A great quantity of it."

"Aye, aye, sir."

"We expected you over an hour ago," Zephyr commented. "And why do you look as though you've been dragged over coral?"

Their camp swarmed with Tahitians playing music and carrying baskets of fruit and another feast of very tasty roast pig. He knew for a fact that some of the crew who'd come ashore were absent, but if he attempted to put a stop to their fraternization with the native women, he would face a mutiny as surely as had Captain Bligh. As for him, despite the stinging sensation ringing his neck he was quite . . . content to be precisely where he was. *Content*. It was a new word for him, and he knew precisely the reason for it. She sat beside him, just close enough to touch.

"The chief wanted to thank me for keeping the French away from the village," he said aloud, nodding his thanks as a pretty, bare-breasted chit handed him a banana leaf platter of the roast pig. According to Sir Joseph pigs weren't native to the island. Wherever they'd come from, the Tahitians were damned masters of roasting them.

Zephyr lifted an eyebrow. "He wanted to thank you, how?"

Warmth swept down his spine. "Jealous?"

"Perhaps, until you suggested it. Explain."

She did look more annoyed than anything else. Before she could hit him in the chest and kill him, Shaw gingerly pulled the open collar of his shirt away from his skin. "Apparently it's tradition," he said. "And a great honor."

"Good heavens." She reached out, then stopped herself. "Does it hurt? May I touch it?"

"Yes, and yes."

Abruptly she blushed. "That sounded naughty, didn't it?" she whispered.

The stinging eased a little. "Excessively," he agreed, grinning.

"Mm hm. Take off your shirt. You must tell me what the designs mean, and then I want to sketch you."

With an exaggerated sigh he complied. "For God's sake, make me look devilishly handsome."

"I fear I'm not that skilled." Pursing her lips, she leaned in to peer at the black ink coloring his skin. When she brushed one finger along the pattern, he flinched—at least as much from the contact as from the pain. "Oh, apologies, Shaw."

"I said you could touch me."

Gray eyes met his, the soft blush still coloring her cheeks as she looked down again to continue her examination. "It's raised a little. Is it swollen?"

"Why yes, it is."

"Shaw, hush."

It was his turn to lift an eyebrow. "I was only answering your question." Her father appeared from beyond her shoulder, and he clamped down on the no doubt foolish expression of amused affection on his face. "Sir Joseph," he greeted the botanist, before Zephyr could say something incriminating. "I seem to have become part of the tribe."

Sir Joseph moved in with a magnifying glass. "You said this was to honor you for keeping the French at bay?"

"That is my understanding. Though considering that we've been here three days and I haven't actually done much of anything but glower at the *Courageux*, the symbols could just as easily say 'death to all foreigners.' "

"I don't believe so," the botanist said thoughtfully. "The markings mirror those the chieftain has on his own face and arms. Make certain you sketch them, Zephyr, both in detail and as they appear around the captain's neck."

At least Sir Joseph agreed with his assessment of the markings. After another close look the botanist handed his daughter the magnifying glass and strolled over to finish potting the day's plant specimens. Shaw returned his attention to Zephyr, who continued to scrutinize his chest and neck very closely. "What do you think?" he asked after a moment.

"It's actually very attractive," she mused slowly, running her fingertips gently below his throat. "You know, I can carry a parasol and be mistaken for a lady. These marks, my friend, will not come off. As soon as you remove your cravat, no one will take you for a gentleman."

Shaw grinned again, wishing mightily that he and she were alone by the fire. "I never claimed to be much of a gentleman. But whether you tote about a parasol or not, you are every inch a lady. Quite possibly the finest I've ever met."

"Goodness. If you continue saying such things, I'll begin to think you're smitten with me."

"I'd describe it more as being clubbed into submission," he murmured, aware both that her palm had come to rest just over his heart, and that his men and the Mayfair mob across the fire pit could see it. "But yes, I am rather smitten with you."

Her pretty gray eyes regarded him. "If you're jesting, then stop it. If you're not, then, well, please continue."

His smile deepened. "If you keep your hand there much longer, our feelings won't matter as much as their wagging tongues." He angled his chin toward his other passengers.

She blinked, then abruptly removed her hand from his bare skin and picked up her pencil so swiftly she dropped it and then had to retrieve it again. "You should have said something."

"I like your hands on me."

Finally her expression eased into a grin, and then she stuck her tongue out at him. "Do be quiet. You'll ruin the sketch."

Shaw relented, more because he wanted to take a moment to think than because she'd asked him to stop teasing. He *was* taken with her. Smitten. God knew he liked and enjoyed women, but they'd always had their place. And it hadn't been aboard his ship. Or buried in his heart. Until now. Until Zephyr Ponsley.

Someone brought him a large mug of rum, and he downed it between questions about the various symbols as she sketched him and his tattoo. Most other navy captains with whom he was acquainted would not have allowed themselves to be marked by savages unless it happened to be a wound while they battled each other. And he could have escaped this if he'd truly wished to do so. Quite simply, it had been a new and unique experience and it had been meant as an honor, and so he'd agreed to it. If only all his decisions were so easy.

"How is Dr. Howard faring?" Zephyr commented after a time. "Have you reconsidered his punishment?"

Shaw glanced at her sharply, the sting of his tattoo disappearing in comparison to the dark tightness in his chest. "You want him about to accost you again?"

"He didn't accost me. He suggested, and made up some absurd lies to justify it. I've been propositioned before, you know."

"It's not the same thing," he snapped, grabbing up his shirt and pushing to his feet.

If he stayed where he was, he would say something he couldn't charm his way out of, something they would both regret. Because it sat on the tip of his tongue to tell the damned chit that he loved her.

Once he did that, he would have to admit that he hadn't deciphered what he wanted for his own future, other than the fact that he wanted her to be in it. And she was just as likely to comment that he should know that he was a sea captain, and didn't he remember that botanists stayed on land?

"Shaw?"

"I need a breath of air," he said without turning around, and kept walking.

Christ. He *loved* her. He'd appreciated that two of his brothers had fallen in love and married, but he'd expected his life to continue to be at sea. Going to all the bother of finding, courting, and marrying a chit just to leave her behind when he sailed away again made no sense. Things had changed—his feelings about his career had changed—but it was a damned boatload to take in all at once.

She'd brought up another point in this mess, as well. Christopher Howard had influence—or rather, his family did. Once the story circulated that Captain Carroway had locked the good doctor in his cabin in order to woo the woman they both apparently wanted, Shaw would be reduced to captaining a prison barge. But knowing what he did about Howard, and feeling as he did about Zephyr, he refused to believe that he'd been in the wrong.

"You're on a tropical island, Shaw," Zephyr's voice came from behind him. "I doubt you'll find more air anywhere else."

Sighing a lungful of that plentiful air, Shaw slowed to allow her to catch up. "It was a figure of speech," he retorted. "You were bothering me."

"Because I pointed out that you haven't been able to justify your treatment of Dr. Howard?"

Out of the reach of the fire and torches where only the moon lit the path before them, Shaw offered her an arm. "Because he had every intention of ruining you and then likely informing his Mayfair cronies where they might have a bit of fun."

"You ruined me."

"I—" He stopped in the middle of the palm tree–lined path. "Of course I ruined you, Zephyr. There was no other way for me to get my hands on you."

"What is the difference, then?"

A growl rose in his throat. "If I have to explain that to you, then . . . then there's nothing I can say *to* explain it to you." He shrugged free of her hand again. "Now go back to the tents and leave me be."

"I don't want to leave you be. I want you to explain it to me."

"You are so damned aggravating," he exclaimed. "You know I'll return to camp later, so explain why you're chasing me now, why don't you?" *There*. A bit of a turned table should slow her down.

"I'm not chasing you."

"You most certainly are."

She put her hands on her hips. "Very well, I concede that I am chasing you. It's only because you're so damned obtuse!"

Shaw jabbed a finger into his own chest. "*I'm* obtuse? Me?"

"If you would explain yourself in a halfway intelligible manner, I wouldn't need to pursue you at all. So would you rather me call you obtuse, or idiotic?"

That was bloody well enough of that. "Fine," he snapped. "I don't have everything deciphered. I didn't swoop in and use your blasted rules simply to get you into my bed. I like you. I like becoming acquainted with you. I . . . You make me consider things that I never expected to have cross my mind. But I don't know the answers yet. So go away and let me think."

Zephyr shook her head. "Obtuse," she muttered, and turned her back on him. "You might ask my opinion, you know."

If he had any sense at all he would keep his damned mouth closed and let her go, then conjure something he needed to do tomorrow so he could avoid her until he found an even keel once more and could talk to her without blathering like the idiot she accused him of being. *Damnation.* "Zephyr," he said aloud.

She turned around. "What?" Her expression remained unchanged, but he could practically feel the frustration coming from her. Or perhaps that was his own aggravation seeping from him.

Very quietly, half drowned by the sound of the surf and the myriad insects around them, he heard a click. *Christ.*

In the same second he threw himself forward, catching Zephyr around the waist and driving her to the ground beneath him. The ball whistled over his head so close he could feel the heat of it. "Stay low," he whispered, shifting to put his legs beneath him. He grabbed her hand. "And run."

Chapter Sixteen

My son John was tall and slim,
He had a leg for every limb.
But now he's got no legs at all,
For he run a race with a cannonball.

"MY SON JOHN"

Zephyr ran. With Shaw holding her right hand and hurtling over rocks and ducking behind palm trees, she had to either run or be dragged. She had no idea how he could see where he was going in the moonlit dark, but as another weapon cracked close behind them, she didn't care as long as it was away.

He pulled her down behind a pile of boulders. The shore and sea opened up behind them, which seemed terribly exposed, but Shaw had always seemed to know what he was doing. She made herself as small as she could in the deep shadows. "Shaw, wh—"

"Shh," he breathed, his mouth pressed against her temple.

His hand in hers remained as steady as if they'd

been strolling on the beach. Perhaps being shot at was nothing to him; after all, what was musket shot compared with a cannonball? She, on the other hand, was quaking in her shoes.

"My men will have heard the shots," he whispered almost soundlessly, squeezing her fingers. "I headed us toward them, but I don't want us caught in the middle."

"But who is it? The French?"

"That's my guess. The French navy carries rifles, and those were definitely not muskets."

Good heavens. He could tell the difference? Clearly she'd chosen the right man in whose company to be during a shooting. "So what do we do?"

"We listen."

"But what if they—"

"No harm will come to you, Zephyr," he cut in, his voice taking on a harder edge. "I won't allow it."

Any other time she might have argued that he couldn't assure her safety no matter how strong his declarations. Tonight, however, she very much wanted to believe him. When the undergrowth just beyond their stone shelter rustled, she had to clamp her lips closed over a gasp.

Shifting silently, Bradshaw slowly drew a very sharp-looking knife from his boot. He freed his other hand from hers, but even without the connection she could feel him tensing, coiling like a great panther about to strike.

"Captain! Captain Carroway!"

The voice came from closer than she expected. A quiet curse drifted over to her, and then with a shuffle and crunch the rustling retreated. Relieved, Zephyr started to her feet.

Shaw gripped her shoulder, keeping her on her knees beside him. "What I was attempting to avoid saying a few minutes ago," he whispered, his blue eyes silvery and glittering in the moonlight, "and what now suddenly seems ridiculous to avoid, is that I seem to be in love with you. Stay down until I know for certain we're safe."

He stood, putting two fingers to his mouth and whistling. A moment later marines and sailors surrounded them, all of them armed and clamoring to know what the devil the shooting was about. Zephyr belatedly rose when Hendley offered her an arm.

For heaven's sake. She'd been attempting to goad Shaw into saying . . . something nice about her, but she'd thought at the most that he would admit to bearing her some nebulous amount of affection or admiration. This, however . . . goodness.

He loved her. They'd known each other for only two months, but in that time she'd seen him daily, spent hours and hours in his company, and they'd chatted—or argued—about everything.

After priding herself for being a logical, science-minded female, it was odd that she hadn't known which word to use to describe her own feelings until he said it first. Love. *Love.* When her father took her arm, she jumped. "I'm well," she managed, though she had no idea what he might have been saying to her.

"Do you think they were merely attempting to frighten us away?" he asked, facing Shaw. "Because I intend that we should remain here at least another fortnight. This is my best chance to learn what the natives know of the uses for their local botanicals."

"Someone just shot at your daughter, sir," Bradshaw retorted, anger seeping into his voice for the first time. "And they weren't trying to miss."

The brief annoyance on her father's face didn't surprise Zephyr in the least. For the first time, though, it disappointed her a little.

"Zephyr just stated that she was well," her father returned, his nostrils flaring. "And subsequently I need to hear your assurance that we will be remaining in Tahiti."

"I can tell you at this moment that we're not going anywhere."

"Good."

"I reserve the right to reassess that decision, depending on the circumstances," Shaw continued. "Now if you'll excuse me."

With a glance at her, Shaw said something to Major Hunter and then strode into the darkness, trailed by half a dozen marines. So he thought he could say something so important and then simply walk away? Especially when he seemed to have intentionally left her no time to respond?

Zephyr started after him. Before she'd managed a half-dozen steps, though, Major Hunter blocked her path. "Apologies, Miss Ponsley," the marine commander said, "but you're to remain close by our camp and in my sight."

"I believe the danger has passed, Major," she returned, wondering for a brief moment if Shaw might not want to hear her reply, uncharacteristically cowardly of him as that seemed.

"Even so, I have my orders."

Scowling in the direction Bradshaw had vanished, Zephyr nodded. "Very well. Lead on."

Perhaps a bit of time to consider . . . well, everything, would serve her better, anyway. However, as she walked in the center of the very fierce-looking circle of the remaining marines and sailors—her father a bit to one side and clearly benefiting from the attention while not its focus—her mind refused to engage in any sort of logical process at all. He *loved* her. That aggravating, argumentative, witty, brave, handsome man was in love with her.

It seemed for the best that no one expected her to carry on any sort of conversation, because with a half-dozen words or so, Shaw had performed what he claimed to be a miracle—rendering her speechless. And now she couldn't continue to dwell only on the questions of where she wanted her life to go. She needed to decide, to find the answers.

Stupid man. Shaw had to know she wanted to talk with him, to argue through her own feelings. He'd done this deliberately, then, left her to figure out where reason and logic had to stop and she had to listen to . . . to her heart. "Major, we can see the camp from here," she finally said aloud. "Shouldn't you be assisting Captain Carroway?"

"The captain said to see to you and your father," the marine returned, his expression grim. "I imagine there'll be enough shooting to go around later."

"Please remind Captain Carroway that we are not here to shoot things, Major." Her father slowed as they reached the edge of the firelight. "We are not at war with France."

"We may not be at war with them, Sir Joseph, but they seem fairly free with shooting at us." The major gestured toward the tents. "If you please. The lads and I will keep a good watch here until the captain returns. You'd best get some sleep. We'll likely be in for a long day tomorrow."

"I—"

"Papa," Zephyr broke in, taking her father's arm. "Shaw hasn't disappointed yet. And honestly, I'm a bit . . . frazzled."

His brow lowered. "Yes. Of course. Please keep me apprised of any developments, Major."

"I will, sir."

So she stepped in as she always did, to point out to her father that most people would consider his priorities somewhat skewed. Luckily that sort of diplomacy had become second nature to her over the years, because she was quite occupied with something else entirely. If she knew one thing, it was that she was not going to get a wink of sleep. And it wasn't because someone had shot at her. It was because she'd finally realized that Shaw had pierced her heart.

Shaw settled beneath the undoubtedly precious and rare shrubbery that covered the north point of the rugged Matavai Bay harbor. Beyond the island's protection the sea was still restless, but between the *Nemesis* and the *Courageux* the water was as flat as glass. Even in the light of the setting moon he could make out the launch just arriving at the French frigate.

"It looks like you had the right of it," Gerard murmured from beside him. "They're French, not from the merchant ship."

"Even if Captain Wright isn't above piracy, he'd rather have us here than the French," Bradshaw noted. "And at this point I don't care if this happened because Gardanne has a personal grudge or because of whatever it is the Frogs are up to out here. They attacked me and mine. I will not give them a chance to do so again."

This time there was no moral ambiguity, no hesitation, no questionable politics. Zephyr might have been killed tonight. And it was only a happy coincidence that the Admiralty had indicated he should feel free to deal with the French. They were finished, regardless.

"How do we accomplish that? There's a second ship just a few hours down the coast. The odds might be even now, but they won't stay that way."

"I'm aware of that, William. And I'm not willing to risk my passengers or Sir Joseph's botanicals in a brawl." He moved back from the view and straightened. "I want someone watching that ship at all times," he ordered, brushing leaves from his trousers. "If anyone so much as leans over the railing, I want to know it."

"But what—"

"We're going to sink her, Mr. Gerard," Shaw broke in. "I'm not about to wait for them to fire directly on the *Nemesis*. The trick is to put her into the bottom of the harbor without risking our cargo."

"So we need to sink her without giving her time to fire at us," the first mate mused, gazing at the wide, dark harbor again. "And we need to do it before her sister ship returns and they both blow the hell out of us."

"We need to do it before dawn and they decide to make another strike." With a grim smile, Shaw clapped Gerard on the shoulder and then headed back down the hill.

Out on the open sea, with two ships moving and maneuvering around each other, options were fairly limited. They could either fire at one another, or disguise themselves as other than what they were and strike first. He'd had success with both techniques. But here in the harbor, stealth seemed to be the wisest route, and the safest for the animals and botanicals stuffing the hold of the *Nemesis*.

As he walked back to camp, Shaw couldn't help but wonder how angry Zephyr would be at him. After all, he'd practically blindsided her by declaring that he'd fallen in love. He hadn't meant to say anything, but the rifle fire had rather . . . accelerated his sense that they did not have an endless amount of time to figure out what they meant to do.

Or rather, what *he* meant to do. He'd never let a chit catch his fancy before; it had seemed a foolish and useless thing to do when his life was so transient. This chit, however, had knocked him off his feet. And now he had two sets of options to consider; the first for putting a pair of French naval ships out of his and England's misery, and the second for leg-shackling himself to a stubborn, aggravating lady more changeable and enticing than the sea.

Shaw stopped at the outer edge of their makeshift camp. He'd been promoted to captain only a handful of years ago. And while he'd never given much thought to becoming an admiral, before the battle with the *Revanche* he had looked forward to another twenty or thirty years sailing the ocean.

On the way to Australia he'd spent endless hours considering his future. Wondering if his general malaise would fade with time. Speculating over whether he could tolerate captaining a merchant ship just to remain at sea. Looking for another path that wouldn't leave him contemplating putting a ball through his head.

Knowing that Zephyr was in the world, however, changed everything. It put the answer there in front of him, in large black letters. He needed to retire. He needed to have this scientific expedition be his last voyage. Bradshaw took a slow breath. His last set of storms, his last days of a following breeze and the bright stars guiding his way. And a lifetime of adventure and exploration knowing Zephyr—if she would have him.

If this was his last assignment, he was damned well going to make certain it ended successfully, and that no bloody French captain was going to feather his cap by stopping or sinking the *Nemesis* or killing any of her passengers and crew. Blowing out his breath again, he walked forward, nodding at the sentry, and slipped back into camp.

"Captain," Hendley said, joining the others as they stood and saluted him.

"As you were." Shaw accepted the mug of hot American coffee the cook's mate handed him as he sat on one of the wooden folding chairs. "Any noise from anywhere?"

Major Hunter sat beside him. "No, sir. Other than Miss Ponsley wanting the lot of us to set up a protective perimeter around you, that is."

With a short grin, Shaw took a swallow of the strong coffee. "Do me a favor, will you? Ask around quietly to see who knows how to swim."

The jolly furrowed his brow a little, but nodded. "Do you have a number in mind?"

"Five seems reasonable."

"Captain Carroway. I demand to know whether we are in danger," Lord John Fenniwell said, stalking up with half the Mayfair contingent behind him.

"That's what I'm attempting to prevent," Shaw returned. "Stay in camp, and don't go anywhere alone."

"But—"

"Panicking will only make you look like a fool, Fenniwell. Remain calm, and do as you're told. Good evening."

Looking affronted, Lord John retreated again, no doubt to complain to his companions about the captain's autocratic behavior. Shaw didn't much care, as long as they followed his orders.

On the far side of the fire, the flap covering Zephyr's tent shifted, and her scowling face peered out at him. Taking another drink of coffee to cover the sudden acceleration of his heart, Shaw stood again. "If you'll excuse me for a moment, Charles, I need to go have an argument."

Hunter followed his gaze. "Better you than me, sir."

"Mm hm. Good swimmers, if you please."

"Aye, aye."

Keeping his expression neutral, Shaw reached Zephyr's tent and tied one of the flaps back to keep it open. Yes, he'd already ruined her, but no one else knew that. And for the moment he preferred to keep it that way. Of course there was also another benefit to witnesses—she would have to mind her tongue.

Generally he enjoyed arguing with her. This was the first time, though, that he'd ever told a woman he loved her. He did not look forward to having either that or his character thrown back in his face. One of the perils of falling for a chit with both a mouth and a temper, he supposed. "You should be asleep," he said aloud. "It's late."

"Was that your plan, then?" Zephyr retorted in a low voice, sending an annoyed glance beyond him at the camp beyond. She crossed her arms over her chest, not budging from her spot at the center of the tent. "To declare yourself and then go off and get killed while I fell asleep?"

"I didn't go off to get killed, and I didn't declare myself. I said I'm in love with you."

This time he had the opportunity to see her eyes widen a little, her quick intake of breath, the soft blush that crept into her cheeks. Whatever she said, then, at least she felt something. Determining what that something was, however, seemed vitally important. After all, she'd helped him regain his sanity and his bearings in the midst of both of them slipping away.

"Why are you?" she finally blurted.

"Before I say anything else, I think you should sit down. You look like you're about to punch me in the nose."

"I've been considering that very thing." Her lips twitched, and she sank down on a crate of glass jars.

Shaw took a seat on the edge of her narrow bunk, facing her. He wanted to touch her, to stroke her face with his hands and to kiss her soft mouth. He rubbed his palms against his thighs. "If you're looking for logic, I'm afraid you're not going to find any. I can't explain it."

"Mm hm. Try."

He flashed her a grin. "Zephyr, you annoy and aggravate the devil out of me. You ask too damned many questions. You don't take my word for anything, and you constantly make suggestions that contradict my orders."

Zephyr furrowed her curved brows. "That sounds like a list of charges with which to force me to walk the plank or something."

"In the navy we prefer keelhauling or stringing men up from the yardarm. But you know, I've never tolerated any of those annoyances aboard my ship before, and with the exception of my own family I've avoided most of them in my civilian life, as well."

"This doesn't sound terribly flattering. Are you certain you haven't mistaken lust for love?"

At least she was keeping her voice down. Shaw refrained from pointing out that she was still arguing with him. "You have . . . seeped into me. Things I wouldn't tolerate from anyone else, I crave from you. I crave *you*, Zephyr. Not just your very lovely body, but . . . everything."

A tear ran down her cheek. With a sniff, she wiped it away. When she didn't say anything, Shaw abruptly began to worry. If she was searching for a diplomatic way to tell him that since he'd satisfied her curiosity and lust she was no longer the least bit interested, then he'd spent a great deal of time in useless contemplation.

As the silence lengthened, his worry began to heat into anger. Yes, he found her stubbornness and independence exhilarating, but this was ridiculous. If she didn't care for him, she could damned well say so.

He cleared his throat and stood again. "Well. I apologize, then. If what I've said doesn't make any sense to you, then clearly I've misread the circumstances. Don't worry; I'm not Howard. I won't press unwanted attention on y—"

Zephyr leapt to her feet and flung her arms around him. Her soft lips met his, and he kissed her back, relief flooding through him. She did like him, whether she would say the words or not. Lifting her off her feet, he held her close against him, feeling the joy in her kiss.

"What the devil is this?"

Shaw jumped, letting Zephyr go so quickly that she stumbled backward and sat down hard on the bed. Then he shook himself and took her hand to pull her to her feet again. "Sir Joseph," he said, facing the open door of the tent.

"I came to ask Zephyr whether we needed to send to the ship for more specimen jars," Sir Joseph said stiffly, his face red. "I did not expect to find . . . this. Explain yourself, sir."

He hadn't said *the words* to her yet, but with her tendency to disbelieve everything without proof to the contrary, a witness—or several—might help his cause. "I mean to marry your daughter, Sir Joseph, as soon as I can convince her to have me."

"Shaw," she breathed.

"I don't—" Narrowing his eyes, Sir Joseph took another step forward. "You've been very helpful to us, Bradshaw, but I won't see my daughter married to a navy captain."

Damnation. He'd wanted to discuss all the ramifications with Zephyr before he said anything to anyone else, much less the chit's father. But there was a chance he wouldn't be alive to see the dawn. Best to have everything said that needed to be said, then. "She won't be. I mean to retire. This is my last voyage."

She shot to her feet again. "Shaw! You can't—"

He faced her. "I'm not asking you yet," he broke in. "I have a few Frenchmen to see to first. But perhaps you'll take this time to consider how you want to answer me. Because I do mean to ask you." He took her hand and squeezed her fingers. "Now if you'll excuse me, I need to return to the ship. I have a favor to ask Dr. Howard."

Another tear ran down one of her soft cheeks, and she brushed it away before he could do so. "Shaw, this is mad."

Shaw nodded. "That's what I excel at." Releasing her fingers, he brushed past her father and left the tent.

He'd heard of some bungled declarations in his time, but he had to rank this one fairly high up the ladder of nonsense. He'd stumbled into this like a complete nodcock, and then tripped over his own attempt to explain in front of her father. Ignoring the gawping aristocrats beside the fire pit, he topped the slight rise between the camp and the harbor. "Damnation," he muttered, swinging his fist at a low-hanging branch as he descended to the harbor. He'd best manage the French better than he managed that woman, or they were all done for.

Or perhaps he would drown this evening, and he wouldn't have to straighten out the considerable mess he'd just made. And he wouldn't have to wait to hear Zephyr say that she merely viewed him with the same interest she did a beetle in a specimen jar.

* * *

For the second time since sunset Shaw had managed to say something unexpected and . . . vital, then walk away before she had a chance to decipher what it all meant. Zephyr took a quick, hard breath. *Damn that man.*

"Did you know about this?" her father demanded, closing the tent's flap as though that turned the heavy canvas into solid stone walls. "Have you been encouraging Shaw's attention? I know we've been in fairly close quarters, but surely he's aware that circumstances and the importance of this expedition simply dictate we cooperate."

How in heaven was she supposed to respond to any of that? And how could she tell her father about her feelings when she hadn't said anything about them to Shaw? "He would retire," she managed, putting a hand to her throat and abruptly realizing what Shaw had meant when he'd said he'd needed some air.

Her father eyed her. "I would think that whatever Shaw does after the end of this expedition is his own decision."

"But not if he does it for me."

"Then there *is* something between you."

What had Shaw said? That she'd seeped into him? As she ignored her father's blustering for a moment, she tried to conjure a single amusing, surprising, or exciting second that didn't share its place in her memory with Shaw. There simply wasn't one. Even though she'd been traveling for eight years, she hadn't come alive until that night at Admiral Dolenz's home. Until she'd set eyes on that aggravating, wonderful man.

"I insist that you tell me what's afoot, Zephyr."

"Apparently I'm going to marry Bradshaw Carroway," she said, her voice unsteady. *Goodness.* Saying it aloud made it seem suddenly real. No more transience. No more passing through life without truly experiencing it. She would have an anchor—albeit a very odd choice for one, since Shaw had likely spent as much time away from England as she had.

"I— No."

She blinked. "No?"

"When we return to England, the Royal Society will expect papers, reports, cuttings, plantings—and more than likely an exhibit, quite possibly at Kew Gardens alongside Mungo Park's specimens. And then, God willing, I may be offered the leadership of an even grander expedition."

"Even as a married woman I can certainly assist you with everything but the last portion. We'll have to find you a new assistant for that."

"So you simply abandon me, after I've worked so long and so hard to accomplish this for us?"

"Papa, I've been very happy to journey with you and assist you. But you didn't do any of this for me."

He scowled. "This is ridiculous, Zephyr. I've given you a life of science and exploration, and this is how you repay me?"

The swiftly deteriorating ribbon of her patience snapped. "What you have done, Papa, is drag me halfway around the world to take notes and make sketches while you study plants."

"I—"

"As I said, I've enjoyed this life," she cut in, unwilling to let him pull her argument astray. "I have.

But I'm not a shrub. I require more than water and sunlight. I require Shaw."

"You didn't even know he existed two months ago. You were content with your life, then."

"How do you know that? You never asked. The moment Mama died you were off, me in tow. Did you think because you named me Zephyr that I would want to travel?"

"You've never complained before this."

"No, I haven't. But don't deny that you've always put me second to your botany."

His face continued to redden. "So now you rebel, in the middle of the most important expedition of my life."

"I'm not rebelling." Zephyr looked down for a moment, still attempting to gather a thousand different and scattered thoughts. "I'm living. I'm finding what *I* want, and I'm pursuing it. Wherever it may lead."

Her father took a deep breath, clearly summoning every ounce of patience he possessed. "And what you want is Captain Bradshaw Carroway. You're certain of that."

She smiled, her heart so full of excitement and anticipation that it startled her. "Yes. He is what—who—I want."

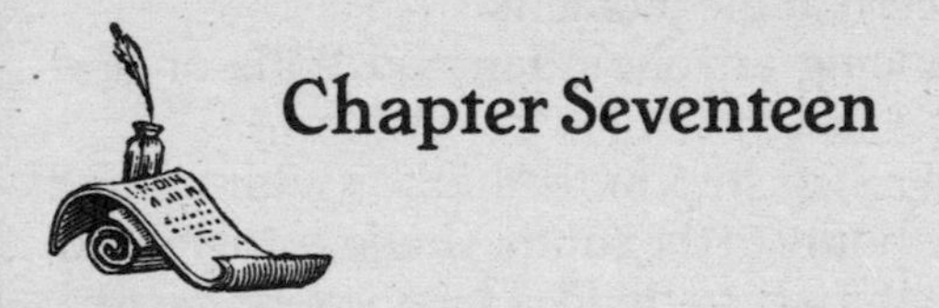

Chapter Seventeen

His coal-black eyes and his curly hair
His pleasing tongue did my heart ensnare.
Genteel he was and no rake like you
To advise a maiden, to advise a maiden,
To slight the jacket blue.

"THE DARK-EYED SAILOR"

Shaw rapped his knuckles against the cabin door and then pulled it open without waiting for an answer. "Dr. Howard."

The earl's brother looked up from his correspondence. From the size of the stack of closely-scrawled-upon pages, he'd been writing a great deal. "Captain. Don't attempt to apologize after all this time. You'll have to murder me to silence my protests."

"I'd considered asking you whether my reputation in hitting a civilian attached to my crew would be damaged more or less than yours in verbally accosting a young lady after having ruined two others and fleeing England because of it."

"You will n—"

"However," Shaw interrupted, "I have a more pressing concern at the moment."

"I'm not lancing anyone's damned boils or blisters."

"There's a French ship in the harbor with us, and another a few hours to the south. I believe them to be harvesting materials to build a fortification nearby. And considering that they attempted to shoot me earlier this evening, I don't think they have anything good in mind for England."

"Then sink them. You seem to prefer violent action, anyway."

Shaw refrained from pointing out that with one exception he'd gone to great lengths on this voyage to avoid maiming anyone. "I intend to do just that. But I can't risk the *Nemesis* with its present cargo, and I can't let the French see me offloading or they're likely to either strike first or summon help."

The physician scowled. "And how the devil does this concern me? Other than encouraging me to thank the captain of the other ship for attempting to kill you and suggesting that he not give up so easily."

"I'm going to hole their hull. You, as I recall, are a fair swimmer."

"I am not going to risk my life to assist you."

"Yes, you are. Because I'm going to be out there, as well, and I could be killed. You wouldn't want to miss that. And because if you don't, I'll make it known both that you're a coward and that you propositioned my fiancée."

Howard's eyebrows disappeared beneath his overhanging brown hair. "Your fiancée? Does Miss Ponsley know you're claiming to be engaged to her?"

She should, considering that he'd stated in front of her father that he meant to propose to her. *Idiot*. "She does," he said aloud. "We're going overboard just before dawn. I'll expect you on deck at four o'clock."

"I'll consider it."

"I've relieved the guard at your door; do as you will." Shaw left the small cabin again, shutting the door behind him. At the moment their odds of mutual ruination were fairly even, so if Christopher Howard had any sense—which he generally did—he would go along with this reconciliation and otherwise keep his bloody mouth closed.

The problem at the moment—or rather the most pressing one of many—was that in order to sink the *Courageux* without becoming involved in an exchange of cannonfire, they would have to engage in subterfuge. He preferred a swim to the French ship to bore strategic holes beneath her waterline. Most of his men, however, didn't swim.

He was well aware of the superstition that allowing the sea to get a taste of you meant it would thereafter look for a chance to have you back. Personally and privately he thought it ridiculous; if he fell overboard he intended to be capable of staying afloat until the ship could come back around for him. Out loud he agreed with whatever would give his men the courage to serve.

Out of a hundred and eighty men he could likely find a dozen who could swim well enough to assist him. The decision to include Dr. Howard had been more strategic than practical, but for the rest he wanted men on whom he could depend.

Shaw entered his cabin and closed the door behind him. This was one log entry he needed to begin beforehand, on the chance that he wouldn't survive to explain himself later. Niu barked and fluttered over to perch on his shoulder. He scratched the parrot beneath the chin. "You love me, don't you, Niu?" he murmured.

"Damned chit. Stap my anchor," the bird rasped.

"Good enough."

He might have kept his own mouth shut, he supposed, but not saying anything about his . . . obsession hardly kept him from being in love. Shaw quickly outlined his plan in the logbook, then sat on the edge of his bed to remove his boots. Frustrating as it was to say something he considered rather momentous and life-altering and then realize that perhaps he'd misjudged *her* feelings in the matter, he preferred knowledge to ignorance. And so did Zephyr. If he knew anything, it was that.

It had been no one but Zephyr since the moment she'd snorted at him for not being much of a reader. Just *when* he'd realized that he wasn't certain, but this was a truer course than any he'd ever sailed before. The idea of shaking her until she admitted she loved him back began to seem more and more appealing. Generally he had more patience than that, but generally he didn't wait until he felt full to overflowing, announce that he loved someone, and then hear . . . nothing. Well, some kisses, but nothing he could lock away in his heart and hold on to.

Good God. He was beginning to sound like a chit. His brothers would be rolling about on the floor, laughing at him. In fact he was fairly certain that he'd laughed at them for badly expressing very much the same thing.

Once he'd shed his shirt and exchanged his white

officer's trousers for an old, dark pair of breeches, Shaw looped a satchel over his neck and one shoulder. The strap hurt where it lay across his new tattoo, but that couldn't be helped. After he jammed a knife into the back of his breeches he gave Niu another handful of nuts and padded barefoot back up to the main deck.

Lieutenant Gerard was there already, one stripped-down jolly and five shirtless sailors with him. "Has Mr. Gerard explained this jaunt to you, my lads?" he asked, accepting a large hand-cranking drill from Ogilvy the carpenter and dropping it into the satchel.

The six men tugged their forelocks in near unison. "Aye, aye, Captain."

"Captain, you shouldn't be risking yourself," Gerard commented, as a shirtless Lieutenant Abrams joined them. "I can swim, and so can Jamie."

"I appreciate that, William, but I want you here to see that our passengers and this expedition remain safe if anything should happen to me. And I won't risk my men where I wouldn't risk myself."

"But you'll risk me," Dr. Howard said, shedding his shirt as he approached.

"Yes. Choose a weapon." Shaw gestured at the small pile of boring tools the carpenter had assembled, and then indicated on a swiftly drawn plan of the French ship where to concentrate their sabotage and how to go about doing it. "Dr. Howard, Hendley, Garnett, Pettigrew, and I will spread out along the starboard side of the *Courageux*." He glanced at the physician. "That's the side furthest from us."

"I know that."

"Good. Mr. Abrams, Lewiston, Dobbs, and Everett

will take the port side. Do as much damage as quietly as you can beneath the waterline."

"It'll be sunrise in less than two hours," the physician noted.

"Yes. When the *Nemesis* sounds six bells, be certain your companions have heard it, and my group will make for shore. Mr. Abrams's group will return here. Silently. Are we clear?"

"Aye, aye." Belatedly Howard nodded, as well.

"Good. Let's go sink a ship."

They slipped overboard on the starboard side of the *Nemesis,* keeping the dark hulk of the ship between them and any watching eyes aboard the *Courageux*. The water was nearly the same temperature as the air, and it stung his fresh, ink-filled scars.

Shaw dunked his head, then swiped hair from his eyes and took the lead. In a quiet, ragged line they swam around the aft of the *Nemesis* and set off for the large, dark shadow halfway across the harbor.

In ten minutes they'd reached the steep, towering side of the French warship. Shaw and his small group continued around her, while Abrams and his men pulled out their drills and bores and went to work.

Unfortunately they wouldn't be able to open her up the way a few well-placed cannonballs could, but they would be concentrating the damage in areas that would be difficult to patch. A few dozen smaller wounds would kill the *Courageux* just as dead. It would only take her a bit longer to die.

Freeing his knife and the drill, Shaw took a breath and submerged. A hard jab of the blade into the wooden underbelly gave him something to lock his knees around, and then he placed the iron tip of the drill at the joint of two planks and began to crank it. Even when he had to surface for air, the knife marked his place.

In five minutes he moved the drill and placed his hand over the hole. Water rushed into it past his fingers. Shaw wrenched his knife loose and then moved a foot or so aft to repeat the procedure.

He knew by heart the weakest points of his own ship's hull, and he knew where the corresponding places would be on the slightly larger French ship. With his crew, his passengers, and his heart—his love—to protect, he meant to see that this ship never fired a cannon again. As for the crew, the natives could do as they pleased with any who survived. Without a ship and without weapons, they ceased to interest him.

By the time he surfaced to hear the dim, familiar sound of the *Nemesis*'s bell, he'd lost count of the number of holes he'd drilled. Both his hands were wrinkled and blistered and cut and riddled with splinters, but he didn't much care. Even in the dark he could see the *Courageux* settling lower in the water.

The widespread holes had her sinking fairly upright, but someone was bound to venture into the hold and notice it was rapidly filling with water. He and his men needed to go. With one more dive to retrieve his knife, he stroked slowly toward the bow.

Garnett and Pettigrew were already partway to shore, and he tapped Hendley on the shoulder as the sailor broke the surface. "Six bells," he murmured. "Go."

With a brief flash of a grin Hendley nodded and began paddling away. That left Dr. Howard. Shaw continued forward. On the far side Abrams and his men would be headed back to the *Nemesis.* A large bubble plopped to the surface in front of him. The schooner was beginning to settle faster.

"Howard," he whispered. "Howard. Six bells."

"I heard."

The deep breath of voice came from directly behind him.

For a heartbeat Shaw froze, waiting to feel the jab and hard slice of steel into his spine. Nothing touched him. "Then let's be off, shall we?" he whispered. "The ship's beginning to list."

Silence. "We're even now," finally came from behind him. With a light surge of water against him, he felt Christopher Howard kick away toward shore.

Shaw followed him. After this he would have to give the physician slightly more credit for possessing restraint. In one instance, anyway. His legs began to feel like dragging weights as he neared the rocky beach at the southern edge of the wide harbor, but the first sliver of sun across the treetops encouraged him forward.

Just as his bare feet touched solid ground, he heard the yelling begin. The brass bell of the *Courageux* began ringing frantically. With a last hard push he staggered out of the water.

"Here, Captain," Hendley hissed, waving at him from behind a barricade of broken and tumbled boulders.

Panting, Shaw joined his men and Howard. The sight that met his eyes as he turned to face the harbor struck even him, and he'd caused it.

The *Courageux* lay half sunk, listing badly to starboard. Her crew ran across the slanted deck like ants, everyone scampering to reach the swinging launches. He'd seen ships captained by friends go down in the middle of the Atlantic at the hands of the French. Those men hadn't had a chance of swimming to shore; and damned few had survived the chaos of battle to be rescued by their countrymen.

"Let's go," he said, turning his back and heading into the jungle.

"What about the crew?" Dr. Howard asked.

"As long as they can't fire on my ship, I don't give a damn. But I want to get back to camp before any of them make it to shore."

Because even if the chit he loved didn't love him, he wasn't about to allow any harm to come to her. Not for anything.

Zephyr awoke to excited shouts. Blinking, she sat up on the narrow camp bed and then hurried over to untie the tent flap and peer out. Goodness. She felt like she'd fallen asleep only minutes ago, but low morning sunlight already streaked the tops of the trees.

Men ran by, headed toward the harbor. As she caught sight of the half-dressed Major Hunter, she stepped out. "Major! What's happened?"

He slowed. "The French ship's going down. Captain Carroway did it, by God, without firing a bloo—a single shot."

Reaching back inside the small tent, Zephyr grabbed her dressing robe. She yanked it on as she ran barefoot up the small rise separating their camp from the village and the harbor beyond. The sight opening up before her stopped her in her tracks.

Halfway across the shallow curve of the harbor

the *Courageux* lay partially on her side, water washing over half the main deck. Canoes and launches and floating debris littered the water, everyone hurrying about, collecting floundering sailors. Three launches from the *Nemesis* had joined the rescue, and another left the beach as she watched. The *Swift* had sent out a pair of small boats, as well, and much closer by a handful of sailors crawled onto the shore on their own.

"Zephyr," Juliette Quanstone hissed, taking her by the arm to pull her back toward camp. "Come away! For heaven's sake, you're nearly naked."

She, of course, looked as though she'd been awake for hours—though the maid behind her looked exceedingly frazzled. Zephyr shrugged free. "I want to know that our men are safe," she retorted. "That is far more important than having my hair put up."

"Hm. Have you ever thought that Captain Carroway might be so enamored of you because you know nothing of proper behavior? I daresay he's glad not to have to abide by any of polite Society's rules out here. You may find things different back in England."

Zephyr stifled an unexpected smile. "Shaw follows the rules quite well, thank you very much. Now please leave me be." Turning her back, she topped the rise again. The shore and the harbor teemed with people, but where was Shaw?

A hand touched her shoulder. Zephyr jumped, twisting to see a very wet, nearly naked Bradshaw looking down at her. "How did you manage it?" she asked, her pulse speeding.

"A few well-placed holes beneath the waterline." His blue-eyed gaze held hers for a moment, before he looked away. "The natives seem to be rather pleased, don't they?"

"The French were using them as slaves. I would be pleased, too." She took in his lean profile, the exotic pattern of ink circling his neck, and his bare chest and feet. His skin would be cool to the touch, she imagined, her fingers twitching with the abrupt desire to find out. "Shaw?"

He glanced at her again. "Once all the sailors are rounded up, I'm going to offload all of your father's specimens, plant and animal. I want them safe before I go after the second ship."

"But what if something happens to you?"

Shaw shrugged. "See if you can arrange something with Captain Wright. I imagine you could persuade him to take over your transportation." He straightened. "There's Major Hunter. Excuse me."

She didn't like this Shaw. He felt cold and distant, as though he'd said his good-byes and had only neglected to leave physically. This man was nothing like the one whose bed she'd shared, or even like the witty fellow with whom she'd bantered on the night they'd met. "Don't do that," she said.

"I have to sink the other ship," he returned, slowing his retreat.

"That's not what I mean."

He faced her again. "I'm sparing you my presence. Don't ruin it."

Zephyr put her hands on her hips. "That's idiotic."

"You are impossible." Scowling, he took a half step toward her again, as though he couldn't decide whether to attack or retreat. "Stop talking to me."

"No."

"No?"

"No. It isn't fair, you know, that you say . . . what you did and then just waltz away without giving me a chance to figure out what the devil is going on."

"Ha." This time he took a definite step closer. "I gave you time to say something back to me, and you didn't. You just stood there."

Zephyr had heard the expression "mad enough to spit" before, but this was the first time she truly understood it. "When? The first time when you ran off, or the second time when you made a point of *not* proposing to me—and in front of my father?"

"Then I apologize," he said stiffly. "I'll attempt to do a better job of it when I return." He looked away. "Major Hunter, if you would be so kind as to assist in gathering our unfortunate French neighbors and bringing them before the chieftain, I have a ship to offload."

The major saluted. "Aye, aye, Captain. With pleasure."

"What does he mean, 'a ship to offload'?" her father asked, joining her at the top of the rise as Shaw trotted off.

"He's taking the *Nemesis* after the second French ship, but leaving your specimens behind," she returned, watching Shaw as he disappeared between the village huts and feeling as though she'd somehow said the wrong thing and missed a moment. *The* moment.

"Good thinking on Shaw's part, then."

"Yes, because this way he'll only be risking himself and his crew, and your miniature pear will be safe."

Her father put a hand on her shoulder. "I know you think me callous, Zephyr, but he is a navy captain. A warrior. That is his life."

It had used to be. What was she supposed to tell her father, though—that Shaw had tired of hunting and killing? That he'd seized on her as a remedy for the loneliness that had unexpectedly struck him? Shaw *was* a warrior. Just not in the way that her father thought. "People change," she said aloud.

"Not happily or willingly."

"You're wrong about that."

The look he sent her said that he was never wrong, but before she could find an adequate retort he hurried away to oversee his plants being taken to shore. Zephyr knew she should be assisting him, but for the first time in her life she simply didn't want to. Instead she wandered back to camp and closed herself inside her tent again to dress.

Clearly Shaw was put-out and angry. And while she enjoyed annoying him, she preferred that it be with her wits rather than her protests over timing and word choice. But there was more to this than simply saying a few words. Both their lives would be irretrievably altered. The idea excited her, but she wasn't quite as certain about him. After all, he was in quite a hurry to go into a battle now, when he'd made it clear to her previously that he'd lost his taste for such a thing. Situation unresolved.

Her father wanted her to take reality as it was. That certainly sounded simple enough. Zephyr pulled her sketchbook from beneath the bed and opened it. The drawing gazing back at her, faint amusement on his lean, handsome face, was Bradshaw. He wore his uniform, the jacket and waistcoat unbuttoned and his throat bare, a breeze stirring a lock of dark hair across his brow.

She could say no if he did bother to propose to her.

She could walk away—at least to the far end of the ship—and go on with her life as it was. After all, she had sketches and botany with which to satisfy her. Brushing the tip of her finger along the pencil line of his jaw, she sighed.

Flat, cold, lifeless paper. It in no way resembled the warm, solid, arousingly alive Shaw she knew. The man she craved being close to. The man she loved.

Oh, dear. Her legs went wobbly, and she sat down hard on the edge of the bed. She did. She loved Bradshaw Carroway. If she didn't, they would both have known it immediately, because God knew she always spoke her mind. The problem had been listening to her heart.

That deceptively intelligent organ began to beat faster. Shaw hadn't asked her to marry him. Not outright. But she wanted him. Whatever turbulence might surround them, they needed each other. Zephyr stood, smoothed out her skirt, and went to find him.

He was aboard the *Nemesis*, of course, but with the launches busily ferrying plants to the island, simply climbing into one and riding back to the ship only took ten minutes. As she ascended the rope ladder and stepped onto the main deck, everything felt fuzzy and unreal, as though she was walking through a dream.

"Excuse me, Miss Zephyr," Dobbs grunted, staggering by with a potted tree in his arms. Hendley, likewise burdened, nodded at her as he passed by.

Blinking, she swiftly stepped backward—and into a solid male chest. "Oh. Pardon me."

"That depends," Shaw said, setting her away from him again. "What are you doing here?"

Somehow she'd expected she would fall into his arms and they would be kissing by now. Shaking herself, she caught his sleeve in her fingers before he could retreat. "I want to talk to you."

"I'm busy."

Belatedly she noticed that Captain Wright of the *Swift* stood across the deck eyeing the aviary as some of the sailors attempted to catch the birds inside. Shaw had been serious about vacating all of her father's specimens from the ship, then. "You trust him now?" she asked aloud.

"Not particularly. I'm including him to remind him which side of this he would be safer on. If you go to him for passage, make certain you emphasize how celebrated he'll be at the end of the expedition. That'll give him incentive to see you safely to England."

"I wish you would stop making it sound so final."

"It could be. The *Audacieux* outguns us, and she'll see us coming."

A cold shiver ran down her spine. "I know you would prefer to avoid a battle," she said, pitching her voice low.

"Actually, I'm looking forward to this one. No one shoots at those precious to me and lives to try it twice."

Well. That settled that. "Come below for a moment. Please."

"Zephyr, I don't have time t—"

"Bradshaw, do me the courtesy of at least looking at me when I'm talking to you, or I shall punch you in the nose."

His lean jaw twitched, but he folded his arms across his chest and faced her. "What is it, then?"

She took a deep breath. This would have been so much easier in a more intimate setting and if he wasn't glaring at her. "Shaw, I just wanted to say—that is, I mean—I . . . I love you."

Something crossed his expression so swiftly that she couldn't decipher it. But then he very obviously scowled. At her. "You're only saying that now because I bullied you into it."

Oh, that was enough of that. "Idiot. You have no idea how much considering I've been doing. And you have never bullied me into anything. I said I love you because I love you."

He hesitated again. "Very well. Thank you. Now you won't have to worry that you drove me to my death if I don't return."

Zephyr narrowed her eyes. "All you did was say you loved me and then run away. I'm standing here saying it back to you, and all you can do is try to make me into a liar. It's *your* fault, for surprising me. I don't keep a response to that sort of thing in my pocket, ready for use."

"I know that. And I said thank you."

She punched him in the chest. As he winced, she caught sight of Captain Wright watching them curiously. And then it occurred to her—a thought so unexpected that it literally made her knees shake. When she glanced back at Shaw at least he wasn't scowling, but he still bore that uncertain expression, as though he didn't know how her announcement actually changed anything. Well, she did. If she had the courage to do it.

Slowly she leaned up along his hard chest. Sliding her fingers into his hair, she drew his face down and softly kissed him. At first his lips remained tight and still, and Zephyr thought she'd made a terrible mistake. Then his mouth molded to hers, his hands sliding around her waist and crushing her against him.

"Does this feel false?" she murmured against his mouth, wishing they had been all alone on the ship.

"No, it doesn't," he returned in a low, husky voice, kissing her breathless. "It feels very, very not false."

"Then marry me, Bradshaw Carroway. Have something in your future beyond another battle. Marry me right now."

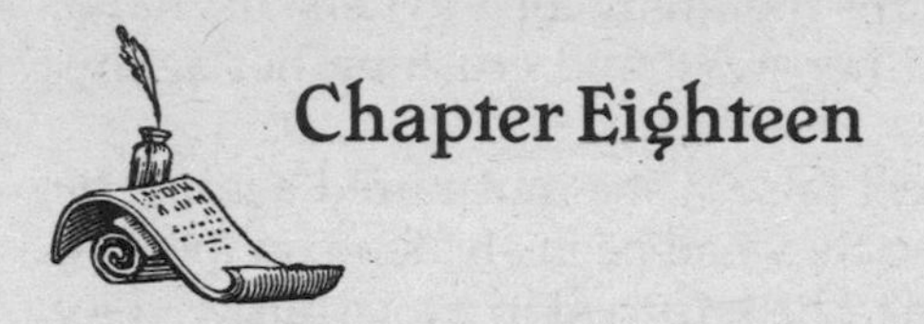

Chapter Eighteen

Now let ev'ry man drink off his full bumper,
And let ev'ry man drink off his full glass;
We'll drink and be jolly and drown melancholy,
And here's to the health of each true-hearted lass.

"SPANISH LADIES"

Bradshaw prided himself on his ability to think on his feet. It was only very rarely that either a person or an act took him completely by surprise. As he stared down at Zephyr, however, he couldn't recall ever being more astonished in his life.

"What?" he blurted.

Zephyr's gray eyes practically sparkled with a heady combination of excitement and terror. "You heard me," she returned, her voice shaking. Her fingers dug into his arms. "Do I need to sink down on one knee?"

"No. No. But if you're saying this out of guilt—if you think I'm about to go off and do something stupid . . . well, I do stupid things anyway. And I've a better reason for this battle than most I've been in."

A quick, nervous chuckle broke from her lips. "This is merely one more lunatic act, then."

Shaw tilted her chin up with his fingers. Electricity seemed to flow from her into him, all around and encircling them. "You will never regret this, Zephyr," he murmured, taking in every bit of this moment, wanting to memorize everything about it. The bustling sounds of a ship readying for battle, the bright sun bathing the deck with gold, the breeze making her blue muslin gown swirl about her legs—everything. "I promise."

She nodded, pushing past his fingers to kiss him again. His. In a handful of moments she would be his, and for the rest of their lives. He brushed her warm lips with his, feeling her trembling against him. Then she took a deep breath and pushed away.

"Captain Wright?"

The captain of the *Swift* straightened his spine with a nearly audible snap. "Aye, miss?"

"Would you be so kind as to marry me to Captain Carroway?"

"I— It would be my pleasure, miss."

Good God. He was getting married. Shaw took her hand in his. "What about your father?"

"I told him that I would continue to assist him. Beyond that, I don't think he cares."

She made a good point. And while he didn't wish to begin a marriage being disliked by his father-in-law, neither did he intend to let this moment pass by without seizing it. And the last time he'd seen Ponsley, the botanist hadn't been terribly pleased at the idea of his daughter marrying a naval captain anyway. "Potter!" he called.

The midshipman stepped forward from the group that had surrounded them. "Aye, sir?"

"Fetch my dress jacket from my cabin."

"Aye, aye, Captain."

"And if Miss Jones and her companions—and Sir Joseph—are in sight, have someone fetch them, as well. I want witnesses from damned Mayfair."

With a grin and a salute the sailor ran from the deck. In truth they had witnesses aplenty already, but to the peerage a loyal, sweaty, and barefoot group of sailors would count for nothing. The only way to avoid any rumors of impropriety or undue haste would be to have some of their own to attest to witnessing the marriage.

Potter returned, and while Captain Wright busied himself with moving sailors here and there and checking the view from the wheel deck, Shaw pulled on his coat. Zephyr brushed out one sleeve, and he smiled. "Whatever the devil we're in for," he said softly, "I am very glad I met you."

"And I'm glad you're much more pleasant and brilliant than I might possibly have thought at first."

Laughing, Shaw kissed her forehead. "Thank you."

Ten minutes later Miss Jones arrived on deck, her frivolous friends following along behind her. "Captain, your man said we're to witness a wedding. What is he . . ." She trailed off, blinking her long lashes as she took in Zephyr standing beside him, her hand held in his. "Oh."

Juliette Quanstone swept forward, clapping excitedly. "I love a wedding!" she exclaimed, her voice a bit shrill. "But Zephyr, you can't mean to wear that! Ladies, surely we can find something for Zephyr to wear so she'll look presentable at her own wedding."

Perhaps risking a small amount of censure would have been worth it. "We only ask for witnesses to attest that they've seen us properly wed," Shaw broke in. "Miss Ponsley . . . takes my breath away just as she is." He turned his gaze to her. "Change your gown if you wish, but I prefer this."

"I brought my parasol," she returned, and Dobbs retrieved it for her. "Will this do?"

"You are every inch a lady with or without it, my love." Shaw cleared his throat. "However, I do have a ship to go sink."

Her grip on his hand tightened. "Frederica, did my father come aboard with you?"

"I haven't seen him all morning, dear."

Shaw looked at her disappointed expression. "This can wait until I return," he murmured.

She shook her head. "You're mine, Bradshaw Carroway, whatever happens. I will not wait." Taking a breath, she squared her shoulders. "Captain Wright, will you begin?"

"Aye." The barrel-chested captain folded his hands in front of his waist. "Dearly beloved, we've gathered here on the deck of this fine ship off the shore of Tahiti to marry these two good people. Do ye h—"

With a loud squawk, Niu flapped up from below, circled over the mainmast, then fluttered down to land on Shaw's shoulder. "I apologize, Captain," Potter whispered loudly. "I must've left yer door open. Shall I catch 'im and stow 'im back below?"

"Don't you dare," Zephyr commented, tilting her parasol in her free hand. "I think it's quite fitting."

"My youngest brother will perish from envy," Shaw noted with a grin. "Continue, Captain."

"Aye, aye, Captain. Do ye have a ring?"

Freeing his hand from Zephyr's for a moment, Shaw pulled the ring bearing his family crest off his right hand. "This will have to do for the moment."

"Put it on her, lad. Do ye, Captain Bradshaw—"

"George," Shaw supplied.

"—Captain Bradshaw George Carroway, take this lady to be yer lawful wife? To take no other or be forsaken?"

The vows weren't quite traditional, and for a heartbeat Shaw wondered just how much of this Captain Wright might be inventing on the spot. Nevertheless, he nodded. "I do."

"Splendid. Do ye . . ."

"Zephyr Patricia Ponsley," she offered.

"Truly?"

Shaw scowled. "Captain. If you please."

"Aye. Do ye, Zephyr Patricia, take this man to be yer lawful husband? To take no other and to love as long as ye both shall live?"

Zephyr grinned. "I do."

"Give 'er that ring, lad."

Trying to keep his fingers from shaking, Shaw took her left hand in his and slipped the ring over her third finger. It was too large, of course, but when they returned home he would choose her a proper one. "Now you're mine, my warm, following breeze," he murmured.

She blushed. "I prefer 'companion breeze,' if you don't mind."

"I like that better myself."

"By the power vested in me as captain of the good ship *Swift* and as a former proud navy man meself, I now pronounce ye husband and wife. Give 'er a kiss, my boy."

"With pleasure." Dipping her in his arms, the parasol waving wildly, Shaw leaned down and kissed his bride.

He knew what it meant—retirement, finding a permanent home, no more squalls or fast currents—but all he cared about was that Zephyr was laughing in delight, the sound only muffled by his mouth as he continued to kiss her. The sailors cheered and whistled, while the handful of Tahitians on board began a spontaneous dance.

"Damned chit," Niu squawked, fluttering to keep his balance on Shaw's shoulder.

"Ignore the parrot," Shaw muttered, chuckling. "I do love you."

"I love you," she returned, holding on to him as he swung her upright again.

"My only regret is that our wedding night will have to wait until after I return." Holding her gaze, Shaw brushed his fingers against her cheek. "I mean for this to be the last time I leave you," he said quietly. "Thank you. I can do this knowing—"

"Just please be careful."

Zephyr wanted to stay on board the *Nemesis*. She wanted to sail with him off to do battle with the *Audacieux*. But that would be mad. What would she do, hold his pistol for him? Brush splinters from his coat while he shouted orders? Ridiculous.

Rolling her shoulders, she gave him one more kiss and then walked over to pick up a small potted fern.

Her husband sent her a swift smile, and then returned to readying the ship for battle. Married. She was a married woman.

And her father was wrong. Bradshaw was not only the perfect man for her, he was the only one. She couldn't imagine anyone else who would understand her lapses of finesse, her enjoyment of arguing, and her insistence on logic. Yes, she had just given up her days of traveling, but so had Shaw. She hoped he felt as much joy thinking about their future together as she did.

When she couldn't put it off any longer, she left the ship and returned to shore. The rest of the crew returned to the *Nemesis,* save for the two dozen jollies Shaw had ordered to remain on the island to assist with keeping the French sailors in check and to watch over her father's—and her—safety.

"That's an unhappy sight, isn't it?" Captain Wright asked from beside her.

As she watched, the *Nemesis* weighed anchor, unfurled her white sails, and floated gracefully for the entrance of the harbor. "They'll be back," she returned.

"In the meantime, it would be my honor to have you and your papa and the other ladies and gentlemen on board the *Swift* for dinner this evening," he said, nodding at her father as he appeared from farther along the shore. "Carroway did me a good turn, sinking that French bastard—however he managed it."

"That would be grand of you, Captain Wright," the botanist said, offering his hand. "I can't speak for the others, but my daughter and I will be happy to join you."

"I think it will be lovely to visit a different ship,"

Frederica Jones said. "We've been aboard the *Nemesis* for weeks and weeks. It's very . . . military."

If the choice had been up to her, Zephyr would have refused the invitation. Captain Wright might have just performed her marriage ceremony, but Shaw didn't entirely trust the man. And she trusted Shaw. "Are you certain you wouldn't rather join us in our camp?" she asked. "It's a bit rustic, but the scenery is lovely."

Emily Quanstone made a face. "I detest food cooked over an open fire. It's either nearly raw, or burned to a crisp."

"That settles it, then," the captain commented, smiling. "I'll send a launch for ye at six o'clock."

"Thank you, Captain," her father took up. "We shall be there."

"Excellent. We'll drink a toast to the newlyweds."

Oh, good heavens. Forcing a smile that felt more like a grimace, Zephyr took her father's arm. "I need a word with you," she said, pulling him away from the shoreline.

"I need to keep an eye on my specimens," he protested, looking over his shoulder at them.

"I'll just be a moment. It's important."

He sighed. "You've chosen poorly, you know. When we return to England you'll be celebrated, just as I will be. If you've decided to abandon me, you might have netted someone titled, someone with enough wealth to see you esteemed and me able to continue my botanical studies. *That* would have been the aim of a dutiful daughter."

"I'm not abandoning you, and I chose Shaw. *You're* the one who declined to attend your daughter's wedding."

"You never used to speak to me like this. A dutiful child would never have accepted a proposal from the first man who asked, simply because he did ask."

"He didn't propose to me. I proposed to him."

Finally he looked more surprised than angry and frustrated. "*You* proposed to *him*?"

"Yes, because I didn't think he believed me when I said that I loved him. I can hardly blame him, since I had to think about it for an entire day after he said it to me, but I do love him. More than I can articulate to you."

Her father looked at her for a long moment, his brown eyes very serious. "Well. All I can say to that is that you're married, Zephyr. Married. To a man you've known for two months. You may have just stepped into a life of misery and dissatisfaction, but if you think you're grown enough to walk without my advice or assistance, then you're grown enough to live with the consequences. I do wish you well."

He turned on his heel and returned to ordering his plants moved up from the high tide mark on the beach. She watched him for a moment, then went to go help.

After speaking with him, she was glad he'd declined to attend her wedding. His recitation wouldn't have changed; in fact, it would only have begun earlier and likely would have spoiled those moments of . . . of absolute joy when Shaw put his ring on her finger. Sir Joseph saw every event only as it affected him. And he never considered that she had already asked for his advice and assistance, and he'd failed to offer it in the way a father should.

The botanist glanced over at her several times, but

didn't approach again. Well, she hadn't anticipated marrying today, and she hadn't anticipated spending the hours after her wedding moving plants, but then again, nothing since she'd boarded the *Nemesis* had been ordinary. Zephyr smiled. And when Shaw returned, she imagined that her wedding night would be rather extraordinary, as well.

As soon as she could manage it without looking overly suspicious, she walked into the village to find Major Hunter. Two of his men accompanied her there—apparently either Shaw or the marine commander had ordered that she be protected at all times.

"Miss—Mrs. Carroway," the major said, doffing his hat. "My best regards and congratulations."

"Thank you." She glanced beyond him at the makeshift compound being constructed, apparently from the timber that had come floating up from the sunken *Courageux*. "Do you know what the natives mean to do with their new guests?"

"I think they're waiting to see whether the *Nemesis* or the *Audacieux* returns. My money's on Captain Carroway. He's won against worse odds than this."

A slight tremor ran through her, and she clenched her hands together. Shaw would be successful and return, because she couldn't imagine him not doing so. Losing him now would be unthinkable. "And when the *Audacieux* doesn't return and the *Nemesis* does?"

"I have the feeling that the Tahitians and the French are going to become great friends," he said with a grin. "The chieftain's no fool, and when another French ship comes by he's going to make certain everyone's been well-treated—and that they're all in his debt."

"Good for him." She took a step closer, lowering her voice. "We've been invited to have dinner aboard the *Swift*," she told him.

"You can't."

"My father and Miss Jones accepted on our behalf before I could say anything. If we refuse now, Captain Wright will be suspicious."

The marine blew out his breath. "At what time are you going?"

"Six o'clock."

"I'll be inviting myself along, then."

She touched his sleeve. "Thank you." Zephyr started to turn away, but the major put a hand over hers.

"I've known Bradshaw for eight years," he said. "We've drunk rum and bled together. He's a good man, and he enjoys life, and I know losing Dr. Griffeth gutted him. And I've still never seen him as happy as he is when he's around you."

A tear ran down her cheek, cool in the warm air. "Thank you, Major."

"I just wanted you to know that." He saluted jauntily. "And I'll be about, if you should require anything."

Well, that was a very nice counter to her father's pessimism. If she hadn't been so worried over Shaw and his men, so occupied with listening for the impossibly distant sounds of cannonfire, she would have been skipping and twirling as she continued past the round, thatched huts.

A small group of women, chatting and laughing among themselves, approached her. "Hello, miss," the youngest of them, a girl of twelve or thirteen, she estimated, greeted her.

"Hello."

"You is missus to handsome Captain Shaw now, yes?"

Zephyr glanced back at her two marine companions, who looked terribly amused. "Yes, I am Shaw's wife."

"We make you pretty for when husband return."

Oh, dear. She rather liked Shaw's tattoo, but from what he'd said, it had hurt. And she would never be able to show herself in proper Society if her neck was dotted with Tahitian mythological symbols. "Thank you, but I have a dinner to attend."

"No, you come. Come see how we dress for marry."

Zephyr considered that. "No tattoos?"

The ladies laughed. "No. The church men say no lady tattoo. Come. We show."

With a grin, Zephyr inclined her head. She was something of an explorer, after all. And she'd just embarked on quite possibly her greatest adventure. "Thank you. I would be delighted."

After several hours, Zephyr took the bundle of things wrapped into a large roll of decorated tapa cloth and hid them in her tent. Even with Frederica Jones and her friends in their small camp this afternoon, the area seemed quiet and deserted.

She spent a long moment gazing out over the harbor in the direction of the lowering sun. This was the first time she and Shaw had been apart in two months, and already her breathing felt tight, the pinch in her heart making her want to sit and weep.

What might have happened if he'd still been that wild, devil-may-care captain of repute, she had no idea. Just the idea that he might wed her and then sail off for years at a time left her feeling ill. She wanted him with her. So much of her life had felt transient, with brief friendships set aside in favor of her father's travels. It was only natural, she supposed, now that she had Shaw to not wish to let him go. Thank God he felt the same.

"Aren't you going to dress for dinner?"

Jumping, she turned around to see Juliette Quanstone tying a bonnet over her light-colored hair. "Most of my clothes are still aboard the *Nemesis*," Zephyr returned. "And I wore this to marry in, so I suppose it'll do."

"Yes, congratulations."

"Thank you."

"I owe you an apology, I think. I accused you of being unpolished. But I've seen Captain Carroway with ladies before—I even pursued him myself, you know—but no one's managed to get him to the altar." She lowered her light green eyes to Zephyr's abdomen. "This is to be a long voyage. Perhaps too long to hide certain things. Well done."

Zephyr frowned. "I thought you and I might be friends, Juliette. I've had so few close friendships that I cherished just the idea of it. Apparently because of that I overlooked things I should not have—like your pettiness and your propensity for gossip."

"I—"

"Since we will be traveling together for several more months, I think we should remain cordial. But I don't care much to hear your opinion or receive your advice."

"You'd best be careful when you return to London, Zephyr, because Shaw was quite popular. And no one knows who you are."

"Yes, but you won't be there." Beyond Juliette, she spied Major Hunter approaching. "Now please excuse me. My dinner escort is here."

Her jaw clenched, she did her best not to stomp as she walked up to take the major's arm. He lifted an eyebrow, but continued on with her toward the beach and the waiting launch from the *Swift*.

Her father approached from farther along the shore, and she squared her shoulders for yet another battle. Until this voyage she'd thought Sir Joseph's view of the world and the resident flora and fauna therein to be the correct one. Now, however, the way he placed his specimens squarely in front of any man, woman, or child—even her—seemed both wrong and rather sad.

"Look at this," he said, lifting the specimen jar he held. "One of my guides found it. Some sort of beetle, but look at the gorgeous coloring."

She peered at the small insect with its black front, bright yellow backside, and red and black segmented legs. "It's very pretty," she agreed. "Is it joining us for dinner?"

He handed the jar to one of the natives standing with them. "No. Is it time already?"

Major Hunter nodded. "It is. I thought to join you, if you don't mind."

"Of course not. That seems wise, actually, given Captain Carroway's reservations. Is there any word on when Shaw intends to return?"

"No, sir. I would imagine late tomorrow or early the next day, if all goes well."

"This way, ladies and gentlemen," one of the *Swift*'s sailors called in a striking Cockney accent. "The captain's laid out quite the feast for ye."

Even with Major Hunter and Dr. Howard joining them they all managed to squeeze aboard the launch, and in five minutes they reached the *Swift*. Captain Wright had rigged a board-bottomed swing of sorts to bring his guests aboard one by one, and Zephyr fleetingly wondered whether Shaw knew of such a thing or if he'd simply preferred her to climb the rope ladder with her boy's breeches on beneath her skirt. Hm.

The *Swift* was much smaller than the *Nemesis*, and her crew was quite a bit more ragged-looking. They all seemed friendly enough as they guided the captain's guests below to his cabin, but she kept half her attention on Major Hunter and the other half on memorizing the route back to the main deck. Yes, Shaw was quite possibly being overly cautious in his mistrust of Captain Wright, but she'd already realized that her husband had a rather uncanny way of being correct.

"Welcome, my friends," Captain Wright said, greeting them as they squeezed through the narrow door of his rather expansive cabin. Goodness. He had more space than Shaw did—but then again, there weren't rows and rows of cannon directly outside the merchant captain's door.

"Thank you for inviting us aboard, Captain," Lord John drawled. "If we've discovered one thing about evenings spent on tropical islands it's the abundance of biting insects."

The captain laughed. "I made that discovery myself, quite some time ago. Please, tell me all about your voyage. My cook traded a butcher's knife for a very fine young pig, which I'm told now comprises the finest roast pork ever prepared."

They all seated themselves at the large table. Thankfully Lord John and Lord Benjamin Harding seemed to remember Shaw's warnings about kidnaping and ransom, because they maintained their rather plausible tale about a group of friends whom Shaw as a personal favor had agreed to transport so they could forgo the expense of seeking private passage.

"Captain Carroway has himself quite a shipload of friends and family, he does," the captain commented, gesturing for everyone's wineglasses to be refilled. He'd been doing that quite a bit, Zephyr noted, though only she and the major had refrained from imbibing. "And some very unusual plants. I know a breadfruit tree from a coconut palm, but beyond that I'm afraid I'm quite lost."

"It would be my pleasure to show you some of my treasures," her father said. "For terrains of such similar elevations, the islands have an astonishing variety of flora."

Captain Wright nodded. "We've had success growing the transplanted breadfruits in the West Indies, but before we brought 'em there, not a single one grew on its own."

"I've begun work on a hypothesis concerning air and sea currents and their effect on the propagation of species," the botanist returned. "It's quite different from my land-based theories concerning elevation and rainfall. If you're interested in a deeper discussion along those lines, I would be happy to lend you my latest book."

Zephyr winced. Once her father began discussing botanicals, everything else—including common sense—fell by the wayside. "Papa," she said aloud,

"Captain Wright has already told us that the French have put him behind schedule." She turned her gaze to the captain and forced a smile. "Please don't feel obligated to humor my father. He has quite enough to keep him occupied, himself."

The captain straightened. "I'd be pleased to read yer book, Joseph. I have a suspicion about ye, if I may. Carroway introduced you as Joseph, but yer daughter there gave her maiden name as Ponsley. That put in my mind that you might be Sir Joseph Ponsley, the famous botanist. I'd never say anything, of course, but if it's true, I am truly honored, sir."

Drat. Now it was her fault, for thinking only that she was getting married and not about her father's identity. She took a gulp of wine; keeping her wits remained vital, but blast it all, it hadn't helped thus far.

"I suppose the secret is out, then," her father commented with a rather professorial smile. "We're attempting to keep our expedition quiet, so I appreciate your offer of discretion."

After that everyone seemed to relax, and soon they were all chatting like old friends in a London drawing room. The fact that back in London most of his guests wouldn't have so much as acknowledged Captain Wright didn't seem to trouble any of them—except her. Slowly she put her fingers over her table knife and then slid it onto her lap beneath her napkin.

"Ye know," the captain commented as sailors removed the last of the dishes from the table, "I've been thinking. With the *Nemesis* gone and damned insects aplenty on the island, I'd be happy to give over my crew quarters to you fine ladies and gentlemen."

Alarm bells began ringing in Zephyr's skull. She gripped the knife beneath the edge of the table. "Oh, thank you, but that's not necessary, Captain," she returned before anyone else could respond. "We've been sleeping on shore to this point, and we're here for a bit of adventure, after all."

"Speaking of which," Major Hunter said, pushing back from the table with an exaggerated sigh, "I have a watch to relieve."

"Oh, by all means, Major," Wright agreed. "We'll be happy to see ye to shore. But yer passengers deserve a bit better than sand and thieving natives."

"Thank you so much for your kind hospitality, Captain Wright," Zephyr took up, pretending not to hear the threat in his voice, "but we do have to be going."

"And I think ye should stay."

By now even Miss Jones and her idiotic brother began to look troubled. Of their party only Major Hunter was adequately armed, and on the *Swift* they were hopelessly outnumbered. If this became a fight they would lose, and the major would more than likely be killed.

In the past two months Shaw had taught her about more than sex and simply being alive. He was also a master of strategy and subterfuge. And she hoped that she was as good a student as he was a teacher. She cleared her throat. "Did Shaw tell you the particulars about the demise of the *Courageux*?" she asked, the calm sound of her voice surprising even her.

"He inferred that he sank the damned thing."

"Yes. Someone from the *Courageux* shot at us last night. With my father here—well, Shaw didn't like that one bit. Finishing this expedition is quite important to the Admiralty and the Royal Society." She chuckled. "I mean, my goodness, we're not at war with France, and he simply went over and sank their ship before they ever knew what was happening. And he's doing it again at this very minute—to a ship that hasn't even set eyes on any of us." She glanced at Hunter. "Major, what was the name of that pirate ship he sank shortly before the *Nemesis* sailed to the Pacific?"

"The *Revanche*," the marine answered. "We hunted her for six months. The rest of the fleet gave up on ever finding her. Captain Carroway said we weren't returning to England until she was ours."

"Imagine that," Zephyr continued, looking back at Captain Wright again. "Did he have a personal grudge against the *Revanche*?"

"No, Mrs. Carroway. He likes the hunt. All he requires is the shadow of an excuse."

If she had any say in anything, Major Hunter was going to receive some sort of medal. "I find that very enlightening." She stood, keeping the knife concealed in the folds of her skirt. "There are so many things I still need to learn about my husband. But at the moment I'm quite tired. I hate to cut our evening short. Do you mind terribly, Captain Wright?"

Captain Wright stood, as well. "I'll have the launch lowered. Ladies, gentlemen, if you'll follow me?"

"Certainly, Captain. Thank you so much for a wonderful evening."

As Wright passed by Zephyr, he slowed. "Remind me never to play cards with ye, Mrs. Carroway," he murmured, then pulled open his door and led the way out.

She headed down the corridor toward the main deck, the rest of her companions behind her. Then someone took her arm. "I believe I owe you an apology, Zephyr," Dr. Howard whispered. "Not only did I behave inappropriately, but I made an even worse error."

"What was that?" she asked, genuinely curious.

"I underestimated you. You are quite formidable, and I'm sorry to have missed a chance for a friendship with you. And your husband."

Zephyr nodded. Under other circumstances she would likely be feeling quite pleased with herself. As they returned to the launch and then stepped back onto the island, however, the only thing she could think of was that the man who'd shown her how to be . . . alive was facing death, and that she wouldn't sleep a wink until he returned and she shared a bed with her husband.

Chapter Nineteen

Full ten thousand miles behind us
And a thousand miles before,
Ancient ocean waves to waft us
To the well remembered shore.

"ROLLING HOME"

By the next evening Zephyr decided she more than likely knew the harbor at Matavai Bay better than any foreigner ever had or ever would. By her estimation it was a little more than a mile from one side to the other, and she'd walked it five times.

She had no idea where her father was, though she had noticed him set off shortly after sunrise with a dozen natives and half that many marines in tow. As for the Mayfair company, the last she saw of them was as they walked into the village. They were safe from Captain Wright, and other than that they no longer concerned her.

As for her, she couldn't concentrate on anything. After several attempts to sketch her father's newest beetle and then a scene of Tahitian girls dancing, she put the paper and pencils aside and began walking.

Her head ached from staring at the sun-tipped waves for hours and hours, but she kept looking anyway.

"Missus Carroway. Zephyr."

She jumped, slowing her pace as she realized she'd reached the shore directly in front of the village again. The two marines who'd been assigned to her were discussing something with Major Hunter, who wore a bemused expression on his face. "Major," she acknowledged.

He left his men and walked up to her. "Garnett and Brist just begged me to speak with you, and to ask you to sit and have something to eat."

"I'm not hungry."

"But my men are wearing holes in the soles of their boots."

"Oh." When she considered it, her own feet were terribly tired. All day she'd felt separated from her body, with every ounce of her soul and spirit looking for Shaw and praying that he and his men were safe and well. "I'm fine on my own, then."

"No, you're not." Hunter looked from the village to her and back again. "I'll have a chair brought to you, and you can sit here. You can see the entire harbor from this spot."

"Don't patronize me." She scowled. "And yes, please bring me a chair."

"Aye, aye, Mrs. Captain Carroway."

If she hadn't been nearly out of her mind with worry, her new moniker would have been amusing. But then she saw it—a white kite flying just over the tops of the trees at the south end of the harbor. Except that it wasn't a kite. It was a sail.

"Look!" she shrieked, running onto the sand.

The *Nemesis* soared in grandly, furling her sails

and slowing as she neared her previous anchorage close to the middle of the harbor. A section of rail was missing and her fore topsail had a hole through it and looked tattered on one edge from a black powder explosion, but if Zephyr hadn't been so familiar with the ship she never would have known they'd been through a battle.

Behind her Major Hunter and her guards whistled and waved. Villagers began appearing, as well, dragging out canoes to meet the ship as they had when the *Nemesis* had first arrived in Tahiti. As she watched them piling into the water, an idea touched her, making her heart beat even faster. She caught the arm of one of the men she recognized from his assistance to her father. "Wait for me," she said, motioning for the canoe to stay.

As soon as he nodded she sprinted over the low rise to their camp. Her sore feet forgotten, she dove into her tent, grabbed the roll of pounded bark and the items therein, and ran back to the beach. The canoe and its four-man crew had waited for her, thank goodness.

"Come, Missus Captain," the fellow called, taking her bundle and settling it into the bottom of canoe as she scrambled over the side and took a seat. Laughing, the men pushed the boat into the water and jumped in to grab their paddles.

It felt like they were flying across the surface of the harbor, but it still wasn't fast enough. The *Nemesis*'s anchor plunged into the water, and the ship rocked to a gentle stop.

A familiar tall, lean form appeared at the railing and stepped over to the rope ladder hanging above the lowering launch. "Shaw!" she called, her breath catching and keen relief flooding through her. He was alive. *Thank God. Thank God.*

Bradshaw spotted Zephyr the moment the *Nemesis* rounded the point and entered the harbor. He hadn't slept for over thirty-six hours and his eyes still stung from the smoke and black powder, but none of that mattered. She stood on the shore, watching for him. His wife.

Once they'd set the anchor he ordered the launches lowered. Before he could do more than step over the railing, however, he heard her voice. She was in a damned canoe, rowing out to greet him.

Grinning, Shaw returned to the deck. When he'd first joined the navy he'd craved the adventure, the battle of arms and wits. Then it had become an exercise in stupidity and waste. Yesterday he'd been impatient, baiting the *Audacieux* into aggression and then maneuvering her onto the rocks, working toward doing just enough damage that she would no longer be seaworthy. The moment he'd been waiting for, craving, was back here.

"Mr. Gerard, you have the command," he said, ignoring the snickers and muttering going on around him.

The canoe reached the side of the ship, and Zephyr handed up a bundle of something, then climbed the ladder herself. Shaw stepped forward, lifting her over the railing and into his arms. She felt warm, and vital, and alive.

"Shaw," she muttered, her voice muffled against his mouth as he kissed her again and again. "You're not hurt? You're well?"

"I'm fine now." He closed his eyes for a moment, just holding her.

She feathered her fingers through his hair. "I want my wedding night," she whispered.

Shaw straightened, shifting his grip to her hand. "Carry on, gentlemen," he said, and pulled her toward the hatchway.

"Wait. Bring that," she ordered, pointing at the bundle Hendley still held.

Taking it, Bradshaw left the deck with her in tow. He'd meant it when he'd said he would retire; he wouldn't leave her standing there again. He took a moment to wonder how married captains managed it, sailing off for years on end while their wives, their hearts, stayed behind. Or perhaps that was why so many captains never married. The thought was unbearable.

He pushed open his cabin door, but Zephyr pulled back against his hand. "Wait."

"What is it? I broke every speed record imaginable to return here before sunset, you know."

"Give me a moment inside." She took the bundle in her own arms and slipped past him. "I'll tell you when to come in." Then she closed his door on him.

"Don't tell me someone found you a wedding gown," he said to the door, concentrating on images of sag-faced old women and arithmetic to avoid embarrassing himself in front of the sailors who suddenly had business below decks. "I'm only going to take it off you again."

"Hush," her voice came distantly, and he swore he heard her laughing.

"I'm an impatient man, Zephyr."

"And I'm an impatient woman. I nearly walked my shoes to pieces today, waiting for you. So now you can wait a damned minute."

"Damned chit," Niu said from inside the cabin. "You tell her, lad."

Finally, after a great deal of muffled rustling and bustling and a few fairly unladylike curses, she cleared her throat. "You may enter now," she called.

He wasn't waiting for a blasted second invitation. Shaw pushed open the door—and froze.

"Close it," she ordered, blushing.

Without turning away from her, he closed and latched his door. Zephyr was naked. Well, not entirely. Around her hips she wore a grass skirt that hung down to her knees, with an anklet of shells just above her left bare foot. Her long chestnut hair with its brass highlights hung loose down her shoulders, not quite obscuring her bare breasts or the necklace of shells and stones she wore around her neck. More shells adorned her left wrist. And she had a flower tucked behind one ear.

"Well?"

"Just a moment. My heart's stopped beating."

"It's traditional," she explained, swirling in a circle that made her hips sway and his breeches feel uncomfortably tight. "Because I didn't get a chance to wear one when I became Mrs. Handsome Captain Shaw."

"That's quite a moniker for your stationery," he noted, pulling his jacket off and dropping it somewhere behind him. "I thought you might have taken the past day to realize what a dreadful mistake you'd made in marrying me."

Putting a hand to her heart, she shook her head. "I only . . . I only hope that you don't regret it," she said thickly.

Bradshaw shed his waistcoat and then pulled his

shirt off over his head to drop it, as well. "Do I look like I regret it?"

"No, but we're going to have sex. You like sex."

"I do like sex. But I love you."

She smiled. "Then come here."

"Just a moment." Shaw took the cage where Niu perched, watching interestedly, and put it outside the door. "I don't want him learning any new vocabulary," he explained, locking them in again. Then he sat on the edge of his writing chair and pulled off his boots. "Now. You come here."

Zephyr swept forward, circling her arms around his neck and settling on his thigh to kiss him, soft and openmouthed. She intoxicated him. Brushing her hair back from her shoulders, he dipped his head to take her left breast into his mouth.

With a groan she arched against him. God. Even when they weren't arguing she aroused him no end. And in that costume . . . He put his palm on her knee and slid upward, beneath the stiff blades of grass. "You are keeping this skirt," he murmured, shifting his mouth to her other breast.

She chuckled breathlessly, the sound lifting into a gasp as he slid his hand between her thighs and slipped a finger inside her. Sweet Lucifer. She was hot and damp and ready—for him. For her husband.

"Stand up."

After she did so, he rose as well, unfastening his trousers. Zephyr decided to trace his necklace tattoo with her lips and tongue, and he nearly ripped his buttons off in his hurry. Once he was naked, Shaw put his hands around her hips and drew her up against him, lowering his head to take her sweet mouth again.

"How do I get this off you?" he asked, running his fingers around the band of her skirt. Then he found the knot on one side. "Ah. Never mind."

With a rustle the grass skirt fell to the floor. Orange sunset filtered in through the aft windows, bathing her in gold. Perfection.

He swept her up in his arms and laid her down on his bunk, her shell necklace looping beneath one full breast. "You're keeping the necklace and bracelets, as well," he breathed, dipping his head for another taste of her soft, smooth skin.

"I want you, Shaw. Please." She pulled on his shoulders, tugging him up over her.

Another statement with which he had no argument. Bradshaw settled himself between her knees. Kissing her again, he angled his hips forward, entering her. Tight warmth engulfed him, and he stilled for a moment, trying to steady himself. A man with experience he might be, but she rendered him taut and panting with just a look. And she was looking at him now.

He entered her again and again, watching as her expression grew tighter and then she shattered, pulsing, around him. When she began to relax again he rolled them, putting him on his back and letting her ride him. Her shell beads clicked and bounced—in fact, he didn't think he'd ever be able to hear that sound again without going hard.

Finally he let himself go and surged up into her harder and faster until he came deep inside her. With a satisfied groan she collapsed against his chest and they lay there in a tangle of beads and limbs, panting.

The sun had set, leaving them in candle-lit darkness, before she lifted her head to look down at him. "I love you, Bradshaw," she whispered, kissing his mouth.

"I love you, my warm, companion breeze."

Nineteen months later

Bradshaw heard the shouts before he even stepped down from the hired hack. Stifling a grin, he helped Zephyr to the ground. "I did warn you, didn't I?" he muttered, kissing her fingers as Dawkins the butler pulled open the Carroway House front door.

"Several times, but I think I'll manage."

"Damned chit."

The red parrot on his shoulder echoed the sentiment as the Runt flew out the front door and launched himself at Shaw's chest. "You do have a parrot!" he shouted.

"You've grown, Runt. How old are you now, twenty?"

"I'll be thirteen next week," Edward announced proudly. "And I'm nearly as tall as Andrew, so you can't call me Runt any longer."

"Duly noted." With a grin, Shaw pushed him back to arm's length. "Aside from a parrot, I also have a woman. Edward, this is Zephyr. Zephyr, my youngest brother, Edward."

She dipped a curtsy. "Hello, Edward."

His brother faced the doorway. "You're wrong, Andrew! She does not have a fish tail or a mustache!"

"Oh, good God," Shaw muttered. "Move aside, will you?"

They all waited in the morning room, aunties and

brothers and their wives and several more children than there had been when he'd left. He introduced Zephyr to the ones he knew, looking on as his large family enveloped her the way they always had one another.

"Now who's this?" he asked, squatting down to eye level with the young man holding on to Robert's knee.

"This is Bradshaw," Bit returned, fondly ruffling the toddler's black hair, his other hand holding that of his wife, Lucinda.

Shaw blinked. "Really? I'm flattered. Thank you, Bit."

"We call him Barnacle, for obvious reasons."

"Well, that makes more sense, now." Straightening, he peered into the blankets that Georgiana, Tristan's wife, held. "And this?"

"Alexander. I'm sorry, but you're no longer my heir apparent, Shaw." Tristan grinned.

"Thank God for that. Well, tell me what else I've missed."

"You first!" Edward demanded. "And how do you pronounce your parrot's name?"

"Niu," he said, putting a finger beneath the bird's feet and then settling him on his brother's shoulder.

"Stap my anchor," the parrot announced.

Zephyr watched as Shaw regaled his family with the tale of their voyage, from the near battle at Tonga to the pirates they'd run off just beyond the coast of Onotoa, to the wondrous statues they'd seen on Easter Island. He'd spoken of his family a great deal, and she already felt she knew them.

What a difference they were from her rather solitary, transient life with her father, and she adored it.

From their first meeting it felt as though she'd been living in one room of a house and now suddenly discovered there was more than just the library.

For weeks after their return to London they went daily to see her father, to help him prepare for his presentation to the Royal Society. She didn't know if she'd been forgiven for choosing Shaw over botany, but once he seemed to realize that Bradshaw wasn't going anywhere, he at least became more civil. The presentation itself was fascinating even to her, and she'd lived the expedition. The entire Carroway clan—or at least the ones who had learned how to walk—attended, as well.

Friends, family, people with whom she could chat and in whom she could confide without worry that some socially awkward comment of hers would end up on the dance floor of the next soiree. She loved that they'd attended her father's presentation, and she loved that they'd done it for her.

"Do they mention me?" Shaw asked, leaning over from his seat at the breakfast table to see the newspaper article she was reading.

She perused the report of her father's presentation. "Hm. Let's see. Oh, yes. Here you are. It says that the unnamed captain of the vessel in question married the eminent botanist's eminent daughter."

"You are such a liar."

Zephyr laughed. "Isn't it enough that my father said so many nice things about you during the presentation?"

"He should have said more nice things about you. That presentation would have been dull as dirt without your illustrations."

"He thanked me for my assistance. And I didn't even require that much. I'm more interested in looking for a house with you."

He kissed her cheek. "We'll leave Edward behind today. I don't want to be run out of a home by torch-wielding neighbors before we even claim residency."

Laughing harder, she took his hand, kissing his fingers. "Are you certain you're happy?" she asked more quietly.

"The only way I could be happier is if you would stop worrying that I'm not happy," he returned. "Yes, I miss the smell of the sea from time to time, but not enough to make me want to return to that way of life."

Tristan, Lord Dare, strolled into the morning room, then paused. "Should I exit again and make more noise out in the hallway?"

"No," she said, releasing her husband's hand.

Shaw, though, took her fingers again. "We're going out to look for a house again today, Tris. Keep Edward occupied, will you?"

"You don't have to leave. There's more than enough room here."

"Yes, we'd love to have you stay," Georgiana, Lady Dare, seconded, following her husband into the room. "I'm still full of wonder at seeing Shaw civilized."

"Semi-civilized," Shaw countered, reaching over to take a slice of peach from Zephyr's plate. "I always stayed here because we all knew I'd be leaving again before long. I want my own home now." He brushed his lips against Zephyr's temple. "Our own home."

"Well, I can't say I'm opposed to you moving those

crates of weapons out of the spare sitting room. We have children about, all of whom may possibly have worse aim than you do."

"My aim is just fine, thank you very much. And the door is locked." Shaw patted his pocket. "I have the key."

Back down the hallway someone knocked at the front door, and the butler hurried out to answer it. Dare sat at the head of the table while Georgie took a seat opposite Zephyr, and the two ladies began talking about gloves while a footman poured the viscount and his wife cups of tea. Georgiana knew everything about fashion, and thank goodness she wasn't at all condescending about it.

"How many pairs of gloves does a chit need?" Shaw asked, handing over the newspaper to his older brother. And then the butler hurried back into the room again.

"What is it, Dawkins?" the viscount asked, lifting an eyebrow.

"The Duke of Sommerset, my lord. And Admiral Arlington, and several other gentlemen. They wish to see Captain Carroway."

Oh, no. Were they going to deny Shaw's request to sell out his commission? Zephyr clenched her hands together beneath the table. Her father had been *very* liberal with his praise of Shaw's participation in the expedition. What if they ordered him to sail again? What would he do? What would she do?

Shaw stood, then offered a hand to her. "Care to join me?" he drawled, only the steel in his blue eyes betraying that he was less than unconcerned.

"I wasn't invited."

"I just invited you."

"Shaw?"

"Stay close by, Tris. There may be a brawl," Shaw said over his shoulder.

She rose and walked with him out of the breakfast room. Behind her she could hear her new in-laws talking, but she had no idea what they were saying. She had no idea what even to expect.

Six men stood about in the Carroway House morning room. Seven, she amended, frowning in surprise as her father turned to face them. "Papa? Is something amiss?"

He walked up and took her arm, guiding her to one side of the room. "I have noticed that our . . . relationship has altered since your marriage. I want to make things right between us."

"Papa, th—"

"You've never met His Grace, have you? Your Grace, my daughter, Zephyr. Zephyr, the Duke of Sommerset. He sits on the board of the Royal Society. And this is Admiral Arlington, of the Admiralty. And these gentlemen are also members of the Royal Society."

"What can we do for you, gentlemen?" Shaw asked, his stance cautious. "You're aware that I've tendered my resignation to the Admiralty."

"Yes, we are, Captain. It hasn't yet been accepted, however." Admiral Arlington took a seat on the low couch. "So you might attempt a salute to a superior officer."

Taking a breath, Shaw stiffened his spine and delivered a crisp salute. "Admiral."

"At ease, Captain."

"You're aware that Sir Joseph's presentation painted you in a very positive light," the Duke of

Sommerset commented. "I'd venture to say you're being seen as the hero of the expedition."

"We wouldn't have succeeded without Captain Carroway. His experience and enthusiasm and skill were essential."

Zephyr stared at her father, surprised. She had no idea what might be afoot, but at least it was interesting. "I agree," she said for effect.

"It's still early to tell, but we estimate that Sir Joseph discovered seventy-three new species of plants, and at least two dozen heretofore unknown insects, reptiles, and birds."

"Congratulations, Sir Joseph," Shaw said. "That's impressive." He frowned. "I still don't see, however, why this would bring all of you here."

"Ah." Sommerset leaned against the fireplace mantel. "The Royal Society has come to a majority agreement to ask you to do it again."

"Beg pardon?"

"We'd like to mount a second expedition," another of the gentlemen took up. "In the manner of Captain Cook."

"Captain Cook was killed on his second expedition." Shaw folded his arms over his chest. "And I'm married."

The admiral cleared his throat. "Yes. About that. As you know, Sir Joseph gave you credit for the drawings and sketches, Mrs. Carroway."

"Given his persuasive argument," the duke began again, "the Society and the Admiralty thought that something could be arranged."

The duke kept excluding himself from all these decisions and thoughts, Zephyr noticed. This was the man who'd sent Shaw to find old King George.

The man whom Shaw credited with keeping him sane while he sailed to Australia. She stepped forward. "Your Grace, might Shaw and I have a word with you in private?"

Her father frowned. "Zephyr, that is n—"

"Certainly." The duke straightened again, motioning Shaw to lead them out of the room. While the other distinguished gentlemen looked at one another, baffled and a bit affronted, she hurried with her husband to Tristan's office.

"You don't think Shaw should go," she said, as soon as she'd closed them inside.

"You're invited as well, Mrs. Carroway," Sommerset countered.

"This is my father's way of trying to set things right." Scowling, she dropped into a chair. "He has no idea."

"He thinks he'll be able to keep utilizing you as his assistant, and that you'll be happy because I'd be along." Shaw looked from her to Sommerset. "But she's correct, isn't she? You don't think I should go."

The duke shrugged. "That's not for me to decide. I will say that I voted against it."

"Should I be insulted by that?"

"Not at all." He glanced at Zephyr. "May I speak freely?"

"Of course."

"Very well. When I saw you last, you were a man who was . . . discontented with the trail his life had taken. Now that you've returned, I don't think it's my imagination that you're more satisfied, or that you've made some drastic changes that have brought you to this point."

Shaw wrapped his fingers around Zephyr's hand. "It's not your imagination."

"That is why I voted against you." His gray eyes assessing, Sommerset returned to the office door. "Do you want to sail away again? This expedition is expected to last between three and five years."

She'd just found a family and friends, and lately she'd begun thinking that she might wish to add to the Carroway clan numbers. If they left again, even both of them together—well, she wouldn't want a child or children to be born and raised out on the ocean so far from home. Not when she'd only just found a home.

"Zephyr, do you want to go?" Shaw asked quietly. "And tell me the truth; not what you think I want to hear."

Taking a deep breath, she resisted the urge to close her eyes. "I would prefer to remain here." *There.* She'd spoken the truth; now their future rested in his hands.

"Good." He faced the duke. "We thank the Admiralty and the Royal Society for their flattering offer, but we must decline."

Sommerset actually grinned. Nodding, he pulled open the door. "Wait here for a moment. I'll see to it." Halfway through the door, though, he stopped, facing Shaw again. "Have I thanked you for delivering that package for me?"

"Yes. And have I thanked you for tasking me with it?"

"You seemed like the man for the job." The duke inclined his head. "Mrs. Carroway."

"Your Grace."

Once they were alone again, Shaw drew Zephyr

to her feet and kissed her long, and slow, and deep. "They have no idea," he murmured.

She tangled her fingers into his black hair. "No idea about what?"

"That I couldn't possibly crave adventure when its very goddess sleeps in my arms every night. In all my imaginings, Zephyr, I never expected this life. I never expected to fall in love. I never expected to want children or to be so . . . full of joy simply waking up to see you every morning. You are my adventure." He kissed her once more. "Now do you believe that I'm happy to be where I am?"

Tears filling her eyes, she nodded. "Yes. Now I believe you. And I feel oh, so much the same."

"You are my warm, companion breeze. I think we'll have enough adventure together to satisfy even us."

"And a home."

"Yes," he murmured with a grin, lifting her into his arms and spinning her in a circle. "And a home."

New York Times bestselling author

SUZANNE ENOCH

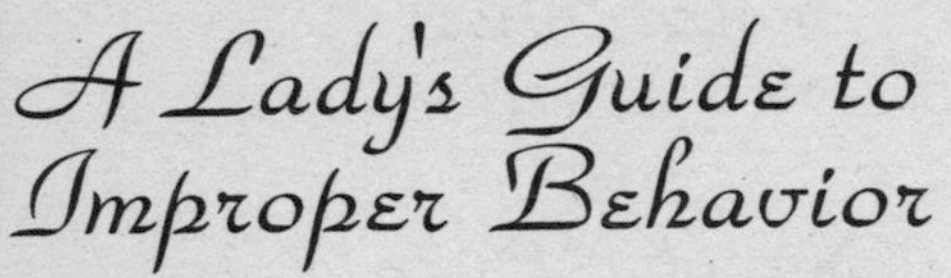

978-0-06-166221-8

Rule #1: A truly improper lady *always* surrenders to her desires . . .

The Care and Taming of a Rogue

978-0-06-145676-3

There's nothing civilized about the passion between Lady Phillipa Eddison and rugged adventurer Captain Bennett Wolfe.

Always a Scoundrel

978-0-06-145675-6

Lady Rosamund Davies is suspicious when the unrepentant rogue Lord Bramwell Johns shows a sudden interest in her.

By Love Undone

978-0-06-087525-1

Madeleine Willits has no idea how to resist the importunate young rakes who deem her ripe for the plucking, but there is only one rake whose attentions she truly desires.